D0057188

A MILLION REASONS WHY

ALSO BY JESSICA STRAWSER

Forget You Know Me

Not That I Could Tell

Almost Missed You

A MILLION REASONS WHY

Jessica Strawser

ST. MARTIN'S PRESS
NEW YORK

This is a work of fiction. All of the characters, organizations, and events portrayed in this novel are either products of the author's imagination or are used fictitiously.

First published in the United States by St. Martin's Press, an imprint of St. Martin's Publishing Group

www.stmartins.com

Designed by Devan Norman

Library of Congress Cataloging-in-Publication Data

Names: Strawser, Jessica, author.
Title: A million reasons why : a novel / Jessica Strawser.
Description: First edition. | New York : St. Martin's Press, 2021.
Identifiers: LCCN 2020040964 | ISBN 9781250241627 (hardcover) | ISBN 9781250241634 (ebook)
Classification: LCC PS3619.T7437 M56 2021 | DDC 813/.6—dc23
LC record available at https://lccn.loc.gov/2020040964

Our books may be purchased in bulk for promotional, educational, or business use. Please contact your local bookseller or the Macmillan Corporate and Premium Sales Department at 1-800-221-7945, extension 5442, or by email at MacmillanSpecialMarkets@macmillan.com.

First Edition: 2021

10 9 8 7 6 5 4 3 2 1

1
2
3

For my parents,
who always cheered the loudest—
and whose love story remains
the real deal

A MILLION REASONS WHY

1

Caroline

Long before Caroline ever felt compelled to seriously consider the split between nature and nurture, she knew exactly which traits she owed to her dad.

Number one was that growing up with a father like Caroline's, you couldn't not learn to look at just about anything from a new angle when you needed one. He was a market research analyst who never could quite take his brain off duty—and was perhaps a bit too remiss to disappoint his favorite clients. Thus, when Caroline was down after, for example, getting only six out of ten correct on a surprise quiz, he'd say, "Well, if this were a sporting event, you *would* have beat the test." The "glass half-full" question was not even debatable in his eyes.

"Anything point five and above, you round up."

Disarming though he was, as an adult Caroline begrudgingly grew to understand why her mom could be a killjoy in those moments, calling him out for oversimplifying things or excusing poor behavior. But by then, his influence was inherent. Caroline was no math whiz, but she did pride herself on being a quick-thinking and creative problem solver—an instinct that, as an event director and mother of three kids in the single-digit age range, she called upon no fewer than a dozen times a day.

Besides, he'd taught her a valuable lesson: that data, while itself trustworthy, could always be skewed—and often was.

So when she first saw the email from a woman she'd never heard of, claiming Caroline was her half sister, her mind skipped right over the *half* and immediately to the *sister* part, with no half measure of alarm. But then it backed right up to the starting line and dismissed the whole idea as nonsense.

She'd been in her office, fielding a call from a new staffer who was unsure how to break down that day's trade show—Caroline *knew* she should have insisted on going along to the conference center—and packing up her laptop bag, when the new message popped onto her screen. She had exactly forty-five minutes to pick up Owen at preschool, retrieve the girls from her in-laws', run guiltily through the most wholesome drive-through she could find, and unload them all on the sidelines of Riley's soccer practice. This was the level of busy she thrived on: There was reassurance in being indispensable at work, in shepherding her children from one well-rounded activity to the next. Already on a roll, she sped right on through the cascade of emotions that trailed the email: with scarcely a passing glance at initial shock on to doubt to dispossession.

What lingered, as she snapped the laptop shut, wished her staffer luck, and ran across the parking lot to the minivan she'd caved and stopped feeling embarrassed by, was annoyance.

This was *exactly* why she never saw the appeal of those mail-in DNA tests the rest of the world had gone gaga over. Seemed like she heard about erratic results as often as sought-after ones—but when Walt applauded his genius at gifting them to the extended family last Christmas, she hadn't rained on his tee time. For one thing, she appreciated his willingness to divide the holiday shopping—too many of her fellow working-mom friends shouldered the whole burden, citing husbandly disinterest or incompetence or procrastination, and thus spent the last two months of every year in a frenzy. In the well-oiled system she and Walt had developed, *not* arguing over stuff like this kept the gears greased. Christmas morning, she'd merely exchanged a knowing side-eye with Dad, then smiled and volunteered to coordinate mailing the kits and creating their log-ins on the spot.

Obviously, it wasn't possible she could have an unidentified sister, half or otherwise. The family compared scorecards as they came and found them unremarkable, though Walt did lament their post–St. Patrick's Day arrival, as his side discovered a surprise sliver of Irish ancestry. As if he hadn't spent the holiday downing Guinness anyway. No one received a bombshell that their much older sister was actually their mother, or that they were adopted or had ties to a loathed enemy—and even if they had, what meaningful difference would it make? When it came to families linked by marriage, theirs was one of the few she knew that genuinely got along, merging traditions and celebrations, the more happily the merrier. Perhaps this owed a lot to her and Walt both being only children, but a decade in, she was more grateful than ever for the gift they'd given Owen, Lucy, and Riley in having four grandparents so involved in their lives.

Sure, they squabbled, and Mom in particular *could* be a little judgmental, but the prevailing feeling was that together, they were stronger and could withstand any storm life blew their way.

Or, in the words of Caroline's best friend, Maureen, who had zero tolerance for her own family and even less for harmonious ones, they were "the sort of thing you'd picture if you'd eaten something bad and needed to make yourself throw up."

Secrecy was antithetical to who they were. Caroline had seen her parents' results firsthand. Case closed.

It irked her, as she drove from one pickup to the next, that this dared vie for space in her at-capacity brain. She tried to focus on asking the kids about their school days, playing their daily game of each naming a high point and a low one. Owen was proud of his finger-painted art project but less enamored with that day's "yucky noodle" lunch. Lucy had befriended a new girl in kindergarten and, true to mediating middle-child form, could not think of a single bad thing to report. Riley had scored a goal at recess but was annoyed to have homework. In short, everything was perfectly ordinary in their little worlds.

Everything except Caroline.

An hour later, in her folding chair on the sideline, as Riley ran after her teammates and Owen and Lucy divided the fries and apple slices from their kids' meals and Caroline choked down a rubbery dish purporting to be salad, she pulled out her phone and read the email again. More carefully.

The woman's name was Sela, and she was the same age as Caroline—their birthdays a couple of short months apart, thirty-five years ago. She lived a half day's drive away, in a North Carolina town that, oddly, Caroline had once considered moving to, and had *just* completed her test with the same company Walt had patronized. Only then did Caroline register that this woman's results wouldn't have been available when she reviewed her own. But if the database had flagged them as such a close genetic match, wouldn't she have been notified? This had to be some clerical or technical error. If she waited to respond, maybe it would resolve itself—the company issuing an apology about notifications gone haywire or Sela realizing her own mistake and retracting her inquiry.

Caroline felt a twinge of sympathy for the woman. She said she'd never known her dad—and Caroline couldn't help but think of what a different person she herself might have been without her own. A lesser person, certainly. She'd wait a day or two and, if no further email arrived, break it gently that Sela was barking up the wrong family tree.

But that night, by the time the kids' stories were read and the calls for one more drink or one last snuggle had subsided, her conviction had, too.

"You don't think . . . ?" she asked Walt. They were changing at last into lounge clothes, alone for the first time all day, in their large master suite—his and her walk-ins, jetted soaking tub, reading nook—the one upgraded indulgence in their otherwise middle-of-the-road suburban home. Walt insisted that after having three kids in five years, they'd earned it, and though she'd have saved the funds if left to her own devices, she was glad. So many of their friends' marriages had already failed, and a common denominator seemed to be letting parenthood trump all else. Walt kept the room immaculate, a sanctuary, and feeling as if she belonged here was enough to remind her that she was more than just an especially resourceful woman at commanding chaos.

Even if she did secretly like being known in their playgroup as MacGyver Mom.

He was returning his suit to the closet now, lips pursed, thinking before he answered, and she wondered if he was regretting having purchased the tests, just as she was regretting never voicing an objection. No one in their family took a particular interest in genealogy. If she'd come up with something better last December, they would not be in this awkward position now.

"Still have your parents' log-ins?" he asked.

She cringed. She'd hoped he would dismiss it out of hand, the way she itched to. Which was when she realized that somewhere between her initial scoff of impossibility and this moment of naked truth, she'd become legitimately scared to look.

The house wasn't cold—Ohio Septembers remained fully rooted in summer at the start—but she shivered, and he tossed her the microfiber robe from the hook on the closet door. "I guess, if they haven't changed their passwords . . . I don't even know if mine still works."

"One way to find out."

"It just feels a little—"

"Wine. I'll pour us wine."

By the time they'd arranged themselves side by side, cabernet by cabernet, at the built-in desk that divided the kitchen from the family room, Caroline just wanted to get it over with. To laugh at how easily a misdirected email had thrown her off and feel a welcome stab of guilt over doubting her parents for even a second. She peppered Walt with questions about his day as she located her browser's bookmark for the provider's website and keyed in a handful of her go-to passwords before hitting on the right one. He was midway through a not-distracting-enough story about his boss's allergic reaction to their banquet lunch when she caught sight of the red star indicating a *New Match!* from the "Relative Finder." Walt fell silent mid-word.

She met his eyes for a nervous instant before clicking on the alert, checking box after *Are you sure?* box, agreeing that *yes,* she did want to see the result, though in truth she did not, and then holding her breath while an icon spun on the screen, working away. Then it was gone, and in its place appeared a name with an italicized tag highlighting the connection.

Sela Bell. Half sibling.

"Click here," Walt said before she could process what she was seeing. He pointed at a prompt to *see what other relatives you have in common.* Robotically, she obeyed.

No matches at this time.

She exhaled, leaning back in her chair. "Well, neither Mom nor Dad is here, and they're both in the database. Obviously it really is a mistake." She gave a nervous laugh. "Thank God!"

"Hmm." Walt didn't laugh. He was reading the fine print beneath the subhead *What Does This Mean?* "You'd better verify that your parents opted in. Looks like you can decline having your info be searchable."

"I seriously doubt either of them messed with the defaults. I did the whole thing."

"Only for due diligence, before you get back to this woman."

Caroline logged out, then in as her mom: Hannah Shively. The password she'd set for the rest of the family still worked: *MerryXmas.* The in-box lay dormant. She scrolled to her settings and found the opt-in box checked. "See? I don't think they've touched this." She glanced at him, realizing how that might sound. "Not that they didn't appreciate the gift, I'm sure."

Walt still didn't crack a smile. "Now your dad."

He was too kind to point out that it had been pointless to check Mom's account in the first place—or that she was stalling. She logged out, then in as Fred Shively, and felt her heart lift when she saw his notifications blank as well. "See? We've already confirmed my parents *are* my parents, and they don't match her, so—" She stopped scrolling.

His database opt-in box was unchecked.

An oversight on her part? Or something he'd logged in himself and removed? If he had something to hide, surely he'd have changed the password from the one Caroline had chosen. She checked the box, clicked *OK,* and watched the spinning icon reappear. The room had fallen the conspicuous kind of silent, the breath in her own lungs and Walt's again stilled.

New Match!

She couldn't click fast enough. Yes, yes, I'm sure, show me. More spinning. Then:

Sela Bell. Daughter.

Caroline's hand hovered over the mouse for a terrible moment, then dropped to her lap. "Doesn't mean it isn't an error," she said, not looking at Walt. He knew her too well, and she was afraid of what he'd see if she allowed him to meet her eyes—and of what he'd reflect back. "It only means they're being consistent about it."

"Right. Let's check the FAQs. I'm sure there's a procedure to follow if you believe they've made a mistake." She slid the laptop across the counter to him—summoning all her willpower not to actually say the words *You got us into this, you get us out of it*—and he pulled it closer, lowering his head to the screen in concentration. She gulped her wine, her mind racing. This simply could not be true. It would mean Dad had somehow fathered another woman's child while he was a *newlywed.* Her parents had had her so fast.

She risked another glance at Walt. He frowned at the help menu. "I'm not sure this is covered. . . . We might have to contact customer service."

"Say it's correct." The words fell out. "What's that even mean? Dad maybe cheated on Mom? It would've been over thirty years ago." Much as she hated the idea, was that worth broaching now? Whether a hurtful truth was better off known was an age-old, unresolvable debate, one she had no desire to be in the middle of. Certainly not between her parents.

Walt pushed back his chair and turned to her, warming her clammy hands between his. "First of all, there's a chance of a real explanation here. Maybe he donated sperm to a friend in need—or for beer money in college."

"But there's no way to ask without risking drudging up something worse."

"True. But I'm not sure that's up to us. There's another person at the other end of this now, and—" His head shot up. "We better go back and uncheck that box. What if he's already displayed in her account as a new match? She's only found you so far."

"Oh, God." Caroline's mouth went dry.

He dropped her hands and navigated once more to the account settings. "Done. Let's see if her name disappears now. . . ."

"I doubt he'd ever even log—"

"Shit."

"What?"

"This is set to notify him of updates to his account. I think—I think when you opted him in, it might have sent him the result."

She blinked at him in horror. "But my account had a new match, and I didn't get an email! Not until Sela's." She felt disloyal even saying the name aloud, as if doing so might conjure this stranger whom she wanted to remain exactly that. "I don't remember messing with my settings any differently from his."

Walt was a step ahead, logging out as Fred and scooting aside so she could sign in again.

A few clicks and he had it. "Looks like you unsubscribed from everything. That wasn't the default—I still get their emails sometimes. Nothing important, but . . ."

Oh God. She *had* unsubscribed, in a fit of cleansing her inbox of things that did not "spark joy." This was Marie Kondo's fault.

She dropped her head into her hands. "Maybe we unchecked the box fast enough?"

"Maybe." But she could tell he doubted it. "Maybe this is one of those sites that mails off a daily digest of activity after the fact."

"How could I be so stupid?" she moaned into her palms. "What did clicking that even prove?"

"Well. Maybe it's better to have a chance to clear up the confusion sooner than later."

"Better?" She lifted her head so he could see for himself she hadn't been born yesterday.

"I'm not sure doing nothing was ever going to be the best option," he said gently. "Do you really want to go on suspecting something this serious that might not be true? Something that could be explained away if only you'd ask? That would eat at you." This seemed unfairly easy for him to say. Much as he loved her parents, no rando was claiming *his* dad as their own.

She looked down at her fingers. Mom's fingers, really. Caroline might have been a computer-generated image of her parents' predicted child: Mom's body—the dancer-like build, fair coloring, and thick blond hair—with Dad's facial features superimposed on top. The slightly wide-set eyes, crook in the nose, heart-shaped chin . . .

Was it possible someone else out there had them, too?

"Let's just contact a rep and find out how to challenge the match. Or call it into question, or whatever."

Walt reached for his phone, then stopped, pointing instead at the details on the computer screen. "Call center keeps regular business hours. First chance is nine a.m. tomorrow. How's your schedule in the morning? Can you swing it from the office?"

She pictured all the personal calls she'd had interrupted by one coworker or another: detailing a toddler's rash for the pediatrician, or apologizing to daycare about a biting incident, or begging for school pictures to be taken even though she'd forgotten to send in the order form. This was not the same kind of potential embarrassment, breezily shrugged away.

This kind might require space to process.

"I don't know if I want to."

"I could call, if you want? Or we could send an email. Says to allow one to three business days for a response, but it might not take that long."

"Both?"

Walt pulled up the contact form. "You know, if he does get the email, he's going to assume you got one too."

"Well, then maybe he'll save me the trouble of figuring out how the hell to bring this up with him."

Mere hours ago, she'd almost laughed this off. A miserable sinking feeling overcame her. She felt nonsensically angry at Sela. She didn't want to put herself in the woman's shoes, the way she briefly had at first when it seemed such an improbability, the way Walt was now that it was not. She just wanted her to go away.

But if so much could change so quickly, it had to be as likely that by this time tomorrow, she and Walt would be sharing a belly laugh over the false alarm. Over the agonizing they'd done for nothing. It *had* to be a mistake. Dad would never let a possibility like this be.

After all, he'd been the one to teach her: If you have half of anything, you round up.

2

Sela

She knew Doug's SUV by the headlights, even through the dream-like fog that had descended from the mountains overnight, even in the yawning blackness of the dawn before sunrise. So often had Sela watched him come and go that the exact curvature and yellow white glow of this particular broken promise had imprinted on her mind, and as it approached now she dipped her head, tightening her grip on Oscar's leash and hoping that if she pretended not to see, Doug would take his free pass and drive on.

Willing Oscar to follow suit was futile, but she did it anyway. As a puppy, he'd been such a curmudgeon, completely uncharacteristic for his retriever breed, let alone his youth. He'd resisted walks, digging in his paws every step that took them farther from home and then pulling so eagerly when they turned back he'd choke himself the whole way. He'd stared with mute skepticism at balls, squeaky toys, and anything else he was actually supposed to mouth or chase or chew, and gave his plush bed a wide berth no matter which corner of which room Sela moved it to. But he'd grown into one of those dogs who clearly identifies more as human child than canine adult, and as such he showered his "parents" with a love so enthusiastic it made a bighearted joke of his name. If he noticed their new shared custody agreement carried for both parties a regret-laden sadness, he showed no sign.

With her eyes averted, it was hard to tell which came first: the vehicle slowing along the curb or Oscar yelping and flinging his tail in jubilant recognition. Either way, the result was the same: her ex-husband meeting her reluctant smile with his own, cutting his engine, and taking a knee in the dewy grass at Oscar's side, burying his hands in the golden fur to say hello.

"You're up early," Doug observed, sounding forcibly casual. "Sleep okay?"

He likely hadn't been awake for more than a few minutes but nonetheless looked rested, ready to go. Although he'd always been fit, his tall frame had hardened, broadened since he'd left her; everything about him was suddenly so intentional, down to his mussed hair, as if determined to become opposite of her in nearly every way. She'd never been especially athletic but once had a litheness, elegance even. Now, she was more spindly, unable to hide her fragility. Shadows permanent beneath her eyes. Shine gone from her hair. Everything she tried to mask this—cutting her brunette waves to this pixie cut, dabbing on concealer before running even the smallest errand—seemed only to call attention to the problem.

Doug heading to the gym at this hour was normal—she knew without looking that the front seat held a forest green duffel of everything he needed to shower there and head straight to work—but her standing in the front yard was not. Concern was plain on his face, and she hugged her hooded sweatshirt in a posture of self-preservation. The term *ex-husband* was still foreign enough that Sela sometimes found herself rolling it around her mind, partially because technically they remained married, for reasons exclusive to health insurance. She'd protested the arrangement, already foreseeing the awkwardness when he got serious with someone new and they had to have all the big, teary talks all over again. But he'd insisted. Least he could do, seeing as she was self-employed and thus had limited benefits.

That, and him having left her with a pair of vital organs slowly failing.

"Slept fine," she said. With declining kidney function came a nighttime restlessness that was cruelly disproportionate to the fatigue she battled all day: swelling, muscle cramps, a bladder that begged to be emptied in the incessant manner of a kid on a road trip—*Are we there yet?* But admitting this was why she was up at 5:00 a.m. was akin to admitting defeat. Though Doug's former address really was on his new commute, she never shook the feeling that he was checking up on her, that passing inspection was paramount to avoiding further scrutiny. "I wanted to get a jump on some mock-ups for a new client."

This was true enough. Working from home with a toddler underfoot was a game of strategy, but in relinquishing every other weekend and stray weeknights to Doug, she wasn't about to rely on childcare more than absolutely necessary. So she made the most of nap times and playground benches, and her clients grew accustomed to emails time-stamped at all hours. She tried to think of sleepless nights as "found time."

Sometimes it even worked.

"New clients are good." His relief at having something positive to say was palpable.

"You bet."

Doug straightened and jammed his hands into the pockets of the baggy sweatpants he favored for workouts, and Oscar buried his nose in the grass, resuming his investigation of every animal that had touched his territory overnight. "Did you send it?" His face strained with the effort of bracing for another argument, and she wished the tension were enough to make him look like someone other than himself. Like the Doug she'd lost wasn't the same version she'd loved. "The email, I mean."

"I did." She hadn't needed his nudge—she'd *known* she needed to do it—but their last blowup was bad enough to give her the push.

"You did?" A nervous laugh escaped him. "Good! I mean, good for you. When did—Have you heard back?"

"Not yet. I expect it might take her a few days. To process."

"Sure." He scuffled his feet. "How much did you *give* her to process?"

As if Sela didn't have the sense not to scare off someone she'd been reticent to contact in the first place.

"I only introduced myself. But even that is a lot."

He ran a hand through his hair. It needed a cut. "Good," he said again. "I, uh. I went to that seminar they recommended. The Big Ask: The Big Give? Really helpful. You should definitely sign up for one, once you're looking at broaching the subject with her."

Sela tried to smile. In the whirlwind years since her chronic kidney disease diagnosis, she'd managed to wrap her brain around a lot of unavoidable realities. The careful tally of every nutrient that went in or out of her system. The inconvenience of monthly blood draws and the mounting disappointment of their outcomes. The head-up determination to maintain a quality of life as close to normal as possible, to give Brody a childhood as normal as possible. But the idea of being coached on how to ask someone to consider giving you a piece of their *body* was not yet in her comfort zone. Ironic her husband had been unable to cope with so much of the rest—to let go of the idea that things could ever go back to the way they were—and yet had made up his mind to earn extra credit on this of all subjects.

"I'm gonna go out on a limb and assume they don't role-play

my particular scenario." There was how to ask family for a kidney and how to ask strangers for a kidney. But her situation was . . .

Well, it was both, while managing to feel like neither. And though she was no opportunist, she hadn't worked out yet how to come across as anything but.

He gave her a look that said, in no uncertain terms, rehashing this would not be helpful. "What they do is raise your comfort level with the topic. Have you watched their videos online?"

She looked away. Too bad she couldn't come out and ask him for the kind of advice she'd actually find useful. Like how he managed to avoid exhausting himself with this worried energy that constantly depleted her.

"I know you chose to tune out social media . . ." He was selecting his words carefully, as they'd butted heads over this, too. Doug had accused her of doing what he'd been warned about, isolating herself, retreating, when she'd wanted only to maintain her sanity, to block out the toxicity inherent online, and yes, to avoid the barrage of well-meaning inquiries about her nothing-good-to-report health. But in Doug's newly hypervigilant eyes, she'd been morphing from his individually human wife into a case study who refused to behave by the book. He took her noncompliance as a personal affront in a way she didn't grasp until too late. "But you should know I posted my Big Ask on my accounts, on your behalf."

She squeezed her eyes shut. She should be grateful, probably, that he was willing to swallow her pride and do the thing she could not yet do. But she could practically *see* his friends rubbernecking at how desperate her situation had grown and what a stand-up guy he was to try to help. "The seminar says the more people who see or hear the request, the better," he went on. "Even acquaintances, friends of friends. You never know."

"But Doug, you know finding a nonrelative match in my case is *super* unlikely—"

"Of course I know that." He'd sat through the lesson on her

antibodies, too. *Highly sensitized,* they called her. In fact, even if they found a live donor candidate, she'd almost certainly have to undergo something called a desensitization process to lower her body's defenses before being green-lighted for the transplant. "But it's even more unlikely if you don't try." This was why he'd been on her to send that email in the first place. Her mother would turn in her grave if she knew about this: that Sela had, if the DNA ancestry test could be believed, located her father's family via a half sister—something her one and only parent had expressly forbidden her from attempting. People didn't come much more understanding or nonvindictive than her mother, so Sela trusted that she'd had good reason—that whatever was on the other end of her parentage would be explored at her own peril.

Doug insisted that had her mother foreseen these circumstances, she'd have felt differently—anything to give Sela a fighting chance. At the time of her mother's death, they'd had a slim, if fading, hope that Sela's kidneys might plateau at a reduced but livable level. When they didn't, it became hard to argue with the facts: That a transplant was highly preferable to dialysis at her age especially—and the slow crawl of bureaucracy required she be proactive about her options well in advance. That even now that she'd initiated the process of getting on the transplant list, it could take a year just for approval to *officially* start waiting. That a living donation would extend her life years longer than an organ donated in death.

That no one on her mother's side was a match.

Nor was Doug, who turned out to be disqualified regardless thanks to—of all things—growth hormones he'd briefly taken as a cocksure underclassman trying to make varsity. It would have been almost funny, had it not solidified his new stance that no misstep was innocent enough to be laughed off.

Besides. Sela *had* ordered the DNA test: Deep down, she must have come to terms, let herself hope it wasn't a lark. Although . . .

If this were just about a kidney, she'd never have reached out. With her mother dead and Doug gone, Sela's world had shrunk to a perfect triangle: Brody, her work, and her illness. An unnaturally rigid shape for a life, which was meant to be soft, bendable. Expandable.

That there might be a half *sibling* somewhere outside those points was the real temptation. Depending on whom she was talking to, the possibility that the half sister might also be a pathway to a one-day donor was either a cover story or an icing-on-the-cake scenario.

But at both ends of the spectrum, this feeling applied exclusively to the mysterious Caroline Porter. Had Sela found her father, she'd have rather died, honestly, than combine his flesh with hers. He was likely either too old or too unfit to donate, anyway—assuming he was about her mother's age, most people had by then lost the impeccable health required. But a sibling . . .

"The response on my pages has been encouraging. If you want to take a look, maybe chime in—"

"Please." Sela held up a hand, chagrined to find it shaking. She *was* touched by Doug's frustration, even in this early-morning ambush. It meant he still cared. If only that translated to something that mattered. "I'd like to set this conversation aside for later before I say something that makes me sound ungrateful."

A counselor had provided this script in the weeks after Brody's birth, when it became clear that Sela's condition was both escalating and irreversible—and that neither of them was handling the strain well. She suspected Doug found the line as enraging as she did, but neither of them could say so, since the words did at minimum acknowledge the sensitivity of the situation. Which was more than either of them had accomplished without them.

Doug looked at her now as if he couldn't decide what he wanted more: to press her to talk or to get away as fast as he could. A well-worn combination—she already knew which would win out.

"Well, the email is a big step," he conceded. "I'm glad I drove by at the right time to see you."

She might have invited him in for coffee but figured she'd save them both the humiliation of him saying no. It was tough enough to be standing here at the far reaches of the porch light, staring into the eyes of the person to whom she'd be forever linked in catastrophic failure. They'd disappointed each other, let Brody down, even complicated the simple life of their perfectly innocent dog, who sat between them now, looking from one to the other with his ears cocked expectantly.

Doug meant well. He didn't know how to let go all the way. But she found things easier without him. With no line of sight to this tormented look on his face, she could pretend, if she needed to, that he was gone temporarily, tending to a business trip or family issue as dutiful people like Doug did. When she knew he was coming, she could pull on a protective layer of numbness, a barrier to keep any particular feeling about him from touching her directly. But when he caught her off guard like this, when she didn't have time to reach for that coat, it was like being woken from a bad dream to find out things weren't as she'd feared after all.

They were worse.

"I'm glad you came by too," she said.

With people like Doug, lies could be a form of kindness.

He bent to give Oscar one last pat. "See you Friday, pal. If your mom's still okay with me taking this weekend?"

It made the most sense to treat Oscar and Brody as a package deal, keeping the same schedule for both. "Of course."

She leaned into the thought of Brody asleep upstairs, resisting the cruel temptation to linger and watch Doug's taillights fade into the fog. She'd recently converted the crib to a toddler bed, and ever since, Brody would randomly wake and come looking for her, simply because he could.

A powerful thing, really—to have someone rely so wholly on finding her where she was supposed to be. She liked to think it meant she could still rely on herself.

After all, she had no choice.

Neither of them had anyone else.

3

Caroline

"Mommy?" A little voice deposited the word so directly into Caroline's ear, she could feel the vibrations carrying the sound. Her eyes flew open to find her younger daughter's bleary face inches from her own, smiling expectantly. "What do you think?" As Caroline blinked properly awake, Lucy jumped back and twirled, showing off her outfit: a sparkly heart-covered cap-sleeved shirt, tucked into a metallic silver tutu that billowed around purple leggings, over which had been pulled candy-cane-striped knee-highs resurrected from the holiday drawer. Rainbow cowgirl boots that Caroline had learned too late shed more sequins than a Rockette completed the ensemble.

"Wow, you got yourself all dressed," she said, sidestepping the question.

Lucy nodded proudly. "Everything but my underwear!"

Caroline squinted at her kindergartner, who was potty-trained, of course, but still slept in training underpants. "You put on all that without panties underneath?"

Lucy giggled. "Whoops!"

Behind her, the door to the master bath clicked open, and Walt stood buttoning his dress shirt in the dissipating humidity. He sniffed conspicuously. "Do I smell . . . glitter?"

Lucy let out a squeal. "Not the glitter monster, Daddy!"

His voice turned ragged, goofy, as he draped his bath towel over his head. "Daddy not here. Only me. Me want glitter!"

The pair took off running down the hallway, and Caroline pulled a pillow over her face, groaning. She was surrounded by morning people in this house. It was inhuman.

Sleep had eluded her for much of the night. As Walt's breath had grown slow and deep, his arm draped across her turning to dead weight, she'd admonished her brain that worrying about this could wait until morning. Things would look clearer once she had answers from the test provider. No reason to exhaust herself in the meantime. But when she at last drifted off, it was to that off-kilter place where consciousness hovers and waits for an uncertain outcome.

Caroline couldn't deflect the feeling that a stray cat had been let out of a bag that may or may not have been delivered by mistake. Even if it did have the wrong address, there was a decent chance she'd have to face off with the feral animal.

If only there was some way of knowing whether it had been contained here or escaped to Dad's in-box.

Why had she not checked the other settings before she opted him into the database? Until that gaffe, she hadn't thought of logging on as violating his privacy, only trying to disprove an erroneous claim he need not know about. But now, if this did find its way to him, she'd have some uncomfortable explaining to do.

Then again, so would he.

She tossed the pillow aside and grabbed her phone. No missed calls, no new texts, nothing but junk mail unopened in her inbox. She was not reassured.

Lucy trounced back into the room, wearing her most angelic poker face—and a pair of Hello Kitty underwear atop her head. "Fixed it, Mommy!"

Caroline yawned and sat up. The thing about morning people was, they always won. "How about pigtails today? I can pull them through the leg holes."

"Mommy! I was *joking*!"

For all her resistance to the frenetic starts to her workdays, Caroline could say this: Their get-five-people-out-the-door-with-everything-they-need routine, or lack thereof, *was* distracting, whether you wanted it to be or not. This day, she threw herself into it, mediating arguments over toaster waffles and misplaced school library books with appreciation for small problems she could actually solve. Walt gave her a tight squeeze on his way out the door, mouthing, *Call you later,* but she didn't meet his eyes to acknowledge the reason. It was easier—steadier—to be in her most natural, most capable state of busyness once she got going. She doodled notes in the girls' lunch boxes and led Simon Says at the bus stop and lingered at Owen's drop-off, chatting about an upcoming field trip for so long that she ended up volunteering to chaperone. When there was nothing left to do but go to work, she texted her boss an apology for running late—rarely a big deal, given how often she ran shows on evenings and weekends—and turned out of the preschool parking lot in the opposite direction.

She'd decided: She couldn't face this day without getting a look at Dad. One look at his normal, unsuspecting, *did not get the email* self—*that* would reassure her. At least until they heard back from customer service and could decide if there was cause to pursue this at all.

And if he *had* gotten that big red exclamation point message? Well, let him bring it up—or not. If he seemed off, she'd know there might be something to this. Which would leave her . . . well, exactly where she stood.

Dad had retired early and reluctantly last year, after worsening high blood pressure flags provoked Mom's threats to damn well give him a heart attack if he didn't slow down. Their siblings had collectively died young, one cautionary tale after the next, and though Caroline's parents were just creeping up on sixty, they'd spent conservatively and invested well. Why wait and risk never getting to enjoy retirement, especially with three grandbabies nearby? Now, Dad started every day with the lazy luxury formerly reserved for Sundays: reading the newspaper front to back while savoring three slow cups of coffee—though he'd crankily switched to decaf. He habitually rose as early as every other senior she knew, but that didn't mean he liked it. Caroline never wondered where her aversion to her alarm clock came from.

Mom, who'd been a homemaker until Caroline left for college and then worked at a handbag outlet "just for fun"—fun being an obvious euphemism for "employee discount"—was the opposite, all get up and go, and collected comments that she didn't look old enough to be a grandmother the way other people collected vinyl or coins. By now she'd be at one of her fitness classes, a rotation of yoga, water aerobics, and senior spinning. Dad poked fun at the latter title, bringing to mind the ridiculous image of oldsters getting dizzy on swivel desk chairs. But for all Caroline cared, Mom could be off turning cartwheels—as long as it meant she'd catch him alone.

She stopped at Busken Bakery for a half dozen of their heart-shaped, low-fat glazed doughnuts, which no amount of fruit-topped yogurt, egg white omelets, or eye-rolling could stop him from calling "the *only* edible heart-healthy breakfast in town." Mom would frown upon this, but Caroline needed a ruse. Nothing would disarm him like fried dough.

She scarfed two of the pastries while she drove. She'd claim to be bringing leftovers. His house was only ten minutes out of the way—it was conceivable she'd detour just to treat him.

At least, she hoped so.

The morning was dreary, gray clouds sagging with the threat of rain, and the porch light still glowed as she eased the minivan into the driveway. Same old house as always. With same old Dad inside—surely. Probably combing the dining and entertainment sections by now, looking for some new restaurant or show Mom might like. He was so good at that sort of thing, the mere thought of it made her feel disloyal for giving this question any thought at all, test results be damned. He'd loved his Hannah from the day they met, married her straight out of college, and never looked back. Not like Caroline and Walt, who'd traversed the same spheres for years before taking interest in each other. The doughnuts suddenly seemed more preemptive apology than excuse.

She was halfway up the front walk when she caught sight of it: the *Enquirer*, in its plastic weather sleeve, leaning between the front door and the stoop. Usually, no faster could the courier toss it than Dad would be out here, waving thanks. Unease tickled the nape of her neck, but she fought the urge to turn on her heels. One small detail out of the ordinary did not mean her fears about the *New Match!* were being realized. The lack of sleep was clouding her thinking, swinging her suspicions willy-nilly. Two steps ago, she'd been brimming with confidence.

She grabbed the paper with her free hand, pressed the doorbell, and waited.

And waited.

No answer.

She rang again, wondering for the first time if a rogue email was the least of her worries. What if her intuition was firing for a different reason? One or both parents sick? Hurt? Could they have been robbed? She'd seen that news story about seniors as easy targets. She tried the knocker, three times, each thud of brass on brass carrying the metallic echo of mounting panic.

She was about to knock again when the door flung open, and

she felt before she saw the *whoosh* of anger behind it. Mom glared at her through puffy eyes in a face hardened with determination, a boxer bruised to the point of staggering but adrenaline-ready for the clang signaling another round. As she registered Caroline, her relief was obvious—this was not the bell she'd thought it was—and her rage diminished to exhaustion, pale and drawn.

The older Caroline had gotten, the more she'd begun to resemble Mom outwardly, if not inwardly. She'd always kept her unruly locks longer than Mom's dyed-to-her-natural-color bob, lest she look *too* much like the matriarch. But now their mannerisms had become alike, the no-nonsense way they moved about the kitchen, the unconscious habit of talking with their hands. They even grew to share physical oddities—the same mixed astigmatism, one meridian of each eye farsighted and the other near-, the same slight bunions on their left feet, the same random flare-ups of dermatitis. Now, as she took in the woman standing barefoot in her nightgown on the flowered doormat, all Caroline could think was that she didn't look like herself at all. Which was to say she didn't look like Caroline, either. She looked like a stranger.

"Mom?" The house was dark behind this shadowboxer version of her mother. Maybe Caroline had woken them—maybe they *were* sick, the kind where all you wanted was sleep. "You okay?" Mom sniffed, and Caroline almost believed she was about to invite her in, laugh whatever this was away. But she didn't smile, didn't speak. Instead, she seemed to shrink inward, like Owen at the end of a tantrum.

"Where's Dad?"

"Not here." Monotone, she eyed the newspaper and doughnuts with disgust. "Those for him?"

Caroline nodded, once—the bare minimum, as Mom's expression made it plain this was the wrong answer. "I had some left over, from a—a meeting. But finders keepers, if you're here alone . . ." She held them out, a peace offering, but Mom didn't move. "Where'd he go?"

Mom opened her mouth as if to give some pat response, but her expression caught there, a scratched track on an old record—and what came out was part cry and part laugh, the twisted combination of a roar to back off and a whimper to pull her close.

"Mom, what's *wrong*? What's going on?"

This was a woman whose wifely restraint was legendary in Caroline's circle. A child of messy divorce from an era when divorce still meant scandal, Hannah Shively let it be known she had solemnly vowed never to argue in front of her child. Thus, if she had something *constructive* to say to her husband, she'd whisper it into his ear. So infallible was her approach that the teenage Maureen and Caroline had perfected a hilariously believable *SNL*-style skit of the couple communicating this way even when they were alone. Rare disagreements that escalated peaked at a cold shoulder, never a confrontation, until harmony was restored, things presumably resolved offstage.

"It's between your father and I." With that, Mom seemed to remember whom she was talking to, but that wasn't enough to stop the tears from spilling over. They streaked frustration down her cheeks, and she swiped at them as Caroline stood slack-jawed, clinging to an unlikely hope that the timing of this fallout was a coincidence.

Because what if what she was witnessing was the wake of the email alert—already? This was at least partially Caroline's fault for triggering it.

"You had an argument?" she prodded, her own voice quivering.

"A spat." Mom cleared her throat, but the tears kept coming. "I'm only tired. I was up all night—you know I get emotional when I'm tired. . . ."

But why on earth would he have shared it with Mom right away, without even verifying its validity? *Unless he already knew. . . .*

Not possible. Dad wasn't perfect, but he was no deadbeat.

"Doesn't look like a spat."

That put her tears on pause. Mom took a moment to compose herself and when she spoke again, she was firm. "You should go. Thanks for the breakfast. It's just not a good time."

"I can't leave you like this."

"You certainly can."

"Let me come in and make you some coffee."

"You're expected at work."

She rocked the box of doughnuts side to side. "Aren't you the one who taught me we get free passes on calories every time a guy acts like a jerk?"

"I *don't* want to talk about it, Caroline." It was telling, that she didn't chastise her daughter's word choice, and Caroline blanched. "And even if I did, you know how I feel about couples who drag their kids—"

"For Pete's sake, Mom. It's too late to scar me like that, okay?"

"It would scar *me*."

She had her there. Caroline shrugged. "Don't talk to me, then. Just let me make coffee."

"I don't even want coffee," she muttered, losing steam.

"Liar." The woman ran on the stuff, her one true vice, morning, noon, and night.

With a heavy sigh, she turned and headed up the stairs, leaving Caroline in the doorway. "Let me put some clothes on."

"Take your time." Caroline shut the door behind her. Now that she was inside, coming here seemed an even worse idea than it had obviously been from the start. She flipped on the overhead light and blinked into the sudden brightness. In her childhood, this entryway had been shabby chic, with well-worn hardwood and rose-patterned wallpaper, but now gleaming white tile and fresh paint reflected the new LED light to an artificial effect. Mom had fretted that the house should be ready for resale, lest Fred's health decline to the point where a condo without upkeep made better sense. She never complained that in the interim, the renovations meant living in a space that didn't suit her.

In the eat-in kitchen, Caroline placed the doughnuts in the center of the farmhouse table and opened the box invitingly. Yesterday's dregs remained in the coffeepot, and she cleaned the carafe and filter, then filled the brewer to capacity. As the percolator putted and hissed in the empty room, she set out mugs and small plates and rifled through the pantry in search of napkins. Anxiety twisted her gut as she strained for the sounds of Mom's return. She no longer knew what would be worse: leaving here without knowing what had gone on, or finding out.

There were no napkins to be found, and the paper towel holder sat empty. Extras were usually shelved in the garage. She crossed to the far end of the galley and pulled open the door.

Her hand flew to her throat. There, standing in the dim light, was Dad. Through the open bay behind him, his old Buick was parked next to her van.

"Dad! You scared me."

He shifted from one foot to the other, and she got the feeling she'd caught him debating whether to come in after all. "Sorry, sweetheart. It's these new garage doors. Eerily silent, aren't they?"

"What are you—I mean—"

"I saw your Honda. I had a feeling . . .

"That coffee *does* smell good," Mom called behind her. Caroline turned to find her bent over the doughnuts, looking marginally better: She'd washed her face, pulled her hair into a neat nub of a ponytail, and traded her nightgown for a fitted velour jogging suit. She swiped a pastry and took a swift bite.

"Heart-healthy, my ass," she said, half-smiling. Then she looked past Caroline and stopped mid-chew.

"I asked you to leave." Instantly, the strain returned to her voice, the tears again a breath away.

Dad looked stricken but held his ground. "Hannah, listen to me."

"I've listened enough!"

Caroline slunk backward, but no matter how she angled herself, she remained caught in the middle. Literally.

"Why is she here?" he asked calmly, tossing his head in Caroline's direction as he filled the doorway.

"She brought your beloved doughnuts."

He faced his daughter. "Is that all?"

"Don't bring her into this!" Mom was verging again on hysteria.

"I saw the van," he shot back, "and had a bad feeling. That she might have also gotten . . ." His words trailed off, and then both pairs of eyes were on her. She swallowed hard.

"An email?" she ventured.

Mom burst into tears.

"I saw it first," Mom whispered, tossing an accusatory look at her spouse. "If I hadn't, who knows if he ever would have shown me."

"We still don't know there's anything to show, Hannah." He was matching his wife's exhaustion point for point, but without the anger to fuel it, he just looked older than usual. They'd formed an awkward triangle at the kitchen table, though no one had made a move to fill the mugs. The heart-shaped doughnuts mocked them from the box. He turned to Caroline. "We saw it at the same damn time. When it came into my phone, she was on the computer. She puts in for these sweepstakes. Uses my email address so she can enter twice."

"You need to go into the in-box for that?" Caroline asked. Stalling, really.

Mom looked defensive. "You do if you want extra entries for sharing, liking their social media—"

"You never told me you were doing all that," he interrupted. "No wonder I'm flooded with irrelevant ads."

"Somebody's got to win," she snapped. "Might as well be me."

"Or Dad," Caroline added.

"Same thing." At that, Mom buried her face in her hands and started to cry again.

Dad cleared his throat, turning to Caroline. "So you got this same—notification?"

This did not seem the time to admit she'd had a hand in sending the thing. "Not until I logged on. What I got was a note from her. Sela." It was odd to see two people wince so fiercely at such a musical name. A *sea,* followed by a song. Across the table, Mom dropped her hands and stared. "I can show you . . ."

They shook their heads in unison.

She focused on Dad. "Is there *any* chance this could be true?"

He looked away. "I'd need to know more."

"I have it all here in her email. Her mother's name, where she lives—" She stopped, realizing what he'd said. "If you need to know more, the answer is *yes.* There's a chance."

In the silence that followed, her cell phone began to croon at full volume with Walt's ringtone: "It Had to Be You." He'd programmed it as an inside joke. She yanked it from her pocket and silenced it mid-note.

"Be that as it may," Dad said, "it's premature to be discussing the details." So much for Walt's theory of an easy explanation.

Mom laughed mirthlessly. "Guess retirement has made you a little rusty on spinning the data."

A text pinged in, and Caroline glanced at the screen nestled in her palm.

Got through by phone. They're "confident" in familial matches, but they can't be used in court, etc. So, not exactly official.

"I don't think Sela would agree," she said flatly. It seemed mean to say her name again, seeing how it stung them—Mom especially. But what else was she supposed to call her?

"How did she get your email address?" he asked, as if it mattered. Her phone pinged again.

> A 25% DNA match indicates grandchild/grandparent, aunt/niece, or half sibling. They estimated relationship based on your ages.

"It's public on our corporate website." Another ping.

> You can always retest, blah blah blah. No discount for those retesting "because of something they didn't want to hear."

Smug bastards.

"Your public awaits?" Dad looked critically at her phone.

"Sorry." She placed it screen down on the table. "Walt called the company, to see if it could be a mistake."

"And?"

"Unlikely."

Mom's head dropped, while Dad looked on with such anguish Caroline didn't know how to stay.

"Can you give us a day, sweetheart?" He was asking his daughter, but his eyes didn't leave his wife. "Give us a day to talk this out, and then we'll decide where to go from here."

"You two take a day." Mom's voice had returned to a whisper. "When I asked you to leave, Fred, I did not mean to drive around the block."

Caroline could practically hear the bomb inside her mom ticking, and it suddenly seemed possible that maybe it had been there all along, waiting to explode on them all. Much like Sela herself. Caroline got to her feet, reeling in disbelief. There was no *if* about this. This was happening. In the foyer, she turned. They were both watching her go.

"You know what's really weird?" Caroline couldn't help it. "She lives in Brevard. I came so close to moving there. We could have passed each other on the street and not even known."

Mom stiffened. "Yet another reason it's a very good thing you didn't go."

A new layer of confusion wrapped around her thoughts. Caroline had been anything but glad when those plans fell through. Nothing had before or since laid her flat like the raw wound of that heartbreak, Keaton leaving her behind. She'd had to move home, where her parents spent weeks piling on sympathy, never once expressing relief that the split was for the best.

"*Yet another* reason?"

Very good thing?

"Leave it," Dad barked, as if Caroline were the one in the wrong. She blinked at him in surprise. "Give us one day," he repeated.

She turned without another word, childishly slamming the door on her way out. She had the curious feeling of floating above herself, watching her own exit while surveying the formative part of her life—all of their lives—from an angle she'd never had access to before.

It wasn't Dad's admission alone that carried her there, to this dizzy new height. She'd had since yesterday to allow for that possibility, however slim.

But she had not been the slightest prepared for what she saw in Mom, in that final moment. In the moment that pertained, most directly, to Caroline.

When she'd unmistakably looked as if her husband were not the only one who'd been caught in a lie.

4

Sela

Brody zigzagged the playground as fast as his squat legs could carry him, giggling and panting through a one-boy game of chase around the support poles, under the slides, and through the tunnels as if on some secret challenge to explore them all before a buzzer announced time's up. From her perch on the closest bench, Sela might have envied his energy were the force of it not such an amazing feat.

For other toddlers, the physicality of their exuberance was a prerequisite, a default mode set to exhaust their parents, but for Brody it was his hard-fought reward in the endless game of catch-up he'd been playing since birth. Doug was so tall that by rights Brody should have dwarfed his infant counterparts, but instead he'd begun life barely big enough to join their ranks at all. Even now his height and weight were in line with the smallest one-year-olds, though his verbal and motor skills were *almost* on par with the two years he was about to mark. A child whose abilities so outpaced his size might have drawn attention among the parents of his peers, but in this park, dominated by older kids thanks to the rec center across the street, the other moms—and occasionally dads—rarely acknowledged Sela, as most were past the point of close supervision and thus engrossed in whatever was so interesting on their smartphones. At the moment, she and Brody—and Oscar, back on his leash and collapsed at her feet after a raucous game of Frisbee—had the place to themselves, the normal crowd at school.

"Sela!" Leigh came rushing down the sidewalk, breathy and late as always, pushing a mountain of gear in front of her. Annie strained against her stroller straps, having caught sight of the playground, kicking her little legs beneath the lap bar in excitement. In a pouch strapped to Leigh's shoulders, her six-month-old looked right to left, in search of whatever her sister's happy shrieking was about. Between them, an overflowing diaper bag swung like a pendulum from the stroller handles, a bottle and sippy cup rattling in the crossbar's ill-fitting holders. Oscar raised his head and quickly ducked it again, wisely lying low from the toddler's affinity for fur by the handful.

Seeing her best friend like this, laden and frazzled, always made Sela grateful Brody was so low maintenance in that respect, rarely demanding toys or snacks on the go with the impatience she'd seen from Annie. Then again, she and Brody spent an awful lot of time at home; when given free rein to explore, he took it.

"Have you been waiting long? I'm *so* sorry. As usual." Leigh brought the stroller to an abrupt halt beside the bench and kicked the brake on, wrapping a protective arm around the baby as she bent to release the flailing Annie from the torturous confines of her straps.

"No worries. Although I did start without you." Sela held up the half-eaten apple in her hand. "Bad me, I know."

"Good you. That's so much healthier than what's about to pass for my lunch." Leigh caught her misstep instantly, but Sela waved off her cringe. Though poor nutritional choices were a forbidden luxury for Sela, she was past being sensitive about it.

"Hi, Annie girl." Sela smiled down at the toddler. "Love your dress." It was zebra striped from top to bottom, the kind of thing only a certain kind of adult could pull off—the kind that wasn't Sela. Annie rewarded her with a lopsided curtsy before running to join Brody beneath the jungle gym.

"Did you get your steps in?" Leigh plopped next to her on the bench and peeled the waxed paper from a salami sandwich. It couldn't have been more pedestrian—white bread, yellow cheese, no garnishes—but Sela's mouth watered. She quickly sank her teeth back into the apple.

"Most of them. I walked the long way here, so the round trip should do it." They used the same fitness tracker app, Sela focused on getting in her prescribed thirty minutes of daily activity and Leigh aiming to lose the baby weight. Neither had seen the desired results—Sela did usually meet her goals, but her disease didn't seem to care, and her friend was wearing maternity pants even now—but they cheered each other on nonetheless.

"Dizzy at all?" Leigh had dealt with anemia in college, when they'd met as randomly assigned roommates, though hers was self-inflicted by overcorrecting to avoid the freshman fifteen. Neither necessary nor wise for someone burning mad calories on an athletic scholarship. Her extreme diet ended the day Sela dragged her, pale and trembling, to the student health center.

"Leigh," she said gently, "no need to parent me. I think you have enough kids to worry about."

The words held only affection, but Leigh dropped the sandwich into her lap and burst into tears.

"Oh, no. You know I didn't mean—"

"I'm *pregnant*," she said through her sobs.

Sela blinked, her gaze falling to the little face peering up at her from Leigh's carrier, oblivious to her mother's distress. Though her name, Piper, was as whimsical and sweet as her demeanor, she'd come along so soon after her sister that she was more often referred to as merely "the baby." As in, *I barely sleep, between Annie and the baby.*

Only now, there was going to be another one.

"Wow. Um . . ." The thing to do was congratulate her. But she wasn't sure how to go about it while her friend was weeping over the news.

While a part of herself that she despised was struggling not to join her.

"I didn't even think it was possible yet." Leigh's words spilled out in a rush that sounded too much like a protest. "I'm nursing around the clock. I could count on one hand the number of times Van and I've had sex since Piper was born—hell, practically since Annie was born. Yet every test I pee on says it's true." She dissolved again into tears, and Sela's eyes went to Annie. The fearless ball of moxie was on her fifth attempt at climbing up the spiral slide, a feat she had yet to manage more than halfway. Brody had worn himself out and plopped down in the mulch, which he was busy scooping into piles, paying Annie about as much attention as she was paying him. Sela knew this parallel-play stage was developmentally normal, but Annie was an attentive big sister to Piper. In months, the baby would be out there trailing after her—and another would be on the way. The most natural cycle there was.

But not for Sela. Her doctors not only cautioned against another pregnancy, they forbade it. A danger to both her and the fetus, which would likely not make it to term and, regardless of that outcome, endanger her own life in the process. The fact that she was already blowing through late stage three owed a great deal, she'd been told, to that shift in hormones and bodily function, a nine-month-long high-risk complication that could not be avoided unless it was, well, avoided.

For Sela, there would be only Brody.

"I was not going to tell you this"—Leigh sniffed—"until I was prepared to pretend to be happy about it."

"You don't have to pretend with me."

"I sound like a callous bitch." She covered Piper's ears with her hands, too late. "Not only am I resistant to what I know will be a blessing, but I'm selfish enough to cry about it in front of you of all people."

"Leigh, look at me." She'd seen this anguish in her friend before. When the giddy road they'd been traveling in carrying Brody and Annie at the same time—weekly prenatal yoga dates and shared registry links and even the same childbirth class—abruptly forked. Sela's routine urine tests coming back abnormal, leading to diagnosis. The pregnancy itself escalating the decline of her kidney function before anyone could stop it. Brody coming much too soon, the long hospital stay that followed. She'd been left to navigate sharp turns at the top of a steep, deadly cliff while Leigh's road continued straight and smooth, and then even Doug had stopped walking beside her, while Leigh and Van were nesting into a new stage of love with their baby miracle.

Both she and Leigh had tried, earnestly, but neither had known how to bridge the widening chasm between them when the forces quaking their worlds apart were so visceral and raw. The crevasse had grown almost impassably wide before they finally found a way across.

Sela had no interest in going back to that lonely place. No one, least of all Sela, liked someone who couldn't see past their own misfortune to be glad for a friend. And she was through with not liking herself. She'd never *meant* to resent Leigh before, and the difference now was that she was self-aware enough to push back against the reflex. Her eyes flicked to Brody. Small, yes, and weak, maybe, but every bit as fierce as Annie beneath the surface. He was what no one else could ever be: the child of her heart.

"It's just . . ." Poor Leigh was still trying to explain. "When you said I have *enough*—"

"Poor word choice. I hadn't guessed, I swear."

"But it's not fair." Leigh's voice wobbled. "I do have 'enough.' And you . . ." She shook her head. "I know how much you wanted another shot at this." Sela put an arm around Leigh, overcome with an odd gratitude that even when things got awkward, Leigh didn't try to brush them under the rug the way Doug had.

Thank goodness Sela hadn't driven both of them to divorce her.

"I did," Sela admitted. "But that doesn't mean I can't be excited for you. And I am. Or will be, whenever you're ready to feel excited for yourself." Her own eyes had grown teary, but she smiled and could see her friend's relief, though something else hid there, too. Fear.

"What if I don't?" The words were barely audible, but Sela heard.

"You will," she said with conviction. "What does Van think?"

"You know, I was so busy cussing him out I didn't get around to asking." She laughed joylessly. "I'm so *tired*. The idea of remaining awake at all hours for however many more years . . ."

"Sleep is probably what you need now. Why don't I take the girls for the afternoon?"

Leigh's eyes slid sideways. "I can't ask that."

"You didn't ask. I'd enjoy them—honest."

She picked up her sandwich from where it had fallen onto her jeans and took a big bite, as if to prove she was better already. "Thanks, but Annie will be so worn out after this, she'll nap well. I'm just hormonal. And hungry."

"My mother used to pack salami in my lunch," Sela heard herself say.

"Really? Rebecca? The same Rebecca who coaxed us off campus with elaborate home-cooked spreads and regaled us with horror tales about processed food?"

"The earlier version. The broke single-parent version. Once her work took off she had the luxury of becoming more of a nag."

"I never thought I'd *miss* being nagged."

"You and me both. Although she'd be super proud of my diet now. I don't know what she'd find left to concern herself with." They both laughed. Sela had been about a year into her diagnosis—and a mother herself for only six months—when her mother died unexpectedly, having carried to the end a black leather-bound journal filled with meticulous notes—tracking every symptom, researching every drug, calling Sela first and last thing each day, and recording whatever seemed important. *Saw a funny movie—that helped, but misses popcorn. Need to find her a low-sodium sub.* Doug called it the Sela Bible, teasing that if his mother-in-law went so far as embossing the cover, he was *out of there.*

Of course, he'd stopped joking about that once they both realized how much he'd welcome the excuse.

None of them had had reason to look ahead to a life without Rebecca, who at fifty-seven had been far too young and vibrant to pass the way she did. Natural causes, they called it—but vague underlying conditions be damned, it didn't feel natural that such a big heart had simply given out. For Doug, Rebecca's singular devotion to Sela had been a safety net for him shirking his own. For Leigh, it was more personal. With her own family out of state, Sela's mother had been a surrogate parent since college. That her death brought the friends back together was the only good that had come of it.

That, and the fact that Sela didn't have to worry about how she'd pay for treatment. At least, not for a long time. Even with health coverage, patients were advised to have a staggering hundred thousand dollars banked before they even thought about pursuing a transplant. Her mother's life insurance payout took care of that.

Sela would have rather fundraised, groveled, panhandled, a hundred thousand times over.

"You know . . ." Leigh's poker face was horrible. Especially when she was bracing herself to share an unpopular opinion. "If your mother had known she was on her way out, she might have revisited her stance on your father."

Sela fought the urge to say Leigh sounded like Doug, though it would have gotten her to stop. He'd never been so uptight before all this. In fact, his old devil-may-care gleam was the first thing she'd ever noticed about him—the thing that had drawn her near. He'd been waiting on a bar stool for his blind date, who was running late. Sela had popped in for a carryout order, they'd gotten to chatting, and when the date finally arrived, he'd leaned to whisper in Sela's ear, "I don't want to have dinner with her. I want to have dinner with you."

She'd smiled coyly. "Tomorrow?"

And he'd replied, "Not soon enough."

His date was not amused.

Sela wasn't the only one who'd grown so different she was unrecognizable now.

"No," she told Leigh. "Ecca had opportunities aplenty to reverse course on dear ol' Dad."

When your mother raised you around a steady stream of artist friends and students and buyers, when she spoke of herself in the third person as if to reassure you both—*There, let it never be said your mother can't manage dinner on a dime*—and when you had no father or sibling around referring to her as *Mom,* you ended up creating your own version of the name you most often heard her called. In their case, the only bit Sela could pronounce as a toddler stuck. When she started school, she saved *Ecca* for home and publicly opted for *Mother,* even though her friends sometimes asked, *Why so formal?* She never knew why *Mom* felt strange on her tongue. Maybe it had something to do with the fact that Ecca, though they made a tight pair, was so obviously not meant to belong to anybody, least of all in a supporting role. She imagined Brody would have called his grandmother *Ecca,* too, had she lived to see him thrive.

"But if you hear back—when you hear back—from this sister, we all know it's not just her on the other end of this. This could be big: a whole side to your family you didn't know about. Maybe they'll be glad to hear from you."

"Given it's already been a few days, we can probably rule that out."

"Premature."

"Plus, we've been over this. My father isn't on the table. That way, I don't betray Ecca's wishes, he doesn't have to feign some heartfelt explanation for the past three point five decades, and all I have to do is handle the small matter of winning over his other daughter enough to . . . well, you know. It keeps things the simplest possible version of clusterfunked."

Leigh sighed. "I understand the boundaries you need to draw around this to feel okay about reaching out. But we all know there's a lot more to this than a potential, maybe, compatible kidney donor. All I'm saying is to keep an open mind. Having more support in your life could be a positive thing, no matter what else happens, or doesn't happen. I worry about you, Sela."

What to say to that? That of course the possibility of there being "more to this" had not only entered her mind but consumed it? That Sela could think of little else but what Caroline must be thinking—whether she'd ever suspected, whether she even believed her? That hinging hope on this far-flung chance—the idea of a prospective sister relationship as slim and foreign as that of a donor match—was too thick a risk when she was hanging from so thin a thread? That she still longed for her mother with the fervor of a lost child?

Do the DNA test, her doctors had urged upon learning half of Sela's parentage was unknown.

Contact her, her friends had urged upon learning the test had turned up a half sibling. Leigh herself had helped her look up Caroline online: A husband and three kids, her bio said. That meant half nieces, nephews. Maybe not too far off from Brody's age.

Did people really think it was only the DNA on her mind? Sela let it stand—though a less biased party might have thusly seen her as cold, calculating, in spite of all the nudging required to carry her this far. Better than the unbearable vulnerability of admitting that the idea of a family was a far stronger pull even than a kidney her life might depend on.

"We'll see. Like I said, you won't catch me driving to Ohio, knocking on doors."

"Has anyone told Doug that?"

"I take it you saw his Big Ask."

"Is that what they call it when you're trying to assuage your guilt in public?"

"That's what *he* calls it."

"Should I put out a call too? I didn't realize we'd reached that point, but if we have, I will not be upstaged." Leigh had done the initial blood test last year, in spite of being advised she should be sure her family was complete before donating. A moot concern: no match.

"We have not. But I appreciate you putting your competitive nature to work for my cause."

"Competitive kidney culling. And here I thought I'd missed my chance at an Olympic medal." Sela laughed—it wasn't just a lame joke. Leigh's onetime Olympic hopes were what had brought her to town; Brevard College's cycling team was about the only thing putting it on the map. But when her times didn't improve enough after a year of hard training, she acquiesced to her coach's doubts. *I love it,* she'd said then, *but I don't live for it the way those people do. I can accept that what I'm willing to offer is not enough.* That was it: no wallowing. Sela always admired that her friend had somehow managed to quit without ever behaving as a quitter.

Sela didn't think she had it in her to let go of a dream that way.

These days, her dreams consisted of things other people took for granted. But she did live for them—fought for them harder than she'd ever fought for anything before. On the online forums she canvassed, fellow patients talked about the upsides they'd found to their illness, and though Sela found it difficult—laughable, offensive—to feel anything but spite toward hers, if forced to cite a silver lining, it was that she'd found the fight that had been within her all along. She was here, wasn't she? Out in the world, breathing the air? Getting her steps in, rain or shine?

Anyone who thought Doug being out ahead shouting into his megaphone meant that *he* was the one coaxing *her* along wasn't paying attention.

Brody came running, arms outstretched, her own sudden fatigue reflected in his eyes. She gathered Oscar's collapsible water bowl and got to her feet, grateful for the excuse to go before the conversation turned back to Doug. She wanted to think she was over him—how could any self-respecting person not be?—but she'd never get over what had happened between them.

Annie followed Brody's lead, throwing herself into her mother's lap. Leigh wiped the smears of tear-streaked mascara from her cheeks and smiled down at her daughter, maternal adoration clouding out the angst of her earlier confession.

"Don't count that medal out yet," Sela told her. "In the mom events, you're going to be a triple threat."

Leigh looked at her with such compassionate gratitude that

Sela had to look away. "You'll call me, right? As soon as you hear anything back at all?"

Sela rested her hand atop Brody's fine hair and smiled as bravely as she could.

"Who else would I call?"

5

Caroline

Dad had asked for a day. On the heels of that surreal morning, Caroline had forwarded Sela's email to both parents—*FYI*—without further comment. Beyond that due diligence, she wasn't about to break the silence, make the next move. Not after her inadvertent role in what had happened so far, and the odd note things had ended on.

Thus, she went through the motions as if time itself had slowed as "one day" stretched into two, then three. Caroline didn't appreciate being avoided. She wasn't the one who'd done the wrong thing. At least, not the big wrong thing. So when Dad called on Friday, she answered with a gut feeling that fell oddly between relief and dread—that she might finally get some answers but might not like them.

"I've been at one of these extended stay places, but they're sold out Saturday for a wedding, and between Oktoberfest and the Bengals/Steelers game, I can't find anything that isn't a small fortune. Any chance I can stay with you?"

They didn't have a bedroom to spare, but their semi-finished basement housed a pullout couch, every bit as uncomfortable as the rest of its breed, with the added misery of subterranean dankness. Still. She wasn't sure any accommodations at her address could be shoddy enough to ward off resentment on Mom's part.

"Just for a night," he added, reading her thoughts. "She has enough grounds for divorce as it is." His tone made light, but they both knew he wasn't exaggerating.

What was the alternative—send him to a friend's couch, where the circle of Mom's humiliation would only grow? Besides, Caroline wanted answers. What could she say but yes?

Walt wasted no time in planning his exit. "You two should talk. Alone." Then, moments later, head up from an events calendar on his phone: "That railroad in Lebanon has a princess-themed ride Saturday afternoon. Think Owen would go along with it since a train is involved?"

Caroline raised her eyebrows. "How much is this talk with Dad going to cost me?" But she couldn't help returning his sideways grin, even as a current of memories tugged at her heart. Every year for Father's Day, Dad used to flip the script with a special daughter date, telling everyone who asked that treating her was the best treat for him. Carousel rides at the zoo until she grew dizzy. Reds tickets behind the dugout, with clouds of cotton candy. An overflowing pick-your-own basket at the blueberry festival.

Sela never had any of that.

Would *all* Caroline's memories be colored this way—like her ignorance-as-bliss childhood had been at the expense of someone else's silent sacrifice? She desperately didn't want that to be true.

She desperately needed to know if it was.

"Let Owen take that foam sword we got at the Renaissance Festival," she suggested. "He can be a knight, or a prince."

"Good call. Has anyone told you that you're pretty good at this mom thing?"

Silly as it might sound, they made a point of trading compliments almost on a schedule. Maureen had noticed once, called her out, and rather than owning up to the weekly reminders set on her calendar, Caroline had shrugged and said, *Don't knock it till you try it.* But this was gentler, kinder: Walt sensing without her saying so how anxious it would make her to juggle Dad and the kids at once and how she was not currently feeling *pretty good* at anything. Maybe it was Walt, then, as much as her memories rendering her in this moment verklempt.

Alone in the quiet house Saturday morning, Caroline found she could do little but wait. She flipped through a magazine but retained nothing. Unable to locate the TV remote, she launched a top-to-bottom search and recovered it in the fridge. That sent her hunting for the coffee creamer, which sat warm and ruined in the living room console.

At last, the doorbell rang—but even the chime was out of place. Usually Dad flung open the door and yodeled, "Yoo-hoo!" The formality had her bracing for how he might look—like he hadn't slept or kept up with the blood pressure meds Mom usually monitored. But here he was—not tired or pallid.

Only sad.

"I have some 'splaining to do," he said by way of greeting, holding up a plastic bag of Thai lunch carryout, a peace offering she wasn't sure she could swallow. She tried to smile, to go along—as if he weren't someone other than the man she'd seen him as before. If there'd been no end product of his infidelity, the issue would have remained between her parents and them alone. Did it have to involve her now, just because said end product not only existed but found her first?

It was a question only she could answer, which made it all the more miserable. Because the answer she kept coming back to was yes.

The warm aroma of ginger and sweet basil filled the kitchen as he unloaded the noodle bowls onto the table. She grabbed silverware and ice waters and took her seat across from him.

"Have you talked to Mom?" She'd meant to let him speak first but couldn't stand the quiet.

He leaned back in his chair in a manner that suggested she wouldn't like what he was about to say. "Your mom has given me an ultimatum: She'll have me back if I promise not to pursue a relationship with Sela."

This was not where Caroline had expected to begin. This wasn't the beginning, thirty-some years back, but the end. Present day. She blinked at him. "She wants to just—pretend this hasn't happened?"

He cleared his throat. "I'm not sure Hannah is as surprised as she's let on, to be honest. It might be more accurate to say she wants to *keep* pretending."

A puzzle piece clicked into place—the hollow darkness in her mother's eyes the last time they'd said good-bye. It had the depth of an old, unhealed wound, not the fresh cut of a new one. "Are you saying she knew about Sela's mother all along?"

He sighed. "Well, she knew Sela's mother. The message you forwarded confirmed that."

In the beat of silence that reverberated between them, Caroline tried to picture someone, *anyone,* she knew sleeping with Walt. How disregarded she would feel, by both of them.

She didn't imagine the torment of that kind of betrayal had an expiration date.

"Rebecca, she was . . . God, this is hard." He picked up his water glass and gulped, spilling a little down his chin and trying to laugh at himself as he wiped it on the shoulder of his sweater. "I don't want you to think worse of me. But I suppose it's too late for that."

"I don't know, Dad. It was a long time ago, okay?"

He nodded again, steeling himself with a deep breath. "Rebecca Astin was a good friend of your mom's. And then, after—well, she wasn't. So I don't know for a fact how much Hannah knew, but I had my suspicions all along."

A good friend? Oh, Dad. How *could* he have? How could Rebecca have? Caroline felt disloyal for having reassured him. This was somehow worse for Mom. And yet . . . "As in, she may have known about your affair, or as in, she may have known about the pregnancy?"

He shrugged.

Caroline stared. "But *you* did not know about the baby?"

"Unequivocally not."

A detail that had been nagging at her surfaced. "Your profile settings, on the DNA site—you'd opted out of the database. Why?"

He squinted at her. "I don't know what you're talking about. And I'm not sure I want to."

She sat stunned into comparing this new picture of Mom with the one she'd had before. How could the spouse whisperer, the doting wife who'd always done everything by the book, be the same woman as the shadowboxer who'd met Caroline at the door, ready for a fight she might have had reason to fear? A fight she might have taken questionable steps to thwart?

"If Mom knew all along, why throw you out now? Isn't it a little late for ultimatums?"

"Turning a blind eye on a hunch is one thing. Having the truth thrust in your face in front of the people you love most is quite another. How else would any self-respecting woman react?"

"But if she knew about Sela, and never said—you'd forgive her that?"

A weighty pause hovered over the table. "You say that as if I'm not asking for a great deal of forgiveness in turn," he said finally. "Would I have wanted her, or Rebecca, anyone to tell me? Of course. Am I in a position to pass judgment on doing the right thing, and what the right thing even was? Hardly."

An incredulous grunt escaped her. "Well, where does this ultimatum leave me? I'm the one Sela reached out to. I can't pretend this hasn't happened."

"No one asked *you* to. I think Hannah knows she can't ask that, which is what makes this such a blow to her, even if it wasn't the total blindside it may have seemed." He shifted uncomfortably. "Listen, she's your mom no matter what, loves you no matter what. Her role as my wife involves more scrutiny of the data. If you maintain contact with Sela, don't expect Mom to want to hear about it, but I doubt she'd begrudge you whatever you decide on your own."

Caroline considered this—the sister she'd sometimes, as a little girl, wished for, but never like this, discovered and then sealed in a secret compartment. A whole part of her life that she'd keep to herself. How would that even work?

Evidently, she could ask Dad for tips. Mom, too, for that matter.

"Without the ultimatum," she said slowly, "how would you be feeling about this?"

"That is what's known as a pointless question."

"This isn't some customer survey you've been hired to pick apart. It's about you. It matters to me."

"I'm—" He slouched, and his face flushed crimson, reminding her how seldom she'd seen him embarrassed. "Fine. To be honest, I'm heartbroken that I never knew. I think that's the other thing that's so difficult for Hannah. That I would have cared, a great deal—I never would have just let it go. But what I want doesn't take precedence over her wishes now the way it might've then. She says that she could never look at this woman and see anything but my betrayal. That inviting her into our lives would unravel everything else in a way your mom can't get past—and in fairness to her, she wouldn't have to get past it if I'd honored our vows. I owe it to Hannah to respect that."

"Sela might argue you owe her something too."

"But I've unknowingly shirked that duty for *decades,* Caroline. Is there really a chance of making that up to her now? It's hard to imagine her directing anything but resentment toward me."

She shook her head. He might have retired, but he was still an *actual* professional at finding a mental path to justify most anything.

"Could you back up and tell me about Rebecca? About what happened? Honestly?"

He held up his hands as if she'd caught him. As if he'd known she would. "What do you want to know?"

She stared at the untouched food growing soggy between them. How many details could she stomach? "How did you meet? Through Mom, I take it?"

He grimaced. "This is going to keep sounding worse."

"If you expect this to be the only time we ever discuss this, I'm not letting it go until I get the whole story."

He looked away. "I met her at our wedding."

Worse indeed. "Please tell me you didn't—"

"Of course not. But it *was* an at-first-sight kind of thing."

"Dad. I distinctly remember you calling that whole concept bunk. Multiple times."

"I wanted it to be. Still do. Rebecca was the friend who Hannah always talked about but I'd never met. She was an artist, talented enough to be accepted to competitive programs before she was even out of high school. They'd been close since they were little, but she'd been studying abroad for as long as I'd known Hannah. A semester in London, a summer in Paris, a year in Italy . . ." The emotion in his eyes turned to something she'd never have expected. Pride. "Their home lives were equally bad, which is how they bonded in the first place. But for Rebecca, not only did her parents not get along, they wouldn't get divorced. They were older—had already raised Rebecca's brother, who was long gone—and the way she put it was that they were over being parents. Her father stopped bothering to hide what a violent drunk he was. Once she realized her talent was her ticket out, she used it. But she and Hannah wrote to each other—your mom wallpapered her dorm room with the postcards."

Caroline already knew how soon after graduation her parents had gotten married. The following weekend, in fact.

"Hannah was so excited Rebecca was coming back in time for the wedding. At the rehearsal dinner, she forced the two of us together and commanded us to not stop talking until we'd won each other over." He didn't look at Caroline when he said this, which was just as well. "I hadn't any qualms about jumping into marriage up to that point. That's what you did in those days. Hannah had been my sweetheart since before I understood what a sweetheart was. When we met, she was the shy new girl everyone felt sorry for. Not only was her parents' split a gossipy disaster, but who moves their kid to a new district senior year? It made me feel good, being able to make things better for her simply by being kind. She was pretty, and loved me back. Why *wouldn't* I stay with her at UC? Why *wouldn't* I marry her?" He shook his head. "But when I got talking to Rebecca, I never wanted to stop. I began to worry I was starting to understand new things about love. The way it can knock you off your feet, blind you to reason."

"You two became friends outside of the group?"

"More like, when the group got together, we'd gravitate toward each other. Rebecca wasn't having the easiest time reacclimating."

Caroline had asked for this, but she found it difficult to listen. Perhaps because he was starting to look genuinely wistful. "Sounds like a pattern," she said coldly. "Like you always had a thing for the new girl."

He blinked at her. "Nothing about Rebecca seemed lost, or wanting to fit in. She was the most self-possessed person I've ever met. On top of that, you had this sense that she was fleeting—that she was far too interesting to stay. I found it impossible not to be drawn in by her." He shook his head. "I'm making it sound much more ordinary than it felt. But doesn't all love?"

"It sounds selfish."

Oddly, he smiled—as if ceding a point worth losing. "But doesn't all love?" he repeated.

It was Caroline's turn to merely blink. Where had this side of him been hiding? What else was in there? "So was the affair a onetime slip, or a long-term thing?"

"In between. We both knew it was wrong, but the idea of stopping was as unthinkable as what we'd already done. I'm ashamed to say it, but I was . . . reevaluating my choices. I'd barely been married a year."

"So what changed your mind? Or made up your mind?"

"Hannah got pregnant."

This was more than a recounting of his wake-up call. It was Caroline's appearance in the story. Her mouth went dry. "I'm the only reason you stayed?"

He shook his head, adamant. "I never stopped loving Hannah the way I always had. Even at my most conflicted, I don't think I'd have brought myself to leave her—she was so wrecked by her parents' divorce that going through one herself, especially that fast, would have destroyed her. I'd have hated myself for it. I only wished, once I saw what love was capable of, that I could love her that way too. I promised myself to try, and that was the end of Rebecca."

But Sela's birthday was so close to hers. "Only Rebecca was pregnant too."

"Evidently." The pain in his eyes was real. "When I told her about Hannah and you, she removed herself, instantly—moved hundreds of miles away so fast it was hard to believe she hadn't planned to all along. And maybe she had. She always talked about setting up in one of those little artisan towns."

"Brevard."

"Yes. And if she kept in touch with anyone here, I never heard about it."

"When I was thinking about moving there with Keaton, what did you—I mean, did it come up again? With you? With Mom?"

"Rebecca has *never* come up again with me and Mom."

"Their friendship just stopped? And you never asked why?"

"Asking why would have been what's known as pressing my luck. Hannah was a newlywed and then a new mother. Rebecca was this free spirit letting her talent lead her somewhere totally different. At least, I *thought* it was totally different. I never pictured her changing diapers and warming bottles, the way we were. . . ." He cleared his throat. "It was conscionable that the friendship would grow apart, so that's the story I told myself. When your move to Brevard was on the table, I do remember hoping Rebecca had moved on from there, and resisting the urge to look—but then it was off the table, so I put her out of my mind again, too."

"What if you'd known about Sela? From the beginning, I mean?"

"You know how I feel about *what-ifs.*" *A waste of time.* His eyes clouded. "I was so sorry to read in that email that Rebecca died. I'd never allowed myself to so much as type her name into a search engine. But I did this week, at the hotel—and she's left so much beauty behind. Paintings, murals, mixed-media collaborations. And a legacy of students—she'd been an adjunct at Brevard College. The world is a less colorful place without her, yet her color is still here. That brings me some peace."

Brevard College. Not only the town Caroline had almost relocated to but the campus. The coincidence poked at her, but she shoved it aside.

"Her *daughter* is still here. *Your* daughter. How can you let Mom dictate whether you meet her?"

She didn't know what had prompted Sela to reach out.

Curiosity, duty? But the fact that she had seemed to indicate Sela would not as easily dismiss newfound knowledge of blood ties. What might those ties hold besides blood? Caroline was Sela's half sibling. But their father? His title in respect to them both was whole.

"Sweetheart, I'm becoming an old man. I'm not a well man. My heart is a ticking clock, and I don't know how much time is left on it. Your mom and I have spent this lifetime together, raised you, gone on to see your beautiful children born, and we're proud of our legacy, if you could call it that. Up until that email, we were proud, damn it." He pounded the table, his dreamy sadness turning to resistance, and Caroline jumped. "The last thing I do on this planet will *not* be disappointing my faithful wife. I've already broken her heart, and maybe Rebecca's too, even Sela's by default. If I can glue only one of those things back together, I choose Hannah."

"If you've already decided, why aren't you back home?"

"Among other things, I wanted to talk with you first. Anything you have left to ask, ask it now, because once I go back Hannah will not be open to us discussing this further."

"Isn't it cold to carry on like Sela isn't out there?" She was disappointing him, not being a team player. But she barely even recognized this team anymore.

"Being your father is the best thing I've ever done. Certainly the only thing I haven't screwed up." She didn't laugh. He leaned in. "It's devastating to know I missed out on that with someone else. But letting her in now would hurt you too, if only because Mom would be . . ." He shook his head. "We all make hard choices to preserve the happiness of those we love." He flipped open a noodle bowl and dropped in a spoon. "Rebecca too. If she'd wanted me to know, I'd have known. In that way, this course feels like respecting her wishes as well as Hannah's."

"But Sela reached out. Don't you think she knows best what her mother wanted?"

He handed over her lukewarm bowl, and she dropped it back onto the table with a thud. "She didn't reach out to me," he said gently. "She reached out to you."

"This is not exactly Six Degrees of Kevin Bacon."

He lifted his hands in surrender. "I don't mean to sound flippant. I know it puts you in a terrible position, and I'm sorry. I can't change what's happened. Even if I could . . ."

Had she ever before realized how much her father's practical, even-keeled attitudes about relationships had influenced her own? Love at first sight nothing more than a fairy tale; what-ifs merely a waste of time; quiet compromise trumping open dialogue.

All based on lies.

He was unmistakably glad of the time he'd had with Rebecca. While Caroline agonized over the revelation, he'd spent the last few days nursing a decades-old thirst. One last time, he'd reopened that sealed-forever bottle and let himself drink in the things Rebecca had left behind. She was the reason he had not looked haggard on Caroline's doorstep this morning. He was sorry, and yet he wasn't.

"You two always said I was an only child because you got it 'so right the first time.' But now I'm wondering if there's more to it."

"There's not. We meant every word."

She was reaching, she knew. For what? She couldn't shake this nagging feeling that there was something left to put her finger on.

"You honestly think you and Mom will go back to being happy now?"

"If we don't, it won't be her fault. It'll be mine."

This was the bolded one-line summary of his analysis. There was no arguing with it.

"Can't have that," she mumbled.

He would tell himself, today and tomorrow and all the days after, that she'd come to understand in time. She knew him well enough to know that.

But for the first time ever, she wondered what life would be like if she didn't. Because if Dad had traded Mom for Rebecca?

He'd have traded Caroline for Sela, too.

Sela

In the back room Sela had converted to a studio, the best parts of her mother still lived.

Last year, when she'd had no choice but to ready Ecca's left-behind bungalow for sale, she hadn't thought twice about boxing up the piles of sketchbooks for her mother's partners at Aesthetic—the storefront their collective had conceived of as part boutique, part gallery. Determined and dutiful, Sela sorted the shelves of art history hardcovers for Ecca's favorite students, the clothes for the women's shelter, the dishware for an adjunct colleague doing "mosaics for public art" installations. It didn't matter that her mother had never spelled out what she'd have wanted; Sela knew. Just as Ecca knew Sela didn't care about those things the way she cared about, say, the stout Amish-built bookshelf that had stood at Ecca's bedside for as long as Sela could remember—that was with her at the unexpected end, even though Sela was not.

Sela's artistic talent was not like her mother's, inherent and deep and inescapable even without the formal training she'd pursued. It was borne instead from years sprawled on Ecca's studio floor with a basket of cast-off art supplies, hoping that wanting to be like her was enough. As a teen, Sela gravitated to graphic design—where even indelicate fingers could pinpoint the right elements and arrange them in pleasing ways. It wasn't easy, waiting for her skill to catch up to the pictures she rendered in her mind, but Ecca saw from the start what she was trying to do and nurtured the best of her impulses. Her designs were never, even early on, conventional. They were unexpected, even if not entirely successful.

"Your imagination," Ecca would say when Sela showed frustration, "is your superpower. Never underestimate what you can do with it."

She kept Ecca's old bookcase in view of her desk now, to remind her. Loaded its shelves with the other precious few things she'd kept—things no one but her would miss. The frayed copy of *Little Women,* dog-eared pages marking Jo's fieriest moments. The Boggle game they'd played when Sela was home sick from school, the letter dice yellowing, the box stuffed with old score sheets she couldn't bear to throw away. The hot plate that had daily kept her mother's mug of tea steaming and now warmed Sela's own. And, tucked out of view, a tiny, hand-carved wooden box she'd promised herself, just as Ecca had promised *herself,* to open only in case of emergency.

Ecca called Sunday evenings "the memory hours." For tucking the best of the weekend away to a place you could keep close, for summoning whatever fortitude you might need to face the week ahead, for savoring the precious time left before appointments and obligations took over again. Sela had taken to spending them here, with these reminders of what life had been like when feeling loved was as simple as a one-on-one game or a classic novel read aloud under a blanket big enough for two.

This weekend had been especially bleak—unavoidable, when Doug took his turn at custody. But Oscar was back now, his renewed commitment to remaining underfoot making her laugh as often as it made her trip. Brody was snuggled across the hall—never fully himself on these transition days when he'd reappear in the house that was most his home, with the parent who was most his guardian. He'd hug her tight but stay quiet, go to bed early a bit too willingly. But by morning he'd be back to normal, and she'd patch the tear in her heart and think, *Okay, we can do this, just us two. Plenty of people do this.*

Ecca did this.

In fact, her mother was still lending purpose to Sela's days. Aesthetic remained her steadiest client, with Ivy, Ecca's closest partner in the collective, hiring Sela to maintain everything from their website to takeaway cards to booth signage at street fairs—though surely as a group of artists, they could have managed on their own.

It wasn't that the work made her feel closer to her mother, exactly. Feeling Ecca's presence, for Sela, had never been about her art—though it adorned her whole house and half the town, too. She'd always known those works would outlive Ecca in the way every artist is aware of this fact, whether consciously dwelled upon or merely accepted as a blessing or even curse of the gig. The art, then, took on no mystique after her death, but the work to carry its legacy did give Sela something to do. It seemed fitting to do it here, where she kept the small parts of her mother's heart that had never been brushed onto canvas for everyone to see.

The parts she'd saved for her daughter.

The parts Sela never liked to share.

On a grade school field trip, when Ecca lent her own coat to an underdressed classmate, Sela began to shiver. Years later, when a down-on-her-luck sculptor took over the guest room, Sela counted the days until the perfectly unobtrusive woman would leave. Even in college, when Ecca joined the cheering section along Leigh's road course, Sela burned with shameful jealousy welling where no one could see.

Maybe it was compounded by having a mother who shared

so much of herself so fully—opening a vein for every project, no matter how small. But Sela—who'd met her grandparents on only a few terse occasions, who'd learned to stop asking about her father, who'd watched her mother claw their way, commission by commission, out of their crammed apartment and at last into that light-filled bungalow—had grown up viewing life as her and Ecca versus the world. It was hard to stop seeing anything that changed that, for better or worse, as a threat.

Sela did stop, though. Doug broke through with his easy laugh and game-for-anything stance, filling pockets of her soul she hadn't realized were empty. Elated that her daughter had found what she herself never could—a true life partner—Ecca loved Doug like a son. But years later, when Sela feigned sleep while her mother, on the other side of her hospital room door, came at Doug with as much compassion as fury, that old jealousy reared its head, and she wanted to spring from her mechanical bed and claw at him, not for leaving her but for making her mother care about him enough to try to accept his reasons.

"The problem with Doug," Ecca told Sela that next morning—when he was gone, *really* gone—"is he has no imagination." This, considering the source, was as close as she'd get to an insult. And Sela, who by then had to reach for things to be glad of, made a fist around this: the fact that once again she had Ecca all to herself.

Until she didn't.

Sela ran her fingers over the shelves of her mother's things, breathing in the comfort that wafted up around her.

Then, she dropped into her desk chair and opened her laptop, intent on designing a print she could frame for Leigh: a gift that reimagined everything news of a new baby should be. The silhouette of a dream so sweet you barely dared to breathe it, stretching its arms triumphantly under a vast field of bright stars.

But bolded and unopened on her screen, she found a new email instead.

Dear Sela:

To say your message came as a surprise is an understatement. I feel as if I owe you an apology, though of course I had no idea there was any possibility you existed. But it does appear likely that you are correct: that I am not the only child I've always believed myself to be.

Out whooshed a breath she didn't know she'd been holding, loud enough that Oscar's collar jangled from the floor at her side.

Her mysterious sister, little more than a name until now, had written back. Here were Caroline's words, tumbling across Sela's screen with reluctance and grace.

She'd written back.

This revelation has stirred up quite a bit of turmoil in my family—which I'm telling you not to shift responsibility or cast blame, but to explain my delay in responding. I don't know how much you might have guessed or been told about my—our—father's situation, but he's been married to my mother since before either you or I were, evidently, conceived. His infidelity notwithstanding, he was just as shocked to learn about you. Suffice it to say my parents have some things to work through, and need space to do it. He has issues with his heart, and . . . Well, I won't make his excuses.

I'm not sure what you hoped for in reaching out, but I'm open to corresponding—I'd like to learn more about you, compare notes. But it would be disingenuous if I didn't let you know I'm the only one in my family who feels this way.

If you're willing to get to know one another independently of other expectations or ties . . . I'd like that. If you think I have a lot of nerve imposing limits, especially when I'm in my shoes and you're in yours—well, you'd be right. No hard feelings if you'd rather pretend you never read this, move on.

Sela tipped her face to the ceiling. She wanted to laugh with incredulity, to cry with relief.

Caroline was so careful, so obviously worried she was about to disappoint Sela. Or, perhaps more to the point, that their father was.

No danger of that. At least, there wasn't supposed to be.

Couldn't be.

That her father had been married, with children, all along was one of the many possibilities Sela had entertained over the years. Learning it was true brought no worldview-altering surprise, no harsh judgment that Ecca was no longer here to defend—even as Sela took in the confirmation that Caroline was in fact, strictly speaking of the DNA, likely her strongest hope: no other siblings. And the heart issues mentioned would keep her father off any prospective donor list—a relief, really, as she'd never have considered him and had no desire to argue the point with Doug, Leigh, or a well-meaning doctor.

For Sela these details merely provided a better frame of reference. Yet clearly her own email had turned the whole picture upside down for Caroline. And Sela hadn't even told her the most upside-down part.

Perhaps Sela had been feeling preemptively guilty for the wrong reasons.

I'm not sure what you hoped for in reaching out. As Sela reread the words, she wasn't sure either. Everything seemed in conflict—things Doug and Leigh wanted for her, things Ecca hadn't, things Sela wished she didn't need. But *open to corresponding* was a good place to start. The only place, really.

I'd love to know more about your mother. I'm so sorry for your loss. Dad tells me he was quite taken with her, and though I have mixed feelings about that, I know she must have been very special. To that end, if she ever spoke of him to you, I'd love to know what she said. This is new to me, though I suspect it's familiar to you: having this puzzle in your mind that is missing pieces. Maybe we can help each other fill in the gaps.

Yours,

Caroline

Sela held onto the desk, as if she were teetering on a high ledge. Although she supposed she *had* thought of Caroline as the one with the answers, this had never been about filling *those* gaps.

But she should have expected it would become so for Caroline.

In those grief-stricken days of cleaning out her mother's bungalow, Sela did search, against her better judgment, for any sign of her mysterious father. She didn't want to regret letting this chance pass her by. But she'd found none, and that alone seemed evidence that Ecca hadn't been *taken with* him in turn. Or that if she had been, she'd wanted to forget.

Caroline clearly thought it charitable to write *our father* instead of *my*. But she could keep him. His stories, too. Who knew if they were even true? For some women, that a man had transgressed out of love would be the last thing they'd want to hear; they'd more easily explain away a physical moment of weakness. For others, love was the *only* forgivable reason to do something unforgivable.

It had certainly been that way for Sela and Doug.

Of course Sela would write back—she didn't have the luxury of deciding not to. She'd open up about herself, starting basic before getting into Doug, Brody, everything that had happened. It would all come out in time—it had to, or this would be for nothing.

But she would see Caroline's limits and raise her a few of her own.

Sela was no more willing to share her mother's memory in death than she had been to share her affection in life. Least of all with Caroline.

Not even during the Sunday memory hours that this stranger of a sister had, miraculously, managed to make the tiniest bit less lonely.

7

Caroline

Caroline had spent a single long weekend with Keaton in Brevard, when they went for their face-to-face interviews at the college. In the year after graduation, they'd coordinated job applications out of town, targeting places they both found interesting—trendy cities, scenic regions—and so far in the responses, this was their only double hit: He was up for a coaching job, she for a position in alumni relations, and both had already passed multiple phone screens.

One of them—neither claimed responsibility—must have suggested taking the scenic route in, because they ended up pulled to the side of a narrow road in Pisgah National Forest, leaning over the guardrail where the Looking Glass Falls plunged into a shallow pool far below, sucking greedy gulps of cool air. Never had Caroline been so carsick: The roads weren't merely curved but coiled, tight and steep and up and down and around in endless circles. But the journey was worth it. The forest around them was impossibly green, thickly carpeted with huge lush ferns that lent an exotic, Jurassic quality to the landscape.

They hiked out and back to another waterfall, a thinner, higher trickle from a limestone ridge they could climb behind, then watched a busload of students queue up to *whoosh* down a natural waterslide called, what else, Sliding Rock. By the time they reached Brevard proper, Caroline was newly stocked on ginger ale, peppermints, and daydreams. She'd always been partial to small college towns, but the surrounding natural beauty made her love this on sight.

Keaton was just as taken, though he'd known better what to expect. The right convergence of geographic features and trails through them made this an increasingly top spot in the country for cyclists to train. Brevard College was so small that back in Ohio its name was obscure, but its cycling team ranked as up-and-coming, and the athletic department was expanding, with sights set on Division I. Keaton had won a handful of collegiate championships before earning his master's in sports science, and was a perfect candidate for the new assistant slot. He pounced on the opportunity like a kid who'd resigned himself to growing up but then found a loophole to keep playing with his favorite toys.

They checked into an inn in a walkable part of town, and she went exploring on her own, giving Keaton time to collect his thoughts for the selection committee. Her job was more straightforward, less competitive, and she'd been given the impression this interview was little more than a formality—to lay eyes on her before making the offer—so she'd come with more curiosity than anxiety. The streets put her in mind of a smaller, mountain-rimmed Athens, the Appalachian town where they'd met when Keaton was in grad school and she was finishing undergrad at Ohio University. To some of her friends who'd stayed in Cincinnati at UC or Xavier, OU's campus was too much of an isolated bubble.

But Caroline loved that bubble, from its bumpy brick streets to its iconic Burrito Buggy, and cried when she left as if bidding farewell to a friend who'd seen her through the best time of her life.

By the end of her self-guided Brevard tour—from the eclectic vintage shops to the coffee roaster selling stamped brown bags of whole bean, from the colorful boutiques to the gem and crystal "mine" filled with oddities and treasures—she was starting to feel about the prospects of this town the way Keaton did about the job. That it was something of a seasonal tourist stop for those going off the beaten path—walls of T-shirts boasting "The Land of Waterfalls" and postcards showing the mountains' beauty in floral bloom, in brilliant fall hues, even in snow—only amplified its appeal. She and Keaton had both moved back to Cincinnati by default, but now seemed the time to explore, see what else was out there before settling. Keaton was living with his parents while he completed one last internship, and she'd moved into an apartment with Maureen, both of them having landed the kinds of entry-level jobs one could bide time in without getting attached.

She'd loved Maureen like a sister since childhood, but after going separate ways for college, they found cohabitation felt too much like a backward step. They hadn't learned yet how to be more than their old juvenile selves together—selves they were ready to outgrow. Rather than dissolving into awkwardness, they agreed that one way or another Caroline would move out at the soonest opportunity. The truth was, she'd have followed Keaton anywhere if he asked her to. But for both of them to find opportunities here? One day was all it took to feel as though she'd won the lottery three times over.

Friday, they bounded out of their respective interviews with confident smiles and spent the rest of the weekend hiking to hidden lakes, eating their way through cafés, and speculating about becoming regulars in the spots they liked best. Which was all of them. They both felt it: They belonged here.

Sure as they belonged together.

On the day Keaton got the job offer, he arrived at Caroline's apartment with champagne and a fistful of flowers. Maureen let him in. Caroline was curled on the couch, staring listlessly at a form letter. *We've decided to go with another candidate.*

She'd never thought of herself as prideful, but she'd never forget the way his face fell. Though it conveyed only a crestfallen fraction of her own disappointment, it should have spoken louder than the words he did say: "Come anyway."

It was hard even now to piece together what came next. She'd agreed, right away, but in the coming days . . . well, they'd begun to argue. Silly stuff, mostly, but they couldn't seem to stop. She started to worry: Was he sorry he'd asked? Had she not made her own feelings reassuringly clear? For reasons she couldn't pinpoint, *Come anyway* morphed into *Why don't you put out some feelers, come later?* The difference was subtle, akin to that between *I'll pick you up* and *I'll save you a seat,* but in her sensitive state, it mattered. Enough to spark their biggest fight yet.

They took a day to cool off, and in that day, Caroline put her emotions in check. Of course they were both on edge. This was a big step. But she'd work the register in one of those cute little stores, for all she cared. As long as they were together.

She asked him to meet her, to talk—not in her apartment, which still held the awkwardness of popping a cork on one-sided bubbly, but at her parents' house, on a night they had other plans. She'd make him a *real* dinner, better than she could in her sparsely equipped kitchenette. Tell him how ready she was for this step together, how the possibilities made her buzz with pride in him and excitement for them both.

Keaton didn't show.

Caroline wrapped up the pesto, the roasted vegetables, and the pasta with a note for Mom and Dad, as if leaving a surprise in their fridge had been her intention all along.

Saving face would soon become something of a default mode.

He never did convince her he'd rather go alone. He was not a sprinter but a man who'd spend months, years, training for a grand-scale race, riding the long game. Yet one day he was sending her links to rental properties, and the next she was moving the things she'd packed not to Brevard but back to her childhood bedroom. Their relationship ended so abruptly, she was left with the disoriented feeling that she'd imagined the entire thing. When she looked back on that visit to Brevard, it was through the heavy haze of this filter, rendering the memory indistinguishable from a delusion of what might have been.

She tried to picture Sela there—spending her whole life weaving through the spaces Caroline had once been so eager to claim. But the setting no longer seemed any more real than the pretenses that had brought her there. And the sister was still little more than a woman whose face, whose mind, she didn't know. Dad was right that Rebecca had a wide imprint online, but all Caroline could find of Sela was evidence of deleted social media accounts—old post tags that no longer linked, search results behind privacy walls.

There'd been something painfully familiar in the way Dad spoke of Rebecca. As if she'd torn him into halves: one part aching for a glimpse into a parallel universe, the other knowing he couldn't bear to look. Caroline and Keaton's story differed in ways she might have been grateful for. They hadn't met too late. They hadn't betrayed anyone to be together. Hadn't tormented each other—at least, not until the end. But their connection had always felt like something beyond her control. The only thing, in fact, beyond her control that she'd ever liked. Loved.

What did it say about her that her father's confession of his least forgivable impulses had left her relating, contemplating an untaken path of her own?

And not just because that path might have collided with her sister's.

Yet another reason it's a very good thing you didn't go, Mom had said.

There wasn't much left to say to Dad. At the end of their strained lunch, Walt and the kids ran in, tiaras galore, and she'd done as Dad asked, putting a full stop on their conversation. That night, when Dad turned in early and Walt slipped out to his monthly poker night next door, she typed out the response she owed Sela before she could lose her nerve. She thought she'd feel better if she at least acknowledged their connection—regardless of what may or may not come with it.

But she didn't. As the weekend came to a close, the kids bathed and tucked in down the hall and Walt shouting at the Sunday night football game downstairs, there was one person Caroline had yet to clear the air with.

Mom answered the old house phone on the first ring.

"Fred?"

"No, Mom. It's me."

The most uncomfortable residue of his visit was a flimsy film of disloyalty left on everything Caroline touched. It was the cloudy by-product of hearing him out while across town Mom was hurting, ears ringing. And of her brain's perplexing response, that looping keyword search on memories of *Brevard,* of what might have been, even as Walt did his best to hold things steady on her behalf.

Disloyalty. It glommed on to her now at the sound of Mom's voice saying Dad's name with such obvious hope.

"Oh." Mom sounded, unbelievably, disappointed. "Is he still with you?"

Their marriage really might survive this, exactly the way Dad had said. And yet—maybe it had already been surviving it. The fact that Mom might have opted him out of that database . . . Caroline wasn't the only one who still needed processing time.

"He's at Deer Creek by now."

He'd surprised Caroline by heading not home but to a state park lodge with Walt's fishing rod on loan, trying to joke that it was better if Hannah had a chance to miss him. She'd asked for space, and this was his chance at some, too—to make peace with the ultimatum that would shut out one daughter and leave the other grappling with questions he'd never answer.

"Right." Mom's sighs were so expressive, she could communicate via verbalized exhales the way other people did with emojis or GIFs. This one was ready for the ordeal to be over.

"I felt strange, not acknowledging that Dad filled me in—at least, on the basics." She cringed at the thought of Mom guessing at his candor where Rebecca was concerned. Was it possible Caroline herself now knew more about Dad's transgression than his own wife did? That was somehow worse. "I'm sorry this happened."

"It's not you who has anything to be sorry about."

"I know you said you don't want to talk about it, but—"

"I'm trying not to feel humiliated, sweetie. Talking about it is—well, humiliating."

And here was Caroline, calling to confront her. Could she really do it? This wasn't only about getting answers to things that were nagging at her, about wiping away that sticky film. There were things she needed to say, too.

"But Mom. Dad said you might have known all along, that something happened with him and Rebecca. And if that's true, the timing of finding out you were pregnant with me . . ." Caroline faltered. "It hit me that you might have sacrificed some things. Not the least of which was enduring feeling humiliated. You might have felt *trapped* by me."

It was equally possible, she supposed, that Mom had rushed her pregnancy to trap Dad, knowing he'd do the standup thing. But Caroline couldn't, wouldn't, go there, not even alone.

"Oh, Caroline." The edge fell away from her voice. "Every

parent makes sacrifices, but I don't know a one who is trapped by a child. By their own choices, their own mistakes, maybe. A child? No. A child is the opposite of a trap. A child opens you in ways you didn't even know you were closed. You know that—three times over now."

Gracious words. But everyone knew parents and children alike were equally capable of not just opening doors but closing them.

Much like her father with Rebecca, as it turned out, Caroline had forbidden herself to seek out Keaton online or even ask a mutual acquaintance how he was. She knew next to nothing of what had become of Keaton, and that was the way she liked it.

Well, not exactly. It was the way she *needed* it. She'd struggled too hard to climb over that mountain of disappointment to risk a backslide. Once she finally accepted that she'd never understand what, or who, had changed Keaton's mind—whether her own failure made him second-guess her abilities, or he got cold feet, or thought they'd moved too fast, or met someone else, or, or, or—she'd never wavered.

Until now.

"Thanks for that, Mom. But I also couldn't help but think . . ." She cleared her throat. "It must have been a hard coincidence when Keaton and I set our sights on Brevard." She debated adding the word *College*. Had Hannah known Rebecca was teaching there, at the very place Caroline interviewed?

Another patented, exasperated sigh. "Forgive me if I don't see how Dad's infidelity—which, I'll remind you, is between me and him—reopens discussion of your ex-boyfriend. This is the second time you've brought him up. What would Walt think?"

"This has nothing to do with Walt." Why wouldn't Mom just admit, as Dad had in a roundabout way, *Well, I didn't love the idea and* was *sort of secretly glad when you didn't go*?

Unless she had some reason not to.

"Given my current position, you'll understand why I beg to differ."

"Walt is far from in your position, Mom." Harsh, but true. She hadn't been tempted by another man since meeting him. Walt was also well aware of how heartbroken she'd been over Keaton. He'd seen it firsthand. "And if Walt heard what you said last time it came up, he'd understand why I'm bringing it up again."

"What on earth did I say?" A nervous laugh gave her away. Neither of them could forget the cold shock of that morning—every word of it. Caroline's unease grew.

"That it's a good thing I didn't go."

"I should think that's obvious. Look at your life: Walt, the kids. You wouldn't have any of that if you'd gone."

"When you said it, I got the impression you'd felt that way all along without telling me."

"Your impression was wrong."

"Please. Be honest."

For a moment, the line was so silent, Caroline wondered if they'd been disconnected.

"Fine. Yes, Keaton's choice of cities was a coincidence I'd have rather avoided."

"Did you do something to avoid it?" She kept her voice calm, even sympathetic.

"What could I do? I didn't dissuade you."

"It fell apart, though. And while I was devastated, you were relieved."

"I hated seeing you hurting. Now that we have the benefit of hindsight, isn't it nice to be able to say it was the right choice in the long run?"

"But it *wasn't* a choice. Not for me. It was Keaton who decided I wouldn't be going." That silence again. So much louder than the things Mom did say.

"He must've known it was for the best."

"In what way? No one could ever explain what made him change his mind." His mom had actually called Caroline to apologize, which only added to her mortification. "No one seemed anything but sad and confused that he left without me. Except, apparently, you."

"Well, if he was going to change his mind, I think it's sensible to be glad he did before dragging you across state lines."

"You're dodging the question: Did you say or do something to change his mind, Mom?"

No response. This evasiveness was becoming terrifying, but Caroline had to push ahead. "You said you didn't try to dissuade *me.* Maybe you couldn't let me think you were interfering—but that didn't mean you wouldn't interfere?"

When Mom spoke again, her voice was faint. "It was so long ago. . . ."

No. No, no, nonono.

She hadn't wanted it to be true.

It took all her resolve not to scream, *What did you say to him? How could you?* But she needed to know. "I understand it's been hard dredging up the past, and you want to move on. But I'm not going along with that until you tell me this. I have a right to know."

"I'm not having a twelve-year-old fight with my daughter, on top of a thirty-five-year-old split from my husband. I can't take it."

"It's not a fight," she lied. "Like you said, it was a long time ago."

Mom cleared her throat. "He came by the house one night, looking for you. Sounded like you'd gotten your signals crossed, but I had that nice meal you'd left here the night before, and your father was out, so I invited Keaton to join me."

Bile rose in her throat at the thought of Keaton eating that laborious dinner after all.

Without her.

The start of doing everything without her.

"Mom! How did this never come up?"

"Well, the boy seemed a little lost, to be honest. I thought maybe I could help."

Caroline clenched her fists. "Lost about what?"

"It's a lot of pressure, navigating a crossroads like that, even when you don't have anyone but yourself to consider. But when you do . . ."

"It's supposed to be a good thing, not having to take a leap of faith alone."

"Yes and no. He seemed very concerned about leading you in a direction that might not be right for you. About you having regrets later."

"Keaton was the direction I wanted. The rest would have worked itself out."

"Look. All I did was try to reassure him. But I wasn't a hundred percent convinced you following him to Brevard *was* your best move. Women in your generation have so many more options, and—" She caught herself. "Anyway, I didn't sugarcoat things. When he left here, I thought he was reconsidering the move, maybe thinking about rescinding the job and finding something else where you both had opportunities. I never imagined he'd do—what he did."

Caroline could scarcely breathe, so tightly was the betrayal squeezing at her lungs. Since when was Mom an outspoken or even self-aware feminist? "You expect me to believe the fact that you weren't 'convinced' had nothing to do with Rebecca being there, on the same campus?"

"On the . . ." Was she surprised by this detail or only that Caroline knew it? She recovered quickly. "Again, I only meant for Keaton to reconsider the job, the town. Never to reconsider *you.* And I don't know that I had anything to do with that! But I do wish I'd never invited him in."

Caroline's mouth dropped open, but nothing came out. The pain in her lungs grew tighter. She wanted to ask whom Hannah had been more afraid of her meeting—Rebecca or Sela? But she was starting to think Dad was right that it was better to stick to questions she was sure she wanted answers to.

"And when he did reconsider me? Did you do anything to stop it?"

"What could I do? I guess I'd underestimated how strongly he felt about that particular next step. I thought Brevard was one of many places the two of you would be willing to try on for size. Not *the* place he'd already decided was a perfect fit."

"He wasn't the only one who thought it was perfect." Caroline couldn't restrain the emotion from her voice. There was more to this, surely—her own pride or Keaton's youth getting in their own way. But that Mom had played any role . . .

"All I can say is I'm sorry."

"You're sorry now? What about then, when I was lying upstairs in my old room with my heart in pieces? It *never* occurred to you to tell me what happened? Even if you didn't think you could fix it, maybe I could have!"

"What's left to fix? You can be unhappy with me, but surely not with how things turned out. Probably I shouldn't have said what I did. But everyone makes mistakes, and sometimes, they're a blessing in disguise. You have no idea how relieved I am that's the case here."

"So because Walt is great, I'm not supposed to be upset that this pivotal moment of my life hinged on a lie? That I lost a year—more—grieving a relationship that didn't need to die the way it did? I made big life decisions out of that terrible place. This isn't just about losing Keaton."

"I think we've had enough for one week." Another heavy sigh: *You promised this wasn't a fight.* "Let's not blow this out of proportion. It's not as if it changes anything."

She was finally right, Caroline had to admit, about something. It didn't change anything, not if you stepped back and looked at things objectively.

It changed *everything.*

8

Sela

"What if you didn't tell me the numbers anymore?"

The words rushed out of Sela, and the nurse appraised her for a minute before resting her clipboard on the table between them. Her name, according to her name tag as well as the many, many voice mails she'd left Sela over the years, was Marie. But though Marie handled most of her monthly blood and urine draws and relayed the results, and though she was the go-between for any questions for the nephrologist—who might as well have been the Wizard of Oz, given how little Sela saw of him versus how much time she spent in his office—Sela did not wish to be on a first-name basis.

She'd seen the other patients, the ones the nurses liked, coming and going with the kind of bright familiarity that put all parties at ease—asking if the receptionist's daughter was over that nasty cold, complimenting the tech's haircut, deflecting teasing about slipups over sweets or wine or whatever other vice. Sela did not wish to be one of them. In fact, she actively wished *not* to be.

Because coming and going anonymously? Well, that was

an anonymous level of sick. Which couldn't be too bad. At least, not yet.

"I understand that sometimes they're difficult to hear?" Marie had a way of phrasing everything as a question—unless it actually was one. *What time would you like to come in.* The reverse inflections came across as condescending enough to justify keeping Marie at arm's length. "Or they can be confusing? But you do need—"

"I need to know when I'm looking at the next stage," Sela cut in. She was well aware that other factors mattered, that most people with kidney disease ultimately died not of kidney failure but of some other problem caused by an underperforming bodily filtration system: haywire blood pressure, heart disease, stroke. Surely her preventative medications could be adjusted, though, without discussion. "What if you just tell me when that signpost appears? I'm not sure I want to know about every single point I pass in the meantime."

She *was* sure: She did not want to know. Her correspondence with Caroline was off to a cautiously optimistic start—she'd written back, and Caroline had reciprocated—each exchange a nudge less stiff, more personal. Sela had learned that her father's only sibling died a career bachelor, that his parents were gone, too, that there was no further extended family dangling on the other end of this teetering balance scale. More important, she'd learned that this tenuous relationship with her half sister would require time and space to develop. The last thing she needed was her kidneys' cries for help drowning out her thoughts.

Caroline's day-to-day life seemed, in a word, full. So much so that Sela couldn't see how she would possibly fit. Sela spent hours obsessing over what to say—not too little, not too much. Even a basic outline of her life circumstances felt like oversharing. This was her opportunity to endear herself, and she had to get it right. To find some way to win her over that would not seem insincere later.

Even if this did, now that she'd begun, seem impossible.

Marie looked skeptical, so Caroline kept talking. "I'm doing everything I can to take care of myself. Following your instructions to the letter, and then some."

This was worth noting, because plenty of people did not. Sela saw them every time she came—smoking outside the clinic, their cars littered with fast-food wrappers and empty slushy cups, brazen evidence of depression or denial or some self-destructive impulse. Part of her hoped they'd get away with it, triumph with their sugar and sodium raised as a stiff middle finger to the disease—but it didn't seem fair that so many of them coasted with a shrug, faring no better but no worse, while she did everything right and still saw her numbers decline at a haphazard rate.

"Let's just say," she continued, "that getting regular updates on what little impact my efforts are making is not boosting my morale."

Would a little self-delusion be that bad? Healthy people engaged in it every day. If Doug ordered a salad with his pizza, somehow that justified polishing off a whole medium. If Leigh enjoyed a glass of wine in her third trimester, it paled in comparison with what older generations had done. And if this very nurse sneaked one of those Camels showing through her pocket on her break, her lungs would recover when she got around to quitting. Any day now.

"You want to be informed about your care?" Marie persisted. "You want to be—"

What she *wanted* was for people to stop telling her what she wanted. What she should be thinking or feeling or doing, or—more often—refraining from thinking or feeling or doing. Even the so-called support forums populated by fellow patients exhausted her, with their claims of magic fixes in keto diets and pharma-driven conspiracies to keep patients sick, with their simultaneous distrust in and reliance upon doctors.

"I don't see how stressing over things I can't control will make anything but a negative impact."

This was not a stretch, either. No one had ever said the stress of her illness might have helped to kill her mother, but no one had said it hadn't. Marie looked Sela over as if she might be called upon to deliver some assessment—physical? psychological?—to support this request. "Which numbers are we talking about. The GFR, creatinine, functionality . . ."

A valid question, posed as a statement. Now they were getting somewhere.

"All of them."

"I see? And do you imagine wanting to know when the next stage is around the corner, or when it's here."

If she were *imagining,* there'd be no stage at all. But this was real, and she'd have preparations to make. Filling in Caroline, for instance, if she hadn't managed to do it by then.

What *was* the deadline, the sweet spot between coming on too strong and holding out deceptively long? And when that moment came to share not only what had happened to Sela but the position it left her—and, by extension, Caroline—in, would she find the courage to seize it? As of now, any point at which she could fathom the reality of coming clean seemed miles away.

Three hundred and eighty-eight of them, to be geographically precise.

"When it's *right* around the corner."

Marie's eyes flicked down to the numbers on the chart, then back at Sela's. "Okay?" She scribbled a notation on the top sheet of paper, the only indication that this was not actually a question. "You ever change your mind and want to know, ask."

"I won't. But I will."

The nurse smiled ruefully. "Numbers aside, how are you feeling?"

Sela had never figured out how to assess the degree of her symptoms—like those pain scales of one to ten—without feeling an unspoken pressure to buck up and assume her discomfort would hardly faze other people. Stronger people.

"About the same, I guess."

"Swelling still bothering you?"

"Some." When she gave specifics, she often lived to regret it—being admitted for observation or earning a nasty new addition to her daily meds cocktail. Spending seventy-two hours collecting her urine in what looked like a gasoline can had been especially fun.

"Now that you have me looking at this again . . . any chance you might have been a little dehydrated at your last visit?"

The corners of Sela's mouth twitched, struggling to maintain their upward position. This one had implications. The need to explain away something.

"There's always a chance, isn't there?" Given that she'd describe her normal state as chronically thirsty, she had no idea how she'd ever tell. "But I follow the limits exactly."

"You're not undershooting it?"

Who in their right mind would drink less than they were allowed? Before this started, Sela had been one of those people who carried a refillable water bottle everywhere. She still did—but rarely got to refill it. Thanks to her body's stubborn new affinity for fluid retention, fifty ounces a day was the max. Whether this was truly uncomfortably little or her ensuing misery was due to that mean mind trick of wanting what she'd been forbidden, it was real all the same. For someone who slept so little—six hours on her best night, never in a row—her daily allotment worked out to 2.8 ounces every waking hour. Sips. If Sela awoke dry-mouthed and greedily gulped a glass of water, she could have only two more before the same time the next morning. If she wanted to throw it back every time the clock chimed, she could use a standard shot glass, but not a double.

Tracking ounces away from home was tricky. At the pizza place she and Doug used to visit weekly, servers plunked straws into clear plastic cups of twenty-four. At the Chinese Buffet, the clay teapot on every table held sixteen and the tiny no-handle teacups three. There was no subtle way to measure—or bring her own beverages—without turning heads. She stayed home more and more.

She knew of dialysis patients who were limited to thirty-two ounces, and tried to be glad she wasn't there yet—but feared the day she would be. It became an obsession, rationing water like an ill-prepared tourist on a desert hike, sucking ice to make it last longer, always trying to anticipate how this moment's thirst compared to her baseline compared to where she'd be an hour from now.

She tried to laugh. "I'm disciplined, not sadistic."

"Good. Even so, I should've . . . Let's retest in a week or two? To be sure I'm looking at an anomaly." *Oh, you are,* Sela wanted to tell her. *I'm nothing if not an anomaly.*

Outside, she was heading to her car when she heard her name and turned to find Doug rushing toward her, buttoned up in his work clothes but without his jacket, a striped scarf billowing around him.

"Doug? What are you . . . ?"

He stopped, trying to catch his breath. "I thought I'd keep you company at your appointment today. But an accident held up the interstate. I'm sorry."

He always apologized for the wrong thing. For finally leaving rather than for wanting to. For continuing to want the things from life that she could no longer have rather than for refusing to compromise. For being late rather than for presuming she wanted him here.

"I appreciate the gesture, but I'm fine on my own." She turned and resumed walking, not caring that it was rude.

Undeterred, Doug fell into step beside her. "How'd it go?"

She shrugged. "I don't know."

"What do you mean you don't know?"

All he ever did these days was follow one question with

another. She never had answers to appease him, and he'd grow so frustrated he seemed to forget she had the same questions, too.

They used to pass hours in companionable silence. In a hammock stretched in the shade of their backyard, she'd sketch while he'd read or throw a ball for Oscar. But he'd lost the ability to be in her presence without needing to know something, ask something, fix something.

"Look, Doug, for all intents and purposes, we're not married anymore."

"We're still on the same health care plan."

It was such a fine-print reduction of everything they'd meant to each other, she didn't know whether to laugh or cry. She closed her eyes and saw Doug standing next to Brody's tiny, wire-strewn body in the neonatal intensive care unit, his unshaven face lost in a sea of beeping monitors while she clung to Brody's fingers through the opening in the Plexiglas. Given the chance, she'd never have traded places with her husband then, stoic as he stood while she withered and wept. Not if it meant letting go of that impossibly small hand.

So he'd drifted further away, she'd let him, and now, they were—

Well, they were on the same health care plan.

"A generous act on your part. But not one that gives you license to insert yourself in my treatment. If I need something from you—if I want to be checked on—I'll let you know. Okay?"

"Not okay." He grabbed at her arm, trying to slow her, but she shook him off. "Sela—"

"These appointments are routine. Don't make it a thing."

"Yeah, well. If anyone knows there's no such thing as routine, I think it's us."

He could have been referring to any number of things. The standard prenatal screenings that led to her diagnosis. The "nothing to worry about" cramps that turned out to be preterm labor. Their uncommonly amicable shared custody agreement.

But he was overlooking the most important one. Again.

"There is no us," she reminded him. Her car came into view. If she could just duck in before he asked about Caroline. She'd come to this appointment determined to ease the pressure on the tenuous exchanges with her sister. She would not now have that progress undone by Doug wanting to know how *that* was going and if she'd told her yet and what her plan was. More answers she couldn't give even if she wanted to.

She'd come here to draw lines today. And since he'd taken it upon himself to show up, he was going to get one, too.

"Look, I appreciate where you're coming from. But none of this is helping. I need space to deal with this, and I'm not just talking about my appointments." She pressed the remote to unlock her car door and opened it, turning to say good-bye. The look he gave held so much pity she had to look away. She was glad she'd dropped Brody at Leigh's rather than dragging him along; if he were here, Doug wouldn't be dissuaded from wanting to stick by them, get lunch together.

"I don't like the idea of you trying to handle so much on your own."

"I'm not on my own." As if on cue, the phone in her pocket started to ring, and she held it up to show him Leigh's image on the screen. His face softened, and she knew he'd back down for now.

If only he'd back down for good.

9

Caroline

"You're not avoiding me, are you?" Walt's tone was playful, but the question was not. Still, Caroline had to laugh. Some inexplicable impulse—guilt in one of its many maternal forms—had compelled her to agree to "just one quick Nerf battle" before she left to meet Maureen for drinks. So she and Walt found themselves crouched behind opposite ends of the couch, youth-sized safety goggles squished onto their faces, awaiting attack.

Funnily enough, Maureen had accused her of the same thing.

"Of course not. I haven't seen Mo in weeks, is all."

"And the suspense is killing her."

Well, yeah. Maureen knew only that a mysterious half sister had surfaced and chaos had ensued. Caroline had promised details as soon as she had them, then promptly commenced stalling. It wasn't that she didn't want to talk to Mo about this—in some ways, Maureen, who'd known her family the longest, would understand her position the best. But Maureen also had a way of making every shared experience feel like an inside joke—from the server-in-training who never brought their food to the shockingly bright DIY paint job that made their short-lived apartment's kitchen look like a Dr. Seuss book. Though she loved her friend's easy intimacy, Caroline would sometimes later wish she'd stopped short of poking fun at the server's shoes or even at her own misguided paint swatch choices. And she didn't want to feel that way about what was happening with her family. Even if they did have it coming.

"You know Mo."

Don't leave me hanging, she'd texted, sweetening her appeal with a GIF of a dangling kitten. Then: *I promise not to delight* in the fact that your parents are less than perfect after all. *Outwardly.*

Mo's inclusion of their signature Asterix dated back to a middle school health class, when they'd taken to passing notes mimicking their antiquated textbook's footnotes—notations on the reproductive systems that struck them as uproariously funny. By high school, not an unaltered page remained in their yearbooks by the time Caroline and Mo got done with them. The superlatives that featured their friends were Caroline's favorites.

*Most likely to succeed.**
**At using the fake ID that looks nothing like any of us—God bless those distracting DDs!*

Walt shuffled toward her in a crouch, his flimsy foam-dart-loaded battle vest swinging over the white button-down he'd worn to work. He came to a stop inches away and blinked at her earnestly through the goggles. "Is the first line item a discussion of how none of this would be possible without your idiot husband's idiot Christmas shopping?"

The smacking of three small sets of bare feet across ceramic tile came from the adjacent kitchen, followed by maniacal giggling. They both crouched lower.

"You're in luck," she whispered. "Considering the other husbandly fail on the agenda, that would make me seem petty."

"Remind me to thank your dad," he hissed, and she elbowed him, hard.

Neither of them knew how to talk about this—how much to analyze or speculate. Walt was not emotionally exempt as he tried to reconcile the family he thought he'd married into with the reality of this particular skeleton closet. He listened in attentive silence as she read Sela's emails aloud but didn't volunteer much beyond prodding for her observations—which Caroline either kept vague (*I guess she sounds nice? I guess I should write back again?*) or kept to herself.

There was no reason not to have told him about that fraught call with Mom. Caroline had done nothing wrong. But that night, after hanging up the phone, she'd been consumed by tears—and letting him see the raw power such a long-ago betrayal could wield over her seemed unkind. She'd gone to bed early, they'd all been in a hurry come morning, and now . . .

"Chaaaaaaarge!" Cries in octaves ranging from soprano to screeching brakes tumbled over the couch, along with a cascade of rubber-tipped darts. Caroline popped up to defend herself, plastic bow in hand, and promptly caught a chair cushion in the face. The force sent her stumbling backward, and Walt grunted as she crashed on top of him.

The kids roared with laughter, doubling over and dropping their toy weapons with a clatter. The rest of the family might be turning inside out, but these three were her constants. They didn't seem to have a clue anything was amiss; in fact, it was Dad's gift of new Nerf for their arsenal that had inspired this battle. They'd been too excited to question why Gramps had come for an unprecedented "sleepover" without Nana.

"I'm going to pee my pants!" Lucy squealed, bolting bowlegged from the room, and Owen and Riley threw their arms around each other and cackled louder.

Walt met her eye as they untangled their limbs and grinned. "You really want to tear yourself away from *all this* and go to *happy hour*?" He turned so the kids couldn't see and mouthed, *Take me with you.*

She laughed. "I must need to have my head examined," she said, winking.

If only it were entirely untrue.

—

"You've *never* looked up Keaton? Come on. Seriously?"

"Seriously."

On the patio of their favorite brewery, Caroline and Maureen had pulled a pair of Adirondacks as close as they could stand to one of the blazing firepits. The place was usually uncrowded on weeknights, but tonight the taproom was packed for a new Oktoberfest release. So they'd brought their pints out here, though the sun's orange-streaked descent was making for the first truly chilly evening of the season.

"Inhuman."

"I'll take that as a compliment on my restraint."

Maureen set her beer on the wide arm of her chair, reached into the pocket of her sweater coat, and pulled out her smartphone.

"What are you doing?"

Her thumbs were flying across the screen, which she thrust toward Caroline seconds later. "Found him!"

"No!" Caroline jerked her head away. "That's not what I—"

Mo retracted the phone with an eye roll. "Fine. I'll look for you." She tapped the screen and smiled. "He looks good. He's—Holy shit."

"What?" Caroline leaned forward involuntarily, then caught herself. "Wait. Don't tell me. I didn't look on *purpose*, Mo. Obviously."

"Don't take this the wrong way, Caro, but you just gave me a ten-minute rundown of your parents' soap opera–worthy fallout, followed by a *twenty*-minute rant on how this subsequent injustice could have happened to *you*."

A flush of embarrassment climbed her chest. "Sitting here with you just got me fired up. I mean, you were *there* that night Keaton came over and, you know. Pulled the plug. You had a front seat for the whole rapid decline."

Maureen frowned. "I still consider it my biggest friend fail that I'd already signed another roommate to the lease. When you had to move out anyway . . ."

"It wasn't your fault! But it is why you're the only one I can vent to. Knowing my mom not only did something to help cause that, but kept it from me? And it's not like she gave me a play-by-play—it's driving me crazy not knowing exactly what was said, or how much weight he gave it. I mean, how did she turn him off past the point that he'd just *talk to me* about it? Give me a chance to set things straight?" She shuddered, as much at her own words as at the memory. "But, you're right. I'm on a tangent." She smacked the knees of her jeans. "The game changer is, I have a half sister."

Maureen picked up her beer and set her phone in its place, letting the screen go black. The tension holding Caroline's shoulders eased a little.

"Do your parents know you've been emailing?"

"I think they're instituting a 'don't ask, don't tell' policy."

"Worked great for the military. What could go wrong?"

"I know. But . . . I couldn't not write her."

"What's she like?"

Caroline took a long, hoppy sip of her pint. "It's hard to tell over email, but she seems . . ." She paused, trying to think of how to describe Sela. "Different."

"Different how?"

"I'm not sure, exactly. She doesn't come out and say things the way you or I would. She'll explain not just that she works from a home office, but that it's *the place she feels most in control of her life.* Not just that she likes her work, but that it *gives her a way to channel her dreams into something she can see.* I think those were her exact words."

"Huh. You must have read them more than once."

"Wouldn't you?"

A tilt of Mo's head conceded the point. "What does she do?"

"Graphic design. She sent me the link to her website—not your average stuff. Creative."

"That makes sense, considering."

"Yeah. I tried to ask about Rebecca, but she ignored the question. Which is fair. Considering." This old habit of parroting each other's speech patterns was more pronounced when they were alone, which wasn't nearly as often as it used to be. Maureen had a whole brood—her husband, Seth, ten years older, already had two school-age kids from his first marriage when they met, and then they'd had a couple more. Mo called herself the evil stepmother, but Seth's sons adored her. The kids all got along great with Caroline's but by numbers alone made for a raucous crew. An uninterrupted conversation was a luxury she and Mo rarely got to enjoy.

And she *was* enjoying it, in spite of the strange subject at hand.

"Any idea what she knows about your dad?"

"None. She hasn't asked, which Walt thinks is weird. But I'm more relieved that she isn't putting me on the spot. I told her I was corresponding independently of my family's wishes, and I have never felt so awkward trying to word something. *Every* way I wrote it sounded awful. Which made it sink in that this *is* awful, what my parents are doing. In her shoes, I wouldn't think much of them. I might not ask either."

"But she has to be curious."

"There are levels of curious. I mean, I've never not been curious about Keaton, but that's not the same as really wanting to know."

"So you say. Any idea why she took the DNA test in the first place? I mean, was she looking for you, or did she stumble upon you?"

"She hasn't said. But . . . I'm not sure she's in a great place right now. She separated from her husband and they have a two-year-old boy. Maybe the timing was right to look for some other connections." Even this Sela had written in a roundabout way. *My husband Doug and I had a severely preterm baby—Brody was born two years ago this fall—and our marriage didn't survive the challenges. It's not my favorite topic, but maybe one day if we get to know each other better I'll fill you in on the sordid details.*

"Divorced with a toddler? Rough. Raised by a single mother, too."

"Yeah. Although I don't *know* that Rebecca stayed single. Sela hasn't mentioned any father figure, but . . . that seems kind of sad." *Unfair* was what she wanted to say. Dad had hardly suffered. Regardless of how much Mom had been on to, she'd let him off the hook, right up until she couldn't. And that had taken decades.

Then again, what kind of woman would sleep with a friend's husband—months after the wedding, no less? Rebecca had spent the rest of her life hiding their indiscretion, and now that it was finally in the open, she was no longer here to face it. Caroline wasn't sure if that made her lucky or the opposite. How would Dad have reacted to Sela if Rebecca were still in the picture?

If she were, though, maybe Sela wouldn't have reached out. Caroline would be home right now, none the wiser. Not gossiping about her own parents, not looking up her *one that got away,* and not contemplating how much she wanted to know about the woman sharing half of her genes.

"Think you'll meet her in person?"

It didn't take much foresight to realize this would become *the* question. As Walt pointed out, there was a big difference between exchanging a few curious emails and fading back to neutral versus inviting this woman to be an in-the-flesh part of their family against her parents' wishes. The implications were so layered Caroline wasn't sure she could anticipate them all, which made an informed decision seem impossible.

She was an event director. It was against her nature to go in without knowing the agenda.

"It hasn't come up yet. But . . . I haven't ruled it out."

"Bet Hannah would flip." Maureen had been calling Caroline's mom by her first name since long before it was age-appropriate to do so. "Would you rather do it in Brevard? Keep things off your home turf?"

"Maybe. Although—okay, back to my self-indulgent rambling, I'd worry about running into Keaton. Brevard is a really small town."

"No need to worry about that." Caroline narrowed her eyes, and Maureen tapped her dormant phone. "The answers you refuse to admit you seek are at my fingertips." Her last words on the subject of Keaton, Caroline remembered now, had been an expression of surprise.

He looks good. He's— Holy shit.

Caroline moaned, squeezing her eyes shut. "Fine. Tell me what you were going to say after *holy shit* before I change my mind."

"I have to tell you. I don't keep secrets from you. Look what happens when people do."

She opened one eye to glare at Mo, then closed it again. "Nothing else, only that. Tell me, and then back away from the profile."

"Uh-huh." She sounded so damn sure Caroline would change her mind.

"Mo!"

"Fine. I can set your mind at ease about running into Keaton in Brevard. Because he's living here. In Cincinnati."

Her eyes flew open. "What? Since when?"

"Guess we'll never know. I'm backing away from the profile."

Caroline ground the heels of her boots into the gravel beneath her chair, furious—not at Maureen but at herself, for still caring.

"You know what," Mo said. "You're not the one looking him up. I used to know him too. You just happen to be sitting close enough to see." She wasn't teasing anymore. Still, Caroline didn't want to get by on a technicality. She was the last member of her family with a clean record.

Well. Cleanish.

Maureen slid her Adirondack closer until the arms touched, and Caroline stared at her lap, ashamed but not enough to protest as Mo set her phone between them and began scrolling.

"A year or two, looks like," Mo said, then stopped short. "Oh. He got hurt. Bad."

Caroline couldn't stop her eyes from snapping to the screen. It showed a photo of a bare masculine leg stretched on a hospital bed, with screws holding something beneath the skin in place. She winced. "On his bike?"

"Yeah. Guess that was the end of his involvement with Brevard's team." She clicked on the *About* tab. "He's assistant athletic director at NKU now—sounds like more of a desk job." Not Cincinnati proper, then, but Northern Kentucky University, right across the river. "No relationship status."

"Doesn't mean he doesn't have one."

"It would be a loss if he didn't, wouldn't it? Keaton's a good guy."

She'd thought so, right up until the end, when even in her shock she'd struggled to reclassify him as a jerk, someone who'd so abruptly hurt her. *How,* she'd asked herself countless times, *did he never once reach out to see how I was?* Not the morning after he ran out and left her sobbing, or the night after he unpacked in Brevard without her, or the next week, or month, or even year. Her disbelief had ebbed over time but never quite disappeared.

She'd tried to convince herself he'd obviously not loved her the way she'd thought, but it never felt true. Meeting Keaton had been the sweetest revelation: She'd looked at him looking back at her and thought, *Ohhhhhhhh. I'm in one of* those *stories.*

But it hadn't been the story she'd thought it was.

Only . . . maybe it had. Maybe Keaton had been waiting all these years for Caroline to reach out. Maybe she was, in his eyes and unbeknownst to her, the jerk.

It depended on exactly what Mom had told him. And since she was adamant about not revealing those details, there was only one other person who could.

"Is it weird that I feel like I might owe him an apology? For whatever Mom said? She didn't just mess up my plans. She messed up his. It's possible that all these years, he's been thinking something about me that isn't true."

"Only one way to know." Maureen waggled the phone again. "Whatever Hannah did or said, it was pretty messed up for her to intervene at all, even if it was a caught-in-the-moment thing. Let alone without telling you."

Caroline raised an eyebrow. "You're supposed to tell me to leave it alone. That it's too late to set the record straight."

"You've already told yourself that. It clearly isn't working."

"That's why *you're* supposed to say it."

Mo laughed. "I'm not trying to stir up trouble, looking up Keaton. But I can understand why you'd want closure. For both of you."

Caroline stared into the fire. What had started as a blazing lean-to had shifted so that one sturdy log supported all the rest. She watched as it burned from beneath, turning to white ash. If it gave out, the whole pile would go.

"If it makes you feel better," Mo said more gently, "I wouldn't go there if you and Walt weren't so solid. I agree with Hannah that you're better off, only because—well, we'll never know, right?

You're doing well, so we can assume this is how it was supposed to be. If you believe in that *meant to be* junk." They both laughed, knowing full well how many decades of heart-to-hearts they'd devoted to that *junk* specifically. "It's understandable, though, to want to know what happened. You said yourself it's driving you crazy, so why not get his side? Best-case scenario, you find out it had nothing to do with Hannah and feel better. Clear this out of your head so you can focus on Sela, and where you want to go with that."

Caroline had to admit Mo had a point.

"Do you know the last words he said to me? *Take care.* The kind of thing you say after having a pleasant chat with a stranger waiting for your number to be called at the DMV. Not after a year of the most intense love of your life."

Mo raised an eyebrow. "Of your life, huh?"

Walt was many wonderful things. The sort of husband who could order for Caroline almost anywhere if she was running late and rarely gifted her anything that wasn't her style. Who could—and, importantly, would—recognize her limits and take over before she cracked. He was the person she most wanted to share any moment with—good, bad, or in between. Walt made her laugh, held her when she cried, made most things subtly, gracefully, better.

He did not, however, approach relationships the way a racer pounds the pedals—exhilarated, determined, simultaneously in control and free. *No moment but this. Nobody but us.*

She'd had intense, once. Walt was not it.

"You know what I mean. My life to that point. Both our lives to that point, if you believed Keaton." She shook her head. "How would I even approach him? It's been so long."

Maureen rolled her eyes. "Friend him. Message him. People do it all the time. For way less valid reasons, I might add."

"And say what? 'Um, hi, just wondering if my mom might have

talked you out of marrying me?'" There went that eyebrow again. "What? Is there a different next logical step after you move hundreds of miles together?"

"Let's start with: 'Long time no see. How about catching up over coffee?'"

"But he might think . . ." What? What was she so afraid of? What did she have to lose?

"Think of this as getting out ahead of fate. You're bound to run into him sooner or later, right? This way, you're in control. Last time I ran into an ex, I was at Kroger in PJs, buying out their supply of lice shampoo. Thank you, summer camp." Mo got to her feet, ready for a refill, and gestured for Caroline to finish her dredges. "Besides, his profiles are set to public."

"Meaning?" The blood rushed from her head as Caroline got to her feet, and she had to steady herself on the chair back before following Maureen toward the bar. The last few weeks had felt this way—like a head rush that was by turns dizzying and, for that brief second before she regained clarity, bizarrely exhilarating.

"Meaning," Maureen called over her shoulder, "he's a man who wants to be found."

10

Sela

At some point during the night, Brody had climbed into Sela's bed. She must have reflexively curled around him, because that's how she awoke—breathing him in, not minding that she'd been roused well ahead of her alarm by his little body shifting and sighing beside her.

He nestled his tiny hands beneath her sleep shirt, pressing them into her bare stomach. When he was an infant—scarcely qualifying as a newborn by the time she'd finally, at last, been allowed to hold him—they'd practiced skin on skin as the doctors recommended, and sometimes she still felt he was making up for time lost to those long weeks when a barrier of cold plastic reality separated them. His deep, steady breathing kept her calm—the rhythm of living. Of staying here, with him. She would not think about what his life would be like if she had to leave this world. He was the reason—the only reason, she was unashamed to admit—leaving this world was not an option.

Early mornings, Doug used to slip out of bed without her

noticing, and she'd wake to him climbing back in, with a tray of breakfast and an appreciative eye on the thin-strapped nightgowns she used to sleep in, before she needed heating pads to ease her night pain. These days, she woke with the pads gone cold from the auto-shutoff and her husband gone from the same. Brody's warmth now was an unexpected treat; she'd lie here as long as he'd let her.

Even if her bladder was crying for relief.

Doing her best not to jostle him, she reached for the computer tablet on her nightstand, open to the email she'd been drafting to Caroline before bed. Every word, every phrase, carried the weight of possibility, the impact of life or death. It was an enormous amount of pressure to work through—though only one of them knew it.

Sela scrolled to reread her half sister's last message, which contained, for the first time, a more detailed introduction to her three children. Owen, *still very much the baby, thanks in part to his sisters treating him like a doll.* Lucy, who had *sparkle—literally and figuratively, no better word for this girl.* Riley, *athletic and brilliant and type A from birth.* Sela envied the ease with which Caroline described them as she struggled to craft her response to the last paragraph.

I was sad to hear about your divorce, so soon after the birth of your son—I can imagine time in the NICU would strain any marriage, and I'm so sorry it didn't work out. How is Brody now? What's he like?

Sela contemplated the sleeping miracle in her arms. How indeed?

Would Caroline warm to her more quickly if she was uncommonly earnest? Especially funny? Unapologetic? Sela was all of these things, depending on the day, except for when she wasn't. When sincerity seemed naïve. When life got so serious that joking became disrespectful. When she had something to be sorry for.

Caroline was looking only to bond over their shared experience of motherhood. Sela could do that, if she didn't hold back. If she didn't censor her every word the way she'd gotten so used to doing to keep everyone else at bay.

If she dared to be herself—as much as anyone grooming herself like her own publicity coach could ever be—was it relatable to say that Brody was all she'd ever wanted in the world, that he *was her world,* or did that read as needy, like one of those women priming her kids so she could live vicariously? If she explained that he was small, still catching up, did that sniff of excuses for his shortcomings? Was it likable to concede that *for now, we're content just us two,* or did that sound as if she were trying to talk herself into a happier place? Even her most authentic feelings sounded false and forced to her own ears.

Your children sound wonderful, she'd written. Now, she added:

> How lovely, to have a home so full. Doug and I wanted a big family—him because he grew up in one, and me because I didn't. Not that my childhood was unhappy; far from it. But I did always wonder what it would be like to have brothers and sisters around, and figured I'd have the best of both worlds if I gave my kids a chance to find out.

Hmm. Maybe she *was* that too-vicarious mom. She deleted all but the beginning and tried again.

> Doug and I always thought we wanted a big family, but things didn't work out that way. I've always thought of Brody as the best of us both.
>
> I know that sounds cliché, because everyone says that, but it's also true, in the way that everyone wants it to be. He reminds me of myself, the way I can tell he's dreaming his stuffed animals to life, bringing them along on his adventures. And of Doug, too, the way he acts like a little man of the house, sometimes even checking on me like I'm his responsibility, instead of the other

way around. Doug is still there for us, in every way I could expect him to be, and for that I know we are lucky.

That was better, maybe. It was amazing how many different ways you could tell the same story.

And how hard it could be to keep your own questions in check. She hadn't realized how much she'd been determined *not* to ask Caroline until she had her on the line, offering undeniably tantalizing glimpses into the other part of her mother's past, the other side of their collective story. Sela's disinterest in their father hadn't exactly changed, but it had slid aside to reveal how much uncharted ground remained. What was Cincinnati even like? Ecca never talked of her time there, never took Sela on the six-hour drive to see where she'd grown up. Sela's grandparents had fled the town not long after their daughter did, retiring to a remote area of Kentucky where, in Ecca's words, they had "more peace and quiet to ruin" with the loud, persistent hum of their misery.

But Ecca had spent nearly two decades in Ohio. Had presumably conceived Sela there. Sela had always thought she'd like to retrace her mother's footsteps in Europe—so many old, beautiful schools and museums where she'd honed her talent—but she'd wanted a family of her own, memories of her own, more. *First.* Then it turned out Sela got the order wrong. It became too dangerous to be so far from specialist care, even if she had the energy to go. Which her depleted iron levels made certain she did not.

Cincinnati was one last place within reach that held the gift of a part of her mother she'd never known. Sela couldn't help thinking it would bring comfort to stand in the outlines left behind, however faintly, by someone who would never cast a shadow again.

She had to remind herself it was a place her mother had not wanted to share with her. But it was getting harder to resist the repeated assurances of Leigh and even Doug: *If your mother had known she'd be leaving you in this position, she would have felt differently.* Sela would never be sure of that, but she could grant that Ecca might have *reconsidered* it. And even that would justify . . . well, more action than she'd planned to take.

Thanks for the link to your website, Caroline had written:

> Your designs are beautiful, and I admire the way you talk about them with such drive. I wouldn't want to blur a line, but if you're looking for assignments, maybe I could use you sometime. With the events I direct, sometimes we want more than our in-house creative team can provide. My budget doesn't stretch as often as I'd like, but I bet you could create some concepts that would wow my clients. And I'd feel good knowing I was helping you.

Sela had tried to respond to that bit last night, but she'd gotten hung up on Caroline's phrasing. *Wouldn't want to blur a line.* Given that Sela was biding her time until she annihilated any perceived boundary between them, this seemed foreboding. But then came that closer: *I'd feel good knowing I was helping you.*

Would she? So much dread and hope tangled up in an innocent, oblivious paragraph.

She repositioned the tablet alongside the soft hair of Brody's head and tried again.

> Thanks for your kind words about my work. I keep a pretty full client load, but you can always try me if you think I'm a fit. I'm flattered you'd consider it, but won't hold you to it.

Noncommittal, but open. Or did it come across like one of those form rejections she used to collect cold-calling with her portfolio? She typed a smiley emoticon, then deleted it, then typed it again.

"You have one job," she whispered to herself through gritted teeth. To find a sliver of an opening in Caroline's heart to climb through. Much as she'd been trying to play it cool—to *not* gather all her shiny, hopeful eggs in the long-lost sister basket—she was terrified of blowing it.

Brody lifted his head and smiled sleepily. She laid the tablet aside and pulled him into a good-morning hug. "What job?" he asked, looking almost comically up to the challenge.

"Professional pancake tester." She'd always wanted to be the kind of mom who was famous for her pancakes. A typical Saturday morning in her own childhood involved waking to find Ecca already in the studio and resigning herself to unheated toaster pastries straight from the wrapper. But in college, she loved having Leigh share the breakfast table and took to experimenting with batter. Leigh favored buttermilk; Sela preferred banana walnut.

"Mini?" he asked.

She touched her forehead to his and smiled. Silver dollar pancakes had been Ecca's go-to on the rare occasions that she used the griddle. She arranged them in designs on Sela's plate—smileys on sick days, snowmen when ice closed the schools. Now that Sela had been reduced to a low-sodium recipe that not even the best home chef could brag about, making them small and artful was the best she could do. A miniature picture of what she'd thought motherhood would be, for a miniature version of the boy Brody would grow into.

"You got it," she told him. What would she do without Brody? He *was* her world, even if it sounded too over-the-top to say it. The whole vast, miniature thing.

11

Caroline

Caroline and Walt prided themselves on playing by different rules than other married couples did. There was no keeping score, not even for so-called brownie points. No bitching about each other to their friends. No hinting around things they could and should come out and say.

But that didn't mean they were lax about the rules they did have. Honesty was a big one—even when it came to protecting each other's feelings. *I'd rather hear just about anything from you than from someone else,* Walt had said once. *Besides, I'm tough. I can take it.*

She found herself repeating this silently now. *He's tough. He can take it.*

No: *We're* tough. *We* can take it.

Mo was right: Messaging Keaton was easy, once Caroline took a few days to settle on a safeguard. She'd mention the kids in passing, disclosing the likelihood of a husband, a tethered life. She hoped this would both ease her conscience and increase her odds of a favorable reply: no fishy motives beyond catching up.

Hey, stranger. Heard through the grapevine you're back. My kids keep my schedule full, but . . . Would it be weird to meet for a cup of coffee? My workday breaks are flexible.

Hey yourself! Never weird to meet an old friend. How's your Tuesday? I'll be driving around interviewing PTs. Can work my appointments around a coffee hour.

Just like that, she was "an old friend." Too easy, really, minus the twisting of her gut.

Saying his name aloud to Walt for the first time in more than ten years was harder.

She waited until they were on the deck, watching the sun dip behind the tree line, a ring of citronella around them to ward off unwanted intruders. You could get eaten alive out here if you didn't take precautions.

"Guess who's back in Cincinnati?"

No matter what mental gymnastics she did, she couldn't bend around the need to tell him. If their marital code wasn't reason enough, there was the glaring contrast of her parents to consider. She knew Dad was back home now—had been for nearly a week—and as far as Mom was concerned, that was the only detail worth knowing. Evidently they were all supposed to fall into step now, as if nothing had happened. Caroline was "giving them space" to navigate this period, and they were taking it, for now. But how long could the pretense last? She wasn't ready to face them yet. Her best hope was that talking to Keaton could get her there.

"Keaton," Walt repeated slowly. "As in the heartbreaking cycling coach?" Walt's expression did not read *jealous husband,* but rather more like Mo's in the beer garden.

"As in the heartbreaking cycling coach turned assistant athletic director at NKU."

"Wow. You had a good run—eleven, twelve years with no sign of each other?"

"All good things must end." She tried to sound droll, but he looked at her strangely.

"This is an awful lot of Brevard coming up in Cincinnati all of a sudden."

She let the silence coalesce long enough to form edges.

"Oh." He understood then. Enough, anyway. They'd puzzled over the coincidence together from the start. And she hadn't held back relaying all Dad had told her—including Mom's possible suspicions all along. "So you want to make sure there's not more to the story?"

She tried to imagine how she'd feel in his shoes, but it was too big a reach. His family hadn't been hiding anything like this—not just a secret but a *person.* And his ex-girlfriends were a blur, a parade. Not one of them had a name that would still hold meaning for her or, she honestly believed, for him.

She nodded. "What would you think about me meeting him for a cup of coffee?"

"I'd think . . . *that* could be interesting."

I couldn't help but notice how uninterested you are in dating, Walt had said on the first night they'd really talked. For years they'd traveled in overlapping circles, but he'd never said more than a few words to her until they wound up the only two singles at that party.

I've sworn off love, she'd told him. Keaton had been gone nearly a year at that point. Not seeing Walt, or anyone, as a prospective anything—because she meant it—she'd given him an earful. The topic of Keaton had never been taboo. Hell, Walt was probably as curious to learn what had really happened as she was.

"I love you for being cool about this."

Their *I love you*s always had a purpose. *I love you for finding this hidden gem hotel. I love you for putting that brat next door in his place.* Sometimes Walt would even sing it: *Have I told you lately that I love* *you for talking me into this smoker? Have I told you there's no food else above these fall-apart tender ribs from this smoker?*

"Same," he said now, simply.

She let it rest, at the polar opposite of cool, undoing all her so-called honesty in one innocuous word.

"Caroline?"

She knew the voice before she turned her eyes to the figure standing in the doorway. She'd spent years replaying the last words it said to her.

Take care.

Their eyes met across the coffee shop, empty at this mid-afternoon hour save for a few loners hunched over laptops, ears cloaked by headphones. Caroline stood alone at the register, where the barista had ducked into the back after she declined to order right away. They had an audience of no one, but she'd never felt so painfully exposed.

Not for the past decade, anyway.

"Keaton."

He stopped to take her in, hands in his pockets, looking fit in his polo shirt in the maddening way of a man whose physique actually thinned when not in top form. His face retained its summertime tan, splashes of gray the only change in his wavy brunette mop. Her hand went to her own hair, blown out with the maximum care that could pass as normal. She'd settled, with an equally shameful pang, on her third-favorite wrap dress. Walt would notice if she tried too hard.

Keaton didn't have to try. Not then, not now. He just looked so damn good.

"Gosh. It's been a minute, huh?" He approached, arm out for

one of those tentative half hugs. She patted his shoulder, trying not to breathe him in.

But not even the espresso-laden air could block the olfactory wave of memory. After he'd left, she'd spent weeks trying to duplicate his fresh-from-the-shower smell on her pillow, with an embarrassing combination of left-behind toiletries and one unwashed T-shirt. It didn't work, of course. There was no substitute for the real thing.

The kitchen door clattered behind them, and Caroline jump-stepped back. The barista smiled expectantly.

"Cappuccinos?" Keaton suggested. Their old late-night studying ritual. Perk's, the corner coffee shop at the main intersection on campus, had been so much less pretentious than this hub of gleaming hardwood and stainless steel. She'd gone back one Homecoming Weekend, longing for its cozy mishmash of armchairs, only to find the space occupied by a franchise custard shop. "My treat."

She nodded numbly, waited while he fumbled for his wallet. Her phone buzzed, and she pulled it from her purse to see Mom's picture flashing on the screen. What, did the woman have some kind of echolocation system for Keaton, even now? Caroline switched the phone to silent and followed him to a two-top in a back corner, away from the windows.

He grinned at her across the table, broadly, slowly, and she couldn't help returning the smile, even as she chastised herself. What did he really make of seeing her, after all this time? Were it not for the events of the past month—events she had to remind herself he knew nothing about—she'd have felt quite differently about this encounter. Had she run into him by chance, she'd have been cold, if not outright confrontational. Did he think her openness odd? Or did he simply assume enough time had passed that old hurts had faded?

"So," he began as the barista plunked down two fat, steaming mugs, the foam on top swirled into works of art.

"So," she agreed.

They watched the woman move out of earshot.

"You stayed in Cincinnati, huh?"

More like: You left me in Cincinnati.

"I did." Her voice, at least, sounded neutral. "And you returned."

"Last year. Renting in Hyde Park and commuting to the athletic department at NKU."

He looked as if he belonged in Hyde Park, on trend. She and Walt had been priced out of the neighborhood—the most desirable gem in city limits—the second they even thought about trading their apartment for a house.

They were so *suburban* now.

"Good for you."

"Well, long story. But my parents are happy to have me back." He cleared his throat again. "Heard you married Walt Porter. I remember him running with Mo's crowd—seemed like a nice guy. Three kids, is that right?"

She nodded, noting it was more than she'd known about his life until she—or, rather, Maureen—had looked him up such a short time ago. "Where'd you hear all that?" Fishing around never did sound casual. Least of all when you wanted it to.

He shrugged. "Grapevine." She had that coming—her own lame pretense parroted back.

Mo had so confidently pegged him, though: *a man who wants to be found.*

"And you?" She wondered if he thought this was posturing. She wanted, rudely, to boast that she'd never asked anyone about him. To demand he ask the grapes—they'd corroborate.

"Came close—I was engaged, a few years back, but it didn't work out."

"Sorry to hear that."

"Don't be. It was for the best."

Exactly what Mom had said about their split: *He must've known it was for the best.* Maybe he really had changed his mind—more than once. She nodded again, pointlessly, and took a tentative sip of her cappuccino. It was just on the tolerable side of scalding.

"And Brevard?" she heard herself asking. "It was a good move?"

"I had a lot of good years there," he said carefully. Not exactly an answer. "It's still as beautiful as you remember, with more to it. Outfitters, breweries—a few of my friends opened one, with a big outdoor space, food truck—you'd love it." Maybe, if she ever dared visit Sela, she could get the details, go. "And the cycling program draws better talent every year. I'd be there now if not for some slick leaves on a hairpin turn."

She cringed, trying not to conjure the pictures Mo had shown her. "Bad crash?"

"Depends on whether you consider a full-body cast *bad*."

"I'm so sorry. I can't imagine." Everything changing, just like that.

Then again, maybe she could.

"You know, in hindsight, it's an interesting perspective check. Every team I've ever been involved with, there's a collective fear of these kinds of injuries. To miss a big race, a season . . . disaster, right?" He paused to take a long sip of his drink, undeterred by the temperature. "I'm not saying it isn't, for a serious athlete—but the stuff I saw in that rehab hospital redefined unimaginable. When it was over, I was one of the lucky few who got to actually walk out of there. And you realize it's nowhere near a disaster. Nowhere near."

Keaton's hands sprawled emphatically on the table between them. He used to get a numbness from long rides, cyclist's palsy, and she'd massage them until it eased. The key was maintaining consistent pressure, transferring heat, working her thumbs over his palms and up his fingers in small circles. She'd known every crease, every bend, as if his hands were her own, and the intimacy of the act had become a soothing ritual for her, too. Least of all because of how it always ended—him raising her fingers to his lips and saying, "What did I ever do without you?"

How wildly inappropriate it would be to reach out and touch them now.

How jarring it would still feel when he startled and yanked them away.

She leaned into the high back of her chair. "Nothing like some light conversation to break the ice."

He laughed. "Sorry. I get a little . . ." *Intense,* her mind supplied. And he didn't *get* that way; it was his way. He cleared his throat. "Don't want anyone feeling sorry for me."

Translation: *Don't want* you *feeling sorry for me.* She shook her head. *Wouldn't dream of it.* But it was hard, even now, not to imagine that parallel life. Her cheering him through his recovery. The two of them deciding, together, where to go from there.

"Did it cost you the job?" she asked. "Can you still ride at all?"

"Yes and no, on both counts. But it's okay—also on both counts. All good things must end, and all that." The exact words she'd spoken in sarcastic jest to Walt. A wave of contrition washed over her at his sincerity.

"No regrets?"

He could read whatever he wanted into the question—everything, nothing, something. In any translation, she genuinely wanted the answer to be yes. She'd wished, incessantly early on, that he'd come back for her, change his mind. But she'd never just plain wished he'd come back. Especially not like this. That would have been closer than she'd ever come to wishing him ill.

His mouth twitched. "Maybe just one or two." His eyes met hers, then fell away. "Enough about me. Tell me about you."

A deep breath. No time like the present. "Funny enough, you came up recently. It's actually why I messaged you."

"Do tell."

"Turns out," she began, "I have a half sister. Product of my dad's affair." She rushed on before he could react. "Weirder still, she lives in Brevard. Any chance you know her? Sela Bell."

His eyes went wide. "Holy wow. No, I've never met any Sela. Is she a student?"

"No, my age. Almost exactly."

He slouched, though whether he was absorbing her curveball's impact or dodging it, she couldn't say. "Well, that's—did your mom manage to whisper her way through *that* bombshell?" He pulled a face, unsure if it was appropriate to joke, but she conceded a laugh.

"She did not. First time for everything. Turns out she knew about the affair at the time, though—or at least suspected. Minus the pregnancy. That part was a surprise." Allegedly.

"Guess so."

She took a deep breath. Her entire impetus for coming, and she still didn't know how to broach it.

"The Brevard part, though, she knew." She watched his face closely. "She knew that was where the other woman lived. Turns out she taught art classes at BC. Rebecca Astin?"

He blinked at her. His expression betrayed no sudden revelation, no suspicion. But it did hold a sadness he hadn't let her see before.

Take care, Caroline.

"Small world," he said finally.

Her hands clung to each other in her lap.

"What did my mom say to you, Keaton?"

"Nothing." He managed to look taken aback. "This is the first I'm hearing of it."

"Not about the affair. About me, you, Brevard. Funny neither of you ever mentioned that you came by the house, stayed for dinner." She let the words rest, and his face fell as the unspoken *what-if* echoed between them. If he hadn't mixed the nights up—or was it she who'd said the wrong date?

He frowned. "It wasn't a big deal."

"Wasn't it? Her memory is conveniently fuzzy on the details."

The sadness was all over him now, gathered at the corners of his eyes, in the twitch of his jaw. So prevalent that everything before seemed a facade.

"What does it matter, Caro?" His voice was so soft, she had to lean closer to hear, even as the intimacy of the nickname made her want to pull away. "This isn't why I came. I only wanted to—" He shook his head. "Even after moving back, I resisted. I thought it unfair, actually, to reach out, after . . ." He cleared his throat. "But once I'd heard from you? I couldn't. I wanted to know that you're happy. That you're . . . still yourself."

The word grabbed her: *still.* She might have gotten *back* to herself, even grown *into* herself, but by no stretch was she *still* herself, as if he'd caused nary a ripple.

"It matters because you never fully explained why you ended things the way you did. Not in a way I understood. And now I'm getting a new sense of what might have happened, and I don't like it." A hint of the old resentment crept in, disguised as frustration.

He shook his head. "We went separate ways. It turned out well for you. I'd love to hear more about your life now, about—"

"*That* isn't why *I* came. We parted on your terms. Can we at least do this on mine?"

"Sounds like your mom is going through a rough patch. Dredging this up is the last thing she needs." He was still playing at this as if he didn't want to be caught in some family feud. As if it didn't involve him in any consequential way. Caroline hoped, she realized now, he was right. Even if the very idea of the two of them having *any* talk behind her back made her hair stand up.

"What about what I need? My parents are opting out of any communication with Sela. But I'm trying to do better than that.

Whether it's connected or not, the past is officially dredged up, okay? Even if you think it's 'no big deal,' I'm getting weary of secrets, and of being the last to know them."

He pushed his mug away, as if it, not she, had talked back to him.

"Did you ever get the feeling your mom might have made different choices? If she could go back, do things over?"

"No." Unequivocally no. Even now, she didn't get that feeling. Hannah hadn't shown remorse or wavered on the topic of Rebecca, Caroline herself, or even Sela. It wasn't her style.

"Well. I did."

"What does that have to do with me?"

"Following some guy to another town? Throwing over your own goals for his?"

"I don't recall throwing over my goals."

"That's because I didn't let you."

She swatted away her knee-jerk frustration at anyone—Mom, Keaton—thinking they knew better what was best for her. This was getting away from her, too quickly. Again.

"Back up," she said. "You went to my parents' house. In what mind-set? We'd had that fight. I invited you there to clear the air, talk things through." She remembered playing over all the things she'd wanted to tell him as she sliced the zucchini, chopped the onion. Not with a nervousness, a sense that the other shoe was about to drop. But excitement. Clarity.

She'd known, in that moment, exactly what she wanted.

He nodded, looking a degree more sheepish. "I came in the mind-set to apologize. It seemed stupid to be fighting just because we were both disappointed about the same things. I mean, we were on the same side."

"We were," she agreed. So everything didn't line up as perfectly as it could have for the move. So what? "When you didn't show, I thought—well, I assumed you felt the opposite. You weren't really ready yet to talk. You were still stewing."

He shook his head. "I don't know how we got our calendars crossed. Doesn't matter." It wouldn't have. Except.

"When you did show and I wasn't there, why not just come find me? Call me?"

"I was going to. But Hannah seemed so glad to see me. Your dad was out, and—they're pretty codependent, you know? She'd never really let it show that she minded the idea of you moving, but all of a sudden it was so obvious. And I was the one taking you away. Seemed like the least I could do was keep her company this one night. Next thing I knew I was at the kitchen table, eating pesto."

"And?"

"Well, she asked about the job. When I told her more about it, she got all wistful. Said she hoped you'd find something you could be as passionate about one day. She said she sometimes wondered what she'd have done or been if she hadn't gotten married right out of school." Without recent events, this didn't ring true. In fact, Hannah often joked her college major had been Fred.

"I could have found plenty of other opportunities in Brevard."

He looked doubtful. "We both know the college was your best shot."

"Asheville is a short commute—" She caught herself. "That's beside the point. That was not for you to decide. Or my mom. Or the two of you, behind my back."

"I'm not just talking about your slim odds of landing one of the few jobs you'd love outside of a bigger metro. I'm talking about the slim odds I'd already beat to land mine."

He crossed his arms, as if this were acknowledging some meaningful revelation.

"I don't follow. Why don't you tell me exactly what she said?"

She mirrored his posture until finally he broke and rolled his eyes.

"We're really doing this? Fine. She asked how long I thought it would take to get the coaching gig 'out of my system.' She strongly implied that you hoped this would be a brief stepping-stone for me. That you—your whole family, as I understood it—thought it childish. Which, maybe it was. I mean, if falling off your bike can derail your career, how much of an adult can you be?" He tried to smile, but when she didn't laugh, it dropped.

"But you said she was applauding you for following your passion."

"Yeah. My silly, get-it-out-of-my-system-while-I-waste-your-time passion," he said dryly. "I couldn't start that new chapter of my life that way. Feeling like I was holding you back. Wondering how long you'd be happy treading water until we could move on to someplace that was a better fit. It wouldn't have been fair to either of us."

Caroline thought back to what she'd been doing the night *after* she waited at her parents' house for Keaton. The night he actually showed and found Hannah instead. Mo had cooked her a fancy dinner, since Caroline didn't get to enjoy the one she'd slaved over. Wild mushroom risotto and boxed wine, a combination destined to become an inside joke for future girls' nights in. Mo had kept her laughing that night, told her Keat probably just needed another day to "fully extract his head from his ass" and everything would be fine.

"Are these impressions you got or things my mom actually said?"

"Both? It was a long time ago," he said again.

Twelve years. Still not long enough to erase that special, humiliating breed of heartbreak—the ache of loving someone who simply does not love you back enough. Of wanting a life you cannot have, resigning yourself to another one, making it work. Telling yourself it's better.

And maybe you're not wrong; maybe it is. But can anything built on false pretenses remain sturdy when the cracks in the foundation are exposed?

"*Why,*" she demanded, her voice barely controlled, "did you not *talk* to me about this?"

"I knew if we talked about it, we *would* land on a compromise. That was what we did—really well." He was getting visibly upset now. They were back there, both of them, in the heat of an argument they'd never resolved. An argument that had gone entirely one-sided.

"And that was bad?"

"Yes! No. I don't know. She got me thinking we did it *too* well. I didn't want to be one of those couples who wants fundamentally different things, and so torments themselves for years, dragging out the inevitable. Once it was pointed out to me that's what we were, it seemed better to just call it, rather than prolong the inevitable."

"You were a coward." She glowered at him.

"Maybe. But after I got home from dinner that night, I realized: I'd made my decision. Leaving the way I did was the only way to be sure I'd stick to it. Even if it did hurt like hell."

She felt dizzy from shaking her head so hard. "I did not then, nor do I now, believe we wanted fundamentally different things. We always seemed so in sync—I don't get how you were convinced otherwise, just like that."

He shrugged—not dismissively, but hopelessly—and she had the feeling that whatever he said next would be the real reason he'd left. Like the last thing you ask the doctor at an appointment. "We'd been fighting so much, and . . . Hannah didn't say anything I wasn't already feeling insecure about. She'd always liked us together—I had no reason to think she'd mislead me. And I didn't expect you to be honest if I called you out. Some opinions, you keep to yourself when someone you love is involved. Kind lies."

Someone you love.

Her old anger began to unwind, revealing the spool of grief it had been tangled around. What a waste, for something so definitive to come down to something so insubstantial.

His eyes searched hers. "Are you honestly telling me *none* of that was true?"

"I'm honestly telling you *none* of that was true."

"You think Hannah was projecting her own regrets, insecurities, whatever, on you? Being an overprotective parent, not wanting you to sell yourself short the way she maybe did?"

"That's a very charitable way of putting it."

"What then? She was afraid you'd meet Fred's old flame?" Even as he clung to his skepticism, the first hint of outrage flashed. It was oddly comforting, made her feel less alone.

"Or maybe that it would give him an excuse to look her up. I wouldn't even rule out that she knew about my half sister. I want to believe she didn't, but . . ." She sighed. "She said she underestimated how much you wanted that job. That she set out to talk you out of Brevard and talked you out of me instead."

They stared at each other for a terrible, incredulous moment. She couldn't absolve him of responsibility for what he'd done. Then again, Caroline had been just as proud. Too proud to fight harder, to do anything but silently scream as he slipped away. Those years after college *were* tough. The terror of what everyone called "the real world" was real, particularly on the heels of the "happy little bubble" of Athens. They'd been so young, bent on getting things right.

He forced a laugh. "Do you know I used to think it was lucky I ran into her? I thought that accidental talk ended up saving you and me from making a mistake."

"I guess if you were so easily swayed, it wasn't meant to be."

He took her in, head cocked again, measuring his words.

"It wasn't easily," he said quietly. "And I'd been taught that if something seems too good to be true, it is." His voice broke, and something in her did, too. This was not what she'd wanted to hear. What she'd wanted was proof that whatever ill-considered things Mom had said, they'd been secondary to the deciding factor. Not that her own mother had made Keaton believe Caroline was throwing over her goals for a man—while waiting for him to change, no less. A cringeworthy cliché any way you looked at it. No wonder he'd left.

His eyes were wet. "But you have a family now. We should be talking about your life."

"We *are* talking about my life."

"The part that's still relevant, I mean."

"This is relevant, Keat. You don't know what I went through." She caught a glimpse of what it meant to him to hear her say that before he tucked it behind the more accepting *bygones be bygones* expression he'd been wearing.

She'd needed him to know what had been true for her, before. Now he did.

But what did she really expect, want, in return? Other than the sad truth?

"If I could do it again, Caro, I—"

"There you are!" She looked up, dazed, to see Maureen rushing at them.

"Mo." Keaton straightened, flushed pink. "Good to see you."

Caroline met Mo's eyes, expecting a mischievous gleam. But all she saw was sorrow.

"Your phone's off. . . ." Mo puffed, out of breath. "I told them I'd get you."

Not sorrow. Controlled panic. Caroline scrambled to her feet. "What's happened?"

"It's your dad. He's had a heart attack."

12

Sela

An unfamiliar nurse greeted Sela and led her down a long corridor of numbered exam rooms to the back area where lab collections were done. "Where's Marie?" Sela asked, just for something to say as she walked obediently through the last open door and plunked into the gray vinyl chair, reminiscent of the dentist's office—high back, padded arms, reclining function in case anyone felt woozy.

"She's at Disney World? In Florida? With her family?"

Sela barked a surprised laugh, then clamped a hand over her mouth. It seemed wrong to poke fun at the woman with her colleagues, and yet . . .

"Spot-on," she said, raising an approving eyebrow.

The nurse glanced furtively into the hall, then flashed Sela a mischievous grin and sat down at the computer alongside the chair. "There's more where that came from, if you like impressions. Amateur Night at the Grey Eagle, this Sunday." She tapped at the keyboard, presumably pulling up Sela's lab order, while Sela squinted, trying to discern whether she was kidding. This woman seemed about her age and about as plain. Her ponytail hung down the back of her scrubs, small silver hearts dangled from her ears, and her face was bare aside from a little mascara and lip gloss. Tough to picture her in a spotlight, at a mic, but you never could tell about a person just from looking.

"You do stand-up comedy?"

"I try."

She cocked her head, wondering if this should make her more at ease with the woman or dramatically less so. "Any patients ever make the act?"

"Fear not. I have no need to cross that line. My coworkers give me plenty of fodder." She winked. "Though I limit myself to the ones I'm confident would never show up to support. So don't bust me."

"Your secret's safe with me. I could use a little comic relief."

What was she doing? This kind of friendly chitchat violated her rules. Sela sniffed and sat up straighter, ready for business.

"Couldn't we all," the nurse said, scrolling through her screen. "Okay, so when I haven't seen a patient before, I like to look over . . ."

Sela saw the instant the words escaped her—the way her expression flickered and froze. What had caught her eye? New test results, or something in her history? The nurse caught her watching and adjusted her face back into a smile.

"The whole picture," she finished. "I'm Janie, by the way."

"Hi."

Janie's chatter did not interfere with her efficiency. She moved Sela through the usual in record time—whipping on and off the blood pressure cuff, mercifully finding a vein on the first try—all while answering the questions Sela had wondered but not voiced. She didn't aspire to be a comedian instead of a nurse, it was just a fun outlet on the side. She'd been at it a couple of years, met some great people on the circuit. Didn't have kids, so didn't mind the occasional travel. Didn't have a boyfriend, so didn't mind the occasional fanboy. At that, Sela laughed.

"What about you?" Janie asked. "Married?"

"Divorced. Almost."

"Ah." Janie's eyes glanced almost imperceptibly back at the screen as she adhered labels to the vials of Sela's blood. If she was calculating timelines, she was kind enough not to show it. "Do you have an anthem?"

"An anthem?"

"Say you walk into a pub and there's your ex, perched on a bar stool. What perfect song would start blaring on the speakers when you stride past him?"

"It's been strongly recommended I avoid pubs."

Janie frowned. "Oh, come on. Play. Your kidneys have no role in this fantasy."

What a question—she'd never thought about it. "Hmm. Fleetwood Mac, maybe? 'Go Your Own Way.'"

"Ooh. *Layered.*"

"That's one word for it."

"But fierce. That drumbeat? Plus, you can *shout* that song."

"You can't not shout that song."

"'You can call it an-other lonely day,'" Janie whisper-shouted in tune, and Sela dropped her chin to her chest and punched her fist in the air.

"Take that, ex," Janie said, standing. Sela thought that they were done, that Janie would show her out, but instead she shut the door and sat down again, turning serious. "There's a note here that you don't want to know about your progress."

"That's—" Sela wriggled in her chair. This was exactly why she never let her guard down at these appointments—it invited scrutiny. Then again, if that's what Marie had written, she'd need to clarify. "Not what I said," she finished.

"Good. What did you say?"

She held her palms out: Nothing shady here. "I just don't want the play-by-play on these monthlies. I thought I'd do better on a need-to-know basis." She made a *Please don't say I can't* face, but Janie didn't laugh.

"This isn't a monthly," Janie pointed out. "It's a recheck."

Sela bit her lip. "I know."

Janie smiled then, more sympathetic. "Since I haven't seen you before, I haven't reviewed your entire file. But if we're talking about redirecting your energy to something productive, have you started asking around? For potential donors willing to get tested?"

Sela sighed. It was far too complicated to explain that she was redirecting her energy toward the one untapped relationship that had a worth-mentioning chance of being a match. Or that, for human decency reasons, she hoped to separate that relationship from the matter of her health for as long as possible. Never mind that telling Caroline all this later, even if they did forge some bond, would not necessarily make her *more* decent. "Sort of. But my antibodies are what's known in layman's terms as *oversensitive assholes*."

Janie laughed, but her expectant expression didn't change. "That's exactly why it's never too early to pound the pavement for a match. I love when my patients are able to circumnavigate dialysis entirely. Doesn't happen often, but when it does, it's like beating the system, you know?" *My* patients, she'd said, implying that Sela was now one. That she felt responsibility toward her. Sela hadn't felt that from anyone in a while, and though she'd been actively avoiding it, she couldn't honestly say it felt bad.

She cleared her throat. "Um. Yeah. So, my ex volunteered, my best friend got tested . . ."

"With sensitization issues, I'm sure you were told family might be your best bet."

She nodded. "After my mother's funeral, some relatives kept in closer touch. Her family isn't large, or close, but they were concerned that she was gone and I was—" Sela's voice broke. Over a year later, and she wasn't sure what she hated more—that she had to talk about Ecca in the past tense or that whenever she did, she wound up sounding like a child. "Once my grandmother caught wind of the way this was headed, several of them stepped up. My grandfather is an alcoholic, so he was out, but my grandmother got tested, even though she's way older than recommended. Also my mother's brother and his grown kids, even though they live on the West Coast and barely know me. It was very kind. I don't know if anyone would've gone through with it, but no one matched anyway."

"And your father's family?"

She'd already given an uncomfortable level of detail. "Not in the picture."

"Sometimes it's appropriate—" Sela held up a hand, and Janie took the hint. "Okay. I'm sorry to hear about your mom. Do you feel as if it's worth asking around again, family-wise? Or do you get the sense everyone who was going to step up did?"

"Definitely that everyone willing did. My grandmother was persistent. I think she felt bad about the state of her relationship with my mother and hoped to make up for it."

"Has she been a support to you beyond that?"

"She tried to be, but I—" She shook her head, looking down at her lap. She tried so hard to keep her disease separate from everything else—her marriage, parenthood, family, friendships—but there *was* no separating it. It made no more sense to try than it did to keep the nurses at arm's length so she wouldn't feel like the regular patient she was.

"Okay. I'm sorry, I'm not trying to get overly personal." Janie touched her arm gently. "Have you been to one of the Big Ask seminars yet?"

Sela shook her head. "Since my best chance is family . . ."

"Best, but not only. There's always a chance—you only need one match out there, right? When it comes to this particular need, if you're not trying, you're effectively giving up. And if you're going to be in my rotation, you can't give up. It's bad for my act."

Was she going to be in her rotation? Maybe someone like Janie would be better for Sela after all. She tried for a smile. "Hey, I thought you left your patients out of it."

"Out of the joke, not out of my mind? And I'm supposed to be *funny*? So you gotta work with me on this? So I can sleep at night?" The Marie impression was so damn accurate, it almost made her wish Marie were here so she could hear them side by side.

Almost.

"I'm not giving up," Sela said. She wasn't going to get into it, but that didn't mean it wasn't true. "And my ex went to the workshop. He's been using the . . . approaches."

"Did he run it all by you? Before he put out bulletins or whatever?" Bulletins? Good grief.

"He told me about it after," she said. "I mean, during. He told me he was doing it."

Janie cocked her head. "One of the things discussed in the seminar is to obtain the patient's permission before employing the suggested strategies. This is *your* story to tell. Not anyone else's. It's great to have help, but from your expression—it should be on your terms, or at least terms you're okay with. He should not *go his own way* with this."

This was news to Sela. The Fleetwood Mac faded from the white noise in her mind.

"It's okay," she said awkwardly. "I wasn't mad." As soon as she said it, she realized it wasn't true. But she hadn't wanted to seem ungrateful. Not even when Leigh poked fun at his outreach.

"I can tell you don't feel comfortable with this idea of asking," Janie said softly. "That's why I think you should go. That's what the seminars are for. There's one Friday, in fact." She spread her arms wide. "Go and see what they say. What do you have to lose? Besides a poorly functioning kidney?"

What *did* she have to lose?

She gave a nervous laugh. "I'm kind of a textbook denial case, I guess."

"You told me your situation in plain terms. That's not denial. It's normal to not want to shout it from rooftops. But even though you're just coming in for lab work at this point, it can help to have someone here who you feel connected to. Marie, me, whoever. That's one thing the dialysis patients have on the rest of you—the *only* thing they have that's worth envying: They spend so much time with the staff and each other that it's one big support group over there. Made me want to become a nurse, in fact. And a comic, come to think of it."

Become? Sela blinked at her. "You were a patient?"

"Got my first living donor kidney twenty-two years ago."

Sela gaped at her. Janie couldn't be past forty—at least, not much.

"Third time's a charm, as they say. This one's going strong ten years in. Belongs to my sister. We take a girls' trip on the anniversary every year to celebrate."

"Wow." Sela didn't know why she felt she should've somehow sensed this.

She also didn't know why she was crying. Maybe it was the shock of seeing someone so capable out on the other side. Or maybe it was the mention of Janie's sister—that not only had she been willing but it was something they *celebrated.* Something bringing them even closer. Janie handed her a tissue from a wall-mounted dispenser. "I had no idea anyone here had been through it themselves," Sela managed.

"You'd be surprised how many of us have. Like I said, that 'big happy family' vibe *really* carries you through those dialysis days. Especially young. A lot of people have this sense of wanting to help others that way—or feeling we'd be good at it, because we get it, you know?" She fixed her eyes on Sela's. "I won't pretend to know what you've been through. Everyone's experience is different. But I can tell you that at a base, gut level, I do get it."

Sela's head bobbed in manic agreement, like a doll on a dashboard. Janie gave her hand a squeeze, and Sela felt the folded brochure slide into her palm.

"Promise you'll think about going Friday."

The people on the glossy trifold cover smiled, arms around each other. Through the blur of her tears, she recognized one of them as Janie.

"If I do, any chance of you moving me from Marie's book to yours?" A whisper was all Sela could manage.

"Already done," Janie whispered back.

13

Caroline

Mo did not say, *That looked like some intense shit I walked into with you and Keat.* She did not say, *Holy fuck, not fair that he looks that good.* She didn't say, *Tell me everything on the way.* She didn't say much at all, other than insisting Caroline not drive herself to the hospital.

That's how Caroline had known it was bad.

What if Dad was already gone by the time she got there? The last thing she ever said to him would have been—what?

She couldn't remember the words but knew the emotion behind them, felt it still. Disappointment. Distrust. Disbelief. All of it, though, borne from the infinite depth of her love for the man who had raised her, shaped her. Always been there for her, so dependably and so well that she resented having to think of who else he might have failed along the way.

They drove in silence, while Caroline fumbled with her phone, shame mounting at the way she'd scoffed like a melodramatic adolescent at Mom's incoming call. While she'd been caught up with Keat, she'd missed nine calls from Mom, three from Walt—who'd given up and texted that he'd pick up the kids from school and meet her at the hospital—and two from Mo. None from Dad, no matter how long she stared at the log, willing his name to appear. She dialed his number, just to hear his voice on the outgoing message. Tears filled her eyes.

She should have foreseen something like this. Should have known better than to have the nerve to be *glad* she hadn't heard from him this week. Should have sensed the danger in her marrow, instead of focusing on the wrong worries. The selfish ones.

"Don't worry about responding," Mo said gently. "Hannah's phone can't get service in the waiting room." *On my way*, Caroline texted anyway. With a silent plea: *Let it not be too late.*

Mo dropped her at the main entrance and went to park the car. Caroline rushed through the hospital's maze of corridors as fast as her sling-backs could carry her, skimming the wall-mounted signs, following the shaky instructions Mo had relayed. Above her, fluorescent lights emanated the aggressive artificial glow of a bad dream.

She loathed everything about this place. The way every event that had previously brought her here had started out as routine, then escalated in spite of assurances to the contrary: Walt's "food poisoning" that revealed itself to be appendicitis. Riley's broken arm from an innocuous-looking sliding board tumble. Owen's jaundice, days after discharge from maternity. She loathed the way it made her bargain with God even when the odds were in her favor, the way it smelled of antiseptic desperation, the way it hummed and beeped and vibrated, a conduit for things she'd never understand. The way it held the people she loved in its grasp and decided unilaterally whether to let them go.

Never before had she stepped inside and thought that maybe they had done something to deserve this turn. But even as she ran toward her dread, she couldn't help wondering.

And somehow, it felt like her fault.

She rounded the corner and spotted Mom, spine straight in the middle seat of a row of empty chairs. How long had she been here alone? A torturous hour, two? A magazine lay open in her lap, but her eyes were on a muted flat-screen TV tuned to the news.

Caroline went for her, arms open. The magazine slid to the floor, and then they were hugging tight, swaying, the way they'd stood in all the most wonderful and most terrible of Caroline's daughterly memories. They were almost exactly the same height, and Caroline could feel the neck-and-neck footrace of their hearts' anxious pounding.

"Oh, sweetie." Mom pulled back to look at her. "You look lovely."

The comment was as inane under these circumstances as the reasons Caroline had put in the effort. It already seemed as though a different woman had donned this dress, dabbed foundation over her sunspots, and wielded her neglected round brush while Maureen's voice in her head—*Think of this as getting out ahead of fate*—talked over the preemptive guilt playing on her conscience.

"How is he? Is he out of surgery?"

"Not yet. But, it's just an angioplasty, not a bypass. So that's encouraging. They said it was lucky that he wasn't alone when it started, that I recognized the signs—we got him here fast. As of now, the doctors don't seem terribly worried."

Caroline swallowed hard. "Was it—was it stress that brought this on?"

"Who can say?" Mom dropped wearily back into her chair, tugging Caroline down next to her. "All the more reason to put it behind us."

Lucky that he wasn't alone. One week earlier, and he almost certainly would have been.

For years, Mom's care to his health had been the picture of unconditional love, as she overhauled everything from her diet to her home in solidarity. But the many forms of her devotion—nutritionist consultations, new appliances, salable remodeling—proved useless against the real threat to his heart: a mail-in DNA test. If this attack took him now of all times, Mom would never get over it.

And for what? What had happened with Rebecca was an *actual* lifetime ago. And Sela had yet to express any interest in Dad anyway. Besides, if Caroline hadn't logged in to his account, these bombshells would have gone off differently. Less dramatically.

"Mom, I'm so sorry. That you couldn't reach me. That I . . ." Tears flooded out her voice, and then Mom's arms were around her again, pulling her close.

"None of that. It's okay. You're here now." She seemed calm, reassured, though Caroline was not. Wouldn't be, until she saw Dad with her own eyes.

If he pulled through . . . No, *when* . . . Her parents' love—for each other, for her, for her children, and even for Walt—that was what should matter, carry with it the implicit gift of forgiveness. Life was too fickle for anything less.

"It's not okay," Caroline said, sniffling. "Last time you and I talked, I was—"

"Let's forget it, sweetie. Dad is our only concern right now, which is as it should be."

She nodded numbly. *As it should be.*

She closed her eyes against the image of Mom seated across the table from the first man Caroline had ever truly loved, pouring fuel on his insecurities, carefully, casually derailing their future together. The same woman had called 911 today, saved Dad's life. For better or worse, Hannah was never afraid to do what she thought was necessary, thought was best.

It wasn't such a bad trait when she turned out to be right.

—

"You have to hand it to the guy," Walt said. "He knows how to time a brush with fatality."

He and Caroline watched from the hallway outside Dad's hospital room while Owen, Lucy, and Riley pushed every button on his bed—reclining the top, elevating the bottom, cranking the TV volume, and accidentally calling the nurse three times. Under threat of losing their evening screen time, they now knew which button *not* to push again, which freed their Gramps to direct them in folding him into a pretzel.

"A little higher at the top . . . Now at the bottom . . . There! Perfectly comfortable!" The kids burst into giggles.

He'd been here for three days. With any luck, he'd be headed home tomorrow. Caroline and her crew were taking this shift while Mom was off filling his new prescriptions and stocking the fridge with what few of his favorite foods he was still allowed to have.

She tried to smile at Walt, though his comment had been only half in jest. "If you're going to have a heart attack, might as well double as a perspective check," she agreed.

That's what Keaton had called his own hospital stay. *I was one of the lucky few,* he'd said. *Nowhere near a disaster,* he'd said. Then again, he'd confessed to feeling *lucky* he'd run into Hannah that night, too.

"Is it working?" Walt put an arm around her shoulders. "I mean, for your parents, obviously. But for you?"

Mom had gone so far as to express gratitude that this happened in a treatable way. "Now that he's out of the woods, I mean," she'd rushed to add. "Obviously his other medications weren't doing the trick, so hopefully the stents will." In those moments, Caroline tried hard to see Mom as glad, not smug. Grateful for the right reasons, not relieved for the wrong ones. Embracing his new start rather than getting her way.

Now, Caroline braced her free hand against the painted cinder block of the wall. The sturdiest thing, by far, in the hallway where she and Walt stood.

"All week, I've been telling myself this trumps everything else," she said, not taking her eyes off the kids and their Gramps. "And it does. I mean, look at them."

Walt knew what *everything else* referred to. The first night here, after she'd finally been able to squeeze Dad's hand and reach between his IV lines for tentative, tearful hugs—him taking one look at Caroline and croaking, *Sorry to scare you, kiddo,* her instinctively brushing him off, *Don't be daffy,* and meaning it—they'd given her parents some time alone. Mo, the day's hands-down hero, took the kids to her house, and Caroline and Walt headed to the cafeteria. Over grilled cheese and coffee, he asked about her talk with Keaton, and she told him.

Not the way it felt, but what was said.

He knew her well enough, for better or worse, to deduce the rest.

Which was why he was asking this now.

"But?" he prodded.

She turned away from the window, away from him, to stare blankly across the hallway. "But," she said slowly, "now that the initial panic has died down, I'm realizing that trumping everything else is not the same as erasing everything else. I can be glad my parents are okay and together and here, and still be hurt that Mom sold me out. I can accept that it's useless to rehash what either of them did again, and still need time to get used to the things I learned."

Useless was putting it kindly. They'd been warned not to stress Dad. Which conveniently meant not stressing Mom.

She risked a glance at Walt and caught a flash of worry in his eyes before they met hers. Reassurance took its place. "Of course you can," he said. "I'm right there with you. This is a lot for anyone to take in. We can't all be as selectively harmonious as Fred and Hannah."

Whispering through arguments. Going years without acknowledging an infidelity aloud. Pretending an illegitimate child was just that, nothing more. Then burying it all—doctor's orders.

Keaton had talked about not wanting anyone to feel sorry for him, back when he'd been laid up. Dad's thinking was clearly not the same. Eager as Mom was to have him home—and earnestly as he lapped up that eagerness—he seemed to like it here fine in the meantime. Boasting to the nurses about "his girls" whenever Caroline and Hannah walked through the door. Sweet-talking his way into extra visiting hours. Riding the bed right now, like a carousel.

She nodded her agreement. "Selectively harmonious. Good one."

"I always think I'm funny until Mo sweeps in with her Asterix army and conquers me."

A smile twitched at her lips.

His arm slid back around her neck. "Seriously. You okay? Anything I can do?" He must have asked this ten times a day since this had happened. Draped beside her, his fingers curled helplessly around the empty air, itching to repair whatever was broken. Yet even in calling out Dad's uncanny timing, Walt had no idea how precise it had been.

If I could do it again, Caro . . . Keaton didn't get to finish. Never would. As she'd run out and left him sitting, stunned, him insisting of course she had to go, they'd both known the conversation had gone far enough that there'd be no reason to pick it back up just to add a final word. It was over. Done, in every way.

She laced her fingers between Walt's now, stilling them. "I'm trying to be."

He leaned over, kissed her cheek. "I'm sorry this has been so—"

The ring of her phone cut him off. She'd left the volume

cranked ever since this had happened, taking no chances. She couldn't imagine ever silencing it again. She fished into her purse and saw an unidentified number flashing on the screen. *North Carolina,* in big letters.

Walt averted his eyes. "Did you give Keaton your number?"

Could it really be him?

"I didn't. Maybe Mo did? He might be worried about Dad, the way I ran out."

"You should answer."

She met his eyes, frozen. Only when he nodded encouragement did she lift it to her ear. "Hello?"

"Is this Caroline?"

A woman's voice. Embarrassing, how her heart fell.

The voice didn't wait for a response. "This is Sela."

Oh. That unknown number in North Carolina.

"Wow. Sela, hi." Walt's eyes went wide. He turned back to the window, flashed a thumbs-up that the kids were still occupying their Gramps, and motioned for her to go ahead, find some privacy. "It's so strange to hear your voice," Caroline ventured, heading obediently down the hall toward the elevator bank. Did they sound alike? Or, rather, half-alike? Over the din of the cardiac wing, she couldn't tell.

"It is," Sela agreed. "Yours too, I mean. Is this a bad time?"

Comically bad. But would there ever be a good one?

"I have a few minutes. What's up?"

Gah. That sounded juvenile. Cavalier, for a first conversation. What should she have said? *How are you?* Walt would have gone corny to break the ice: *What can I do you for?*

"Oh God." Sela laughed. "I feel like we've been online dating, and this is that awkward first offline thing."

Caroline found herself smiling. "Is that what we've been doing? I *knew* I should have used a fake headshot."

"Didn't you? Wow, those are really your boobs?"

They both burst out laughing. It was doubly ridiculous, between Caroline's flat chest and the photo she'd sent: of the whole family posed in front of the fireplace for their Christmas card.

And though it was hardly the time or the place to laugh about anything, it felt good to let it out. Like a horrifying giggle she'd been suppressing at a funeral.

Sela cleared her throat. "I hope this isn't weird," she said. "I actually did try online dating once, and in my experience, the longer we went without talking offline, the weirder things were when we finally did."

"You'd think it would be the opposite," Caroline said amicably. Of course this was weird—how could it ever not be, let alone now, when steps away their father's heartbeat was being tracked by a sea of monitors? But the window for analyzing whether she wanted to take Sela's call had closed when she answered the phone, expecting Keat. Served her right, too.

"I know. But I found that in between emails or posts or whatever, your imagination fills in the blanks. And when you fill them in wrong, the real thing is a little disorienting."

Caroline's imagination *had* been doing a lot of filling in lately. There was kindness, too, in what Sela didn't say: that it was Caroline's turn to write back, and she'd left Sela hanging. That the aforementioned time between emails had been lengthened by, unbeknownst to Sela, this all-consuming family emergency. One she'd be part of if things were different. "I can see that."

"I didn't plan this," Sela admitted. "I was thinking of writing you again, and then—I don't know, I picked up the phone before I could talk myself out of it."

How many hours, days, years, had Caroline squandered *not* calling Keaton, back when she still could have?

"I talk myself out of good ideas all the time."

"Do you? Okay, so. Um. I'm in the process of talking myself out of another one."

She sounded so tentative. Though her voice was soft, it spoke loud and clear: that the one who'd gotten lost in all of this was Sela. Sela, who didn't have the luxury of keeping vigil with family she felt maddeningly, simultaneously grateful for and furious with. Sela, who'd gotten only half of the parenting she was entitled to and yet cheerfully called her sister up and joked about her bra size, as if everything else were water under the bridge. Sela, whom neither Caroline nor Walt had the decency to consider, even now, when a Brevard area code appeared on her phone.

"Try me," Caroline said.

"Well. When they sent my DNA results, they left out tips for our particular scenario."

"They were under *disclaimers*." They dissolved into laughter again, the kind that goes on and on and starts up again every time you think it's going to fade.

"See," Sela squealed. "That's the kind of thing you would never type in an email. Or you would, and then you'd worry the other person would take it wrong."

"Even now, I'm grateful you didn't take that wrong."

"That's just it. So what if we just—meet? Would it be too soon?"

All week, she'd been looking from her parents to Walt and the kids to her newest memories of Keaton and thinking three words, over and over: *It's too late.*

Too late to do anything different.

To hold her parents accountable, go back, reverse course. Even if she wanted to.

Now, here was Sela, wanting to know if it was too *soon.*

Though her blinders had slid away, slowly, since receiving Sela's very first email, Caroline truly hadn't seen anything clearly until now.

There was one path not taken that she *could* still turn and follow, see where it might lead, without letting someone down, breaking a promise. One chance denied her that she *could* still take, better late than never.

Better soon than never.

Sela.

14

Sela

So, she'd gone to the damn seminar. The Big Ask: The Big Give.

The big never mind.

By the time it was over, Sela was certain that all of her angst over Caroline—what to say, when to say it, how to endear herself, and all the rest—had been unwarranted. Pointless, really.

Because no way could she ever ask her for a kidney.

"Maybe this workshop shouldn't even be called The Big Ask," the opening speaker had said. He might have been a student at Brevard College—he was about that age—and, like Janie, was a lifelong kidney patient. He'd months ago received his first donation and was still basking in the glow, having begun his speech by raving about the life-changing magic of things as simple as a long, hot shower, things he hadn't been able to do with a dialysis catheter in place. Things Sela hadn't grappled with yet; things that made her feel less sick by comparison—less deserving of the help he'd received.

"Sometimes people just need to know that someone they care

about needs help, and that they might be able to give it," he went on. "That's it. Don't ask, just tell. Tell them what it's like, living with kidney disease. Tell them what the kidneys do, and what happens when they fail. Tell them what a big difference a donor's generosity could make to your life. For me, that's all it took for someone to come forward. And, when he wasn't a match, for someone else to." He beamed gratitude at the donor he'd introduced earlier, his uncle, seated in the front row. "People who care about you want you to live—and live well. Everyone here can speak up that way, for yourself or someone else. Spread the word. With all of you as advocates, maybe one day we'll simply be able to call this program The Big Give, period."

Applause rippled across the hospital's small, half-filled auditorium, but Sela couldn't will her hands to join in.

She'd arrived early, choosing a seat near the back and taking the temperature of the room, which was more of a lecture hall than a theater. *Hesitant,* she'd decided, at the risk of projecting. *Uncertain.* Fellow patients trickled in with people she took to be family, significant others, and close friends. They sat in clusters, saving seats. Sela was the only one who didn't seem to know anyone else, and she recalled what Janie had said about the bonds formed in the dialysis center. She busied herself taking faux notes on her laptop, lest anyone feel inclined to approach.

But then came the recipients. A handful of men and women of varying ages, lining chairs behind the podium, waiting their turns to speak. A few indeed wore scrubs and hospital badges, patients turned providers—Janie's observations on this checked out, too. What Sela couldn't stop staring at, though, was how healthy they looked. Unencumbered, unafraid.

What would it be like to be among them? Sela hadn't let herself think that far ahead, to the mind-blowing reality of a second chance. Yes, it was true that even with a transplant, her condition was chronic. That she'd be pressing a reset button on something that would then inevitably resume its slow decline; that she'd never go back to an unmonitored, unregulated, unmedicated life. But there could be good, even normalish years in between. Maybe lots of them.

Could she really have that, even if someone gave her the essential gift to make it happen? What would it look like, feel like, to still be without Doug, still without her mother, and yet be healthy again? To peer into the mirror and see someone other than a sick, left-behind woman?

As the welcome speaker thanked them again for coming and took his seat, the slide glowing on the whiteboard flipped from the program logo to the first topic of the day: "The Donor Experience." Sela already felt skeptical about summoning enough self-delusion, enough audacity, to think plopping herself in front of Caroline and merely explaining her situation would be enough to inspire life-altering generosity in a relative she'd just met. Still, this was the part of the seminar she most needed.

And most dreaded.

Because it was the only part of the process she had not yet fully researched. She'd had to draw a line somewhere—she'd lost enough sleep googling things that were beyond her control as it was. Immersing herself in what things would be like for the donor seemed the very definition of putting the cart before the highly unlikely horse.

More honestly, though, she hadn't wanted to know. She was afraid to find out precisely what her own inescapable need could *electively* put at risk for someone else. Because she'd never be naïve enough to think "just telling" someone what she was going through and then looking at them expectantly was anything other than asking. It was more like pleading as if her life depended on it. Which it did.

Sela didn't begrudge the optimistic young intro speaker his point of view, or his plump pink new kidney, his bond with his loving uncle, even his assumption that everyone was surrounded by *people who care about you, who want you to live well.* She'd known that the lion's share of this seminar would not apply to her, that she'd very likely end up on the endless nationwide list, where not everyone got what they were waiting for. She'd known that the idea of bypassing the all-consuming hell of dialysis was a pipe dream and that even if Caroline agreed to get tested, it was a long shot that she'd match.

When she'd accepted Janie's challenge to come here, what she'd really been talked into was this: facing up to what she *hadn't* known, inescapable now as the applause died down and a surgeon took the mic to elaborate upon the bullet points of The Donor Experience.

Each statistic, Sela could tell, was meant to highlight the odds in the donors' favor. But what jumped out at her—*screamed* at her—were the worst-case scenarios offsetting each one. Hiding between the lines, and yet right there, if you only looked.

That three in ten thousand donors have a fatal complication from the surgery.

That other, minor complications were rare but did occur. Infection. A longer or more arduous recovery than expected.

That dietary restrictions for *the rest of the donor's life* were typically reasonable things you should do anyway—eat healthfully, moderate vices, drink plenty of water—but more in-depth maintenance was required if the remaining kidney did not rise to the occasion.

That occasionally the transplanted kidney did not take, and the donor would need to come to terms with their sacrifice having been for nothing.

That any complications they'd endured would also have been *for nothing.*

That in the unlikely event a donor's remaining kidney later

failed, the donor would be prioritized on the list of those in the exact shoes of the person they'd set out to help.

They went on, explaining the vetting process, what it entailed, how it was designed to ensure not only a viable match but the health of the donor. And what the recipient's insurance did and did not cover: the procedure, but not lost wages from the (on average) six- to eight-week recovery period, travel for an out-of-town donor, or other incidentals. But by then, from where Sela sat, the details had been rendered irrelevant.

She was living every day with the consequences of an "unlikely event." The emergence of her disease and everything that had subsequently unraveled—her life's plans, Brody's, her marriage—all of it had been rare, unusual, unfortunate.

She had no choice but to live with those outcomes, but she did have a choice about whether she coerced her perfectly healthy half sister to leave the safe cocoon of her life and join her in this game of risk. A game she now understood could be, if she was one of the unlucky ones, *for nothing*.

Sela's luck had run out years ago. And if things didn't go in Caroline's favor, she would bear responsibility for that, too.

She couldn't.

All along, she'd thought this all came down to forcing herself to pursue something she wanted but wasn't entirely comfortable with. What she took away from the seminar was that she'd been wrong. She *didn't* want it. If something went awry with Caroline's health, it would be a waste for Sela's life to be extended as the only good result, because she'd never be able to live with herself. Crushing as it was to resign herself to this—a long, unhealthy wait at best, a slow, uncomfortable death at worst—it was still more palatable than the alternative.

Funny to have that realization in a seminar designed to have the opposite effect.

Afterward, something shifted in Sela. Gone was any hang-up about speaking with Caroline: She felt freed to converse with her like a real person would and not, as she had been, like a machine learning system doing word-by-word analyses to maximize the probabilities of winning her over.

Also gone? The original life-or-death reason for seeking out her never-known sibling.

But she *had* sought her out. And not merely found her but connected, in a tentative but surprisingly meaningful way. Next thing she knew, she was picking up the phone, hearing her speak. Laughing—together. And spontaneously, unthinkably, blurting out an invitation to meet. Caroline accepting, just like that. As if taking the next step forward had been that easy all along.

The unexpected joy following that call was almost enough to erase the vacant feeling that had overtaken Sela in the seminar's final hour, when the panel of recipients and their donors took the stage. As gratitude and goodwill poured from the stories they shared, the room temperature Sela had taken upon arrival warmed considerably, the trepidation calmed and soothed by more compassion than she'd ever felt or seen in a single place.

She'd taken it all in and understood, at last, what it could mean for Caroline to give her back her life.

Even as she let go of the idea of ever asking her to.

15

Caroline

"Mama, Mama, Mama!" Lucy's terror came through loud and clear, and Caroline took the stairs two at a time, feeling frantic at the tone even though she knew this was no real emergency, only her kindergartner's imagination—again. She forced herself not to cry out that she was coming, lest Owen or Riley by some miracle be sleeping through the yelling.

Somehow, this had become the new routine. Lucy used to be good about falling asleep. So good, in fact, that it took a while for it to sink in that one night's test-Caroline's-patience stalling had become a long, bleary stretch of them.

"It's a ploy for attention," Walt warned, unmoved, each time his wife went to her. But Caroline wasn't so sure. Given the timing, she couldn't ignore the possibility that Lucy had picked up on a tension shift in the house, weeks before it had culminated in her Gramps's stint in the hospital. Even before then, she'd been seeing much less of her grandparents—a conspicuous gap that had resumed now that Dad was home and required idle days to heal.

What were the odds that their world could feel so altered to her and still feel the same to Lucy?

As a parent, if you were going to have a personal crisis, it had better be on your own time. And if such a thing didn't exist anymore—which, of course, it didn't? Too bad.

"Sweetheart?" She burst through the bedroom door and found her daughter not merely whining but full-out sobbing, clinging to the safety rail affixed to her twin bed. Caroline pried the little fingers away from the metal-rimmed netting and wrapped them around her own neck instead, standing and swaying while Lucy breathed deep, tear-streaked breaths into her collarbone. "Shhh," she soothed her. "It's okay. I'm here."

Caroline had always been imperfect when it came to dividing attention among all three children. Her rotation was more reactive than proactive, gravitating to whoever needed her most at the given moment, but even that flawed system was less adept lately. She'd been distracted to the point of apologizing daily for some oversight that was "not like her." But this was no unclean soccer jersey at game time—this was sweet, easy Lucy, and it wasn't like *her,* either.

She waited until Lucy was calm, sniffing away the last vestiges of her tears, before perching them both at the foot of her bed. "Let's talk about this," she said, careful to keep her voice open, warm. "What's going on here? Why the trouble with bedtime all of a sudden? Is this anything to do with Gramps? Did the hospital scare you?"

Lucy sniffled, shaking her head. "The hospital was kind of neat."

She should be grateful to Dad for that, she supposed. "Then what?"

Her daughter blinked at her with wide, earnest eyes. "It's the shadows," she whispered.

As simple as a fear of the dark? Was Caroline projecting her own insecurities *everywhere*? "Okay," she began, summoning her old MacGyver Mom self. Down to business, then. "You have your night-light, and we leave the hall light on too. What else can we do? Arm you with a special flashlight? Something like a . . . a sparkle ray?" She had no idea how she'd make such a thing, but if anything could sway Lucy, it was the promise of sparkle.

Lucy's bottom lip jutted out skeptically. "Can I just have all the lights on?"

"Well, that's not very good for sleeping. Darkness signals to our body that it's time to rest. Don't you see the light through your eyelids, even when they're closed?"

She nodded. "I like it."

"I don't think it's healthy, Lu," she said gently. "Let's think of something else to try."

"But everything looks different with the light off."

"Different how?" Caroline envisioned a systematic approach—removing the humpback of Lucy's fuzzy robe from its hook, turning the vacant stare of a baby doll to face the wall. Frankly, dolls gave her the willies even in daylight. But Lucy only shook her head.

"I tell myself things are the same as always. But now that I've seen them a new, bad way, I can't stop. Even though I want to."

This, Caroline understood. Uncomfortably well.

Without a clue as to how to fix it.

It's the shadows. Dad's transgressions, no matter how long ago, did change the light that fell on everything around him: his wife, his health, his daughter. Daughter*s*. And Mom's meddling further darkened Caroline's memories, almost beyond recognition.

Caroline had always thought she'd been so in charge of her life—everything scripted to her specifications. But now, she couldn't help feeling as if she'd been tricked into that false sense all along.

Hannah seemed so glad to see me, Keaton had told her.

Hannah didn't say anything I wasn't already feeling insecure about.

Things had been crafted to someone's specifications all right. But not Caroline's.

She'd been a fool to think seeing Keaton might help. In that little corner table, she'd sat down across from her worst mistakes—and though they'd been overshadowed in the chaos that followed, she hadn't been able to stop them from tailing her home.

Whereas Keaton long ago made peace with "maybe just one or two" regrets, Caroline had done the opposite. She'd waited him out for as long as she could justify—hoping against hope he'd come back for her, change his mind. And then, when there was nothing left to do but give up, along came Walt, offering her a way to take matters into her own hands.

But a decade of her own best efforts at taking control had landed her here, in a life—in a *family*—she scarcely even recognized from weeks ago.

Caroline didn't want to see these things the "new, bad way" either.

"Well," she told Lucy, "if you can't go back to seeing things the old way, maybe you can come up with a *new* new way. One so good, you won't go back to seeing them the bad way."

"A new new way," Lucy repeated. Her eyes fixed on the wide sliding doors of her closet, and Caroline wondered if she was looking at the posters on them—unicorns, rainbows—or trying to see through to whatever was on the other side.

The way Caroline did with Sela.

"How do you want to do this?" Sela had asked. When Caroline agreed right away to meet, her half sister sounded so happy, so hopeful—almost as if freed from some burden. Caroline would have found the mood contagious, had she not been standing in the cardiac unit that housed Dad's fragile heart, contemplating anew the sign in front of her:

AUTHORIZED VISITORS ONLY.

Was she obligated to tell her parents she'd be meeting Sela?

If it wasn't up for debate, and they'd already made their stance on the woman clear, why make it a thing? The potential danger wasn't just emotional anymore.

"Well, I don't know that I can travel anytime soon," she ventured, suddenly less sure of herself. She *was* sure that she couldn't be hundreds of miles from Dad. Not now. "We've had . . . a lot going on."

"I've never been to Cincinnati," Sela said easily. "I'm curious, since Mom lived there."

Had Rebecca been so set on hiding from Caroline's parents that she'd cut off contact with the entire town? The deepening realization of all Sela's mother had sacrificed—to save face, to protect her daughter, to let Hannah and Fred be—filled Caroline with defiance, a surprise sense of solidarity with her sister. It wasn't as if putting off a visit from Sela would make much difference to her parents' eventual reactions. Dad would still cite his heart as an excuse. Mom would still telegraph her disapproval via sighs.

But seeing Sela sooner than later *could* make a difference to Caroline. Give her something to do with the unsettled energy Keaton left behind and someone to turn to apart from the rest of this mess. Someone who wasn't a cheater, a manipulator, a friend who remembered uncomfortably well, or even a partner who checked the right boxes, and yet.

And yet. She despised those dangerous, self-destructive words.

"Then you should come," she heard herself say. "Bring Brody, stay a weekend."

"I'd like that. Although I might pick a weekend Doug has custody, if that's okay?" That made sense. The kid had been through a lot of change lately. And after a month of corresponding, she could tell Sela grew lonely on those off weekends. Caroline couldn't imagine how quiet her house would get if her brood evacuated every other week.

Come to think of it, how to explain a mystery guest to her own kids?

"Let me look at our calendar with Walt, and I'll give the details some thought too. I'll email you?" *Give the details some thought* suddenly felt like a gross understatement.

"Why don't you tell me one of the bad things?" she asked Lucy now. "We can figure it out together."

It was the response she was still awaiting from Walt. She'd hung up with Sela and found him as she'd left him, keeping watch through the window, looking to her expectantly. *Whatever you think,* he'd said when she told him what she'd agreed to. He wouldn't stop her, though he was clearly uncomfortable enough to omit his usual assurance: that they'd *figure it out together.* Whether it was because he disapproved or because he thought this was something she had to do alone, she couldn't tell.

"Maybe some other time," Lucy replied. It was jarring, having your kids parrot your words back to you. Coming from Lucy, they seemed more dismissive than Caroline ever intended. "Please can I keep the lights on tonight?"

Caroline tried to smile. "Whatever you think," she said, trying out the words. They sounded equally dismissive, to her chagrin.

Lucy nodded once, then looked away, in the half-stubborn, half-apologetic manner of someone who senses your reservations but is determined to do as she pleases anyway.

In a pretty good impression, come to think of it, of Caroline herself.

16

Sela

At the threshold of a house twice the size of her own, the front door cracked open and three small, anxious faces peered out at Sela.

"Are you Mom's friend?" the oldest wanted to know. This would be Riley, giving Sela more of a once-over than was warranted from the mundane cover story she and Caroline had agreed upon: old friends who'd found each other and scheduled the weekend to catch up. *Don't get weirded out when they call you Aunt Sela,* Caroline had written. *That's how they address all our old friends—they'd think it strange if you were an exception.* Would Caroline ever tell the kids, once they were older, that the name was not honorary? Would Sela have any say in the matter if she were still in their lives, a caveat as figurative as it was literal?

"I am." Sela smiled—too stiffly, but her nerves wouldn't get out of her way. A fierce reluctance to leave Brody had overcome her when they'd hugged good-bye at Doug's this morning, but that might have had more to do with Doug himself. He and Leigh were both so proud of her for initiating this step to see Caroline—all *Good for you!* and *I knew you could do it!* before Sela got another word in—she hadn't had the heart to tell them she'd decided not to Big Ask her sister anything. If this visit went well, she hoped they'd be glad enough of her finding some new semblance of family to reluctantly follow suit when she let it drop. And if it didn't? Well, that'd take care of itself. The implied answer to the question she'd never voiced would be no.

She'd tried to leave her hesitation behind as she followed the westbound highway across Tennessee and wound northward through Kentucky. As the miles passed, the greens around her had warmed to brilliant early October hues, and what was autumn, after all, if not a succumbing, a final hurrah?

"Pleased to meet you," she elaborated. The door opened no farther; the three pairs of eyes merely blinked, as if awaiting proof. She held up the large, paper-wrapped frame she'd tucked under her arm. "I made you something."

Bingo: the password. They jumped back with a collective squeal, flinging the door open wide as every one of them turned and ran, bare feet slapping the ceramic tile.

"Mom!" Riley yelled.

"Aunt Sela made us a present!" Lucy finished.

"Present!" Owen echoed, not to be left out.

Whoops. Possibly she'd oversold this. She wouldn't have used the word *present;* the wall art was more for Caroline. She rolled her bag over the doorstep and hesitated, awkward and alone in the entryway—which was plainer, though crisper and cleaner, than her own. The house smelled of freshly baked cookies, of Play-Doh, of children and the good fortune of having them. Pleasantly warmer than the sunlit chill outside. She should shut the door behind her. It was just that no one had exactly invited her in.

"Sela." Caroline appeared at the far end of the foyer, dish towel in hand, kids clinging to her legs, peering out.

Sela ventured another smile. The oddest part of this guise was that they couldn't behave as if they hadn't met before. *The more we get into this, the more I can see why you're not bringing Brody for the first go,* Caroline had written, inspiring a flicker of worry that she might rescind the invitation. But Caroline struck Sela as a person who made up her mind and didn't change it, unless someone gave her cause. Which meant all Sela had to do was *not* drive her to regret this.

"So good to see you," she managed.

"Please come in, I'm sorry—they're just excited." Caroline extracted herself from the six hands and hurried to shut the door, then turned to catch Sela in a hug so brief it ended before she registered it. "You made good time," she said, taking her bag. A good hostess, Sela could tell. She'd probably wiped the baseboards, put single-use hand towels in the powder room, stocked condiments she didn't even like in case Sela did.

"It was a pretty drive. I'm glad I decided to take a half day; I'd have missed some gorgeous horse farms in the dark."

"I took a half day too. Walt just got home from work—he's upstairs changing. I'll show you to your room?" Sela nodded, and Caroline turned back to the kids. "Did you Greedy Gretchens introduce yourselves?" All three yelled their names—a big, loud *Lu-ow-ley-an,* and Sela laughed, glad she already knew what they were. "You guys want to give Aunt Sela a tour?"

The kids scrambled up the stairs ahead of them, pointing out which rooms were theirs, where the bathroom was, and the closed door of the master suite. When they got to Lucy's room, they stopped. "Lucy's bunking with Riley so you can have her bed," Caroline explained, wheeling in her bag. "It's only a twin, but more comfortable than the pullout in the basement."

"That's so nice of you, Lucy," Sela said. "Are you sure? I don't mind pullout couches."

"Totally," Lucy said, barely masking her glee at the sisterly slumber party in store. Sela tried to picture Caroline as a girl—not the one who'd been oblivious to Sela's existence, but one who'd been a part of it. Would they have dressed alike, giggled over the same things, rolled out their sleeping bags with flashlights and sneaky plans for staying up late? Or might they have been the competitive, adversarial type—the kind of relationship she'd been glad *not* to have?

"I love your room," Sela told Lucy. The decor was clearly self-selected and a startling contrast from home. Brody was drawn like a magnet to trucks, monsters, anything muddy. Meanwhile, Lucy's bed appeared to be wearing an *actual* skirt. Of shimmering tulle.

"Mom, can we see the present now?" Riley whispered, and Caroline laughed.

"Let's give our guest a minute to freshen up, and she can find us in the kitchen. Daddy too."

Take your time, Caroline mouthed to Sela as groans of protest followed her out of the room, leaving Sela to grin goofily at an oversized giraffe draped with strands of plastic pearls. Silly to have worried so much about how the kids would receive her. Their ready acceptance of her as one of the random grown-ups who sporadically rerouted their parents' attention made this whole visit seem much more normal.

My half nieces and nephew are delightful, she marveled. *I really am an aunt.*

She would keep hold of her gratitude and *not* think about all this happy chaos she'd missed out on growing up in a house far less full.

Or, more to the point, how much Brody would miss.

Downstairs, Walt went in for a handshake instead of a hug, a two-handed grasp that was somehow both wary and firm, and Sela sensed he was the one she'd need to work to win over. Not that she blamed him; of course he'd be protective of his wife, his children, his home. Or maybe he and the multitasking Caroline—at this moment adjusting a Crock-Pot with one hand while plating cookies with the other—had choreographed more of a good cop, bad cop approach, whereby he'd represent their collective concerns and free Caroline to play the welcoming role.

I don't want anything from these people, she reminded herself. *If things get awkward, I'll just go.* It still seemed novel to think this way; she'd harbored fears about the implications of meeting her half sibling since before she'd even known that Caroline was not merely a biological possibility but a real person.

She heard a scraping noise behind her and turned to see all three kids dragging in the wrapped frame she'd left propped by the door. The *glass* frame. "Open?" Owen begged.

"Careful!" Sela rushed to help them lift it onto the table, glancing at Caroline, who was exchanging an unreadable look with an unsmiling Walt. Maybe it *was* good cop, bad cop. "This is actually for all five of you—" But the kids were tearing away the paper, sharks in a feeding frenzy. She slid into a seat, out of the way, as their parents came closer for a look.

"Ooh!" Riley squealed as Lucy and Owen pulled the corners free. "You *made* this?"

Sela nodded, suddenly embarrassed. She'd lettered the kids' names in an interlocking design, *Lucy* ending with the Y in *Riley, Owen* cutting through at a diagonal, borrowing the E. The letters themselves—in deep tones of purple, blue, and red—fell somewhere between whimsical and sophisticated, with tiny, intricate sketches tucked into their serifs and swirls. A soccer ball cradled in the R. Ballet shoes dangling from the L. A teddy bear sleeping in the O.

Lucy traced the letters of her name with her fingers, delighted, then helped her little brother do the same with his. So this was where Brody would be in a year—even more inquisitive, bright-eyed, and, well, tall. She knew a year wasn't a terribly long time, but the further into Brody's future she looked, the harder it was to see him.

Or maybe it was just harder to see herself. Tears pricked her eyes, and she blinked them away, glad the attention was on the artwork and not on her.

"This is beautiful," Caroline raved. "It must have taken days!"

"I've never seen anything like this." Walt seemed to be conceding something, though he didn't meet her eyes but instead kissed his eldest atop her head. "Kids, what do we say?"

"Thank you!" they chorused, and Lucy and Owen scurried off, the excitement having waned with no new game or toy. But Riley sat fixated.

"Could you teach me?" she ventured. "To do letters like that?"

"Absolutely." When Sela got a mind to bring a gift, she'd known the way to any mother's heart, but hadn't counted on the kids being smitten. "You'll have to show me your art supplies. If you don't have what we need, I'll get you some while I'm out tomorrow."

Her plan was to drive by the address she'd found in Ecca's old correspondence, the house where she'd lived—or, rather, bided time—until her first opportunity to escape. Sela had looked through every old notebook and album she could find, hoping for mention of other places she might visit—a photo with a storefront, a ticket stub, anything—but the address was all she had.

"Oh," Caroline cut in, that predictable maternal backpedal. "You don't have to—"

"I'd love to. Honest." Riley surprised Sela with a grateful hug and ran after her siblings.

Caroline flashed a smile. "I thought we'd just do kind of an all-night munch fest for dinner. Appetizers, drinks, treats—not the healthiest, but hey, it's Friday, right?"

Sela panned the counter, a buffet of forbidden delights. A pumpernickel bowl filled with spinach dip. A plate of cheese and crackers. Veggies, thankfully. Whatever the Crock-Pot held—it smelled like meatballs, maybe, or chili?—and a tray of bruschetta ready for the oven. These were the standby dishes of her mother's old artist dinners. Of book club potlucks. Of Friday night gatherings among family, neighbors, friends.

Of people who aren't sick. Who can indulge without a thought beyond *Hey, it's Friday.*

It had been so long since anyone had treated her like one of them.

"Sounds perfect," she said.

"So why did you take the test, anyway?" Walt didn't waste his first opportunity to cut to the chase. The adults were settled on couches around the gas fireplace, the kids at last silent up in Riley's room, where Owen had insisted he not be left out. Sela was doing her best not to look at the mantel, where in a smattering of framed family photo collages, she'd identified the repeat appearances of a man who could only be her father—though even out of context, he'd look much more like Caroline's. Fitting, really. There he was, proudly walking her down the aisle, their facial features clear variations on a theme. There, teaching Owen to fish from behind matching mirrored sunglasses. There, arm around a laughing woman who must be Caroline's mom.

Sela had stolen a moment, while her sister readied the kids for bed, to peruse these frozen-in-time memories that didn't belong to her, to stare into his face just long enough to deny resemblance beyond a few superficial details. Superficial—that's all they were, and she would not dwell on these, not ask to see more. Not let this visit become about him, which would ruin it. She'd promised Caroline, after all, that she wouldn't. Promised herself, too. Promised Ecca.

Never mind that those promises hadn't prepared her for what it might be like to actually see his absentee face brightly present for his rightful family, in glossy Kodak color. She had to be careful.

She didn't like the way Walt had been watching her all night—not when he came downstairs and caught her looking, and not earlier, when she'd been eating and drinking as little as possible without being impolite. She could pass it off as nerves if anyone asked, but no way could she sustain that for an entire weekend under this kind of scrutiny.

"Caroline has been filling me in," he was saying now, "but that's one thing I'm not clear on. You suspected, I assume, that you might have half siblings?"

"Well," she began. "Obviously I'd never known my father. . . ."

"So you hoped to find your father?"

"Not exactly. My mother made it known she'd rather I not."

"But then she—" He checked himself. "Passed on. And you didn't have to worry about upsetting her?"

She shook her head. Wrong—she would *never* escape the worry of letting Ecca down, even now. Especially now, with her father peering out from the mantel. "Even though I knew there were . . ." How to put this? "Possibilities . . . I don't know that my reasons were that different from anyone else's. I wasn't expecting much, honestly. You send it off and think, *What are the odds?* And then when something actually comes back you have to think the whole thing through all over again. It's different when it's hypothetical, you know?" There. She'd managed a fair, even good, approximation of what the careful, thoughtful Sela who'd sent all those emails to Caroline would say. If she kept talking, she'd spoil it. *Deflect, deflect, deflect.* "How about you?"

"Yeah, how *about* us, Walt?" Caroline laughed loosely. She'd had several glasses of wine, lending a languid quality to her movements as well as her words, and leaned steeply toward Sela, smiling conspiratorially. "Let's just say our family got more than we bargained for under the Christmas tree." She laughed again and, when no one joined in, slapped her own cheek. "Oh God, Sela, I can't believe I said that. It's this wine." She clunked her glass onto the end table and stared at it as if it were poisoned. "I didn't mean—"

"No, I get it. Of course you didn't expect the results to be so . . . complicated."

She'd keep her equally complicated questions to herself. *Did your father ever object to the test? Don't you think a man who'd had an affair would have a nagging doubt in the face of a test like that? Is he a falsely confident sort, brazen, arrogant? Do you think some small part of him wanted to know, to clear his conscience for good, even if he was unprepared to own up to a less convenient truth?*

"It's not that I'm not glad to know you. I mean, we're here. . . ." Caroline looked to Walt, as if he might chime in with help, which even Sela could guess he would not. He was watching too closely, even now. "It's just that—I know I alluded . . . There's been some drama."

"That's family for you, right?" Sela tried not to dislike her sister in this moment. At least Caroline was being real. To have this conversation without acknowledging the trouble Sela had caused would be weirder, wouldn't it?

Nicer, though.

"Not my family," Caroline said, surprising her. Sela saw, then, in her eyes, that this had been difficult in ways she'd not let on. That Caroline might be stirring something, some*one,* by having *more than we bargained for* here in her home. Had Caroline thought of clearing the mantel, decided against it? If she'd taken the collages containing her father away, there wouldn't have been much left on display. Which spoke to how much of her life's picture Sela was altering right now.

"Your side, though," Walt prodded. "What's their take on all this? On you being here?"

"Let's not give Sela the third degree," Caroline said, saving her. "It's bad enough I put my foot in my mouth—no need to corner her into doing the same." She turned to Sela, missing the stricken look on her husband's face. He clearly thought this conversation necessary, was only trying to mediate. "Want me to go along to find your mom's old address tomorrow?"

"I think it's probably something I should do alone. But thank you."

Caroline nodded. "I can point you to the high school too, if you'd like?"

"You know where she went to school?" It dawned on her what that must mean. "She went to high school with your dad?"

She'd pledged not to pry for these details Ecca had preferred she not know. But she did not possess the superhuman willpower to decline if one was offered. Caroline, though, looked caught—as if she hadn't realized she was spilling anything new. "No . . ." Her tone held a friendly warning: She'd go ahead and answer but discuss it no further than necessary. "With my mom. From grade school through being underclassmen. Hannah is her name."

Sela peered at her in confusion. "Your mom? She and my mother were . . ."

"Friends." Caroline averted her eyes.

Of all the possible scenarios Sela had run through, this was not one. Yet she instantly understood it must be true.

Ecca's old, weak explanations were bulking up, building muscle.

Even as Sela's wasted away to expose the bone.

Funny thing about a house—from the outside, anyway. With no one there to tell its story, a house is all it is.

Sela had arrived at Ecca's childhood address expecting—what? A memory that was not hers to remember—that would require, she realized now, someone capable of sharing it. Her grandparents had been gone from this place since she herself was an infant, and from the signs of youth in the neighboring homes—strollers on porches, soccer nets in yards—the surrounding properties had turned over, too.

She'd have to imagine her mother here, before the porch had begun to sag from the aging two-story frame, back when the wood was freshly painted—this same yellow, perhaps, but brighter. There: As a child, poking her head from the lace-curtained window, panning the sky for Santa's sleigh. As a budding artist, sprawled with pastels on the woven rug of the porch. As a lovesick girl on the sidewalk, accepting a shy kiss from a first-ever date.

But those probably weren't right. Ecca's years here had not been happy—though as Sela sat in her car at the curb, she couldn't bring herself to conjure an uglier truth. The neighborhood was the sort of midcentury mixed bag that was halfway committed to regaining its former glory, but this house was among those still awaiting a renovator's eye. Perhaps Ecca would've been glad to see it looking shabby, figured the house's history served it right. Then again, maybe she'd have liked to see it move on from her parents and shine brighter.

That's what Ecca had done. She'd rarely said much about what made her parents such unpleasant people, about what had gone on here. Only that her brother, a full decade older, had graduated high school, hitched a ride to California, and never looked back—and that she was not hurt by this but inspired by it. She'd taught Sela how far your engine could run on nothing but self-fueled fire.

Sela got the feeling Caroline assumed that Ecca's story was sad, that their father had left her hanging on some hook. But Sela had never known her mother to be ensnared by anybody or anything. Once, by her own admission, she'd come close, but she'd fought her way through and boxed up her close call with all the other things she'd rather forget. A lesson in that, too.

Stepping out of the car, Sela tried to breathe in anything

that might be left of Ecca's tenacity, even as she realized that if those parts of her mother lived on anywhere, they were not at this address.

They were within Sela. Within Brody, too—strongest perhaps of all.

"You can walk from the house to the school, if the rain holds off," Caroline had suggested, pointing out the adjacent blocks on her navigation app. "I bet Rebecca used to walk, and probably avoided this main road, unless she had errands to run."

Sela checked her parallel-park job—close enough—and started down the uneven sidewalk, grateful for the suggestion. The day was overcast but, so far, dry. She took in the gentle *brush brush* of leaves being raked nearby, the hollow bounce of a basketball, the *whoosh* of traffic from the parallel thoroughfare. Had her mother once tripped over this same crooked paver? Stopped to tie her shoe in the shade of this thick oak tree? Perhaps on this walk, she'd been happier—not at home and not at school, her own boss for the few moments in between.

The school came into view, behind a chain-link fence. Trailers cluttered the grounds, housing extra classrooms—Caroline had explained that the student body outgrew the building, and a larger facility was under construction elsewhere. For this last shot at her mother's old stomping ground, Sela was just in time.

She caught sight of a figure sitting on the wide concrete steps. The figure didn't stand, but waited respectfully to see whether Sela would continue her approach or pretend she hadn't seen and turn back. Sela was surprised at how glad she was to see her. At how nice it was to say she'd rather do something alone and to have someone realize she might change her mind.

She sat down next to Caroline and looked out at the same row of old houses that had no doubt greeted their mothers after school each day. No ghosts joined them on the steps to share their stories. No Walt with his questions, no kids with their bubbly distractions. Only two sisters.

"Did you know," Caroline asked, "that before they used the clinical term *depression,* they used to diagnose people with *nostalgia*?"

Sela grinned, improbably. She had heard that once, but she'd forgotten.

She hadn't understood it then, probably, the way she did now.

17

Caroline

Caroline leaned into Walt's embrace, sighing audibly with relief. On the other side of their bedroom door, the house was quiet—an early Saturday night. Tomorrow morning, Sela would head home, already and at last. They'd made it through.

"What does that sigh mean?" Walt rubbed her back, not letting go. He gave the best hugs. Better still, she rarely had to ask when she needed one.

"Have I still not mastered Mom's sigh language?" He laughed. Walt and Maureen once tried to make a party game of imitating Hannah's dramatic sigh technique. Dubbed "A Sigh Is Worth a Thousand Words," it involved concocting elaborate translations of each nuanced sound. "Correct" answers included such missives as *So help me God, Caroline, if I have to explain this to you one more time, I might begin to question the way I raised you—which is ridiculous, because we all know I raised you perfectly!*

"I think you can be glad that lesson didn't stick," he assured her.

She grinned, pulling back to look at him. "That sigh," she said, "means I can let go of worrying that having Sela here was not a good idea."

"You two had a good day?"

She nodded, crossing to her dresser to remove her jewelry. After last night, the jury had still been out, and Caroline had started this morning feeling paltry that she hadn't been able to offer Sela more than a lousy tip about Rebecca's old school. It was obvious visiting her mother's old haunts meant more to Sela than Caroline had realized. But she didn't dare ask Dad if he could suggest spots to add to the tour. It was too late to mention the visit now that it was underway. The best she could do was go after Sela—and be glad she had.

"She said you took her to the Gas Light? Blast from the past." The dive bar was a fixture in an old neighborhood they'd frequented when they started seeing each other. They never called those evenings dates, but rather, "bonding over beer."

Caroline grinned. "For some reason it stuck in my head as a good place for bonding."

He ducked into the closet, emerging with the jersey-knit pants he slept in when they had company. "And it was?"

She hesitated. How to explain? It was fair for Walt to be expecting a play-by-play. But it wasn't the things Sela did or said that struck Caroline. It was, as with her emails, the way she did or said them: candid yet thoughtful, even with her tongue so loosened by a couple of watery beers that Caroline wondered if Sela was a teetotaler too polite to say so.

"I feel like everyone looks at this as me coming in and rewriting your family's history," Sela had mused. "But it's not like I was down in North Carolina knowing all along, plotting when I was going to come stir the pot. My history had big gaps, too."

Caroline didn't mind the uncensored take—appreciated it, actually, after her own slipup the night before.

"I know," she'd said simply.

Sela looked straight at her then. "Ever think maybe some blanks are better left unfilled?"

"Lately?" Caroline leaned in. "All the time." She waited a beat. "No offense."

They'd erupted in laughter.

The thing was, confessions had a way of bringing on the best kind of heart-to-heart. All of a sudden they were talking about everything. Caroline got almost as tipsy as Sela and recounted the randomness of her trip to Brevard, how she might've walked right by Sela or even Rebecca back then.

"I knew campus jobs were competitive, but still," Sela sympathized. "Mother was always saying how cheap the administration was. I can't believe they brought you all the way down there and didn't make the offer."

"Quite the blow to my young ego," Caroline admitted. "But the bigger blow was my boyfriend dumping me and going alone."

"Ouch."

Caroline hovered there, debating the wisdom of getting into what she'd recently learned about the role Mom had played. Sela's opinion of her parents must be wary at best to start, and it wasn't wrong. But to her relief, Sela jumped in with her own one-that-got-away story: from how she and Doug met to the day it hit her that things had turned sideways.

"I just looked at him and realized we didn't see the world the same way anymore," she said. "It was this sad, odd feeling that I'd missed my chance to say good-bye to him, even though he was still right there."

They'd had a surprisingly easy time carrying on that way: Anytime the conversation might have taken an awkward turn, it took an authentic one instead.

An hour in, they eyed a tray of paper-lined baskets going past. Burgers, fries, onion rings. The smell of grease could be this enticing only after day drinking.

Caroline snatched the menu from behind the ketchup. "Grilled cheese," she proclaimed. "We need grilled cheese. With fries."

"Coming right up," the bartender said, happening past. She hadn't meant to actually order, but they just laughed, kept talking. It wasn't like making conversation with a stranger. More like uncovering a connection that had been waiting for them all along.

When the food came, Sela took a slow bite and closed her eyes.

"I couldn't tell you the last time I had this," she said. "I feel like a kid." A beat of recognition passed between them. That was what they'd missed of each other. Childhood and all the years since. Until now.

Later, when they emerged from the bar into surprisingly bright sunlight, they both sneezed, on cue, three times in quick succession. Sela burst out laughing, but Caroline couldn't. She knew what Sela did not: That Dad had this same reflex. That it was a running joke for Mom to call them "the achoo duo" when in fact they'd been a trio.

How to put all that into words Walt would understand?

"I guess I'm just glad she's here," she said, trading her sweater for a raglan tee.

He took a moment to observe her, so carefully she almost blushed. "I didn't know you wanted this so much," he said finally. "To like her, I mean. To want to know her."

What she'd wanted *so much* was merely to grab at this chance Mom had taken from her. To hold it by the fist and decide what to do with it, one way or another, on her own. She hadn't allowed herself to think further than that.

But there was something so earnest about Sela, in spite of everything. Like no one else Caroline had known. Mo hooked Caroline even in childhood with her large, loud approach to life—a classic "opposites attract" for a girl growing up in a house where arguments were whispered. Keaton swept her up into a dream-driven world for two, if only for a little while. With Walt, Caroline became a proud partner, fair and equal in sensible joint decisions. And with her parents—well, she was no longer sure she'd ever known her place at all.

Sela, though, wasn't just an extra player to deal in. She was all heart. The way she stopped to think before speaking. The way she talked of her son without resorting to the petty complaints common among moms. The way she withheld judgment, with grace—from speaking charitably of her ex to holding her tongue about their father. Caroline couldn't help wondering now how she might be different herself, had she grown up alongside someone like Sela.

How she might be different still, to know her now.

"I didn't either," she admitted.

"But you feel sure. That you want there to be more visits?"

Every potential relationship has a point where you take a deep breath and decide: *Okay. Let's do this—give it some gas and see how far we can go.*

Or where you don't: *Was worth a try, but let's stop wasting our time here.*

She still remembered that point with Walt.

She'd felt so much less certain then—more so than anyone but Walt would ever know.

"You know what I feel? Relieved." A strange word for it, but Sela in the flesh somehow made the emotions Caroline had been reeling in from afar seem valid. And that alone was something. "I guess I didn't want to admit how scared I was that this would all blow up in my face."

Walt leaned against his dresser, facing her. "Don't take this the wrong way, but it still could. We can't hide that we've met her."

She frowned. "Can't we wait and be overcautious after she leaves?" Not that he didn't have a point. "You've been like this for her entire visit. Last night, now . . . Can I just enjoy her for one day? After how miserable this entire ordeal has been? It's not like I'm going to forget that it's complicated."

He looked stung. "Sorry. I don't know if I really am this wary, or just felt like somebody should be. Your folks are staying out of it, and you're going for it. No one's covering Midfield."

She considered this, chagrined. She hadn't asked, after all, what he thought of Sela coming, and hadn't confided her own second thoughts. She'd merely told him, in a fit of misdirected defiance, it was a done deal. Somewhere along the line, this chaos had flipped a switch from her usual modus operandi—of wanting first to share every revelation with Walt—to sifting out the things marriage *obligated* her to share. Walt had been patient with Caroline during these weeks of floundering, but if his frustration had to leak out somewhere, Sela was the easy target. Caroline couldn't fairly expect him to abandon all reserve so readily.

Their partnership had always been the solid thing when everything else went wobbly. She had to stop letting her head be spun by these past betrayals. What mattered was in front of her—even Keaton had known that: Walt, the kids, her parents' health. And now Sela.

"I haven't been very good at talking about all this," she said. "I'm sorry—it's been a lot. I *wasn't* sure about Sela before. But now? I do think this is the right thing."

He sank onto the bed next to her. "Well, it isn't the easy way out." His *are you sure?* voice.

"I know, MIDFIELD." He jostled her shoulder affectionately, and they exchanged a smile—the kind of wordless apology they were best at. She could tell that even if he didn't quite share her relief, he'd buy in.

At least for now.

"She does remind me a little of Fred," he admitted. "There's this look he's taken on since he retired. You know how some older people give the impression they must have really been something to see in their day? Like, I don't know, a stage presence you can't mute?"

"I never did know you thought of Dad as a retired movie star. No."

He laughed. "I'm not explaining it right. But she has the same, I don't know, aura. Kind of a strange vibe to get from a younger person. Maybe it's her posture or something."

Caroline had an inkling of what he meant. There had been little things, all day, that had brought not just Dad to mind but Riley or Owen. It was a lot to take in. She'd have to do this in baby steps.

"Where do we go from here?" he asked. "Do we give your parents a chance to opt back in? I mean, you could look at your dad's heart attack multiple ways. Maybe he'll rethink his priorities. And do we reevaluate telling the kids? What does that look like?"

"I don't know. But at least now I know it's worth the stress to figure it out, in time. Everything that's happened since that first bombshell email has seemed so negative, but—there could be a positive side, you know? She could be the positive side."

Hadn't Dad taught her that even the most complicated study could be narrowed to a simple conclusion? That if you ever wanted to do anything but spin your wheels, sooner or later you had to boil it down and draw one?

"I mean, she said something about us going there next time, and— Walt, I didn't let myself think about it too much before, but we have a nephew, you know? A *nephew*."

"That is . . ." He met her eyes and gave up a smile. "A great thing I thought it was impossible for us to have."

Caroline slipped into the hall, never able to sleep without one last check of the kids, and caught sight of Lucy, her nightgown a pale flash in the glow of the hallway night-light, padding sleepily from the bathroom toward the ajar door of her own room. Only Lucy wasn't sleeping there this weekend. Sela was.

"Lucy," she stage-whispered, not wanting to wake anyone,

not sure whether her daughter was truly awake herself. But Lucy didn't hear. She disappeared through her doorway, and Caroline padded down the hall after her. Even if Sela hadn't fallen asleep yet, surely she wanted peace. They'd had a long day.

"No need to apologize," she heard Sela saying. "Do you miss your room? I'm sorry for having to borrow it."

"I don't miss it." Caroline slowed, coming to a stop outside the door.

"I wouldn't blame you if you did. It's one of the prettiest rooms I've ever seen."

"I used to think so." Lucy sounded comically forlorn for a kindergartner, but Caroline didn't smile. *What* had changed in her happy-go-luckiest child? Should she be worried that this was more than a passing phase—that something had actually happened to turn her fearful?

"I see," Sela said, not a hint of amusement in her voice. "Which part of it has started to bother you, exactly?"

"The alone part."

"Ah. You'd rather share with Riley?"

"Yes, but she won't let me. She says she doesn't want me 'glittering up her space.'"

At the mocking tone, Caroline bit back a chuckle, immediately punctuated by guilt. Had the girls seriously debated sharing a room? Without coming to her? Their house had enough bedrooms for each kid to have their own, thereby each kid had gotten their own: more of a mathematical equation than a thought process. It hadn't occurred to her any of them might prefer to share.

"You know, when I was growing up, it was just me and my mother, and when I was really little, the two of us slept in the same room a lot."

"You did?"

"She was an artist, and our apartment was so tiny, she had to use her bedroom for her studio. She'd put me to bed and stay up late painting, but then her room would smell like paint, and brush cleaner, and all that other stinky stuff artists use. That's what she said, anyway—sometimes I think it was so crammed with all those easels, she didn't fit. I had this little trundle that rolled under my bed, and I'd wake up in the morning and find her asleep on that, pulled out right next to me."

"That sounds cozy."

"I don't know how cozy she found it, but I thought so. Even though she wasn't there when I fell asleep, I knew she would come. I'd fall asleep waiting. Then she started to sell her paintings and teach art classes, enough of them for us to buy a house. It had a big separate studio, so her bedroom was just for sleeping then. She never used my trundle anymore, and even though I liked our new place—and I even used to feel annoyed that no space in our little apartment was totally mine—I felt lonely then. I was always asking to have a friend sleep over. I didn't have a sister, like you. But I wished I did."

Caroline leaned her head against the wall. She and Walt had talked often about growing up as only children—not bad or good, necessarily, but how they were giving their kids such a different experience, literally surrounded by siblings.

How would she ever get used to the idea that she'd had one, all along? That she'd *been* one, all along?

"So what did you do?" Lucy sounded wide awake now. Caroline sneaked a look through the gap between the door hinges and saw her daughter sitting cross-legged at the foot of the bed, facing her aunt, who was curled up in a pair of flannel pajamas, as if it were the most natural thing in the world.

"I told my mom. When you're struggling with something, it can help to tell a grown-up." This was the kind of thing a lot of people would do only for another parent's benefit within earshot—*Hey, I'm having a moment with your kid, but I'm not stepping on toes!* For Sela to be doing it in private meant a lot.

"What did she say?"

"Well, she used to tell me that my imagination was my superpower. It was cool having a mom who thought like an artist—I never had her talent in terms of technique, but the creativity, I did have. She knew it. And she pointed out that power could be used for good or bad, right? Your imagination can run away from you and you can scare yourself silly."

Lucy nodded enthusiastically. "I think it's my superpower too!"

"Right! So when I couldn't stop the lonely or scary things happening in my brain, alone in my room, she suggested I use the superpower to pretend someone was with me."

"Who?"

"Whoever you'd most like to have with you, in that moment. Could be someone real, like your mom or Riley or Owen, but sometimes I think it's more fun to imagine someone totally new. Like, you might pretend one of these stuffed animals can talk. Or you might imagine that a character from your favorite book or movie is your sidekick."

"Huh." Lucy contemplated this seriously. "Did it work? What your mom said to do?"

"Like a charm. I actually *liked* playing alone in my room after that. Way better than my old tiny one."

Lucy hopped off the bed and marched to her bookshelf, where she carefully selected a white stuffed tiger. "Thanks, Aunt Sela."

"I like talking to you, Lucy. If I had a little girl, I'd want her to be just like you."

"If I had a real aunt, I'd want her to be just like you too."

It was lucky Lucy didn't see Caroline in the shadows as she padded through the darkness back to Riley's room. Caroline never could have explained the tears running down her cheeks.

She was still sorting out their meaning herself.

18

Sela

Sela zipped her bag closed and took a last look around Lucy's room, feeling—what was this? Her thoughts were sluggish this morning; she'd slept even worse than usual, but her mood was buoyant. Something like a sense of accomplishment, mixed with pleasant surprise at the twinge of reluctance she felt about leaving so soon.

When she got home, she knew, Brody would throw his arms around her, and Oscar would nose through her things, trying to suss out where she'd been before reclaiming his place at her feet. She'd been picturing the scene since before she'd even gotten here, the reward awaiting her at the finish line. But now that the time had come, she pictured her homecoming in a different light. How quiet the house would seem by contrast, how absent of the breakfast chatter coming from downstairs now, and how far she'd suddenly feel from these people—not just a half sister but a half family.

She cheered herself with the prospect of a reciprocal visit—how nice it could be for Brody's cousins to bring their big energy into his little space. Owen, she knew, would draw the center of her son's attention—Brody would trail his youngest, most rambunctious cousin like an eager shadow. Riley could spend time with Sela in her studio, lighting up the way she had yesterday when Sela gifted her new colored pencils and delivered a shading workshop on the spot. Lucy might bring an imaginary friend or two. And Caroline—well, she already liked Brevard. They'd avoid the backdrops of that old visit with Keaton, show her an even better time.

That had been a story, a whole parallel universe they might have entered. Sela imagined getting her DNA test results and finding that Caroline had been right there in Brevard for her entire adult life. The bizarre, implausible shock of it. She'd always assumed her father—and his family, if he had one—to be elsewhere. How else would Ecca hide him? Or, rather, from him?

Sela was proud she'd succeeded in leaving him out of this visit—both in her conversations with Caroline and in her thoughts. Facing the mantel that first night was the closest she'd come to tripping up, but she'd kept her footing. She could honestly say she had no desire to smuggle home a photo, or to come out and ask where that distinctive giggle she'd heard from all three kids came from. She was already too sick, frankly, to let him infect her brain or her body further. And if she could get this visit under her belt without overstepping, she should be home free, the precedent set.

"Aunt Sela?" Riley appeared in the doorway looking shy, unsure—a mature cry from the giddy girl who'd run off and left her standing on the stoop upon her arrival. "I know this isn't very good, compared to what you can do. But I made you something."

Riley held out a page from the new sketch pad Sela had picked out on the way back from lunch yesterday. The girl had folded it and on the front flap drawn the letters of Brody's name, varying the weights of the strokes and making tiny doodles in the serifs, the way Sela had shown her. Sela took the card and opened it. Inside,

Riley had written: *Thank you for the art supplies and for teaching me. I'm very glad you came to visit my mom and us too. Sincerely, Riley.*

"I told Mom how much I wanted to thank you and she said I should make you a card."

Sela swallowed the emotion balling in her throat. She would *not* get choked up. Not at Lucy's offhand comment about what it would be like to have Sela as a *real* aunt, and not at this painstakingly crafted thank-you. She couldn't read a special connection into every moment just because on some deep, previously inaccessible level, she evidently hoped for one.

She'd never harbored the predictable fantasy of switching places with her sister, à la those separated-at-birth movies. Not even when Caroline's emails made her ache with envy. But now that Sela was up close, it *was* hard not to wish for a day in this other-half life. Only to know what it would feel like.

"I'll display it on my desk at home. Thanks, Riley."

"You're welcome. And I'm supposed to say breakfast will be ready in fifteen minutes."

Sela had had all the unsanctioned meals her body could take. If there was no fruit on the table, she'd beg off, say she wasn't a breakfast person, and stop at the first market out of town to stabilize her blood sugar and whatever else was haywire in her body.

Two masked superheroes appeared behind Riley. "That means fifteen minutes to battle!" Wonder Woman announced, handing her sister a Batman cape and a blue foam ball popper. Her own popper of choice was, naturally, pink. Owen thrust his wrists out, left and right. "Whoosh, I web you! Whoosh, I web you!" He'd tucked his navy sweatpants into red rain boots, one of which held a flimsy-looking slingshot.

"Well," Sela said, laughing, "better get to it, supersquad."

"You too, Aunt Sela!" Lucy crossed to her closet and, improbably, pulled out a Captain America shield, mask, and plastic sword, handing them over in a flourish. "Meet at the bottom of the stairs in one minute! Every hero for himself!"

Riley tied her cape and flashed a thumbs-up. Owen began trying, unsuccessfully, to scale the doorway.

"Aren't we all good guys, though?" Sela's confusion felt decidedly uncool. "I mean, aren't we on the same team?"

"Come on, Aunt Sela," Lucy called over her shoulder as they scattered from the room. "Your imagination is your superpower!"

Sela laughed. You couldn't get anything past a kid. She donned her eye mask and, surveying Lucy's dresser, chose a tiara and a purple feather boa to complete her ensemble. She'd be Captain *Miss* America. Not a bad Halloween costume, actually.

Before she was down the stairs, the battle was in full swing, foam darts shooting across the entryway, makeshift grenades flying through the air—throw pillows, stuffed animals, one of those inflatable exercise balls.

"Take cover!" Sela yelled, jumping the last few stairs and landing in a dramatic crouch, feathers flying, sword drawn. A squeal of excitement pealed from the dining room at her left, and there was Owen, on the far side of the table. The more time she spent with him, the more he really did remind her of Brody. She gave chase; they lapped the table, twice, three times, reversing course and doing it again, both laughing until their breath came fast. She broke the cycle to run across the foyer, where Batman gave her a taunting wave and ducked into the door to the basement playroom. Sela took off after her, repeated her leap down the second half of the basement stairs.

Riley was hiding, somewhere. Lucy too—her giggles giving her away. And then . . .

And then Sela couldn't breathe.

Her breaths came short and shallow, like the onset of a panic attack. Only it wasn't panic—oh, God. She knew this feeling.

She'd overdone it—the sodium, the alcohol, the *everything*—and now she was paying the price. The morning fatigue wasn't from the unfamiliar bed. The swelling in her legs wasn't from the long drive. The shortness of breath, too familiar, brought the full picture into view, showed her what she'd been cropping out of the frame.

She fell back onto the bottom stair, gasping, putting her head between her knees to ward off the stars that would soon follow.

She'd been warned, many times, about the dangers of grazing buffets and of going off script "just this once." That even when you were mostly behaving, you could lose track of all the little cheats adding up.

"Aunt Sela?" Lucy bent to peer at her. Sela could feel the heat of her proximity, little fingers prodding her shoulder, though she couldn't bring herself to lift her head. Not while she was heaving like Oscar after a manic face-off with their backyard squirrels, her heart racing. She hugged the stairs in defeat, her super status reduced to the world's most out-of-shape woman or a senior citizen who'd forgotten her age.

Or a chronically ill visitor trying to pretend she wasn't.

"Are you still playing?" Lucy persisted. Then Riley was beside her, asking too. Sela couldn't even catch her breath to answer. Least of all because she was crying now into her knees.

She should have known one weekend of normal was too much to ask. She of all people knew that wishing something to be true did not make it so.

The girls yelled for their mom, scrambling up the stairs, leaving Sela to fend off the darkness alone.

Caroline handed her a glass of water—full, cool to the touch—and Sela held it between her shaky hands. She'd managed to move, with Caroline's help, to the small basement couch and sat now in the cool, humid quiet with her sister, who'd shooed the children up the stairs, saying Sela needed only space, some air, though of course she had no idea what Sela needed, seemed even more baffled than her children were. How many ounces did this glass hold? Sela would retain it all, yet her mouth had gone sandpaper dry. She took a small sip.

"Sela? Talk to me. What is it?"

"I'm all right," she managed. Another small sip. "Just got a bit short of breath."

"Short of breath?" Caroline looked worried. Walt appeared behind her, phone in hand, and the bolt of terror that he was about to call an ambulance forced Sela straighter against the couch cushion, though her body cried out to double over, to curl up.

To disappear.

She tried to smile. "Turns out Captain Miss America . . . maybe can't scale . . . half flights of stairs . . . like a runway." Another small sip. Good God, this was mortifying.

"But Sela, I have to tell you . . ." Caroline turned to Walt. "She says she's short of breath." It wasn't a question, but she was searching his face for some confirmation. He nodded once, brusquely, and her gaze swung back to Caroline. "My dad, I mean, our—he had a heart attack last month. Shortness of breath was his main complaint. If you're saying the same we need to take it seriously. There's family history."

Sela shook her head. "I'm not having," she gasped, "a heart attack."

"I know it sounds unlikely at our age, but this isn't normal. Look at you—you're gray. You look as if you've run a marathon."

How to explain that it *was* normal, without *really* explaining it? "She's right, Sela," Walt cut in. "If not the hospital, we at least have to go to urgent care."

Sela looked from one to the other. Their faces did not change.

Up to this point, she could *almost* honestly claim that the subject of her health just hadn't come up. That she hadn't lied by omission; she merely hadn't gotten around to explaining yet. But not telling them now would be deceit. If she was going to remain in their lives, this would come to light eventually, and what then?

What had been her plan, anyway—beyond the short term of surviving this weekend, testing the waters?

She hadn't had one.

"No, we don't," she said softly. She took the deepest breath she could manage, steeling herself. "I already know what's wrong."

19

Caroline

"Chronic kidney disease," she repeated. "My God, Sela. *Why* did you not tell us?"

They'd come up to the kitchen, Walt shuffling the befuddled kids back down to the playroom with their French toast on a tray. Caroline could count on them to remain riveted to the movie he put on the old big screen, but not to keep syrup out of the carpet—though this seemed laughably trivial in the scheme of things. The three adults sat around the table, turned away from the soggier-by-thc-minute breakfast abandoned on the stovetop.

"Would you believe it's not a great icebreaker?" Sela tried to laugh, but it came out more like a cry. Although it was brighter here than in the fittingly grim basement, no light had returned to her face. Caroline suspected it matched her own.

"How long have you had this? How did it happen?" Caroline didn't know what to ask first. She had so many questions. Walt sat quietly, arms crossed in front of him, eyes fixed unreadably on Sela.

"I was diagnosed when I was pregnant with Brody. Things escalated pretty quickly from there."

"Do they have any idea what caused it?"

She shook her head. "Ninety percent of people with kidney disease don't even know they have it, until either some routine test turns it up—like in my case—or the symptoms progress to a point of prompting a diagnosis, usually at a later stage. For that reason, they have a hard time studying the onset and early progression." Sela had switched to a flat, matter-of-fact tone, as if this were just another recitation of the facts, not a game changer that revealed her to be yet another person who had kept yet another secret from Caroline.

Not that Caroline was exactly an open book. But this was more than just a skimmed-over chapter.

"In my case," Sela went on, "I had something called chronic glomerulonephritis, but the cause of that is murky too. I might have had an infection that randomly damaged my kidneys—something as common as strep throat—and an acute onset turned chronic. Or something might have compromised my immune system. It's possible I was predisposed to this. But in a subset of women with declining kidney function, pregnancy speeds it up, irreversibly. I'm one of them."

"And Brody?" Caroline's eyes darted to Walt—mention of their nephew had softened him the night before, but still he didn't so much as shift in his chair.

"Well, I told you he was born alarmingly premature. That is quite common with CKD. It's not a pregnancy-compatible disease."

"But his kidneys?"

"They were the least of his worries," she said quickly, looking down at the table.

Caroline cleared her throat. "What can you do? Are you looking at— I mean, from what little I know of kidney problems, dialysis? A transplant?"

Sela nodded. "Either/or. No one can say how soon I'll need it, but a transplant is preferable. Living on dialysis is . . . all-consuming."

"My God, and with a child? How would you manage?" A flare of anger. "Your husband *left* you in the midst of this? With a baby, no less?" She tried to hold to that sisterly loyalty she'd felt yesterday—on the steps of the school, in the hallway outside Lucy's room. But it was disorienting learning that the whole time, Sela had been holding back something so defining.

"He—we—didn't handle it well. In his defense, it hasn't been an easy thing to handle."

Was she really so forgiving? A better sport than Caroline. "How does getting a transplant work?" She sneaked another glance at Walt, whose silence was growing eerie. The unease pressed in on Caroline, but she pushed ahead. "You go on a list?" Sela nodded. "Do you have to reach a certain stage first, or . . . ?"

"They encourage you to start the process early, because the pace is glacial. I'm late in stage three, of five. Not dire yet, but no one knows how long I have until it's going to be."

"And then?"

"And then . . . ," Sela spoke slowly, as if articulating every syllable was of great importance. "Unless you have a living donor waiting in the wings, you get on the list—I'm pending approval now—and then wait your turn and hope that when it comes, so does a match."

"From someone who checked the organ donor box on their driver's license?"

"Usually. A kidney from a deceased donor doesn't last nearly as long as a living donor's, so if you're my age that's a temporary fix. But any working kidney is better than no working kidney."

How many questions could she ask before Sela got frustrated? Sela was clearly uncomfortable, but Caroline wanted only to understand. To think that all this time Caroline had thought her sister might not relate to what it was like to have your life upended out of nowhere so thoroughly. What Caroline and her parents had been through in learning of Sela's existence was nothing compared to what Sela had already been facing. Alone.

"That's why you ordered the DNA test," Walt said—speaking up at last, but his voice didn't sound right. It was low, too low, the bottom bass line. "Isn't it?"

Caroline blinked at him, caught off guard by his accusatory tone. Sela averted her eyes.

"I—"

"You weren't looking for your father's family. You were looking for a kidney that might reside in a member of your father's family."

Sela's chest started to heave again with short, quick breaths, and Caroline wanted to pull her out of this, to chastise Walt for being cruel. But the look on Sela's face—and the silence. It stretched on painfully long, until Caroline knew Walt's accusation couldn't be anything but true.

"You're hitting the road in, what, an hour?" Walt gripped the edge of the table, his knuckles hard and white. "When were you going to get around to asking? Or did you plan to drive home and then send one of your *emails*?"

"Walt, stop." He might have been correct, but that didn't make this right.

"I wasn't going to ask," Sela said.

He scoffed. "Yeah, right. Let me guess. No one on your mom's side is a match."

"But—"

"And family is the best shot at matching, right?"

Sela shrank back. "That was the other thing about the pregnancy. It increased my PRAs—panel reactive antibodies—making my odds of finding a match more slim."

"But not *as* slim with a family member. Right?"

Reluctance poured off of Sela, but she nodded through it,

holding her head high even as tears glistened in her eyes. "I admit, that is why I let myself be talked into doing the DNA test. But I meant what I said the night I got here: Thinking of it in hypothetical terms was not the same as the real thing." She rushed through the words, choking back tears. "So to answer your question, I haven't been getting up the nerve to ask. I wasn't going to ask." A sob escaped her. "I'm not going to. I'm not asking."

Caroline's mouth dropped open, but the thoughts swirling through her mind couldn't assemble themselves into words. Walt, though, had no trouble.

"You mentioned a possible predisposition to this condition that brought on the kidney disease."

Sela tore a napkin from the holder and pressed it to her eyes. "Glomerulonephritis."

"Right. Glomer—" He gave up on the word. "Does that mean it runs in families?"

"It can."

"In your case?"

"They don't know."

He shook his head, even more incredulous. He was getting carried away, taking things in a direction Caroline couldn't turn back if she allowed him to continue, but she felt frozen, incapable of interrupting. "So there's a chance of a genetic component—which Caroline could also have?"

Sela hesitated, then nodded slowly.

"Riley, Owen, Lucy?"

Another nod, almost imperceptible.

"And you would risk Caroline, a perfectly healthy, *young* mother of three, donating a kidney to you, and then having only one left if her own started to fail? Or if one of our kids ends up needing one?" He was practically shouting now, and Sela pushed her chair back until she was flush against the wall, shaking her head hard.

"I'm not asking," she repeated.

"Like hell you're not asking," he boomed. "You're here, aren't you? *Hey, Caroline, turns out you might be the only one who can help, but don't worry, I'm not asking you to?*"

The request registered with Caroline then—deep and heavy. Not through Sela's words. Through Walt's.

"That's not fair," Sela protested. "If you're saying I'm asking just by being here and in my condition, well—I can't help that much. This is me. This is my condition. I know it's a lot to take in at once. That's why I held off on . . . the details."

"Don't act like you're *just* here. You're not *just* anything. You ordered the test. You sought us out. Do you have any idea what my wife has risked for you already, so you wouldn't feel ousted by Fred and Hannah? She's the only one who has tried to do right by you, and this is what she gets?"

Caroline knew she should correct him—at the very least for implying that this visit was an act of charity. Maybe she'd been a *little* fueled by a sense of duty, but that wasn't the whole story. She'd felt called to do this for herself as much as for Sela—and up until moments ago, she'd thought she'd begun to understand why.

But this was her body they were talking about, as if its rightful owner were up for grabs. She put her hands over her ears, not caring that it looked childish. "Stop!"

"Caroline." Sela's eyes returned to hers, desperate. "Please believe me. This visit was not an ambush. It was exactly what we both thought it was." Her voice dropped at the end, barely a whisper. "It meant everything to me. You. The kids. Just as it was."

"Hypothetically speaking," Walt cut in, unmoved, "if I called your ex-husband, or your friends, even your doctor, to ask why you're here, what would they tell me?"

Sela buried her face in her hands. "I didn't want to disappoint them," she cried, her voice muffled. "I didn't tell them I changed my mind." She lifted her head. "But I did, I swear. I swear on my child's life."

"So you lied to the people who know you, but are telling the truth now, to people you've just met?" Walt stood from the table, his chair rattling backward across the tile.

"You didn't want to disappoint them," Caroline ventured, her voice smaller than she'd known it could be, "because they know your life might depend on me?"

Sela didn't answer.

Walt's gaze met Caroline's and held it firm. Everyone was pleading with her these days. *Forgive me. Let it go. Look the other way.*

She might be able to do that with her parents and the self-serving terms of their truce. With Keaton and his crestfallen assertion that bygones could be only that.

But with this?

"She's not asking," Walt repeated, all traces of sarcasm replaced with the desperate hope of convincing himself.

It was too late now. In his rage, in his haste, he'd gone and put the question on the table for her.

No one had the power to take it back.

20

Sela

Oscar was walking Sela, rather than the other way around. She didn't discourage him from pulling her, stroller and all, down the sidewalk; he seemed to sense she could use the help. Autumn had followed her home from Ohio: Ahead, Main Street cut enticingly through town to a vanishing point in mounds of bright foliage, and the morning was cool enough that pedestrians sported knitted hats and scarves. Not Sela, though—beneath her jacket, her skin itched with sweat. As Oscar dragged them past the solemn concrete slab of the county's war memorial—eleven dead in Vietnam, one missing in action—she looked longingly at the low stone wall fronting its manicured lawn. But she could tell from the eager bounce in the dog's step that he'd spotted Aesthetic on the corner two blocks ahead, so she bore down, trying to catch her breath, conceding they were too close to stop and rest.

She was not old enough for two little blocks to seem so far.

At last, she secured Oscar's leash to the bike rack outside—the one Ecca ordered the day she learned Sela's college roommate was on the cycling team—and doubled over, ostensibly to help Brody climb out of his stroller.

"Mama tired?" He eyed her ragged gasps with concern.

"Mama tired," she agreed.

Even dodging the incessant calls from Leigh and Doug was exhausting. On the upside, she hadn't had to break it to them that she had no intention of asking for Caroline's help. The question was out there all right. On the downside, they were bafflingly undiscouraged when she told them it had gone over horribly, maybe even ruined the sisterhood as soon as it began.

Give her time, they said. *It's a lot to take in,* they said. *She'll come around,* they said.

Sela didn't care about that. She wanted only to reclaim the things she and Caroline had discovered between them in that dive bar booth. The surprisingly easy laughter, the comforting sense of starting from a place of acceptance, understanding. Things she hadn't had for too long. Things she hadn't known she was missing until they were dangled within her grasp, then yanked away.

As soon as she got home, she sat down at the keyboard, wanting to explain, repent, retract, for all the good it did. She spoke her heart and hit send, trying not to trip over the way Walt had sneered: *one of your emails.*

A week of silence from her sister, and counting.

Almost as worrisome: a week of her flare-up of symptoms refusing to ease.

"Good boy," she whispered to Oscar, scratching behind his ears. He wasn't even panting, but his tail wagged at her to hurry up. Ivy still kept Ecca's biscuit bin stocked for him inside, and he wouldn't let her forget it.

The mountain air smelled damp, though the day was dry, and as she took Brody's hand and pushed open the heavy antique door, a familiar combination of warmer smells greeted her: herbal tea, fired clay, and the kind of dreamy ambition people belt out songs about on Broadway. Its melody sounded in the chimes dangling where a door knocker might have been.

"You made it!" To Ivy's credit, she didn't drop her smile—or leap in alarm from her stool behind the register—as her eyes passed over Sela's face to her heaving disappointment of a body. "I meant that as a figure of speech, but you look like it might be worth celebrating."

"Water?" Sela managed.

Ivy slid to her feet. "How's your blood sugar? We might have muffins too."

That was all Brody needed to hear. He clapped his hands and ran after Ivy into the back room, and Sela felt a guilty pang that she didn't bring him here more. She talked to him, of course, about the grandmother he couldn't remember, but maybe here he'd feel connected to her in a deeper way. It was Sela who needed to ration her visits to Aesthetic like sweets.

She pulled Ivy's brochure order from her quilted messenger bag as she looked around the showroom. The gleaming hardwood and exposed brick were the same as ever, but the turnover of inventory displayed on the walls, pedestals, and shelves was impressive. *When you're lucky enough to find a town that puts its money where its mouth is,* Ecca used to say, *you stay put.* Sela had always taken this as equal parts compliment to Brevard and referendum on the cookie-cutter world beyond, but now it seemed more like life advice. Which was why Sela kept the co-op as clients, though the work made her ache with longing for their missing partner.

"Here we go." Ivy reappeared with a mason jar of ice water in one hand, a napkin-wrapped muffin in the other, and Sela accepted them gratefully, though the muffin was a bit of a cheat. How many ounces in a mason jar? She took a long, slow sip, closing her eyes as the cold liquid soothed her throat. She heard Brody run by her and opened them to see him climbing onto the club chair next to the About the Artists table, half-eaten muffin in hand and crumbs across his chin, to flip open one of the picture books Ivy kept there to occupy young visitors.

Beside him, a table talker caught her attention—the only part of the display she had not designed. *You Could Make a Difference,* it read. A group picture showed the co-op artists gathered around Sela in their art fair booth, captioned by lots of fine print—the sob story, no doubt—and, larger, a toll-free number for interested donors.

Just when her breathing had started to stabilize.

Ivy followed her gaze. "What do you think?" she asked, as if unveiling some great surprise. "Worth a shot, huh?"

Ivy—who'd known her mother's feelings on Sela's father as well as anyone—did not know about the possibility of Caroline. Sela had been too afraid of what she might say—first that she'd question her judgment and then that she'd encourage her too eagerly. Sela had come today relieved she wouldn't have to deflect more questions about her sister and her kidneys, and yet . . .

"I thought I did all your advertising." Her voice came out in a croak.

"You do." Ivy gestured at the poster. "Look at your pretty face, advertising away."

"Ivy, I—" Sela stopped. She wanted to say that though this had been done with her in mind, it made her feel the opposite—not worth consulting to speak for herself. But Sela had seen how hard it was for Ivy to move on at Aesthetic without Ecca, whom she'd spent nearly every day here with for twenty-five years. Whom she still wanted to do right by, enough to overpay Sela and forgive late work and put up a damn sign soliciting help.

"Did Ecca ever talk to you about her friends from back in Cincinnati? A Hannah, maybe?"

Sela hadn't realized she was gearing up to ask the question, but of course she had been. That her mother had been friends with Caroline's was the only true surprise from Sela's trip north. And now that she was home . . . she had to at least ask.

If Ivy was put off by the change of topic, she didn't let on. "Once," she said slowly. "But only because she was sauced. You know personal history pre-Brevard was off-limits with her."

Sela raised an eyebrow. She did know. Just as she knew Ecca wasn't much of a drinker.

"Sauced, huh?"

"It was an emotional time. You'd graduated college, moved in with Doug. . . . She didn't let on to you, of course, but letting go is never easy for a mom."

Sela's gut twisted. She thought of the way Ecca had often stopped by with little gifts in those early months. Tea towels embroidered with tiny poppies. Handmade soaps that smelled of eucalyptus and sea salt. A stamped metal umbrella stand. Always with a genuine smile, never staying longer than a cup of tea. So respectful of Sela's space, and Doug's, too, but so present at the same time. Hardly a typical empty nester, and Sela hadn't gone far.

Then again, Ivy's generalization was true. What's more, had Ecca shown any hesitation, Sela would have tuned in to it, maybe even followed suit. Ecca had always been careful of that.

"Do you remember what she said?"

"Oh, sappy stuff. Ever get so drunk you end up crying that you love someone?"

"I don't need to be drunk for that." Sela meant it in a light, self-deprecating way, but Ivy's face fell, and she regretted it instantly.

"Aw, kid." Ivy looked nothing like Ecca—didn't even look like an artist, really, more of a 1950s housewife type, complete with apron and poodle-cut hair—but she sounded like her then, evoking the deep, growly sorrow that had marked Ecca's last year on earth, thanks to Sela.

"How did Hannah come up?" she prodded, desperate not to lose the thread.

Ivy swiped at the air. "Who knows? I was pretty sauced too—friends don't let friends drink alone."

Sela laughed encouragingly. *Come on, remember something. Anything.* "But you remember the name."

"Yeah. Well, once the floodgates broke, she went on and on. That I was her best friend since Hannah, she'd never do anything to hurt me, et cetera. Would've been sweet if she hadn't been so worked up. I had to put her to bed."

Sela frowned. "That was it? The only time she mentioned her, ever?"

"The only time, ever." Ivy's eyes narrowed. "Why? Did you hear from this person?"

"No, no," Sela said truthfully. "Just missing Ecca. Wishing she was still here to ask about—well, everything."

Ivy softened. "Me too, kid. Believe me."

"Do you ever think maybe we should have tried harder? To—I don't know. Get her to open up about that part of her life?"

"I do not. And neither should you. Your mother and I agreed dwelling on the past is overrated. What matters is finding ways to cope with the present." She cocked her head pointedly at the *You Could Make a Difference* sign, and Sela flushed.

"I don't mean to be ungrateful. I'm just uncomfortable trying to talk people into this."

"You're not the one doing it," Ivy said, eyebrows disappearing into her bangs the way they did when she got fired up. "We are. And we have zero qualms. This is your life we're talking about. We don't need to be convinced of what it's worth."

The Aesthetic collective skewed older and did not boast healthy lifestyle choices. A few—Ivy included—had gotten compatibility tested all the same, and a handful of others went out of their way to explain to Sela why they weren't candidates, which was just as touching. The rest she didn't blame for liking their kidneys right where they were.

Ivy always spoke with such conviction. Sela wished she could feel that sure of anything, let alone herself.

"Let's talk about what these are worth," she said, flipping open the box of brochures on the counter. "Everything look okay? Like you expected?"

Ivy didn't look. "Would you tell us, Sela, if it got to be too much, to keep working?"

Too much. They all phrased their misdirected worries this way. How could they so easily assume that Brody might be too much, or that work might be too much, and yet refuse to consider that donation might be too much *to ask*?

"If you're worried about Rebecca's life insurance payout running low, we have ideas. Auctions, benefits . . ."

"I'm fine," Sela said. Ivy looked down at the brochures but didn't smile. Didn't reach for them. "Unless—you're unhappy with these?"

"They are perfectly serviceable," Ivy said, the words coming fast—a telltale sign she was about to get blunt. "But they don't have your spark."

Sela slid the jar of water she'd been holding onto the counter next to her untouched muffin. She wasn't offended. She was *worried*.

"They don't need spark," Ivy went on. "It's a standard trifold. I'm only mentioning it because you do. You *are* spark, honey, always have been. I don't want to see you without it."

On that much, at least, Sela could agree.

Ecca's old desktop computer booted up with a groan. The thing was antiquated long before Sela had brought it here and stowed it away in the cupboard beneath the stairs, with every intention of tossing it once she was sure all her mother's paperwork was accounted for. Ecca was always the last to update her technology—she'd still been using an old flip phone when she died—but when Sela hit the power button, the machine miraculously obeyed.

She waited until the slow grinding of the hard drive stopped before opening the old email client. She didn't have much faith the in-box would load, but then there it was, greeting her with a screen full of unopened newsletters and notifications. All dated after Ecca's death.

She found the search toolbar and typed *Fred Shively.*

No results. She hadn't expected any—just wanted to make sure. Then:

Hannah Shively.

She should have known, even without hearing Ivy's story that didn't sit quite right.

Or, maybe, she should have left well enough alone.

Either way, there they were: four results. One correspondence thread in a folder marked Saved and three unsent replies in Drafts.

Before she could think too hard about privacy violations and what she might learn and whether she really wanted to, she opened the saved thread, checking the time stamp. It was dated more than a decade ago. For the first time ever, she was glad Ecca had been such a Luddite.

Dear R:

I can't even bring myself to type your name, but here we are. Every year, you write to tell me you'll do anything, whatever it takes. And every year, I don't reply, because there's never been anything you could do that would help set things right between us. Until now.

My daughter, Caroline, is up for a job at Brevard College, of all unlikely places. Needless to say, she can't get that offer. You don't want her, or Fred, or least of all me down there any more than I do. Surely as an employee you can pull some strings, call a friend in HR? Whatever it takes. Your phrasing exactly, as I recall.

Do this, and consider yourself off the hook. You won't hear from me again, but you can stop groveling, for pity's sake, move on, ease your conscience. Mine will be a bit heavier for this, but I guess that's the way it goes.

You have my word that I won't begrudge you anything anymore. Just don't begrudge me this one request.

Standing by, —H

A few days later, Ecca had sent a one-word reply:

Done.

Sela read it again and again as her brain put the pieces together. Starting with Caroline's story about her blown shoo-in interview and how it marked the beginning of the end with Keaton. She'd looked like she wanted to say more on the subject—like that end still signified to her a heavy, closed door.

Caroline's own mother had been responsible for that.

Ecca, her coconspirator.

What's more, Sela could only conclude from the wording that Hannah had known she existed. Otherwise, why be so sure Ecca didn't want Fred anywhere near her? Ecca had indeed not given a second thought to Sela's father all those years; she'd devoted all her wishful thinking to his wife. To begging forgiveness for having betrayed her in the most unforgivable way, with the most permanent result. A letter every year—for more than twenty of them. *For pity's sake.*

Ivy had talked about Ecca being emotional after Sela's graduation. But it had never been about Sela. It had been about her sister. And in a metaphoric sense, Ecca's too.

Sela clicked on the drafts and found lengthier replies.

H, You know I meant what I said. If this is really what you want, say no more. But . . . I can't help feeling for your daughter. If this opportunity is really something she wants, you have my word I'd steer clear, never say a word. There's no one else here who'd put two and two together. I've never so much as dropped a hint at what happened, not even (especially not) in my own house.

H, You say this is how it has to be, but please—the idea of never seeing or hearing from you again, even now, after all this time . . . Our friendship was always stronger than all the bullshit, no matter what. I'm so sorry I lost sight, during the weakest period of my life, of how special that was. There are things I never told you. . . .

H, You're right: I've apologized enough. If you could see Sela, you'd understand why it was all worth it. Why I can never regret it, no matter how bad it hurt us both.

So that was it. Ecca had agonized over taking her only chance to say how she really felt. To have some say in how things went down, finished up. And in the end, she had squirreled away the words, unsent, and replaced them with just one: *Done.*

Ecca did not do things on other people's terms—not even commissioned work. She was up front about it, having learned her lesson: No complete creative control, no deal. The fact that Ecca had capitulated told Sela everything she needed to know about how Ecca felt about Hannah. And, more to the point, how Ecca felt about her own trespasses against Hannah.

Unforgivable, maybe. Regrettable, no.

Sela's father truly had never known about her. Not that she hadn't believed Caroline when she'd said so—she believed, at least, that Caroline believed it. But finding confirmation here between the lines was something else entirely.

Not only had Hannah actively kept Caroline from knowing her sister, she'd kept Fred from knowing his daughter.

Then again, whether driven by guilt alone or something more, Ecca had done the same. She'd sent that one-word reply, when it came down to it, for Sela's sake as much as anybody's. At least, that's the way Ecca had seen it. Even as Sela bucked against what her mother had done, she knew Ecca's actions had come at no small cost to her conscience, her dignity, her sense of self.

Sela would not endanger the terms of that tenuously evened score now. She'd already wreaked enough havoc on Caroline's happy family; already come too close to dishonoring Ecca's memory.

Caroline could never know what either of their mothers had done. No matter how bad it hurt Sela to carry yet another burden alone.

21

Caroline

"May I ask," the woman on the line said crisply, "which patient referred you to this number?"

"I—" Caroline was sitting in her van at Riley's soccer practice, engine off, while the team scrimmaged in the rain. It pattered down the foggy windshield in streaks, making the driver's seat feel more private than it was—a shell of unexpected solitude, as Walt had gotten home from work early and saved her from dragging the other kids along. Even so, she hadn't expected names to come into this. She certainly didn't intend to give her own.

"No one. I do know a patient, but I'm calling without her knowledge. My questions are hypothetical." That didn't come out right. It made her sound dismissive. "Preliminary, I mean."

She'd looked up the transplant procedure online, of course. She still needed details, still had questions, but the gist of it seemed to be that, well, it was major surgery. As such, it scared the hell out of her—overall dislike of hospitals notwithstanding. But well-regarded medical professionals the world over would not routinely perform an operation on healthy people if it wasn't by and large safe. Would they?

Data analysis was literally in her blood. After more than a week of obsessing, she'd moved beyond reacting off-the-cuff. She couldn't in good conscience rule this out, couldn't decide how she felt about any of it, until she knew more. More than some website would say.

"I see." The woman sounded wary, and Caroline hoped she was an operator and not the actual point of contact. She'd found this number online, dialed it blind. "What did you want to know?"

Caroline closed her eyes, trying to pretend this was a work call. Speccing out a new venue for a client. Merely the middleman. "If I *were* calling about being tested—to see if I'd be a match for this person—what exactly would that entail?"

"Well, for starters, you'd have called the wrong number. This is the office for the transplant coordinator. You'd start with the living donor coordinator. They'd put the request in the system, and someone from our office would call you back to go through our preevaluation survey. It takes fifteen to twenty minutes, and probably covers a lot of the specifics you're wondering about—your own medical history and whether you might be eligible, but also what the testing involves, first steps, et cetera. I can give you that number, if you'd like?"

"Why do I call them, if you're the ones doing the evaluation?"

A keyboard clacked in the background. "A transplant might seem like one process, but it involves two patients: The prospective donor becomes one the instant they enter our system. As such, donors have their own coordinators for the sake of their own best interests and confidentiality, as well as the recipients'."

"Can you just tell me what that first test is, exactly?"

"If you are deemed eligible—no disqualifying medical condition or obesity—the first step is a simple blood test."

"Just my blood type?"

"Not quite that simple. They're looking for a tissue match. Antibodies, things like that."

"And if I'm not an initial tissue match, that's it? No go?"

"No go."

"And if I am?"

"Much more involved evaluations follow, both to check for other compatibilities and to ensure the donor's safety."

"So I could initially be a tissue match but turn out not to be a candidate?"

"Quite often, unfortunately."

Unfortunately. Right. That *was* supposed to be the mind-set of the people calling.

"Did you want that number for the donor coordinator?"

Did she? That was the question.

Walt was livid with Sela. Incensed in a way Caroline had never seen him, in a way that made her tears-in-her-eyes grateful she was not the object of his ire. He seemed convinced Sela had had some master plan—to lure Caroline closer with bittersweet thoughts of all the years they could've been there for each other, then ensnare her with an appeal only a cold heart would deny.

Caroline wasn't so sure. Once the shock of Sela's circumstances wore off, her mental devil's advocate kicked in. Did reaching out to someone qualify as manipulation if you had independently valid reasons for doing it—aside from something you might, yes, secretly hope they might do for you? Caroline, not Walt, had witnessed the wistful way Sela traced Rebecca's old school-day commute, how she'd hugged herself fiercely on the sidewalk when she'd thought no one was watching. Caroline, not Walt, had heard the way she'd talked with Lucy about her fears, offering a solution that was both empowering and tender—and effective, as Lucy hadn't had a bedtime issue since. Caroline, not Walt, had seen the conflict in Sela's eyes when they exchanged hesitant details about their lives to date. The look not of someone fishing for a sisterly connection but of someone open to one in spite of reservations.

A look a lot like the one she saw in the mirror.

Maybe Caroline *should* have guessed she was missing something big. What if she'd asked ahead of the visit, as any good hostess should, if Sela had dietary restrictions? What if she'd shared the details of their father's heart attack when it happened—Sela *had* called while she was at the hospital, after all—or later, in the interest of relevant family medical history, asking if Sela had information to volunteer in turn? Caroline hadn't willfully avoided these topics, per se; and if they'd come up, would Sela have lied, evaded? Caroline didn't think so. Had Sela been obligated to tell them something so personal from the start? Would Caroline have done so in her shoes?

Maybe she didn't feel the anger Walt did simply because his burned hot enough for both of them—so hot, in fact, she couldn't help backing away from it, for fear that mere proximity could singe her. What she felt toward Sela was sympathy. To have her pregnancy end with such a tragic diagnosis—to be gifted with a new life born from hers, with the very big caveat that she might not live to see it through—and then to lose Rebecca so soon afterward? To see her marriage crumble in the midst of it? Yes, Sela's situation extended to Caroline in ways she'd rather it didn't. The person inside that situation, though, had the worst of it, by far.

But when Sela wrote to Caroline her first night back in North Carolina, she didn't speak of her own plight.

I don't know what the right way to tell you was, but I wish I'd done it better—from the beginning. I guess I got caught up in the possibility of having someone like you and your wonderful family in my life—in any capacity. And, if I'm honest, I underestimated how wonderful it would be to spend time with people who didn't know, who treated me like a normal person and not like some ticking clock. I let it go on too long. But you have to believe me: I don't wish any responsibility for my health upon you. There's nothing I'd like better than to go back to how things were before you all knew, as much as that's possible. For my sake and for yours.

Caroline could not undo the way she'd felt that night before she found out the truth: convinced Sela could be the one positive in this whole negative mess. A sister, a sister-in-law, with a nephew in tow. A "real aunt," Lucy had called her without even knowing. What did it say about Caroline if Sela being sick changed her openness to any of those things? Even if Walt's take did have a grain of truth to it, could you fault someone for trying to save her own life?

In Sela's shoes, Caroline would go to any lengths—if not for her own sake, for her children's.

"Ma'am? Would you like that number? Do you have a pen?"

If Walt knew she was doing anything other than dismissing this option out of hand, he'd be beside himself. Not with anger, necessarily, but worry, protest.

Anguish.

If she wasn't a tissue match, it was a *no go*. She'd be off the hook—no decision to make. And even if she did pass the initial screen, she could still be ruled out—*very often, unfortunately*. Someone else would blessedly do the ruling. Not her. Not Walt. They could be a united front again, at least, on that much.

The real question was, once she started down a path she wasn't sure she wanted to continue, could she stop?

"I might as well get it while I have you," she told the woman. "Thanks for your help."

22

Sela

Janie poked her head through the door to the waiting room and, in lieu of calling her next patient's name, sang out, "You can go your own waaaaaay!"

A few curious heads turned as Sela got to her feet, smiling sheepishly.

"I can't tell you what a relief it is to finally have a nurse who remembers my divorce anthem from visit to visit," Sela told her once they'd reached the relative privacy of the exam room. "It's tiresome filling out the same questionnaire every time."

"I aim to deliver that personal touch." Janie winked. "Says here you haven't been feeling well? Tell me what's been going on."

Janie showed no inkling of suspecting that a real answer to this question would far exceed the time she had available. "Well, I went out of town for a weekend, and made the mistake of thinking I could eat like a regular person just that once."

"Ah. You're back to your strict self now, though?"

"For two weeks. And I swear I didn't slip *all* that much in the first place. But I can't get myself right. My energy isn't back."

"Possibly the problem was never your intake. Anything else different?"

Without Caroline to write to and hear from, without the possibility of what their relationship might mean to Sela—not just to her kidneys, *damn it, Walt*—without that hope of filling some corner of the gaping void her mother and husband and health had left in her life, *everything* seemed different. Unfamiliar, too, was the slow-growing anger she'd found herself directing at Ecca's memory since discovering those red-handed emails. Righteous indignation toward Hannah was quicker, easier. But this—she felt as if she were stuck holding something she'd never wanted to be handed and couldn't find a place to put it down.

"Not really."

"How about exercise?"

It was all she could do to throw a tennis ball for Oscar in her little fenced backyard, to play a simple game of indoor hide-and-seek with Brody.

"Not happening. But I think that's more of a consequence than a cause? My body feels . . . I don't know. Heavy."

"Let's check you over."

Janie did the requisite blood draws and an extra-thorough job of the usual exam. Then she sat across from Sela and leaned in.

"Did you go to the seminar we talked about?" Sela nodded. "And are you following through? You seemed to have reservations, before. Did it help with those?"

"It . . ." She didn't want to disappoint her. "Brought some clarity."

"Good. So how's it going? Putting out the call, I mean?"

Putting out a call *did* seem less daunting now that it was off her to-do list. If she'd decided this was too much to ask of someone she did know, how could she ask it of someone she didn't? But she couldn't see how to explain her stance without passing implicit judgment on the fact that Janie had done this very thing—accepted kidneys from not one but three living donors. Sela *didn't* judge her; in fact, she envied Janie's ability to accept the gift with more gratitude than doubt, with more love than fear that she might prove unworthy.

"I haven't rented a bullhorn yet. But I *was* going to ask my favorite comic about incorporating my ask into her act." A good-natured, far-fetched enough duck of the question.

Plus, she'd found some video of the nurse on YouTube. Just snippets—a two-minute bit here, an improv skit there—but quite funny.

Janie made a *psssshhhh* sound. "If you'd ever seen your alleged favorite comic's act, you'd know she already does."

Sela squinted at her. Surely she was joking.

"Hey, even in stand-up some things are off-limits—unless you're the one *in* the position. You think I'd miss the opportunity to milk my donor kidney for material? I'm taking everything I can from this thing for as long as it lets me."

"Seriously?"

"WebMD describes kidneys as 'sophisticated trash collectors.' My kidneys are more like my actual trash collector, on a windy day. Ever try to clean up that mess strewn across your yard? Turns out the rest of my organs are as lazy as he is, so they're like, *Fuck that, leave it, the wind will pick up again eventually.* And somehow I'm the one who gets stuck with this giant fine for littering. I mean, it says it's a hospital bill, but it feels like a fine. Because the mess is still there, but now I'm broke, too."

Sela burst out laughing.

"It helps when my sister's in the audience so that after I explain I have her kidney, I can punch myself in the side and have her yell, 'Ouch!'"

Sela laughed harder. And then, somehow, she was crying. Aimless, ugly sobs. *Again*. What was it about Janie? How did the only person in Sela's life she could laugh with about this keep dissolving her into tears?

Maybe it wasn't so much Janie as the way Janie made her realize how much she missed laughing with anyone else.

"Oh, God, I'm sorry, Sela. I didn't mean to—"

"No, no." She sniffed, raising her head. "Clearly I do need to come see your set. Just maybe not when I'm feeling so poorly."

"I know not everyone has a sister who—"

She shook her head, hard enough to silence the appeal. Even in cataloging the risks versus rewards, Sela hadn't gotten so far as to thoroughly consider the *physicality* of going about life with a piece of Caroline inside of her. Of anyone inside of her. How could anything seem so intimate and so impersonal at the same time, that humans could be reduced to machines in need of a replacement part?

"Is there anything you can tell about why I'm feeling so crappy?" Janie could hardly begrudge her the subject change. Other patients were waiting.

"We'll call with the results, like always. And I'll spare you the same old lecture on how to take care of yourself. But this, this ask? *That* is becoming the best thing you can do for yourself that you're not already doing."

She took a deep breath. As deep, anyway, as her newly shallow lungs would allow. What if fluid was collecting there? That happened. Didn't end well. "What if I don't want to?"

Janie blinked at her. "Sela, there are millions of *spare* sophisticated trash collectors out there, just sitting around. If everyone who could give did, can you imagine how many lives would be better—would be saved? I have to believe more people would donate if they understood that. So when you spread the word, you're not just doing it for yourself. You're doing it for all of us. When you say you don't want to . . ." Her frown deepened. "I mean, no one *wants* to. But there's no shame in asking for help."

That's where Janie was wrong.

Sela hadn't even gotten as far as asking, and shame was all she felt.

23

Caroline

Caroline had once found such reassurance in having her whole family gathered under one roof—celebrations of milestones big and small, happy and sad, taking best shape in simple togetherness. The way any one of them could order pizza for the group—Walt's parents, her own, the kids—without having to ask around about toppings. The running game the grandfathers had going, trying to outdo each other's corny jokes, the kids wielding and withholding the "scoring system" of their giggling volume with shrewd glee. The trading of recipes and the borrowing of tools and the *remember that times* and the mutual agreement that chocolate was the only flavor cake worth serving. The comfort of having everyone safe and accounted for, where you could hear them, smile at them, reach out and touch them.

She stood on this Sunday afternoon in her in-laws' living room, breathing in the smoky-sweet smell of her father-in-law's birthday meal of choice—pulled pork barbecue—and took in the stack of wrapped presents, the shoulder slaps of adults who hadn't seen each other in longer than usual, the shirt tugs of kids vying for attention. Everything looked as it always had: the Cracker Barrel kitsch decor, the coat closet so stuffed no one bothered to seek an empty hanger, the window seats filled with Walt's old toys that his mom, Brenda, kept "saving" for Owen, safety standards be damned.

But that feeling of comfort was gone.

"I'm dreading this family thing," she'd confessed to Maureen. Dad's recovery time had given her parents both excuse and cover to get their heads straight. Or at least their game faces. But they'd made it clear they expected this to be the start of getting *back to normal.* "It's been a couple months since the last one, but it might as well be a couple years. I feel like nothing has changed with Walt's side, and everything has with mine. I'm not used to feeling like we even have sides."

"Oh, come on," Maureen had said. "It's not like you guys are one of those sappy old-timey couples that calls each other's parents *Mom* and *Dad.*"

Caroline had stammered into silence. "Dear God," Maureen had marveled. "You are? Try being a man's second wife. Sometimes I think my in-laws found it presumptuous of me to even unpack my things. I'm pretty sure it's in our prenup for me *not* to call them Mom and Dad."

"Their loss, Mo." Caroline wasn't in the mood to joke.

"Do Walt's parents know . . . anything?"

"It didn't feel like our place to tell them. At least, not yet. It's not like my parents have been subtle about wanting to keep this quiet."

"And your own parents don't know about the—the kidney thing?"

Mo herself had been eerily quiet on that subject. An unprecedented instance of listening carefully and then offering no advice whatsoever. Her obvious fear of saying the wrong thing scared Caroline worse than any phone call to a transplant center could.

"They don't even know I've met Sela." Keeping this from them had been surprisingly easy, given that she hadn't seen them. Any guilt she might have felt was offset by the anger Caroline couldn't shake toward Mom. The worst part, then, became this new tension with Walt. It made its presence known in subtle ways: A skipped kiss good-bye. A flick of the remote when the news turned to health care issues. A dropped call that went unreturned. They'd gone out of sync, off their game, distracted. She hoped that was all it was.

Caroline groaned. "This birthday party is only family, and still I don't know how to act."

"Welcome to everyone else's family gatherings," Mo had quipped. "I suggest wine."

Indeed. Caroline had brought one of those double-sized bottles, and as she hoisted it under her arm, bending to gather the coats shed on the kids' excited tear into the house, she caught Mom's look of disapproval. *Tacky,* Mom mouthed from her perch on an overstuffed recliner. A childish defiance rose in Caroline. Fat bottles, then, from now on. She made for the kitchen and its countertop corkscrew.

"No one is leaving until we have the next family dinner planned," Brenda announced, joy flooding her face as she lifted Owen, touching noses. "You grew an inch, and I missed it!"

"Fred and I were saying that in the car!" Mom gushed. "We are *so ready* to get back to the rotation. And so thankful for the meal you dropped by when he was laid up."

"I wanted to do more." Brenda shook her head. "We had nasty bronchitis, Matthew and I both. You wouldn't believe how long that cough held on. Wouldn't wish it on my worst enemy, let alone my favorite people."

Caroline tried to soak up some of the goodwill, but she seemed to be made of Teflon today, slippery and unreceptive. She ducked into the den to stack their coats in the usual spot on the desk and found Dad squinting at the laptop.

"Just replying to a quick patient portal thing," he said by way of greeting. Caroline's mind grabbed at the word: *patient.* He would never not be one again.

His unacknowledged daughter could relate.

Caroline had resigned herself to playing along. But again she found herself asking: Would her parents feel differently *if*? If they knew about Sela's health, that this chance at reaching out to her might expire, would they still squander it? Or would they, like Walt, remain singularly focused on Caroline?

"We'll host next. Least we can do, Caroline is so busy." Mom's voice trilled through the open door, right outside, and Caroline turned back toward the kitchen.

Specifically, toward the wine.

She busied herself retrieving stemware from the cupboard so no one would see her face. The passive-aggressive remark was infuriatingly out of context, but why argue? She *was* making a point to be extra busy. This week, she'd thrown herself into multitasking as if it were a competitive sport. When her turn came to supply snacks for Riley's soccer game, she made granola from scratch. When she saw a new park mentioned on their playgroup's messenger chat, she organized an outing. On the most satisfying day, she'd nearly managed to be in three places at once, cheering on Lucy's music assembly while listening, muted, on a conference call, then whisking Owen to his checkup within the hour. In those moments, she felt like her capable self again, albeit a guilty version who was tabling her sister's issue in a way her sister could not.

She didn't feel like herself now, though, not here with their family—where she should be her *best* self. Even Walt seemed more at ease today. Probably happy to be back with his own parents, who didn't require explaining away children or apologizing for self-serving meddling.

There was a loneliness in Caroline's position that none of them could relate to.

She bet Sela could, though.

Caroline burned with shame that she'd let weeks go by without responding to Sela's email. But shame didn't help her figure out what to say.

"Should we do presents before we eat?" Brenda mused. "If we're going to enjoy a glass of—" She turned the bottle so she could see the label, smiled politely. "Red blend?"

"Pres-ents be-fore we eat!" the kids chanted, thundering in. "Pres-ents be-fore we eat!" Their sneakers stomped the linoleum, summoning Walt and Matthew, grinning, from the living room. Dad appeared in the doorway of the den, and she had to admit he looked better than she'd seen him in weeks. She'd focus on gratitude for the things that—well, that could be worse. Was he allowed wine? She set about filling glasses; no one moved to stop her.

"If we're doing presents first," Matthew mused, "might as well do cake first too."

The kids let out a cheer so loud no one passing by the house would have believed there were only three inside.

Did Brody's dad have a family that indulged the boy this way, making up for the lack on Sela's side? What was wrong with Caroline that she couldn't shut out these thoughts of Sela and Brody, no matter how she tried?

What was wrong with her parents and Walt that they could?

"Matthew," Brenda scolded, "they'll spoil their dinner."

"It's my birthday." He pouted. "Don't I get to decide?"

Another raucous cheer.

In the living room, as the adults settled with their drinks into seats and the kids ran for the baskets of munchies on the end tables, Walt put a record on the turntable and dropped the needle. The unmistakable organ keys of his dad's favorite band, the Doors, piped through the old upright speakers. "Oh, that one's scratched," Matthew lamented. "Won't make it past this track."

Walt held up the cover so his dad could see its mint condition. "Gift number one: a shiny new replacement. You can thank the hipsters for bringing vinyl back."

"Oh!" he exclaimed. "What a great idea! Skip to 'L.A. Woman,' would you?"

"Matthew," Brenda repeated. "Not kid friendly!"

"But it's 'Sunday afternoon.'"

"T-O-P-L-E-S-S B-A-R-S!" she spelled. "M-U-R-D-E-R!"

"The lyrics are slurred," Walt said. "I think it's okay."

"I'm impressed you *know* the lyrics," Dad told Brenda, Mom nodding in agreement. They favored singer-songwriters—James Taylor, Carole King—though they played them loud like rock. "Fire and Rain." "It's Too Late."

Something inside has died / And I can't hide and I just can't fake it . . .

Caroline swigged from her glass.

"Which one is that, Daddy?" Riley asked. "Want, or need?"

A couple of years back, their family's gift giving had gotten out of control, both sets of grandparents so intent on spoiling the kids that Caroline would burn with contempt at their privilege by the end of the day. She and Walt put their feet down, and everyone settled on a universal rule of three: something you want, something you need, something to read.

"Well, since it's a replacement, I'm not sure it's either. That's why I didn't wrap it."

"Ooh," Lucy piped up. "That means you still have three more, Grandpa!"

"Are we allowed to give the kids more than three, if they're 'replacements'?" Brenda asked hopefully. Walt shot her a *don't get me in trouble* look, and she grinned. "Worth a try," she teased, sipping her wine. "This is good, Caroline. Does it come in regular sizes?"

Caroline ignored Mom's look of mortification. As if Caroline were the one who should be embarrassed here. About anything. "I'll pick up a bottle for you next time I see one."

Owen and Lucy dove to "help" Matthew with the largest gift, tearing the paper away to reveal a leaf blower.

"This is want," he said admiringly. "Definitely want."

"Sign me up," Dad chimed in. "I want too."

"For you, it's need," Mom chided. "Your heart has no business raking."

"That's snow shoveling. I think I can handle some dried leaves." Everyone was laughing, enjoying each other, and Caroline started to relax. Maybe moving ahead *was* as easy as going through the motions, and the feelings would follow. Maybe she only needed more time.

"Mine next, Grandpa," Riley called. "The one in the bag!" Riley had asked, sweetly, if she could do the *something to read,* and Caroline agreed without asking questions. That her daughter wanted to take the initiative was all she needed to know.

"This was all her," she called out, getting into the spirit. A murmur of appreciation went around the room, and Riley jumped up to stand next to the man of honor.

"We learned about these poems at school, where the first letter of each line spells your name. It starts with an A. Across . . ."

"Acrostic," Caroline supplied. Riley nodded proudly.

"You wrote me a poem?" Matthew engulfed his granddaughter in a squeeze.

"Want me to read it, so everyone can hear?"

"Absolutely."

Riley reached through the tissue paper and pulled a trimmed piece of poster board from the bag. She held it so her grandfather could see and slid onto his chair cushion beside him.

"Grandpa," she read loudly:

Giggles,
Riddles,
A+
Nock nock jokes, and
Dynamite
Puns,
Always.

"How sweet!" Brenda exclaimed.

Caroline was puzzling over the N until the misspelling of "knock knock" dawned on her, and she smiled to herself. Some gifts were better for the flaws.

"Hey now. Are you saying he's funnier than me?" Dad feigned offense.

"That's exactly what she's saying!" Matthew boomed—to boast, but also to be heard over the record player's crescendo. Caroline had never realized how *long* "L.A. Woman" was. Walt lowered the volume.

"I'll make you one too, Gramps," Riley promised.

"You haven't seen the best part," Matthew said. "She *drew* it!" He flipped the board around to reveal the poem itself—colorfully illustrated in Sela's lettering technique.

Caroline froze.

"Oh, Riley, that's beautiful!" Brenda gasped. "Where did you learn to do that?"

Walt's eyes flew to hers in alarm. Caroline opened her mouth to interject, but too late.

"Aunt Sela taught me!" Riley bubbled over. "She's an artist, and her mom taught her, and she's teaching me. Next time, we're going to visit her house, and—"

Caroline stole a look at her parents. Their faces had gone pale, and Mom clutched Dad's elbow as if to keep from falling, though they were sitting down.

She herself had held to Walt exactly that way the morning Sela left. She had never loved being so physically like Mom, but she'd never before been *offended* by it. Now, she could barely stand the sight.

Dad, to his credit, did not look particularly surprised. Only sad.

"Aunt Sela?" Brenda turned to Caroline in confusion. "Who's Aunt Sela?"

The song chose that moment to finally end. You could have heard a feather float through the air, so sudden and complete was the silence.

"Old friend," Caroline blurted out, at the same time that Walt said, "Term of endearment."

Brenda smiled teasingly. "Here I was racking my brain for forgotten family members." She laughed, even as a terrible tension snaked through the room. Caroline's face burned under the laser gazes of Mom's alarm, Dad's discomfort. "I don't remember that name," Brenda went on, oblivious. Caroline could see her flipping through her mental copy of their wedding's guest book. Any minute, she'd ask where Caroline knew Sela from or where she might check out her art. Caroline had to redirect, fast.

Even though damage was already done.

"Aunt Sela drew our names better than *that.*" Owen pointed a critical finger at his sister's gift.

"Can't imagine better than this," Matthew said quickly.

Riley sighed. "It was," she conceded. "You can see it next time you come over. Daddy hasn't hung it up yet, but he's going to, right, Daddy?"

Walt dug at the carpet with the toe of his sock. He'd stashed the frame in the pantry, insisting to Caroline that out of sight, the kids would forget it. *I for one don't want to look at reminders of her right now,* he'd said. *What would you tell your parents, anyway? It's distinctive. They'll ask about it.*

But Caroline liked it as much as the kids did. She'd been hoping to wait him out. No matter that he had a point. The next song began with an unnaturally slow, psychedelic beat, and Walt glared at the turntable as if it had disappointed him. He switched it off abruptly.

"She slept in my room," Lucy chirped. "She helped me like it again!"

Brenda looked quizzically from Lucy to Caroline, the tension finally constricting the parties caught unawares in the middle. Moments ago, Caroline had been lamenting the unfairness of being the only one who felt awkward, unbalanced.

Careful what you wish for.

"Well," Brenda said, clearing her throat. "I can see she made quite an impression. It's a beautiful gift, Riley. I have the perfect frame." She clapped her hands. "How about that cake?"

—

"Start talking, Fred." It was a relief to see Mom's anger redirected, if only momentarily.

"What would you have me say? I didn't know she was here. But we talked about the possibility Caroline might pursue this."

They were storming down the sidewalk away from the house, two paces in front of Caroline and Walt, evidently far enough ahead to forget they could be heard. Either that, or Mom had abandoned her lifelong pretense of keeping their arguments private.

"I'd like to take a walk with my daughter," Dad had announced once they'd survived the awkward meal. Poor Brenda and Matthew kept exchanging glances as if they'd accidentally broken something they hadn't known was fragile and still hoped to avoid paying full price.

"Your wife would like to join," Mom had huffed.

"And your son-in-law." Walt didn't miss a beat.

Caroline worried someone might suggest the whole family go, but by then even her good-natured in-laws wanted an out. They volunteered to keep the kids, saying how good a walk would be for Fred's heart, how nice for him to have time with Caroline.

Hardly nice. But necessary.

"I understood," Mom said now through gritted teeth, "that it was a possibility, but not that she'd keep it from us if it happened."

"To be fair, not discussing it was exactly what you wanted. You can't have it both ways."

She whirled back toward Caroline, though her charge down the sidewalk didn't slow.

"They're calling her *Aunt*?"

"Term of endearment," Walt repeated, sticking to his story.

"I understand how it sounds to you," Caroline said, calm, "but we chose it to maintain ordinary. We use it with all our old friends. Which is who they think she is."

"Ordinary!" Mom scoffed. "Honestly, Caroline. Don't you think I've been through enough with this? I had to find out she's in your life—in my grandkids' lives—like *that*?"

"Look," Caroline tried. "I understand you want everything to go back to how it was. But—"

"Not at all." Sarcasm dripped from the words. "I adore having my husband sleep in the guest room. It's how I planned to spend my golden years."

Caroline's jaw went slack. Her parents had given such a strong impression that things were resolved between them.

Then again, this was a couple that whispered their arguments.

"Tell us straight," Mom said. "Do you plan to see her again?

Riley seems to think so. And speaking of, what if Sela decides to tell the kids who she is? Who's to stop her?"

"It's complicated," Caroline mumbled.

"We're aware of that," Dad said. Was he? He hadn't asked what Sela was like or how the visit had gone. Hadn't done anything but trail behind his wife, biting down on her ultimatum.

"It's more complicated than you're aware," Walt said flatly. His eyes met Caroline's, imploring her that if she didn't explain, he would. This, she knew, was why he'd come along.

"In what way?"

Caroline took a deep breath. For not the first time today, she understood how Sela might have felt in the hot seat. "Sela is sick," she began.

By the time she'd finished telling them, they'd stopped walking, the situation's gravity pulling their feet to a halt. They huddled on the corner of a four-way stop in the center of the development, impervious to the occasional passing car or kid on a bike.

"You can't seriously be considering this," Dad said finally. "If someone has to, for God's sake, let me."

"Absolutely not!" Mom looked stricken, and Caroline put out a hand to calm her.

"You're not healthy enough, Dad. They'd never approve you. Not alive, anyway."

"Caroline!" Mom shook her off, glowering.

"I'm just explaining."

"It's out of the question, then," he said, firm. "There can't be sufficient data on the outcomes of these procedures—they're too evolving, too new. No way can they say for certain this wouldn't negatively impact your life twenty, thirty years down the road."

Irritation flared in her. He was himself thirty-five years past an ill-considered, life-altering decision, hardly in a position to preach. "Let's not get ahead of ourselves."

"Has anyone bothered to study how many donors regret their decisions later?"

"Yes." She tossed her head, smug. "Two percent."

He stared at her for a quiet moment. "Too high," he muttered. But he deflated, seeing how capable she was of approaching this exactly the way he'd taught her to.

Seeing that if she did, he might not like the outcome.

"Backing up, this raises obvious questions about Sela's motives," Walt cut in, unmoved.

"They're not obvious," Caroline argued, turning back to her folks. "I feel awful for her."

Mom really looked at her then, at last. "Of course you do," she said, her defensiveness falling away. "At her age, and with a child of her own? My God, that's sad."

"She doesn't have anyone to turn to, Mom. Even if she did reach out to me for that reason—not just looking for a donor, I mean, but for support at a tough time—would that be so wrong? We *are* sisters."

"Half sisters," Dad corrected.

She looked at him sharply. He was so disappointing lately. "She's the only one I've got."

"Far as we know," Mom drawled.

Caroline looked from one angry parent to the other. This really was worse than she'd thought. "I just feel awful," she repeated uselessly.

Mom touched her arm. "As long as you don't feel *so* awful that you do something crazy. Like cut out a kidney."

"She's not going to," Walt assured her, looking to Caroline for confirmation.

She evaded his gaze. "I don't want to," she said honestly. "But it *is* complicated. And sad. And I'm the one in this position—not any of you. I'm not sure I can dismiss it that easily."

"You're not sure?" Walt exploded. "For all you know, you could have a genetic tag for this condition yourself. Or the kids could. You think I'm unsympathetic to Sela, but I'm not. I'm just more sympathetic to you."

He turned on his in-laws, eyes blazing. "You don't want to hear this, but you are the ones who've made Caroline feel responsibility for Sela. She's been the only one willing to acknowledge this woman's existence, and maybe that was okay when no one knew the load that would put on Caroline's shoulders, but it's not okay now." He stood taller. "I love my wife enough to be the one to say you need to find another way to deal with this."

He slipped his hand into Caroline's, and she let him. This was what had always been best about them: that they could disagree and still be on the same team. That he had her back, was her partner above all else, and had been from the very beginning.

They'd always been different from other couples.

But now, they were different from the couple they'd been at the start, too.

I love my wife enough, he'd said.

He never would have said that then.

24

Sela

Two years ago today, Brody was born.

He came out swinging—fighting, wisely but futilely, against the false start—and she joined him on the front lines, never leaving his side, reassuring him they'd defeat the odds together, come out stronger. And for the next two years, he never left hers—even as his battle wound down and hers was just beginning.

Some mothers spoke of their children's infancies passing in a blur. Not Sela. She'd felt every bit of these one hundred and four weeks. Seven hundred and thirty days, the hardest she'd known, and yet in these same two years she'd fully realized the love only Brody could bring.

For two years, she'd had the gift of seeing him thrive.

For two years, he'd given her the gift of witnessing her *survive.*

The cake she baked was two-tiered, round, orange-cone-colored frosting carpeted with brown sprinkles in her best simulation of a construction site. There was no real party planned, no reason to be showy, but a sleepless night found her browsing toddler birthday cakes on Pinterest, and next thing she knew she was ordering little plastic toppers: a cement mixer, a bulldozer, an excavator, like the ones in *Goodnight, Goodnight, Construction Site*—the board book Doug brought home the day they found out they were having a boy. Hers didn't look exactly like the picture, but it was passable, icing firming up in its hiding place in the fridge now. She was remiss to cheat on her kidney diet, but this she'd earned.

Doug was the first to arrive. "Daddy!" Brody squealed, catching him around the legs as Oscar danced around the doorway, his nails scritching across the hardwood. Doug held a fat bouquet of two-toned roses, and Sela buried her nose gratefully in their cream centers, fingering the red outer petals. She wouldn't protest a gift today—not from the father of her child.

"Come in. Pizza's in the oven." The low-sodium concoction crisping at four hundred degrees tasted more like cardboard than any pizza she'd ever craved, but at least it sounded festive.

Doug hung his jacket on the banister, where he always had, and nodded at the display she'd arranged on the entryway table. "Who all sent cards?"

"My mother's parents—that was nice." She still thought of them more as Ecca's parents than as her grandparents—she didn't remember them acknowledging her own childhood birthdays, after all—but had to hand it to them for trying. She pointed down the line, ticking off the well-wishers. "Ivy and everyone at Aesthetic, neighbors on both sides, even the NICU staff." If Doug noticed that nothing from his parents or siblings had arrived, he didn't flinch. Then again, they'd probably sent them to his address. Sela tried not to pass judgment. Divorce, like illness, seemed more common with age, and she and Doug were facing both prematurely. She couldn't expect the others affected to know how to handle it any better than they did.

He nodded approvingly but didn't move to read the sentiments inside. "How are—" The ring of the doorbell cut him off, and

Oscar started up his dance again. From the other side of the dead bolt came the muffled high notes of Annie's excited chatter and Leigh shushing her, issuing some behavior warning. Sela pulled open the door.

"Piper sleep," Annie stage-whispered. "Quiet, goodness' sake."

Leigh hoisted the infant car seat where Piper remained "sleep" higher on her arm. "We don't have to whisper," she told Annie. "We just can't *yell.*" She smiled sheepishly at Sela. "Sorry. Van got held up at a church thing, and I didn't want to be late."

"We're happy the three of you are here." Sela waved them in. "The four of you," she corrected, eyeing the hint of roundness in Leigh's silhouette as she set the baby inside the relative dimness of the dining room.

Doug looked from one to the other, squinting into Sela's meaning. "Are you—?"

"It's early," Leigh said quickly. "So please keep it quiet. But yes, looks that way."

"Wow. Congrats." He glanced again at Sela, and she busied herself with helping Annie out of her jacket, self-conscious at how obviously he was checking on her and how flat his response sounded. Doug directed so much concern at her that it was sometimes easy for people to overlook the weight of his own version of their tragedy, even if he'd walked away from it, even if he could theoretically start over in ways Sela could not. It was harder, of course, on this particular day, but still. If Sela could be gracious, so could he.

"It's wonderful news," she agreed, smiling brightly at Leigh, who had indeed come around. She hadn't had to say so: Sela had seen it in the way her friend had taken to cradling her abdomen with a soft, unconscious smile. She knelt to Annie's level, trying not to grimace as she did. She'd chosen wide-leg pants to hide the extent of the swelling, but her skin was stretched painfully tight, like an overinflated balloon. "I set some cool new blocks out in the living room, if you want to play?"

Annie scurried in the direction Brody had already gone, Oscar on her heels.

"Drinks? I have plenty of good stuff I'm not allowed to have." This was not to exclude her pregnant guest. In Sela's book, the "good stuff" included most anything that wasn't water.

Within minutes they were gathered around the kitchen island—beer for Doug, crushed ice for Sela, soda for Leigh—while the kids made a loud mess of the coffee table, building towers and sending them crashing down. *A joyful mess,* Ecca would've called it. Sela's childhood birthday parties had been small, simple—a few friends, a few games, a rare junk food free-for-all, and every year a new hand-painted banner reading *Happy Sela Day*—but oh, had they been joyful. Messy, too. She looked on wistfully as Annie erected a taller, skinnier stack, until she became aware that the adults' pleasantries had faded into silence. That her guests were watching not the kids but her.

"Don't take this the wrong way," Doug began, "but you look like hell."

"No chance of taking that the wrong way," Leigh deadpanned. But her smile didn't reach her eyes.

"I think I look pretty decent for stage four." Sela shrugged.

"Oh, no," Leigh and Doug replied in unison, and Leigh flushed, so obviously not wanting to match him. "Since when?" she asked at the same time Doug said, "Because of Cincinnati?"

Sela shook her head. "Can't blame that. None of my symptoms are new, only worse. It happens, I guess: You slip almost overnight, no one knows why. Turns out my kidneys have had a milestone week."

"Besides this?" Leigh bit her lip.

"Along with this. I've made the list. Officially."

"Oh, no," Leigh said again, at the same time Doug said, "Good." So much for matching.

Leigh laughed nervously. "Did they give you, like, a number?

I guess transplants aren't like the deli counter." She cupped her hands around her mouth. "Now serving ninety-two!"

"If your deli has a yearlong line to even *take* a number, you gotta find a new deli."

Doug shook his head. "It takes a lot of nerve to make sick people hurdle so much red tape. But this is a relief, right? First hurdle complete."

Sela commanded her head to nod. She did not point out there was only one more stage to go, synonymous with end-stage renal failure. Or that her reaction had been more in line with Leigh's, as if she now had the label to prove she was at the mercy of too many things.

Avoid unnecessary stress, Janie had cautioned when she'd called with the latest. *It can hold more power over your health than you know.* She wanted Sela to come in, go over things in person, but what was the point? They'd entered the realm of inevitabilities.

"Well, what now?" Doug, reporting for duty. "How do we get you *up* the list?"

"We don't. You remember about the point system."

They'd hashed it out, hypothetically, trying to figure out where she might fall in the database's priority rankings. The vague answer was: somewhere in the middle. At least she wasn't starting from last in line. For instance, she got points for being sensitized, and for being youngish. Until she aged out, anyway.

"Can you imagine managing that process?" Leigh's hand was on her abdomen again. "I mean, it's up to someone to decide who's next, and they have to do it based on a *score*?"

Of course she could imagine. That was *the* question you contemplated in Sela's shoes: whether one life is really worth more than another, when the system is structured not on whether to rank but on how. Did they have points for one's place in the world? Would it be fair for, say, a mother to get a point for each child whose life would be forever altered without her? For a medical researcher to get a handful if his kidneys went out while working on the cure for cancer?

The seminars told prospective donors that if anything went wrong with your remaining kidney, you'd go to the top of the transplant list. But it wasn't quite that simple; what you got were extra points. Not a bypass, a head start. The list itself was fluid, recalibrated every time a kidney became available, as matching was a complex thing. Roughly one hundred thousand people were on it. Three thousand added every month. Of the mere seventeen thousand transplants performed a year, only a third came from living donors.

Thirteen people died waiting every day.

"We all manage the process, in a way," Sela said gently. "If I bypassed the list to find a kidney on my own, that's exactly what I'd be doing. Jumping the line."

Doug looked at her strangely. "That's the donor's decision. And right. It's their kidney."

She'd tried, after that last face-to-face with Janie, to *consider* reconsidering. To allow that maybe her emotional reaction to learning what this would mean—for Caroline or anyone else—needed time to settle. She'd gone so far as to search out donor experiences online and found an essay that had gone viral: "Why I Regret Donating My Kidney." The thousands of comments were a firestorm: The irresponsibility of penning an alarmist piece! The insensitivity toward KCD sufferers! But also: empathy, commiseration.

It didn't matter that the rest of the search results seemed at a glance positive, even happy. Sela read no further.

"I brought you something," Leigh announced, pulling a small package from her purse. A rectangular box, wrapped in brown paper and tied with a simple string.

Sela took her time untying it. Inside was an opaque white crystal, carved into an unlikely spiral.

"Annie spotted these in the Crystal Mountain shop," Leigh began. "She said it looked like a unicorn horn."

Sela took it gently into her hands. That was exactly what it looked like.

"It's called selenite. There's a card in there that explains—it's a healing stone, but more than that. People believe it can reenergize auras. It focuses positive energy, calms worries. . . . Anyway, it was impossible to read about it and not think of you. It practically has your name in it."

"I have always wanted a unicorn," Sela said quickly, before Doug could jump in with some skeptical remark or, worse, suggest building a fortress of them around her. "Thanks, girl."

On the counter behind them, her phone began buzzing with a call. She ignored it, but Doug turned to look.

"Sela? Your phone." She resisted snapping that her kidneys were impaired, not her ears.

"You know how I feel about people who can't detach from those."

"Your phone!" He held it up so she could see the name on the screen.

Caroline.

"Oh." The sound escaped her, unbidden. She was about to stammer that she could still let her half sister leave a message, return the call at a more appropriate time, but Leigh was out of her seat, waving her arms excitedly.

"It's been radio silence between you for, what, three weeks?" Sela nodded numbly. Leigh was actually jumping up and down now. "Quick! Before it goes to voice mail!"

Doug thrust it toward her urgently. She'd been so eager to hear back from her sister at first, but with each day it seemed easier to avoid Caroline, even without an audience. What could she do, though, but take it?

"Hello?" She turned away from her guests, as if that might

afford her some privacy. Like Brody, the way he'd cover his eyes and assume no one could see him.

"Sela? I'm glad you answered. I was worried—I mean, I'm so, so sorry to be just now getting ahold of you." Caroline sounded out of breath, as if perhaps she'd had to run and hide to make the call. After the way their visit had ended, it was feasible that she had. "I've been thinking about, well, everything, and— Shoot, I didn't even ask. Is this a bad time?"

"Well, I—" She glanced over her shoulder at Leigh and Doug, who made no effort to do anything but stare at her expectantly. "A few friends are here. It's Brody's birthday." The two exchanged an unreadable look.

"Oh! I wish I'd known. Happy Birthday to Brody! And his mama."

"Thanks." She walked back down the hall toward the front door, away from the scrutiny.

"I won't keep you, then. It's just that—I've been feeling awful about the way we left things. The way you left."

"Please, don't apologize."

"I need to. Walt was incredibly harsh, and even then you sent that gracious email, and I just . . . needed time to process everything. But it was wrong to leave you hanging."

"It's okay. It was all . . ." What was the word? "Understandable."

"I want you to know Walt didn't speak for me. I'm not the kind of person who'd rule out any way I could help or at least support you without taking the time to learn more."

And I'm not the kind of person who'd discover our mothers conspired against you—us—and have an easy time keeping it to myself. Even if I'm sure it's the right thing to do.

"I appreciate that." Sela kept her voice low enough that she hoped they couldn't hear her in the kitchen. "But my email was not just backpedaling, blowing smoke. You really don't need to give this a second thought."

"I've been giving everything second thoughts lately. Don't get a big head."

Sela laughed in spite of herself.

"This might sound crazy, but I'm running a trade show down in Pigeon Forge next week, only a couple hours from you. The company used to be based here in Ohio, but they kept us on, and—well, anyway. Any chance you'd be willing to come up for a night or two, where we can talk away from everyone else? As director I get a suite at the host hotel—we can share it. There's a lounge where you can work while I'm on the floor, and dinner would be on me."

"That's a nice invite, but really not necessary."

"If Walt hadn't blown up at you that way, would you feel differently about coming?" The breathless rush that had begun the call was back, only now Caroline sounded on the verge of tears.

Sela didn't know how to answer.

"He was just being protective of his family," she said finally. "But I don't want to complicate things for you any more than I already have." Sela didn't mean just Walt.

"This isn't about *things*," Caroline protested. "I still want us to know each other better. That hasn't changed. Unless . . . you've decided you don't?"

"Of course not." In truth, she had no real reason not to go. She could work anywhere, and Doug never balked at taking Brody. Weekdays were tougher, but his new neighbor was a retired teacher who loved to babysit. "I suppose I might be able to swing a day or two. If you're sure my being there wouldn't complicate your job?"

"It would vastly improve my job. This is an easy show, and my coworkers would thank you for occupying me after hours, so they can run amuck on the moonshine distilleries."

"No fair." Sela found herself smiling. "Where are we supposed to run amuck?"

When the call was over, she sneaked a look into the kitchen.

Leigh and Doug were murmuring to each other, while behind them the kids tried to ride ever-patient Oscar like a pony.

They'd be all over this. Strap the unicorn horn on the front of her car, soap KIDNEY OR BUST across her windows, and accept nothing less. Her gut twisted around the precarious hope of a second chance with her sister. Was there any harm in letting them presume whatever they wanted about her intentions with Caroline? All they'd need to know was that it didn't work out, one way or another, eventually. Why mar Brody's birthday with an argument?

He looked up from Oscar then, met her eyes, grinned. This was *his* day. She'd carried on the tradition of the banner, hanging it in his room so he'd wake and see it first thing: *Happy Brody Day.* A day that had, historically, not held the happiness it should have. Too much of his life had already been about her—fear, disappointment, work-arounds. The kid deserved a day. They could talk about this later.

Two years down, how many to go? Without finding a living donor on her own, how long would the wait be? How to make the years ahead more bearable—for Brody, for her, for Leigh, Doug, and anyone else unlucky enough to be stuck with a Sela tie?

Maybe the answer was waiting in a Pigeon Forge hotel. Just not the way anyone else thought.

She opened her arms, and Brody came running.

25

Caroline

She took what was left of that fat bottle straight over to Mo's, was what she did. Mo took one look at her and shook her head.

"If you had wine left over from the family thing, you're doing it wrong."

"What else is new?" Caroline grumbled.

She'd walked out as soon as they were home from her in-laws', leaving Walt to put the kids to bed, not asking permission.

There were plenty of things, if you thought about it, that she didn't need permission for.

"Bunch of overthinkers," Mo proclaimed, once Caroline had finished recapping the day's frustrations.

"Are they?" Not a rhetorical question. They were thinkers, sure. But this was serious.

"Not just them, honey." Mo drained her glass and breezed off the couch and over to the dry bar. By the sounds of things, the boys were playing a raucous game of basketball in the bedroom directly overhead, but she remained admirably impervious to the noise. She held two bottles of Pinot Noir in the air and Caroline pointed to the one with a horse galloping across the label. Oh, to be free that way, wind in her hair, discussing anything but this. Mo plunked it between them on the coffee table and started on the corkscrew.

"It's been how long since the first shoe dropped here? Bombshell email numero uno?"

Caroline counted back the weeks, surprised by how many. "Over two months," she admitted.

"So, you've all had time to get used to the idea, but no one wants to. Let a third party lend some clarity then, okay?" Mo didn't wait for an answer. "I know you and Fred are all about breaking down the data. And the question of the kidney stuff—it *is* heavy. But no one needs to answer that right now. In the meantime, you don't need to dissect why you want to know your sister. It's because she's your sister. Or why you're so hurt to find out what your mom did. It's because she's your mom. Or why you're so angry to have lost the chance at Brevard, and Keaton. It's because you loved them."

Caroline couldn't help noticing the last point was the only one in past tense, and she hoped it belonged there. She didn't like the way Keaton and Sela were all twisted together in her brain now. Didn't like that she still thought of her last minutes with Keaton and wished for the impossible: a chance to set things right. She couldn't keep squandering the ones she still had.

Mo filled her glass and placed it firmly in Caroline's hand. "Stop trying to justify how you feel. Just go ahead and feel it."

Caroline called Sela, right then.

She had every intention of telling Walt, right away, of the plans they'd made. The house was quiet by the time she got home, the kids asleep. But she hadn't been the only one keying up to talk. He started in as if no time had passed since they'd left the birthday party.

"You see now," he told her, his face garish in the glow of the muted TV. "Right or wrong, like it or not, donation isn't the kind of thing anyone should pursue without the full support of their family. And your mom and dad—they're light-years away from coming around to any of this."

"There's more to our family than that," Caroline tried, biting her tongue on the premature word *pursue.* "The kids care for Sela. You see *that* now. If they knew who she really was, they'd be happy."

"Happy to have a cool aunt, maybe. Not happy their mom would entertain the idea of putting her life on the line for her." Mo wasn't always right about Walt—there was too much she didn't know, had never known, about them. But she was right about this: Time wasn't having much effect on his initial reaction to this whole thing. "Besides," he went on, "even if you wanted to go rogue and tell them, this situation is beyond their understanding. Hell, it's beyond mine."

"Maybe we're overthinking it."

His eyes flared. "There's too much at risk. Everything from your health to how well we can get through a family dinner. I can't be objective here."

Maybe it was too much to ask of him. But it was also too much to ask of her to drop it. He was verging on overstepping, and they had rules against that. If Walt knowing about her arrangements to see Sela again was going to make things harder, well, then he didn't have to know.

She could justify flying under the radar, so long as they were both bending rules. So long as she didn't let anything happen in Pigeon Forge that she couldn't take back. She wouldn't reveal to Sela that she'd gotten as far as calling to ask about getting tested. She'd just spend a day or two, see how it went. If Caroline decided against getting more involved—with any of it—she'd have saved Walt the trouble of arguing moot points. And if she didn't?

She'd once been so sure there was no problem they couldn't talk out.

She hoped that, least and most of all, was still true.

—

"Mind some company?"

Walt, impossibly young then—God, they both were—dropped into the lounger next to Caroline without waiting for a response, and her eyes shifted in his direction. The last of the sunset was fading into stars, but she hadn't bothered to remove her sunglasses. She watched as the dark shapes of his legs stretched out in front of him and crossed at the ankles, mirroring her own, then tipped her head back again, staring up through the lingering heat of the summer night.

Here, at the level-two end of the trilevel deck, she and her cocktail were blissfully out of splash range of the pool below and, equally important, away from the drunken foot traffic going in and out of the house above. It was hardly fair to keep the spot to herself.

Cries of "Marco" and "Polo" punctuated squeals of laughter from the lagoon-style in-ground pool. The game in progress was a "couples edition," girlfriends clinging to the guys' backs, which only served to highlight how many couples were at this party. Aside from Walt and Caroline, the only other person not paired off was Maureen, who was coupled off with the house itself. She was house-sitting for her still-new boyfriend (and, few suspected, one-day husband), Seth, who'd taken his kids to Michigan for the week and who, more to the point, was a decade older and exponentially more flush. Most everyone in attendance—a loose crew of twenty-somethings, old high school and college friends that had grown to include friends of friends—resided in apartments, condos, or at best "starter homes." Out here at the edge of the suburbs, Seth's half of his pending divorce settlement was ripe for the kind of house party none of them could throw unless someone's overly charitable parents went out of town.

Caroline had no idea whether Seth had sanctioned this shindig. She also had no idea why his estranged wife had not wanted to stake claim to this McMansion, especially in sharing custody of the kids. All night, she'd entertained visions of the woman driving up, stomping in, demanding, *Who the hell are you people?* with that last-straw expression women wear when they already guess their fool husband is responsible.

Still, she knew Maureen and Seth's relationship wasn't as midlife-crisis-y as it might appear from the current state of his bikini-clad, margarita-wielding belle. They gave the impression of the kind of unlikely combination that was better than either of its parts, and Caroline couldn't bring herself to caution Mo about getting involved with him so soon. Her own judgment was hardly on a winning streak anyway.

Come to think of it, maybe she did understand why Seth's ex didn't want this house. Caroline had had to find a whole new set of haunts in Keaton's wake.

"No date tonight?" she asked Walt, lest he think her unfriendly. Silence suited her fine; she hadn't minded sitting alone, to Maureen's chagrin. It was nothing personal that Caroline didn't enjoy these invites out, but . . . well, she didn't enjoy much anymore.

"Is that so shocking?" She checked his tone: not flirting, only asking.

"Yeah." He always had a date—though rarely the same one. That was probably why they hadn't talked before. "I couldn't help but notice how interested you are in dating."

"I couldn't help but notice how *un*interested you are in dating."

Touché. "I've sworn off love."

Even to her own ears, it sounded run-of-the-mill. A melodramatic postbreakup proclamation at which people would smile with knowing-better politeness, humoring her while confident she'd recant after time had healed her burns.

"Let me rephrase," she said before he could patronize her. For some reason, the idea of it coming from a player like Walt was especially off-putting. If he turned on the charm, suggested he might be the one to change her mind, she'd feel minimized. But if he didn't, that might say more about her than it did about him. Not in a good way. "I've been reevaluating my ideas about love. Trying to figure out what I'd really want it to look like. And the thing is, I'm not sure that version of 'love' exists in real life."

"It doesn't," he said, throwing her. She hadn't explained what that version *was,* much less expected him to agree. Walt was a gregarious enough guy, not the biggest catch at any gathering, but a good one who was frequently caught. She turned to see if he was serious and found his face scrunched in thought, as if she'd asked him to elaborate. "We all expect too much."

"I'm not sure that's true." She knew plenty of people who were infatuated with less-than-deserving mates. She found it tough to watch classic films—men courting women, dressing up for them, learning to dance for them—and not lament how low expectations had sunk. These days, if the guy called more or less when he said he would, and invited you to perch cutely on his couch while he and his friends watched the game, and didn't cheat on you as far as anyone could tell? That was supposed to be a catch.

And even then, if you had the audacity to expect not a ring or an income bracket but simply a kept promise? That was "too much," too.

"Isn't it?" Walt pulled the paper umbrella from his margarita and discarded it on the arm of his chaise. "By today's standards, our spouse is supposed to be not only both friend and lover, but our *best* friend. Not merely our love, but our soul mate. Someone who will become our family, but remain less annoying than our family. A true partner we can count on by day, and a sexy mystery date by night—because we can't let reliable turn into boring. No, we want someone who will be even more appealing fifty years from now than the day we met."

Huh. She'd been coming at it a different way, but—he wasn't wrong. He tipped his glass toward her—*cheers!*—and drank deeply.

"I guess I've been thinking of it with more of a too-many-eggs-in-one-basket feeling," she admitted. "Like, okay, that didn't work out, and there goes not just my boyfriend, but my best friend. And all the comfort that goes with it—but like you said, the excitement too. Aside from how crummy it feels to lose all that, there's also everyone looking at me, like, *Shit, what's she going to do now?*"

"I should probably pretend I haven't heard anything about this, but you were planning a lot of things around the guy, right? Where you'd live, what job you'd get?"

She nodded, nearly a year past caring about the gossip. "Yeah. And this might sound bitter, but I'm not sure I want to even pursue that kind of love again, where *everything* is so tightly hitched to someone else. It's a lot to trust somebody with."

"It's a lot to put on somebody."

Hard not to feel defensive at that. Still. "I guess we both have a point."

She tried to call up specifics of the women she'd seen with Walt. She'd chatted up a few—in line for the bathroom, on the same team of a silly party game. A medical resident, a preschool teacher, a law student. Not arm candy, not typecast. Engaging, intelligent, funny women.

"Doesn't seem to stop you from trying," she observed.

"Is that what you think I'm doing?" He shook his head. "Look, it's not like I've got this all figured out. I like and respect women too much to stay away from them. *And* I like and respect them too much to get too close."

"So you're like, what, an overly self-aware player?"

"And you're like, what, an overly philosophical cynic?"

They scowled at each other. "It's not like marriage was better before people started wanting more from it," she muttered. Admittedly this did dampen the charm of those black-and-white films. The courtship had better be lovely if the man was going to convince the woman to spend the rest of her life making him pot roasts in high heels and not bothering him too much about raising the children.

There had to be a middle ground. Caroline didn't want to be a cynic. And look at her own parents, after all these years. They weren't exactly lovey-dovey, but they had something good going. Something content. Fred still brought Hannah flowers, and Hannah fussed over his health and happiness as if it were her own. Because it was. She'd never seen in either of them a trace of restlessness or regret. They'd never given her a reason to look for one.

"That's the problem," Walt granted. "What's the better solution?"

It would seem crazy even to her, looking back, but she'd liked the way he said it. Plainly, without judgment. And intimately, as if they were the only two people smart enough to recognize the importance of the question, so they might as well stick together in figuring out the answer.

They got refills, started to brainstorm. A good marriage, they decided, would prioritize the needs it should meet. Partnership was key—an equal share in responsibilities, open communication, trust. "A sacred commitment to trust," Caroline clarified. Both partners should maintain close friendships outside the marriage and not just through couples they doubled with. Neither would ever begrudge the other a night out, and in fact, if someone was becoming too much a homebody, the other should call them on it. As two only children, they agreed family was a big part of the package, and both spouses should make an effort to form genuine bonds with the one they married into, make whole-family time a regular thing and not drive wedges with resentment.

A wild sex life didn't seem realistically sustainable under even the best circumstances. "I feel like ten years into a marriage, if you have kids and you both work and you're in the trenches, a date night would be more of a break without the subtext of—oh gosh, tonight's the night, and it's been a while, and we're not what we used to be." Walt laughed at himself, as if realizing this was not a very *player* thing to say.

"I'm not sure you can have romance without expectations," Caroline mused. They were sitting, after all, in a house of divorce, as guests of the next woman in line. She wondered: How did Seth plan for things to be different with Mo? Or did he? Everyone thinks the next time will be better and starts on their best behavior. But how often do things turn out exactly the same?

"I read this article about how by some standards, arranged marriages are actually happier, and the takeaways were more like . . . What about redefining romance as paying attention to the relationship? Don't stop making the other person feel special. Treat yourself by treating the both of you. Don't hold it up to some ideal of what other couples are doing."

"Okay, but for the physical aspect, are you saying *open* marriage?"

By this point they were upright on their loungers, feet flat on the floor of the deck, hunched together intently. The swimmers were toweling off and heading inside for fresh snacks, but Walt had commandeered the tequila bottle, all the sustenance they needed.

"That's tough. You'd have to all but guarantee you could leave emotion out of those other beds." He snapped his fingers. "One-night stands only? And cone of silence—no talking about it."

"Wouldn't that be weird, every time the person comes home from a business trip? You're looking at them wondering if they got any to hold them over?" Caroline pantomimed a suspicious once-over, head to toe, and he cracked up.

"What's the alternative, though? Deciding you don't need sex in your life?"

"Millions of married people have given up on mind-blowing sex."

"But they haven't *admitted* they gave up. If you'd asked them to give it up going in, they'd have said, *forget it.*"

"So go in thinking of it as, what? More like friends with benefits?"

The conversation was . . . well, they both knew it was weird. But it was also *fun.* For the first time since Keaton had left her, Caroline wasn't thinking about the things she'd lost, the things she might never recover. She was thinking about what she wanted, what she *needed* in order to move past this hurt and be happy with someone again, in abstract terms she found oddly empowering. In spite of having never said more than two words to each other before that night, they'd bypassed small talk in a way that was secretly thrilling. It was possibly the most honest conversation she'd ever had. They challenged everything, from conventions to their own misconceptions and fears. It was a little embarrassing, and a lot thought provoking, but somehow they emerged in agreement, and with that came a feeling of triumph, of awe.

That night, she slept better than she had in almost exactly a year.

When Walt called a week later, she briefly wondered if he was joking—putting her on by asking her out. He made no mention of their talk, or of the date being serious or just a way to kill time. He merely invited her to dinner and a concert—a local band she liked. And, with a tight grip on the danger of having too many expectations, she said yes.

It never felt like dating. From the start, it felt more like a test run of something so crazy, it just might work.

Before they decided what to call their relationship, the people in their lives did it for them: a surprisingly perfect match, that's what. How had no one thought to set them up before? Anyone could see they were big on mutual admiration, low on pressure. Natural. And how nice to see Walt settling down and Caroline happy again. Such universal joy abounded on their wedding day, no one would have suspected they were not in love.

At least, not the way anyone thought.

They were great friends, though. And the benefits ended up being pretty good, too.

She knew it might sound like a regimented, lifeless approach, to lay out the rules for a new kind of self-arranged marriage and then go ahead and self-arrange it. And maybe it would have been, had she and Walt both not been so committed to holding up their ends of the bargain. The guidelines were really just conversations they'd gotten out of the way, battles they'd agreed not to fight—rules had never been so freeing. You didn't have to take her word for it: Ask any of the people who outwardly envied their relationship. They'd have been shocked to learn Caroline and Walt played by their own rules.

Which was the way they liked it.

Explaining themselves would only invite debate, defeat the purpose.

Were there days Walt pushed the wrong buttons? Days pettiness got the best of her? Everyone had those. But there was no *Can you believe we ever thought that would work?* There was only a good life together, a partnership that even Caroline thought worthy of the envy it drew, three kids whom she and Walt would both lay down their lives for.

And the sad truth that if not for the deception that tore Caroline and Keaton apart, the arrangement with Walt would never have appealed—and she wouldn't have learned ten years too late that the kind of love she'd sworn off had, possibly, existed after all.

26

Sela

"Are you sure about this?"

Sela pulled the thick white belt of her standard-issue hotel robe tighter around her waist and swiped her keycard at the glass door of the rooftop pool deck. The sensor blinked red.

"If you're appalled," she said, not turning to catch Caroline's eye, "I won't admit how many times it's worked for me before."

She swiped the card a second time, then a third, and waved it in the air, pantomiming frustration, hoping to catch the attention of a man sitting on a chaise just inside the door, talking on his cell phone. He was fully clothed, clearly there only to make the call, and paying them no mind.

"Having trouble?" The voice came from behind them, and Sela turned to see a young employee clad in a hotel insignia polo shirt smiling pleasantly.

Shit.

"I must have demagnetized my key," she said smoothly, curling her fingers around the card so he could not see that its logo didn't match his shirt.

"Allow me." He scanned his own and held the door for them.

"Thank you so much," they said in unison, filing past in their robes, clinging to the canvas totes that held the clothes they'd just changed out of in the lobby's restroom.

Sela walked the open-air deck as if she'd been there before, perusing the trio of hot tubs at one end of the roof, the push-button firepits rimmed by cushioned chairs at the other. A group of laughing, splashing teenagers had filled one of the spas, so she headed for the open circle farthest from them and dropped her bag onto a chair. Turning, she saw through the glass that the employee had walked on, and exhaled a laugh.

"That was a first," she admitted.

"I was worried he'd offer to call the front desk for you! 'What room, ma'am?' 'Oh, whoops, turns out we're at the Marriott down the street.'" Caroline stood hands on hips, taking a moment to admire the high glass walls rimming the deck, the fringe silhouette of the Smoky Mountains, and the cotton-candy sunset beyond. "This is worth the anxiety attack."

Sela helped herself to a stack of towels from the courtesy rack and offered two to Caroline. "Tell me again why you don't use the amenities at your own hotel?"

"When I'm running a show, almost everyone staying there is attending, or exhibiting—I feel strange about them seeing me in a swimsuit."

"No one expects you to be in the hot tub in a pantsuit."

"No one expects me to be in the hot tub."

"You stay for free at all these hotels, and never take advantage?"

"I know, I know. I'm doing it wrong." Something about the way she said it made Sela think she wasn't referring just to hotels, but

Sela laughed anyway, amused that her sister's objection on professional grounds did not extend to their current antics a block away.

Caroline dipped a toe in the water. "Ever check with your doctor about using these?"

"As long as I don't stay in long enough to get dehydrated, I'm good."

"What about a tiny toast?" Caroline pulled a split of champagne and two plastic cups from her bag, eyebrows raised. "No pressure. . . ."

"As long as you don't mind me nursing the same cup forever."

"I will too. That's why I got the little bottle."

Sela eased into the water, savoring the rush of warmth as her sister poured. Much as she'd enjoyed the facade when Caroline didn't know she was sick, needy, weak, maybe she'd been wrong to think pretending was easier. In the weeks of silence between them, mutual understanding had somehow bloomed where tension might have been.

"To new beginnings," Caroline said, flipping the wall timer for the jets and passing over a cup. As she settled in opposite Sela, the teenagers made their raucous, wet exit across the tile and headed for the gas fires flicking through tabletop stones, leaving them alone.

Sela breathed in the chlorinated steam, the quickly darkening sky, the open face of the increasingly familiar woman sitting before her. Was a new beginning really warranted, if everything that happened so far had gotten them here?

"To half sisters," she said instead. The bubbles roared to life around them, drowning out the hollow sound of her plastic cup tapping Caroline's.

"This reminds me of a place Walt took me once." Caroline tipped her head back, closed her eyes. She'd been working all day, setting up what turned out to be a cast-iron convention. Who knew such a thing existed? Sela had arrived a couple of hours ago and occupied herself—carrying her things into the suite, retrieving bedding for the pullout in the living room, while Caroline finished up something to do with an auction. When they were finally face-to-face, it was dinnertime, but neither of them had been hungry. And thus, this: an escapade of sorts, a reprieve. A chance to talk at last. To choose what to address and what was best avoided.

Safe territory still felt . . . well, safest.

"Here in the Smokies?"

"Back home, actually. It was a few months after Lucy was born—Riley had this run of ear infections, and between that and a newborn feeding schedule . . ." Her voice began to sound far away, back there in her mind.

"Oh, that stage," Sela said, right there with her. "You don't know if you're drowning in love or exhaustion."

"That's it. I wouldn't've taken a break, but he arranged the whole thing. I had the nerve to be mad at first." She laughed haltingly. "But he knew what I needed before I did."

"I love a solid good-husband story," Sela said. She felt oddly relieved, hearing that Caroline's marriage had moments like those. That Hannah hadn't chased away something irretrievable with Keaton after all. "People seem to think the opposite, that they should hold back around we divorced cynics. But I don't want to believe that kind of love doesn't last."

"If Walt had romance in mind, he didn't get it. We did spend hours on a gorgeous penthouse pool deck, minus this mountain view. But the only thing we did in bed was sleep. And eat room service at all hours."

"Sounds like romance to me."

Caroline pursed her lips. "Maybe it was." She gestured around them mischievously. "I take it you and Doug were more of the sneaking into hotels type?"

"Hey, North Carolina mountains have a tourist season, and

any self-respecting broke college student learns the loopholes. I could get you into a canoe on a private lake, no problem, and a continental breakfast after." Her laugh faded. "It was always me egging him on, though, not the other way around."

He'd liked it, back then, being led into eclectic adventure. She could pinpoint the moment he stopped finding her charming: in the NICU, when she'd dared fantasize aloud about busting Brody out of there. She only wanted her baby boy to see the sky, feel the sun. Inhale unfiltered air. Weeks in, the life he'd known wasn't much of a life at all, and it chipped away at her soul. Of course she knew he had to stay there, but Doug took her too literally.

Once he started, he never stopped.

"I'm drawn to instigators—my best friend Mo is a big one too. I think they're intuitive," Caroline said amicably. "No shame in being the one who knows what the other person needs."

Sela wasn't sure anyone had ever given her so much benefit of the doubt, and was fairly certain she did not deserve it. But it moved her all the same.

Across the galley, the teenagers started chanting some nickname or inside joke. "Hop-per Twins! Hop-per Twins!" Sela counted three girls and five boys, ranging from upperclassmen to innocents barely old enough to be included, and two of the girls jumped to their feet, on demand, and scrunched up their faces in an indecipherable impression of someone. They were not twins but did look like sisters a couple of years apart. Not just their matching braids, or their thick-framed cat eyeglasses, but the way they draped their arms around each other and moved as if they shared a brain. The boys howled.

Caroline kept her back to them, unfazed by the commotion. She was on about the trade show now, briefing Sela on tomorrow's schedule, the kind of small talk you might expect. But Sela couldn't stop watching the teens joshing and jostling each other. Two men walked in, and more cheers went up—"Dad!" "Uncle

Hank!" Ah, so this was a gaggle of siblings and cousins. Here for a wedding, maybe, or reunion.

What had Caroline been like at thirteen? Sixteen? Nineteen? Had she, like Sela, sung along with the Cranberries at top volume in her room? Stacked rows of woven friendship bracelets thick on her wrists? Harbored a weakness for gas station slushies? Filled hot pink cases with bolder makeup than she'd ever dare use? Made her locker a shrine to Keanu Reeves? Been "just friends" with her prom date? Wished to grow up faster so she could be more independent than her mother wanted to let her be?

Maybe this stage of adulthood was too late to acquire that kind of intimacy with a person's past, to compare inconsequential notes, to bother constructing a timeline. It was more practical to accept that some things can't be reclaimed. To start from now and move forward.

But Sela wanted to know, all of it and more. She wanted to know if she and Caroline would have been sitting like the sisters she was watching now, closer than necessary, shoulders touching. Or if they'd have been more like these boys, slapping each other on the back with an arm's length between them. Maybe she didn't need to know, maybe she even couldn't. But she wanted to.

So when Caroline volleyed the small talk back, Sela set it aside. And instead, she began to ask.

27

Caroline

Caroline had blended business and pleasure plenty of times before. She'd invited Walt along to the more appealing locales, left him to sightsee, and tried not to envy his recaps when they finally met for a late dinner. She'd switched her room to a double so Mo could have a night off from being "step-monster" and save her self-care budget for the spa. She was happy to do it, even if she did find herself looking too longingly at her companions' free hours, more distracted and less content than she would've been left to her own devices.

This night, though, was a first. Their downtime was not the pause before the separate, purposeful days awaiting them both in the morning. It was the whole reason Sela was here, and the whole reason Caroline invited her, though they had no script to follow, no checklist or plan. They'd exchanged a few texts beforehand to confirm specifics—where, when—but didn't get into how or why. That part went without saying and left so much open to interpretation at the same time. She decided going in to follow Sela's lead.

Caroline had watched a documentary not long ago, about triplets separated at birth as part of what turned out to be an ethically dubious psychological study. When the men located each other during college, they became a media sensation, doing interview after interview about how all three, miraculously, smoked the same brand of cigarettes, dated the same type of women, even had the same youthful troublemaking streak. The movie caused a stir, and Caroline got the feeling Sela had watched it, too, from the things she asked. But maybe these questions were just the low-hanging fruit now that their weightier first meeting was out of the way. Human nature was to find common ground. The triplets had latched on to those similarities, too, stabilizing their bond off-screen when the circus faded.

Then again, so had their families, as innocently baffled by the whole circumstance as their children had been. That had been a commonality, too: having someone external to blame.

Sela and Caroline talked their way from the hot tubs to the firepits and back, until their growling stomachs called them away. At the least touristy pub they could find, they sat at a high-top and ordered salads and waters, Caroline matching her sister's order without comment. Later, Sela laughed so hard she fell off her stool—stone-cold sober. On the walk back, they took off their shoes, climbed into a fountain, and took selfies with the centerpiece: a bear wearing a hat. At a wishing well, they collected coins from the crumb-lined bottoms of their purses and threw in every last one. In the tackiest of a string of tacky gift shops, they bought matching flannel pajama pants dotted with cartoonish waterfalls and pine trees.

But the real magic of the night was not in the movie montage, the photo booth strip feeling of it all, the nostalgic carousel ride of emotions and memories and mirrors. It was in realizing that everything else had fallen away. Not just the mental checklist for tomorrow's show but the confusing dynamics of the months before. The scares and reveals that rocked Caroline's reality, and the lonely hardships that made up Sela's, and the daily go-go-go that persisted through it all. The lot of it didn't merely fade: It vanished.

For those short, long hours, the world consisted of two sisters. They might have been anywhere, doing anything. What mattered was that they were together.

28

Sela

When was the last time she'd made a new friend? Not an acquaintance, but a real friend. The kind you'd tell embarrassing things to, text when something reminded you of her, send a card just because. Leave with a smile that stayed on your face for hours, days.

The kind you feel like you've known for years.

No, that wasn't quite it.

The kind you *wish* you'd known for years.

Long after Caroline said good night and closed the bedroom door, Sela lay awake, curled on the pullout couch, listening to the start and stop of the air temperature control and trying to sustain the simple giddiness of the night's good mood. If only she could help but think of how life might have been different if she'd known Caroline all along. If their mothers had worked things out, clued their father in, or if Caroline had landed the job in Brevard and crossed Sela's path some unsuspecting way. Even without knowing their connection, they'd have liked each other,

Sela felt sure. How could they not, when they liked each other now in spite of so many inconvenient reasons not to?

If Caroline had been in her life back when she and Doug and Leigh were living it up around town, oblivious to how short-lived those carefree days would be . . .

If Caroline had been in her life when she'd gotten pregnant with Brody . . .

When she'd gotten sick . . .

When she'd given birth, too soon . . .

When she'd lost Doug and Ecca and very nearly Leigh . . .

It was hard to believe Sela would have fared anything but better with a sister at her side.

Where she could have been, if not for Ecca and Hannah.

The more Sela looked back on these fresh hours alone with her sister, the happier she was to have had them. But the angrier she was to have *only just* had them. The ticking clock of her kidneys was already counting their time down; she could feel it in her lower back, burning for attention.

Nothing about this was fair. Not Caroline being better off not knowing the things she did not know, or Ecca no longer being here to explain herself, or Hannah subsequently being off the hook. And definitely not Sela having to hold on to their mothers' secret through the push and pull of her sickness and pain, unable to ignore the intrusion of so many questions closing in, pressing down.

She'd brought along the selenite from Leigh, feeling silly but also sentimental—*it practically has your name in it.* She dangled her arm off the mattress now and slid it inside the suitcase open on the floor, feeling between the folded clothes until the crystal's cool surface was in her grasp.

It focuses positive energy, Leigh had said.

Sela squeezed tighter and willed the selenite to strengthen her grip on the good feelings that had prevailed all night. To convert the resentment she was battling now into resolve.

They still had a whole day left together. Tomorrow, she'd work while Caroline did. She didn't have the energy she'd once have had to drive into these mountains, which were not quite like her own—more exposed, somehow, and scarred in large swaths from fires years ago. She could find a view, though, create something inspired by them, by this. Something showing peaks at a distance and the unexpected beauty hidden in the valleys between them. When she was done for the day, Caroline would be, too. They'd stay up late, maybe even all night.

Wherever they were headed on this visit, they were only halfway there.

At that thought, at last, she drifted off to sleep.

—

Sela became vaguely aware of the shower running, and the fan, and of Caroline shuffling about, getting ready. It was early, but Sela didn't mind. The soundtrack of not being alone.

Nicer still when a knock at the door proved to be a breakfast cart.

Sela struggled to pull herself to sitting—always stiffest in the morning—as she watched her sister tip room service, then wheel in far too many silver domes for one person.

"Morning!" Caroline looked ready for showtime, in a smart navy midi-dress with her hair pulled back. Sela tugged self-consciously at the old T-shirt she'd slept in, though she caught her sister smiling at her bottoms—the ones they'd bought last night. "Peace offering, for waking you so early. I didn't know what you could have, so this is kind of a buffet."

"You didn't have to do that."

"I wanted to. I even have a few minutes to sit down and eat it. Which means it's officially easier to run a trade show than my own household."

Sela laughed and went to freshen up.

But when she returned, Caroline hadn't touched the food. Instead, she sat hunched at their little round table, staring guiltily at her phone. "My kids want a good-morning video call," she said, not looking up, her tone full of apology and something else. Regret? "It's our ritual, when I'm away. I can't believe it hadn't occurred to me. . . ."

"Don't let me stop you." Sela missed Brody, too. *Hear their voice, lay eyes on them, every chance you get,* she might have said earnestly. But it felt like overkill.

"I—I didn't mention you'd be here."

She could almost hear the click of her mind's lens sharpening focus. "Oh."

"I'm sorry if that sounds bad. It's more about them than you. Not the kids, but Walt, my parents. They're not sold on this yet and I . . . didn't have the energy."

Wow. When was the last time anyone had the nerve to complain of energy loss to Sela?

Still, she'd said *yet.*

"Go ahead, I'll keep quiet. Or—would you rather I leave?"

"Stay, of course. I only—you know how it is." Mother to mother. Sela nodded. "It'll only take a minute."

"Take all the time you want."

Sela picked at the fruit while she listened to Caroline chatting with her kids. Or, rather, to the kids talking over each other to fill their mom in.

"Daddy let us take sandwiches for dinner to the playground, and there was a raccoon in the trash can!" Lucy, comically horrified.

"I went to throw our trash away, and I *told* them I saw it in there." Riley, pointed but cool. "They didn't believe me."

"I thought you were joking!"

"Well, if you'd believed me, you wouldn't have opened it again."

"I had to throw my juice box away." This was clearly not the sisters' first go at this exchange.

"It jumped out!" Owen, finally getting a word in, clapping his hands in delight.

"It knocked the whole trash can over." Lucy again, not untraumatized. "I thought it was trying to get me!"

"It was trying to get away." Riley laughed. "But oh my gosh, the trash was the grossest thing I ever smelled in my life."

"It made a big crash!" Owen had clearly not been grossed out at all.

In the excitement, they didn't ask their mom about her own night. Sela was glad she didn't have to actually hear her sister lie, though she couldn't put her finger on why it mattered. So she and Caroline were apparently on a tryst of sorts. It wasn't as if they hadn't been sneaking around last night anyway.

But the *whole other day left* suddenly felt more like *only one day left.* Then what?

When Caroline hung up, they ate in silence for a while. Waiting for the weirdness to fade.

"I don't miss their squabbling," Caroline said finally, good-naturedly. "But they seem to think I do."

"Do you think they realize yet, how lucky they are to have each other?"

"Their parents are two only children who won't let them forget it." Caroline was still half-smiling when she caught herself, fork halfway to her mouth. It clattered to her plate. "Grew up as only children, I mean," she said. "God, Sela, I'm sorry."

"I knew what you meant. That's—well, it's why I asked." She should have chosen a better segue. Any other segue. But the raccoon was out of the trash can, so to speak.

Caroline folded her cloth napkin into progressively smaller triangles, working her way up to something. Or, rather, down to it.

"Do you ever think about whether my mom knew you existed?" she blurted out.

Sela blinked.

"I mean, by all accounts, she and your mom were really close. They'd stayed in touch long-distance before. How could such a good friend fall off the face of the planet and you never hear or even sense where or why?"

"I don't know," Sela mumbled. Not mentioning the emails to Caroline was one thing. But she hadn't prepared to jump over and around them.

"I keep coming back to this. My dad seems able to forgive either way. But it doesn't sit well with me. Because if she did know, and maybe even helped make sure my dad didn't? It's not just him she kept you from. It's me."

It should have been comforting, to hear her own feelings in Caroline's words. But instead, she felt her own anger and wishes and doubts—everything she'd been fighting to suppress since the day she'd booted up Ecca's old desktop—rising up to meet them.

"Does it bother you?" Caroline persisted. She looked so earnest, Sela didn't know whether to hug her or upend the room service cart in her lap. "That there's a chance she knew?"

Did it *bother her*? As if Caroline were the only one perceptive enough to try to connect the dots? As if Sela cared only about the future, even if she might barely have one?

"No chance about it," she snapped. "Hannah knew, all right."

Caroline's face fell, more disappointed than surprised. But then, curiosity took over. "How are you so sure?"

Don't do this, she told herself. *Especially not now.* This was only a quick breakfast—meant to be a treat. Caroline could have easily sneaked out without disturbing her, but instead, she'd ordered for two and stayed. Any minute, she had to dash off, start her workday. And they still had tonight to talk.

Only, they weren't supposed to be talking about this at all.

"Just for the reasons you said."

But Caroline was squinting at her, seeing more than Sela wanted her to.

Seeing her.

"You know something. You saw something?"

"I'm just agreeing with you. Speculating."

"Please." Caroline drew up in her chair. So flat-ironed where Sela was finger-combed, so powdered and polished where Sela was blotchy and rough. All Sela could think was that Caroline was so much more ready to face the world and so much less aware of how unfaceable it could be. "Be straight with me. I need to know that you of all people will be."

Of all people? Why? Why her?

"Especially after the way our last visit ended."

Ah.

But what was that *way,* exactly? With the truth, and the rejection of everything it might lead to? Which one of them had the visit ended worse *for*?

Sela jumped to her feet, tipping her chair backward onto the kitchenette tile with a clatter. Her chest heaved with the effort as she stood looking down at her sister, watching her breathe so much easier.

"I know," she wheezed, "because your mother said so."

29

Caroline

Caroline must have read the printout of the email ten times, start to finish, before she dared lift her eyes to meet Sela's. Sela had folded the bed back into the couch and sat there now, chin on hands, staring into the silence between them.

"You say you didn't plan to tell me about this, and yet you have it with you." Caroline didn't tame the accusation. Her fury was too hot to hold, and the only person in scorching distance was Sela.

I can't even bring myself to type your name, Mom had written, *but here we are.*

"I had to print it. I didn't know if that ancient computer would ever boot up again."

"But you have it with you."

"I didn't know if you might've found the same, or something else . . . if there was a chance that's why you asked me here." The don't-kill-the-messenger approach. It might have worked, had the messenger not been operating independently. "I stuck it in my bag in case you brought it up, not because I planned to."

Caroline didn't want to believe that the email was real, that what it said was true. But she recognized Mom's voice—so sure she was right, so polite in her hostility.

There's never been anything you could do that would help set things right between us. Until now.

As if she were right there whispering the whole thing.

"Is this a copy? Can I keep this?"

Sela nodded, and without hesitation, Caroline crumpled the paper between her fists, slamming it onto the table with a bang. Both women startled at the noise.

"What my mom wanted, your mother made happen. She could have said no!"

You don't want her, or Fred, or least of all me down there any more than I do.

"She wanted to say no. There were other replies she didn't send, asking Hannah to reconsider—but in the end, Ecca felt she owed her."

Stop groveling, for pity's sake, move on, ease your conscience.

"Yeah, for sleeping with my dad!"

Sela looked like a church lady who'd stumbled into Coyote Ugly and couldn't find the exit fast enough. As if she'd never imagined anyone could speak such ill of her precious Ecca.

Mine will be a bit heavier for this, but I guess that's the way it goes.

A bit heavier. A bit. Meanwhile, the weight of what she'd done had nearly crushed Caroline to death.

"You want me to apologize for something she did before I was born?" Sela's words shook, even as the volume grew to match Caroline's. "Something that brought me into this world? Believe me, there are plenty of days I wish she hadn't. If I could take it back for her, I would."

The hard stop had the impact of an openhanded slap or a cold glass of water to the face. The constant replay of her mother's hurtful words came to a halt, and she could see it now: Sela's pain, reflecting her own.

Only worse.

"Don't say that, Sela, God. I'm sorry. I'd never want that." What a horrible thing to even begin to think—had she honestly thought Caroline would imply that? "No one would ever want that. Think of Brody."

Sela smiled sadly. "I'm always thinking of Brody."

Caroline sighed, sounding too much like Mom for her own liking. "You swear you just found this? You didn't know before you first contacted me?"

Sela shook her head. "I didn't know what to look for, until you told me they'd been friends and dropped your mom's name. I'd been home a week before it occurred to me to look."

"Kind of takes a minute to sink in."

"Yeah."

They'd returned to a baseline calm, but it felt desolate now. "Listen, I was just—I never expected this. From them, I mean. I shouldn't have reacted that way. And the worst thing is, I have to go. Like, right now." How in the hell was she supposed to run a trade show in the mental wreckage of this blowup?

"I know you do. I'm sorry this came out this way." Sela sighed heavily, rubbing her temples. "I hate that this keeps happening."

"Me too," Caroline said. "Please, don't go. Tonight, we can talk more when we have the time. I promise to be more rational."

"You have every right to be irrational," Sela said. *Just not at me,* she did not say.

But Caroline should have said it for her. Because when the day finished its torturous crawl—the auctions settled and the exhibits closed and the attendees headed home happy—she returned to find her room quiet, the living room tidied, and Sela's bags gone. Caroline stood there, forcing herself to breathe it in, wondering when was the last time she'd felt so lonely.

She knew exactly when. It was when Keaton had gone. And when she thought too hard about him still.

The table was cleared of their breakfast, and in its place was a strange white crystal of some sort and a handwritten note. Caroline lifted the paper shakily, unsure if she was more afraid of what it wouldn't say or of what it did.

Dear Caroline,

Your family doesn't know I was here, and maybe there's good reason for that. Maybe I shouldn't be. Maybe our mothers were right to keep us apart, even if we're equally right to find it unforgivable. My friends want too much to come of our relationship, and your family wants nothing to come of it, and here we are stuck in between. There's nothing wrong with a game of tug-of-war, but no one wants to be the rope. Eventually, we'd fray.

This stone was a gift from Leigh—it's called selenite, which she said reminded her of me. It's supposed to reset your aura. I'm not sure if it's powerful enough to replace the awful picture I left you with earlier, but the least I can do is try, and hope it works better for you than it has for me. If that's too woo-woo for you, give it to Lucy, tell her it's a unicorn horn. We could all use a little more of the kind of magic we don't question.

Our fun last night meant more to me than you can know. I'm still glad you invited me, even if I can't stay. Even if I'm not sure we should try this again.

I'm sorry.

Sela

Caroline did not sleep. She went back downstairs, let herself into the conference room designated for prep, and boxed up everything left over for the sponsors. The overruns of the programs, the evergreen signage and branded table covers: All of it she sealed and labeled, numbly, methodically. She collected the rest for recycling and completed what she could of the checklist to square with the venue. Her staffers could handle the rest—simple cleanup, odds and ends. At dawn, she intercepted a hungover few in the coffee line, and they perked up at news of the unexpectedly easy morning, even if their expressions did fall somewhere between concerned and confused. It had to be obvious she'd been up all night: She looked down and found she was still wearing her clothes from the day before. Back in her room, she showered hot and fast and changed into jeans and a fitted button-down. When the manager came in for the day, she was waiting to hand over her exhibit hall keys and retrieve the deposit.

For five hours, she wove from one side of the interstate to the next, eyes on the dotted line dividing them: the passing lane, the slow lane. The life she'd have chosen for herself and the one Mom chose for her. She didn't stop, not for traffic or for a rest area.

Not even to knock.

Mom was in the sunroom, with a mug of coffee and a romance novel, of all things.

"That's rich," Caroline said, nodding at the book. Mom jumped.

"You scared me! You could have knocked."

She could have. But they'd never been that kind of family—knock to announce your arrival, maybe, but walk on in.

Then again, she'd never understood what kind of family they'd really been.

Without a word, Caroline flattened the ball of crushed paper she'd been clenching and handed it over. Watched as Mom grew pale.

"Where did you get this?"

"Where do you think I got it?"

"I can explain . . ."

"Seems self-explanatory." Caroline started to pace. After being confined for so long in the car, her legs had ideas of their own. "You knew where Rebecca was all along, and who she was with— who she was raising. Both of you hid it from Dad, and from Sela, and from me. With no regard to what it might cost any of us."

Mom looked horrified. "That isn't true."

"You sabotaged me! When this little scheme with Rebecca wasn't enough to completely ruin my plans, you cornered Keaton and made damn sure he wouldn't take me along. And for what? Pure selfishness. What kind of mother sacrifices her daughter's happiness to protect her own? I would never! *Never!*"

"That wasn't—" Tears came to her eyes. "I didn't—"

"You don't get to explain. It makes no difference why you did this. Only that you did."

Mom got to her feet unsteadily. "You really are your father's daughter, aren't you?"

"I'm not the only one," she snapped. Then, seeing the stricken look on her mother's face: "I used to beg you for a sister. Even when I should've outgrown it. I used to *beg*."

"You saw her again? In Tennessee." She was a sheet of ice, frozen by fear. "So help me, Caroline. Tell me this isn't about the kidney."

"This?" Caroline laughed mirthlessly. "It isn't about the kidney."

"So we can at least agree that's off the table?"

"We didn't even talk about it."

"How can you not? How can you talk about anything but that?"

How *hadn't* they? They'd been afraid. They'd thought they had more time. And Caroline had promised herself not to say or do anything, without Walt's knowing, that she couldn't take back.

Right up until Sela handed over the emails and all bets were off.

"I guess there's more to her than being sick. Or maybe we were too busy trying to figure out why it wasn't enough for you and Rebecca to screw each other over. You had to drag your daughters in."

Mom sucked in a loud breath. "This is not about some ideal of having a sister. This is a person with motives of her own, and I would caution you not to oversimplify."

"I'm not the one simplifying. You didn't raise me to turn my back on someone I had the power to help without even thinking it through, without at least some basic fact-finding. Yet all I've heard from the rest of you is how scary it would be for *you,* how awkward for *you,* how unthinkable for *you.* And, yeah, how risky for me. But not once has anyone acknowledged the other side: that I could *save someone's life.* You're so focused on the implications to me and my family, you haven't even acknowledged the person on the other end. Who, by the way, is my family too. But *I'm* simplifying?"

Mom straightened. "I will not apologize for having your best interests at the front of my mind."

"Like you did when you wrote this email? And when that didn't quite do it, moved on to plan B?" Silence. "I cannot believe you. I cannot believe the cruelest thing that was ever done to me was done by you."

"I didn't mean it as cruel! It did work out in your best interest. Look around you!"

"But it wasn't based on—" Caroline caught herself. Nothing good would come from revealing something she'd regret. "You can't brush off the principle of the thing. For better or worse with Dad, you chose him."

"Are you saying you didn't choose Walt?"

Sometimes she wondered if she'd kept the secret so well out of loyalty to Walt, out of respect to their pact, or out of shame. That someone might rightly say they'd given up on love.

"I'm saying what you did impacted everything that came after.

I'm saying I wouldn't have ever been in the position to choose or not choose Walt if you hadn't interfered."

Mom shook her head. "I hope you're smart enough not to say any of that to him."

"He doesn't need to hear me say it. He knows!"

"You shouldn't be talking to your husband about old loves. Knowing aside, there's a reason it's not done."

"I'm through taking your advice on what is and is not done."

"Caroline—"

"Stay away from me. Do not call me, do not come by. Do not ask to see the kids."

"You can't mean that."

"Would you rather I show these emails to Dad?" Silence. "Give me space. I mean it."

"Until when? When *will* you let me explain?"

Maybe never, Caroline thought. She turned at the doorway.

"When you're ready to discuss my life without telling me how to live it."

30

Sela

"Sela!" She could hear Doug's voice, muffled through the front door, which he'd been pounding on for the better part of a half hour. He'd stop for a while, and she could imagine him circling the perimeter of the house, looking for an unlocked door or window. Then the pounding would resume. Oscar kept running up to her bedside, whimpering, then back down to paw at the door frame. Brody hadn't been feeling well, either, and she'd cranked up the white noise machine in his room to soothe him through a long nap—fortuitously, given this racket.

She should have gotten herself one, too.

Maybe a neighbor would see Doug prowling, fail to recognize him, and call the police. Anything to make him leave her alone.

For days, he and Leigh had lobbied protest after protest. *Maybe if we talked to Caroline . . . Maybe if she came and saw for herself what this is doing to you . . .*

They didn't really know the details, though. It had been

simpler just to tell them that Caroline was not receptive—that this was over. The cover story was no less true.

Sela would not be swayed to reach out to her sister again—for any purpose. The most decisive thing about the visit, now that Sela was home, was what Caroline had left unsaid, alluded to perhaps without even meaning to.

That she found herself feeling lost enough to hide her actions *because* of Sela.

That fear and conflict had driven fissures between not just Caroline and her parents but Walt, maybe even the kids on some subconscious level. Also because of Sela.

That it was poor Brody who endeared Sela to Caroline, more than Sela herself.

The mere mention of his name—*think of Brody*—made her heart sink at how spectacularly she'd botched things. It was bad enough that because Sela had let emotions get the better of her—breaking her self-made promise to keep her mouth shut, squandering her second chance—Caroline would now have to contend with a history of betrayals that no one could undo. That could only cause more hurt, more harm. And for what?

She aimed her thoughts away from Doug's pounding, indulging a little fantasy of rewinding to her first truly good moment with Caroline. The one that might have led to something better, if only her weaknesses hadn't surfaced and ruined it all—once, and then all over again. Caroline across that table they'd shared in a hole-in-the-wall on a faraway afternoon. The smell of French fries and browned butter, the protective arms of the cozy booth, the novelty of acting normal for a few hours she could still kid herself wouldn't make her sick. She floated on the stream of consciousness to other cozy booths for two, back when *normal* hadn't been an act. Ecca's face smiling at her over steaming stacks of silver dollar pancakes, or the summery scent of chicken clubs and iced teas, or the sunset celebration of enchiladas with no beans, extra rice. Always two of the same, she and Ecca. One would order, and the other would say, "Make that two," not even looking at the menu.

She and Caroline had gotten as far as buying those kitschy matching PJ pants, but she'd kid herself to think they symbolized anything other than a shared laugh at a tourist trap's expense. No one was the same as Sela now—no one kept that easy, "make that two" company. Inside her memories, she minded less. She was finally free of the pounding—whether Doug had really stopped or her mind had simply carried her into this padded state of semi-consciousness, she didn't care.

She had to accept that she was too tired to care anymore.

They all did.

But then Doug was there, shaking her shoulder roughly, fearfully. "See!" Through half-open lids, she tried to focus—he stood next to her bed, leaning over her, eyes wide with concern. So blue, tinged with gray. She'd loved them once. She could have loved them still, if only.

"What?" She managed to infuse the word with all the impatience she could muster.

"Jesus, Sela, I had to drive all the way home and get my key. Why didn't you answer?"

She moved her lips, trying them out. Her mouth was so dry. She pulled the blankets tighter around her neck, not to warm her body but to mask it. It was hard to remember what she was even wearing underneath, but whatever it was, she'd had it on for days. "Maybe because I didn't want to see you."

"Well, then you should have taken my calls."

"Or talk to you."

He sank onto the bed, in the empty spot beneath the bend in her knees. This had been his side. She'd switched when he left, though she couldn't say why. "Sela. What did I do to make you shut me out this way? Leigh, too. She's so beside herself, she's texting the dreaded *me*." An attempt to disarm her with levity. Transparent.

"I just want to be alone."

"I'm not sure that's a healthy idea."

She closed her eyes. Would it be overly cruel to remind him he was the one who'd *left* her alone?

It was cruel to *make* her remind him.

"Doug." She peered out again through the narrowest slits she could manage. Her eyelashes cast blurry lines across his face. "I'm dying. How's that for an unhealthy idea?"

He leaned forward and clutched at her hand, clasping the clammy length of it unflinchingly between his warm palms. "So you're on the list. No one is saying you're dying."

"You're just not listening."

"I listen plenty. So you're approaching twenty percent kidney function. You don't even need dialysis until you're down to fifteen. You have time." His eyes traveled the curl of her body beneath the blanket. "You might feel *better* on dialysis? This could actually be the worst of it."

Was there any pleasure to be gleaned in calculating where your rock bottom might be and how far off the mark you fell? She'd let him deal his own way, but he would *not* foist his methods upon her. She pulled her other hand from under the covers and placed it on top of the cocoon he'd made of his own.

"I'm dying," she said evenly. "Slowly, or not so slowly. Until and unless someone intervenes. Even then, what I get is a deadline extension. Don't argue it's better for me not to accept that."

"It's better to accept what might be done about it. To *talk* to Caroline—"

"Stop! With the pushing and the guilt and redemption and everything else!" She hadn't known she had the outburst in her, and a geyser of surprised tears erupted on its heels. She curled tighter, pulling her hands away. But then she felt the shift of Doug hoisting himself higher on the mattress, followed by his arms around her, cradling her, the shush of his breath in her ear.

"Okay," he whispered over and over. "Okay, okay, okay."

This was bad. If he was hugging her this way, it was . . . worse than she'd thought.

"I only want to help," he murmured. "I'm sorry I always say the wrong thing." Though she kept her face buried in the blanket, she nodded her agreement.

"You do." He managed a laugh, but it only made her tears start again.

"It's okay to be scared," he said softly. His cheek was on hers now—close enough to kiss, if she turned—and his was wet, too. "I'm scared *for* you. For all of us."

She curled her fingers around the soft jersey of the sleeve cloaking his forearm. He didn't belong to her anymore, but damn it, he was as close as she'd get to having anything like that again. She shifted closer, into his chest, breathed in that familiar scent of aftershave and lotion, trying not to think about how she must smell. The fibers of his shirt brushed her lips when she tried to whisper *Thank you,* but no sound came. She swallowed hard, trying again.

"You'll take good care of Brody for me, right?"

He jerked back, alarmed, but she held tighter to his sleeve, pleading with her fingers. Doug had wanted to be a dad almost as badly as she'd wanted to be a mom—and the first moment he'd laid eyes on Brody, she'd seen what a natural he was. Sela knew it was insulting, broaching the subject this way—she didn't blame him for recoiling. It wasn't as if they hadn't been over it a million times before. Still. "I need to hear it," she croaked.

He pulled to sitting and wrapped his arms around his knees, looking shaken. He always did lose steam after he stormed out the gate.

"We've been through this about Brody. Please, don't start again. I thought you were past this."

She'd been on the brink of the exhale that came with a little reassurance. She'd even grown grateful for the welfare check, embarrassing as it was to require one. But this . . .

"Past it?" Past her child? Past her illness? Past a future without her in it? How dare he? All the fury she'd been tamping down—not just at Doug but at everything—loaded itself in her throat and fired at her cowering target.

"I'll never be past it!" She scrambled out of the bed, away from him. Her stained T-shirt and stretched-out leggings hung around her, but she felt naked, exposed. "I don't want to leave him. It's not fair that I have to leave him."

She could see in Doug's eyes that he'd detached—a familiar tactic to them both. There would be no more pulling her into his arms, shushing that things would be okay. He looked at her now with a coolness that was foil to the fire of their exchange.

"Then fight," he said flatly. "If we're back on Brody, that's the point, isn't it? Or have you lost sight of that too?"

The question hit her like a slap. Since when had she needed the reminder?

On cue came the faint sound of Brody calling from down the hall, stirring from his nap.

Doug got to his feet. He didn't offer to make her something to eat, or ask if she felt steady enough to shower, or if she needed anything from the store.

He just followed the sound of Brody's voice out of the room. She knew better than to hope he'd come back.

31

Caroline

"Who are you here for?"

One step past the initial phone call, and Caroline couldn't even bide her time in the waiting room without someone asking. You'd think at a medical testing center, the desire for privacy would be implied. Then again, maybe something about her invited the question.

Even Caroline wasn't sure how she'd gotten here. One minute, she'd been facing off with Mom. The next, she'd been trying to figure how in the world she could go home to Walt without him looking at her and knowing, on sight, that whatever usually held her together had come apart. Where to start when she hadn't even told him about seeing Sela again in the first place? How to explain the hurt of learning what Mom had taken from her without hurting him in the process? How to mask her remorse that what she'd told herself was restraint in her approach to Sela—*I'll ask later, or she'll bring it up when she's ready*—now seemed like cold cowardice? She certainly hadn't given Sela the impression that she could not be written off with a note, that Sela's poor health was of grave concern to them both, that all the little signs she'd missed before—how Sela often rested a hand unconsciously in the middle-back realm of her kidneys, how she gazed at the nuclear families in the restaurant with the same overt longing she directed at the menu—had kept Caroline awake in their suite long after she'd shut the bedroom door between them.

There was only one thing she could think of to quiet enough of her mind that she might temporarily pass for her usual self. And before she knew it, she'd been picking up the phone and making the appointment to come.

It was too strong, the lure of putting all these worries to rest with a negative result, though the alternative still terrified her.

It was too clear that she would never stop wondering otherwise.

She turned warily toward the woman who'd spoken across the waiting room. She was perched a few chairs to Caroline's right, lightly graying hair in a bun as tidy as her outfit: tailored blouse, black slacks. She had fifteen or twenty years on Caroline, but her aura projected palpable energy, ready for anything—a pop quiz, a footrace. Caroline glanced around, hoping for someone else to take up the chat, but they were alone save for the receptionist, who paid them no mind behind her sliding window.

"My half sister," she said, averting her eyes, hoping the woman might get the hint that she wasn't eager to swap stories. This was hardly the stuff of casual conversation with strangers.

She couldn't even talk it over with the people who knew her best.

"Understandable," the woman said. She picked up a home decor magazine and started thumbing through. This was what Caroline had wanted—conversation closed—yet the odd response jarred her.

"I'm sorry? Is your situation not—understandable?"

The woman laughed easily. "Freudian slip, I guess." She flopped the magazine closed, unread. "Depends on who you ask."

"How do you mean?"

"Well, you have a connection to the recipient. Should be obvious to people why you'd want to help. Whereas I . . ." She rolled her eyes congenially. "I'm what they label an 'altruistic donor'—you know, for a stranger? You wouldn't believe the backlash I've gotten."

Caroline blinked. "People *say* things to you?"

"Not that I've asked for opinions. It got so bad I've stopped telling people—but it's not like I can hide going away for six, eight weeks to recover. You can stash a pregnant teenager in a convent, but where the hell do you put a fifty-something psychologist?" She laughed again, seemingly unbothered when Caroline didn't join. "Anyway, you're lucky to avoid all that, is all. I should've told people this guy was my brother. I mean, assuming it's been better for you?"

Caroline hesitated. This woman seemed further along in the process. And was a *psychologist.* Maybe Caroline could learn something.

"I'm just here for prelim testing. I'm probably not even a match, so it seemed premature to mention it."

The stranger nodded. "Well, once it gets rolling, it's rolling. Brace yourself."

Caroline slid over a chair, closer, dragging her purse and coat with her. "Why do you think that is?" she asked. "The backlash, I mean."

"As not just the target but a therapist, I sincerely wish I understood. Best I can come up with is that some actions elicit an implied question, or comparison. You know, like, *My friends are all getting married—should I be getting married too?* In this case, if people find themselves wondering what's stopping them from donating, and they don't like the answer? Say, that they could save someone's life if they were a little more selfless or noble or brave or whatever?

They don't like the way that makes them feel about themselves, so it translates into finding fault with me."

Noble. Well, Caroline did know that not everyone would classify donating as such.

"Why *are* you doing it? If you don't mind a more empathetic party asking?"

"Et tu, Brute?"

Caroline cracked a smile. "I'm not judging," she assured her. "I'm hoping it might rub off on me."

"In that case . . ." The woman held out her hand—not a handshake, but more of a wave. "I'm Kay Adams, by the way."

"Nice to meet you." Caroline hesitated, reluctant to give her name. Assuming the test was negative, would she ever tell anyone—other than Sela, of course—that she'd come? Or would she have them all think she'd let the idea go?

"I'm Caroline." Surely last names were not required.

"Well, Caroline, I never married. No kids. And it's not that I haven't found my purpose—the opposite, actually. I love my job to the point of being one of those annoying people who says I'll never retire. What I love most about it is knowing I've helped make a difference for someone—which isn't as often as you'd think, but just often enough to keep me going."

Caroline nodded, as if she could relate. But if anyone were to press her on what she liked best about her own job, her answer would be simply that she was good at it.

"I've treated patients who are chronically ill, and witnessed what a toll that takes on all aspects of well-being. Then I stumbled upon this story about Selena Gomez, of all people, getting a kidney from a friend, and I got to thinking about how less privileged people might not fare so well, and—I don't know. I guess I'm doing this because I can. Nothing is holding me back other than my own self-absorption or fear. And I'm in a position to equip myself with the tools I need to deal with that. So here I am."

She reminded Caroline of Keaton, the way he'd been moved by those patients who didn't share his good prognosis in the rehab hospital. If there'd been something he could have done to help them, would he have? She wished she could ask him.

Caroline wanted to know about Kay's tools and whether they might work for concerned third parties, too. But she couldn't inquire without confessing to being . . . well, self-absorbed and fearful.

Besides. She wouldn't need them. Because she wasn't going to be a match. *That's* what she'd come to confirm.

"I think it's great," she told Kay sincerely. "And bullshit that anyone would tear you down for doing such a good thing."

"I guess it's healthy to have our sense of social justice challenged. Keeps us sharp. But thanks."

"How does it work, giving altruistically? Do you have a say in who gets your kidney?"

Kay nodded. "There are a few ways. Some people handpick recipients—there are even websites for it, almost like online dating. But I chose the chain."

She was looking at Caroline as if she should know what this meant, but Caroline stared at her blankly. "Basically it goes to the top person on the wait list who you match and who has a willing but incompatible donor," she explained. "Have you heard of donor swap?"

Caroline shook her head.

"They'll tell you about it today. The gist is, say someone is willing to donate to a friend or family member—like you are—but isn't a match." *Like you are.* Caroline couldn't even hear the words without recoiling.

I'm not, really. I just feel so guilty.

"If that happens," Kay went on, "you can sign up for donor swap, which means you'd be willing to donate to someone else if *they* have a willing friend or family member who doesn't match them but matches *your* intended recipient. It's complicated, but when you start the process with an altruistic donor, instead of an even, crisscross swap it can set off a chain effect where it pairs off a bunch of other zigzag swaps down the list. I heard about one donor who spurred *fifteen* transplants." She grinned. "Matching donors and recipients is no small feat, so I find it amazing they can orchestrate all that."

"Shouldn't every donor choose the chain, then?"

"People argue that. But, others say it's your kidney, so you should get to decide who receives it. Like, you might rather give to a ten-year-old than a forty-year-old. That's valid too."

Caroline had to admit she'd find it harder to decline to help if Sela were a child. Becoming a mother had reprogrammed her that way.

"It didn't bother you, though? Not to have any say?"

Kay shrugged. "I wanted a little say. Most important to me was to give to someone who has good odds of their quality of life improving—who isn't too far gone to return to a healthy lifestyle. This pick from the list takes that into account. Sometimes people actually get taken off if they've been waiting too long, because the toll on the rest of their body has been too great."

Caroline nodded along, but her mind was drifting. She'd already known, of course, that she needed to know more about Sela's situation but was beginning to realize all the reasons why.

But oh, that reprogramming. A child was caught in the crosshairs of Sela's disease. It was impossible to hear Kay talk so earnestly about wanting to make a real difference for someone, and about chain reactions, and all the rest, and not think that whoever helped Sela would undoubtedly help Brody, too. It came at a price, a sacrifice, but still.

The least someone could do was try.

The door to the exam rooms opened, and a nurse called Kay's name. Caroline watched the woman leap to her feet—no deep breath to steel herself, no furtive glance at the exit. Her ready energy didn't waver.

"Good luck," Caroline told her. "And I hope you don't stop telling people. For every naysayer, you might inspire someone."

Kay smiled. "Good luck to you too. And your sister." She turned to follow the nurse, then paused to shoot one more look at Caroline over her shoulder. "And hey, if you're not a match, you could always sign up for donor swap. You never know."

The door caught behind her in the frame, stopping just short of latching closed.

32

Sela

Tot Time at the Asheville Art Museum lived up to the promise on the signs: *Mixed-Up & Messy!* The kid-parent pairs had been turned loose in the permanent collection rooms to seek out the shapes they'd just finished painting in the activities corner, and many of the tots sported paint-smeared clothes and fingers. A few sucked applesauce from packets as their mothers pretended not to see the NO EATING OR DRINKING notices, more willing to beg forgiveness than to risk a hangry meltdown.

As the littles ran in an excited clump for the more obvious contemporary choices—there, three circles on a gridded background; there, a pattern of trapezoids floating in a hypnotic black sea—Sela came to a stop before one of her own favorites, George C. Aid's etching of *Carcassonne.* The early-1900s work showed the French medieval fortress in hard lines and deep shadows, and she knew Brody could easily spot the triangles of the turrets, the square openings in the stone walls, the tall rectangular towers.

Ecca had showed her you didn't need to dumb down art for

children, didn't require special programming to take them to a museum. The important thing was to take them at all. But if you showed up on a weekday morning to almost any remotely educational place, chances were you'd stumble into events catering to the stay-at-home parent—or, in her case, the work-from-home-on-a-flexible-schedule parent. So it had been today: She'd arrived expecting a quiet gallery and instead found the program getting off to a boisterous start.

Brody would love this, she'd thought.

But Doug had taken Brody, along with Oscar.

Sela had had to agree that she could use a few days to pull herself together.

Now, though, being here without her son felt wrong.

Her impetus for coming had nothing—and yet everything—to do with Brody. She'd lost her spark, Ivy had said. Well, Sela knew how to get that back. In this, one of her favorite exhibits away from Brevard and its memory-laden galleries, she was nothing if not flammable. Ideas flickered at her everywhere she looked. But so, too, did the children.

Outings like this required energy, and hers was in such short supply that she'd selectively forgotten that whether she possessed said energy was irrelevant. She had to summon it and come anyway, for Brody's sake as well as her own. Doug was right to remind her of that. Of the fact that her own mother had believed the necessary *push-push-push* of Brody would be good for Sela, even if Doug had not been so sure.

That's the point, isn't it? he'd said. *Or have you lost sight of that too?*

Ecca had never worried the way the others had about whether Sela, in her state, could handle motherhood. Ecca had never insulted Sela by wishing Brody away.

Sela used to call Ecca from galleries when something struck her. She missed having her mother's voice a speed dial away. Missed how Ecca always answered by saying Sela's name in a way that made *hello* seem euphoric. "I'm in Asheville," Sela would whisper into the phone. "Stopped in my tracks by—" And then she'd name the work and artist.

"Ooh," would come the breathy response. "Describe it for me." Their game. Sending a picture was cheating.

Sela had called about *Carcassonne,* in fact, the first time she'd seen it. "It's like a fairy tale that hasn't figured out its moral yet," she'd said. "Sepia, waiting for color that won't come."

Ecca had hummed with approval. "I *see* it."

"What are you working on?" Sela had suddenly needed to picture that, too.

"It's . . . what it might look like if the sun could rise and set at the same time."

Her mother's descriptions were always better.

When Brody was born, then whisked away with Doug to the NICU, her mother had grasped her hand and leaned close to Sela's ear while the doctors worked to stanch the bleeding between her legs.

"Stopped in your tracks by Brody," she'd whispered. "Describe him for me."

Sela had caught only a glimpse of the infant, but it had been enough. "The biggest dream," she'd said, "in the tiniest body I've ever seen." And she'd burst into tears.

"Child of your heart," her mother had amended later, resting her unmoving eyes on Brody. "Fighting to give you both the future you deserve."

Ecca had been her only real comfort then. Sela never managed to outgrow that: When something wondrous happened, wanting her mother. When something terrible happened, wanting her mother.

Maybe, if Sela stared at *Carcassonne* long enough now, its moral would find her at last. It still felt right to have come here, wrong as it seemed to be doing it alone.

If you didn't get out in the world, you could forget what a beautiful place it was. Filled with stained-glass windows, and arched doorways, and open arm staircases, and high, curved balconies. With the expansive sound of live music on an outdoor stage. With those big, boisterous families who resemble one another so strongly you know at a glance they're a clan. With wafts of sugar, even now, from the creamery next door, smelling of a special treat, a reward, a smile.

Those things might have been beyond her reach just now—forbidden, even. But if such impossible everyday beauty existed, surely there was more to keep her fire lit for. If the ordinary could in fact be extraordinary, maybe she *could* find the only thing she truly wanted that she had even a slim chance of conjuring: the right actions or words or feelings to draw her sister closer and set her free at the same time. And the strength to embody a paradox of her own: opening herself to one possibility while resigning herself to another outcome beyond her control.

Sela couldn't be half a sister to Caroline any more than Sela could have ever been half a mother to Brody or half a daughter to Ecca. The fact that she *could* be half a wife to Doug was the reason she no longer was. If this second meeting taught her anything, it was that Caroline was the same way—all or nothing, and clearly uncomfortable stuck in the middle. With her parents, with Keaton and Walt, and with her.

No matter that when it came to Sela, her father chose *nothing*. Just as well, unfair as it was that he had *all* in ways Sela never would: a spouse who loved him enough, for better or worse, to go to great lengths to keep him, and stood by him even now; a daughter, son-in-law, grandchildren. He might have suffered a heart attack, but he had people taking care of his heart.

Well, Sela could take care of her own.

She might not have the energy, but she had the firepower to dream up a thousand better ways to live, to reach out and make one of them true. To imagine taking Brody's little hand in hers and stepping with him inside the frame of this etching, up those weathered stairs, into the formidable fortress, and up the highest tower, where they could admire the hilltop view of the whole walled city of Carcassonne, the mountainous haze in the distance, the tiers of green below.

So far away, foreign. Yet not so different after all, once inside, from their Blue Ridge mountain home.

33

Caroline

The suitcase thudded stair to stair as Caroline made her way down sideways, pulling it awkwardly behind her. The bag should've been small enough to lift, but she'd gotten carried away. How to guess what relics of their unshared past Sela might want to see—photo albums, yearbooks, wedding pictures, the last shots she'd taken of their grandparents before they died? She'd given up and packed them all. Choosing a hostess gift was no easier. If Sela was like most KDC patients, she lived with a dizzying array of inconveniences, worries, and pains. Meanwhile, Caroline might as well have dipped the woman's poor kidneys in a deep fryer on that first visit. After an hour of browsing the farmers market, she wound up with an assortment of hand-poured candles, though she worried they didn't reflect the thought that had gone into them.

It seemed important to bring some kind of comfort now, a sensitivity or peace offering.

Especially since she hadn't exactly been invited. Crystal clearly uninvited, in fact.

"Caro?" Maureen threw open the front door as Caroline reached the foyer, just missing knocking her backward. "Shit! Sorry."

Caroline shook her head. "To think I wondered why you hadn't texted me back yet."

"Are you kidding? I came as soon as I heard. How long do we have till Walt gets home?"

"Twenty minutes, maybe?"

"And you're already packed."

Mo shut the door behind her as Caroline rolled her bag against the wall.

"I didn't want to lose my nerve." Caroline sank onto the bottom step, and after an uncharacteristic moment of hesitation, Mo joined her.

"Catch me up all the way. You did get through when you called Sela earlier?"

"The call got through. Not so much me."

"I'm sure you caught her off guard."

"She was pretty firm about not wanting to even discuss it. I—it's my fault. Every time we meet, it starts off well and then ends in disaster. Largely due to me reacting poorly."

"In your defense, there's been a lot to react *to*."

"Yeah, well." Caroline sighed. "I get that she doesn't want to talk to me right now. But I *have* to talk to her. I need to better understand where she is with this and what her life is like and how she feels about the future before I can decide what I might be open to. I have so many questions I don't even know where to start, but I need to start. I'll drive myself crazy otherwise."

"But you're not going without filling in Walt? On everything? Promise."

"Promise. His mom's shuttling the kids to their after-school stuff now, then treating them to dinner—we have all evening to hash it out."

Caroline wouldn't hit the road until morning. But one way or another, she would hit the road.

"And what does he think he's coming home to?"

"An ordinary day."

Maureen put an arm around her. "Can't remember the last time you had one of those."

"Well, some of that is my own fault too. Sela isn't the only thing I've handled poorly." There were few things Caroline hated more than breaking promises to herself. Especially ones she shouldn't have made in the first place.

"Repeat after me: *I am doing the best I can with the information I have available at the time.*"

She shook her head. "I'm not. Either I'm torturing myself with information I didn't have available at the time, or I'm proving myself just as bad by racking up my own list of secrets."

"Walt is going to understand."

"He's going to be mad."

"Doesn't mean he won't understand."

They sat quietly for a few moments, lost in thought.

"While I'm coming clean, do you think there's any point in talking to Keaton too? Not about this, but how Mom cost me the job?"

"Definitely not."

Caroline knew she was right. Still. "I have this irrational urge to set the record straight. All along, the story has been that I couldn't lock down my opportunity, my end of our bargain, and then things fell apart. But I never actually failed at that, you know? Is it wrong to want him to think better of me?"

"He doesn't hold any of that against you. If anything he blames himself."

"Isn't that all the more reason to tell him?"

"I think it's better for you both if you don't. He just wants you to be happy."

Caroline narrowed her eyes, realizing.

"How do you know who he blames? What he wants?"

Mo looked away, but not fast enough.

"Oh my God. You've been talking to Keat? Behind my back?"

"Hey, don't put it that way. Did you honestly think he was going to watch you run off to a family emergency and never follow up to see if everything was okay?"

Caroline faltered. That was exactly what she'd thought.

"I think he figured it'd be easier for all parties if he checked in through me. He still cares about you, more than he'd ever say out loud. But you have a lot to deal with right now, and he doesn't know the half of it." Mo squeezed her shoulder. "And neither does your husband."

"Neither does your husband what?"

They both startled toward the voice. Walt stood in the kitchen doorway; they hadn't heard him come in through the garage. Caroline saw his playful smile fall, his color drain. But he wasn't looking at her—only past her.

At the suitcase.

At the edge of the kitchen, Caroline and Walt sat together, alone, as they had the night this whole mess started. The night they perched on these same stools with the laptop and these same full wineglasses and puzzled out the beginnings of a truth that would make too many things ring false.

"Feeling like you had to sneak around to see her is one thing. I admit I might have made you feel . . ." He shook his head. "But to come home, get tested, and keep that from me too?"

The words themselves were angry, but the man behind them seemed too shocked to be properly mad. He'd listened in subdued silence while she laid down the weight she'd been carrying ever since the rainy night at soccer practice when she'd made the first phone call to the toll-free number. The rabbit hole internet research. The sisterly meet-up on the sly, and the unthinkable email exchange Sela had found. The falling-out with Mom afterward, the visit to the testing center, the talk with the altruistic Dr. Kay Adams while waiting there. The nagging conscience that refused to let her be.

The test results marking her as a tissue match.

"All I did was ask some questions and have blood drawn. I never set out to head down any kind of path without you." The idea was hard for even Caroline to believe, now that she'd cataloged all her transgressions at once.

"But you did. And I think it's worth questioning why. Are you trying to do right by Sela, or are you trying to spite your mom? Because I have to say, it feels a little like you're spiting me in the crossfire."

Beneath her, her knees actually jerked. "Has it occurred to you that you wouldn't be anywhere near this crossfire if not for what Mom did?"

"How could it not? Has it occurred to *you* that you might not have snowballed like this if Keaton weren't involved?"

"I only saw him the once. Which you knew about at the time."

"I'm not talking about seeing him. I'm talking about the idea of him. We promised to be honest with each other, Caroline. It was our deal."

He looked so sad, she had to fight the urge to cry. She had done this. She wasn't the only one who could no longer keep Keat and Sela in separate camps. And for what? *You shouldn't be talking to your husband about old loves,* Mom had warned. *There's a reason it's not done.* Caroline had shrugged it off with her usual ready excuse that she and Walt were different, and Hannah was certainly not one to talk. But why had it stayed with her, if not because it rang true?

"And I wouldn't be holding up my end," he continued, "if I

didn't point out that every time you take a step toward Sela, there's something emotionally charged with your parents to step away *from*. Your dad's heart attack. Your mom's double cross."

It was a fair point. Fairer, perhaps, before she'd gotten those test results. She'd moved beyond spite, but Walt was still catching up.

"When in the last couple months has there *not* been drama with my parents?" she challenged. "Here's what I know: Until now, the closest thing I've had to a sister is Mo. She rushed over here today because she knows she's the only one here willing to acknowledge what being a sister means." But as she said it, she realized maybe Mo was not the only one. Mom and even Rebecca had put enough stock in the power of sisterhood to keep it from her and Sela both, long before things got this far. "If you can't buy into that, can you at least give me the benefit of the doubt? Trust that I know my heart and will do the right thing?"

"Can you do the same for me?" He covered her hands with his. "I need to know this isn't about anything other than you and Sela. I saw that suitcase and I thought . . ."

He didn't need to spell out his fear. She'd read it: in the way he'd eyed her, horror-struck, and made no move to intervene when Mo made her quick exit. Shame burned beneath her skin, but she didn't want to think about what it meant that she'd so easily rattled him in a way that would have been unthinkable mere months ago.

She turned her hands upward, into his grasp. "I swear, this isn't about anything other than me and Sela. If it ever was, it's not anymore."

She watched as he rolled it out of the way—the doubts he'd held, the harsh words they'd exchanged. His relief was unmistakable, but brief. "Now you're in this, though. You're *in it*." He looked more panicked than she'd felt in her lowest moments, and she might have wondered what she'd done to deserve someone who cared so deeply, had she not already damaged that bond.

"Not irreversibly. The testing center assured me that even if I move ahead, I can stop the process anytime, for any reason. All Sela will be told is that I'm 'medically ineligible.'"

"That's their policy. But can you honestly say it's yours? You'd be able to do that when this is already eating at you enough to do—what you've done?"

She couldn't pretend he didn't have her there.

"All I wanted was for them to clear me. You wanted me to stop considering it. I thought if they ruled me out, I could. I didn't count on this. But now that I'm here, the only thing I can think to do is go to her. Talk to Sela, see how I feel. Without the pressure of what everyone back home thinks."

She hadn't realized how badly she needed him to understand this until she said it aloud. He spun his wineglass on the counter, the rotations as slow and careful as his words. "Don't leave me back home, then. I want to go with you."

She thought of everything she'd already piled into her bag. Memories, offerings. It was already so heavy.

"Walt, Sela is self-conscious as it is. Like I told you, I haven't convinced her it's a good idea for *me* to come. And the way you two left things—"

"I'll apologize. And I'll do better this time. Now that I'm . . ." He searched the air for words. "Prepared."

She pictured the trip anew: Walt at her side as she rang Sela's bell, made excuses for showing up unannounced, explained herself, waved hello to Brody at last. Walt following her in as Sela held open the door, reluctant but also—would she be?—secretly glad. Walt sitting between them as they did their best to pick up where they'd left off before things went awry, working their way up to the matter at hand. She shook her head.

A text dinged into her phone, on the granite in front of her. Maureen:

Feeling icky after running out that way. Thinking: Want me to come along?*

Caroline flipped the phone over, screen down, even as it pinged again.

"Look," Walt said. "I'm sorry I didn't hear you on this before. I was upset with your parents for wishing this away, and I see now that I went and did the same thing. But if you're really going to pursue this?" He leaned closer, forcing her to turn her full attention to his face. "I don't want to get details this important secondhand. If there's even a chance you're going to do this, I'm going to be a part of it. We might as well start now. My folks can watch the kids."

"I don't know if there *is* a chance—"

"Your suitcase is packed." He was only being matter-of-fact, but her eyes fell, chagrined, to their entwined limbs. "You've come this far alone. But you don't have to be. I don't want you to be."

She'd missed the warmth of this feeling: she and Walt, together, no matter the chaos around them. The crazier their lives got, three kids in, the nicer it was to have him as her port in the storm. Even if they hadn't been shuttered against these particular winds.

She flipped the phone faceup, to the new message from Maureen:

*I know what you're thinking. But just because I don't have morals doesn't mean I can't offer moral support.

Hiding a grin, she tapped out a reply.

Thank you, love you, but I'm covered.*
*Walt is coming too.

34

Sela

Caroline had protested. "But Sela . . ." Then: the kind of long, weighty pause of disbelief that came in arguing a point that wasn't yours to make. *Of course you should want me to come,* it said. *In fact, why aren't you* begging *me to come?*

"I wasn't going to tell you like this, damn it." Caroline's long intake of breath was clear across the line. The exhale of words came all in a rush. "I'm a match. I mean, initially. We'd need more tests to really know. Before I consent to that, though, I need to—just let me—"

Sela didn't hear anything after that.

Her own certainty was louder.

Knowing what she did now, feeling as she did now . . . Caroline had to stay away. Face-to-face, Sela might not find the strength to say no.

Even as Caroline saw for herself all the reasons Sela was unworthy of yes.

35

Caroline

"That must be it." Walt slowed the car as Caroline leaned across him, checking the number.

Their GPS had led them to exactly the kind of house she'd pictured Sela in: big enough for a small family, but only just; unique enough for a creative soul, but not showily so. The roof sloped at artful angles, like a curtain pulling aside to reveal a swath of gray blue mountains in the distance. They pulled to a stop at the curb opposite the single-car driveway, which was occupied by a shiny blue SUV.

"Have you thought about how to do this?" he asked, turning to her. "What to say?"

Caroline wanted to laugh. Fine time to ask. As they'd passed the hours through Kentucky and across Tennessee, they'd kept mostly quiet. It was the kind of windy day that comes along at some unwelcome point late every autumn and wipes the trees clean, stripping the colorful canopy to reveal the skeletal trellis of branches beneath. There was something entrancing about the dried leaves swirling across the highway, and they watched them in pseudo-companionable silence, occasionally breaking it to wonder aloud how many more exits until the next decent coffee or which of Kentucky's advertised historic sites they should someday stop to see.

Caroline supposed she'd been trying to behave as if Sela were expecting them.

Why, she couldn't say. They both knew she was not.

"Better not to overthink it," she said, clicking her seat belt free, and they stepped out onto the pavement, pausing to stretch their legs. As they started across the street, the front door opened—but the woman who emerged was not Sela. The rounder, darker-haired figure slipped out and pulled the knob quickly behind her in the manner of someone trying to contain something wily inside. Sela had that beautiful dog, Caroline remembered, with the curmudgeonly name. Eeyore? The woman looked preoccupied with worry as she started down the walk, hugging a thick, knee-length cardigan around her. Caroline reached for Walt's hand as they stepped aside, waiting for her to pass. But when those dark eyes lifted and registered their presence at last, she didn't walk congenially by—didn't return Caroline's reflexive smile.

Instead, she stopped short and stared.

"Are you . . . Caroline?"

Caroline exchanged a surprised glance with Walt.

"I am." She kept her voice pleasant, with a good-natured twinge of *guilty as charged.* Sela had mentioned a best friend, newly pregnant with her third. *Any advice for her on number three?* she'd asked Caroline. And Caroline had joked, *To schedule her husband's vasectomy as soon as they reach their deductible.*

Her eyes bounced over the woman's soft stomach. Could be her.

"You're here." The woman said this as if it were a miraculous relief. A lost purse recovered. A stalled car starting right up with the turn of a key.

Caroline smiled again, less certainly this time. Walt surveyed the woman with something like suspicion but extended a hand.

"I'm Caroline's husband, Walt." Her handshake was slow, full of wonder, as if he'd introduced himself as Bruce Wayne. "And you are?"

She blinked quickly a few times, coming to. "Sela's best friend," she said. "Leigh." She looked nervously over her shoulder at the house, then back at them. "I recognized you from your picture. Listen, this is going to seem strange, but I'm wondering if I could speak with you. Before she knows you're here?"

"Oh." Caroline tried not to sound put off. "Well, we've driven a long way—"

"What about?" Walt cut in. But Leigh didn't even look at him. She was homed in on Caroline.

"I don't want to seem underhanded. But I'm worried about her, and you might be able to shed some light." Her eyes did flick to Walt's then, only for a second. "Also, there are some things you should probably know."

"Maybe tomorrow we could all talk," Caroline offered. She wouldn't jump to Leigh's word, *underhanded,* but it didn't feel right, talking behind Sela's back. Or, rather, right in front of it. "I'm glad she has you looking out for her," she added, hoping to appease. But Leigh didn't make a move to let them through. It started to seem a little forceful, the way she was blocking their path.

"Ever since that trip to Cincinnati, she's been . . . off. Worse." Leigh's tone wasn't accusatory, but Caroline felt her face flush.

"We didn't know at first, about her diet restrictions, her condition." But as she explained, what Leigh had said sank in. Not that Sela came back worse. That she was still worse. "Is she not okay?"

"Well. I don't know."

Walt's hands went to his hips. Leigh had, after all, come from inside. "Isn't she home?"

"Yes, but she . . ." Leigh let the words trail into a sigh, then started again. "I'm here because I got a call from a nurse, Janie, who's taken Sela under her wing. Or is trying to. She said Sela's stopped coming to her appointments. Stopped answering their calls." Caroline blinked at her. "I'm down as her second emergency contact," Leigh explained. "Janie wasn't too keen on calling Doug." She let a smile escape, and Caroline softened. How easy, how ordinary, to unite against the most common of enemies: the inconsiderate ex.

"Did Janie say what's going on?"

Leigh shook her head. "Privacy laws. But she wanted me to check on Sela, see if I could nudge her. Seemed like she was stepping outside the lines by calling, so I'm guessing she'd have to be pretty concerned to do that."

"You just checked on her, then," Walt prodded. "And?"

"And . . ." Leigh glanced at the house again. "It's clear she's not expecting you."

Caroline felt the embarrassed flush return. "I tried to explain on the phone," she began, but Leigh shook her head.

"I'm *glad* you're here. I've been beside myself trying to figure out . . ." She seemed to catch herself. "Please. I'd *really* like to talk with you before you go in. Would you come with me? Fifteen minutes. That's all I ask."

Walt met Caroline's eyes and nodded, almost imperceptibly. They could hardly not go, at this point. Even if Caroline did feel uncomfortably like a coconspirator.

"Come with you where?" she acquiesced. The concern melted from Leigh's face, replaced by a genuine but fleeting smile. She was already headed past Caroline, to her car.

"Follow me," she commanded. "There's someone you should meet."

Caroline would not have knowingly agreed to this, but it was too late now.

She and Walt sat on a brown leather couch in the bland, unfeeling second-floor walk-up where Sela's bland, unfeeling ex-husband now lived. Actually, he'd just finished explaining they were technically still married, as if this somehow made the situation—ambush was more like it—more acceptable. Caroline disliked Doug with surprising intensity as she watched him pace to the tiny adjoining kitchen and back.

Then again, she already had, sight unseen.

"I'm so glad Leigh ran into you," he said. Caroline cringed at his sincerity. Where had it been when it mattered to Sela? He held out two cans of soda, and numbly she and Walt accepted, though neither of them ever drank the stuff. The apartment bore the sparse look of a divorcé—or an all-but-technically divorcé—avoiding calling an unloved place home. No pictures on the walls. Few signs of life, save for a fleece throw draping the sofa behind them and a half-zipped gym bag discarded on the floor by the door. He carried over two stools from the kitchen and motioned for Leigh to join him in sitting to face the couple. She'd been hanging awkwardly inside the door, an instigator turned oddly reluctant, but she obeyed, not meeting Doug's eyes.

Caroline watched as Leigh scooted her seat farther away, giving him the wider berth of a necessary evil.

"Sela has been increasingly . . . fragile," Leigh began. "Since Cincinnati."

Must they harp on this? Caroline had made it clear she hadn't known. But before she could go on the defensive, Walt cleared his throat. "I'm afraid that might be my fault." He sounded truly sorry, and she dropped a hand onto the knee of his jeans.

"Our fault," she corrected. "But that's why we're here. To make it right."

"It's not your fault." Doug ran a hand through his hair, in the annoying manner of a parent debating how much complexity a child might be able to grasp. "I don't blame you for saying no," he continued. "I just—selfishly—wish you hadn't made up your mind so quickly. This will be a long haul for her, and—"

"I'm sorry?" Caroline interrupted. Walt peered inside his soda can as if he weren't sure what he'd find and took a tentative sip.

"The kidney," Doug said. "I know it's a big ask. I mean, that's what it's *called.* But I think when you said no so outright, it was her last—"

Walt coughed loudly, choking on the carbonation, or the assumption, or maybe both. She was afraid to look at him.

"I did not say no outright," she said carefully.

Leigh bit her lip. "You didn't?"

Caroline shook her head, suddenly unsure. Sela was no mind reader, after all. "We might have given that impression," she admitted. "At first."

"I gave it." Walt bowed his head, and Caroline observed his new, subversive demeanor with detached fascination. Maybe he was overcompensating, overconcerned about getting off on the right foot with Leigh and Doug, but Caroline wasn't feeling so eager to please. Leigh might have meant well, but Doug had left Sela in the midst of this—even their infant son hadn't been enough to keep him home.

"I'm trying to get her to try this again, talk again," Caroline explained, assuming her *I'm not the bad guy here* stance. A stance typically followed by nervous rambling. "About her condition, her options. *Our* options, now that I'm a match. But she's shut down."

"Did you say you're a match?" Doug's mouth had gone slack-jawed, his eyes wide.

She realized too late she'd missed an opportunity to keep this between her and Sela. Leigh and Doug had been under the impression she'd ruled herself out. Which meant Sela probably hadn't wanted them to know. Caroline could only nod, wishing she could take the slipup back.

"Sela *knows*?" Seeing Leigh's equally wide eyes, Caroline registered the pressure drop in the air.

"Only the first blood test, tissue test." Caroline's voice sounded thinner than before, as if she were speaking into an empty auditorium instead of this boxy storage unit of a room. "It's not that significant. The next round is where most people get ruled out."

But Leigh was shaking her head.

"With Sela, nobody has been even close to compatible. At any point."

Caroline's mouth went dry. Sela had told her she was tough to match, but Caroline hadn't realized she'd been referring to round one, to tissue alone and not substance, shape. Did this mean that if they'd gotten this far, they had a better chance of going all the way? She swallowed hard, keenly aware of Walt's silence beside her. "Even so," she said unconvincingly.

"Look," Walt said, shifting on the cushion. "We haven't made a decision about moving ahead. It's clear how much you both care about Sela, and we're happy she has that support, but you have to understand this has come at us really fast. We have young kids, and there might be a family history—we don't want to subject ourselves to judgment here, with all due respect. It's a personal decision. A private decision. But we don't take it lightly." Caroline felt the tension in her body begin to ease. She couldn't, in that moment, have spoken for herself so well. He really had heard her yesterday. "We're here to understand more, and regardless of what happens from here, we're not going to turn our backs on her. Certainly not on her son."

"Her son," Leigh repeated, the words flat. Beyond flat—concave.

Caroline looked to Doug. While she found it impossible not to soften at any mention of her own children, his face seemed incongruously hard. Maybe that was what happened when your child's mother had her life on the line. Even so, maybe it *was* better that he'd left if he couldn't handle this.

"I haven't even met Brody yet," she said, waiting for him to give in, smile, gesture to the room down the hall where his son came to stay and tell her what a sweet kid he was, how every other weekend together was never enough. "But parent to parent, I assure you he is my concern as much as Sela is. He's the reason I would never 'make up my mind so quickly,' as you put it."

Doug closed his eyes, shaking his head. Beside him, Leigh dropped her face into her hands. For a long, bizarre moment, they both stayed that way—stone still. The only sound in the room was the muffled snuffling when Leigh began to cry.

Caroline reached for Walt, and he caught her confusion in his warm hand, wrapping his free arm reassuringly around the small of her back. Complicated as this trip had first seemed by his presence, she was suddenly and overwhelmingly grateful he'd come—enough to blink back tears of her own, to cradle a knot of emotion in her throat.

She might not have sensed what was coming. Not yet.

Only that something was not right.

Something no parent should have to face alone.

When Doug's eyes opened, they held so much pain Caroline faltered. Maybe she had him pegged wrong. Maybe—

"You can't meet Brody," he said, so quietly she had to strain to hear.

She leaned reflexively into Walt, catching his expression

from the corner of her eye. He looked every bit as defensive as she felt. Caroline didn't understand. Sela had tried to keep her away, but Leigh had said she'd been right to come, only then she'd brought her here to be—what? Guilt tripped? Chastised? Sent away?

"Why not?" Her voice came out as a whisper.

"Brody was born much too premature. He didn't survive."

36

Sela

Leigh was probably telling them right now.

Sela could only watch helplessly through the blinds as her friend intercepted Caroline and Walt on the path. What a loop-the-loop of emotions: the spontaneous jolt of involuntary joy at the sight of her sister, the crash of humiliation at remembering why this was *not* a joyful thing, the mounting dread at the slow-motion sight of Leigh blocking their way, turning their heads, leading them off.

As Caroline climbed back into the car, she'd stopped to take a halting look around, and Sela wanted so badly to burst out the front door and down the walk, she could almost feel the cold air on her face, the exhilaration of Caroline turning, smiling.

"What are you doing here?" Sela would call, delighted, arms outstretched for a hug, legs carrying her faster than the reality of her disease would allow.

And Caroline and Walt would forget all about Leigh and follow Sela instead.

It didn't matter anyway, why they'd come.

She knew they wouldn't stay.

Leigh herself hadn't stayed. She'd come back, sure, but only after Ecca was gone and the guilt got to her. Sela and Leigh's falling-out after their pregnancies diverged did not occur in a vacuum. Nor did her subsequent split with Doug. Ecca was the only one to understand any of it. Maybe if Sela had known her mother's days were so numbered, she'd have tried harder with the others.

She held to the belief, though, that she shouldn't have had to.

Then today, Leigh was so confused about why Sela had told Caroline not to come. Sela found it hard to explain—largely because she did want to see her sister, to *be* sisters—and Leigh's familiar frustration flared. All Sela could think to say was *Sorry*.

Such perfectly terrible timing, for Caroline to pull up right then. Walt, too, for added effect. Sela found herself swallowing the sort of inappropriately giddy laugh that swells up inside you at a funeral. Yet equally strong was the urge to smash something. To revel in the forbidden release: set the giggle free, wind back her arm, and let go.

Where had Leigh taken them? How long until Caroline came back? Surely she wouldn't drive this far and then turn and go all the way home? Maybe she would. She'd been steered off course easily enough—a few words exchanged, an agreeable nod.

Caroline and Leigh would hit it off. Wherever they were, no doubt they were already trading stories, filling gaps. Leigh, of course, would think Caroline's was *good* news. But then she'd go and ruin it by telling her own version.

Sela should have been used to this feeling by now. Of being unmoored, caught in the current, at its mercy. Only for Brody—waiting there on the shore, calling for her—had she found the strength to keep swimming. To follow instructions, no matter how counterintuitive: into the riptide, trusting that if she waited out the exhaustion, the relentless pull would at last let her go.

Now, she lifted her head from the tumbling waves and saw nothing but a barren swath of hot, dry sand.

No Brody.

Nothing to stay afloat for.

She let the slats of the blinds fall closed. She'd been standing here since they'd left, icy fingers curled on the windowpane, bracing against collapse. Waiting, she supposed, for what came next. Her best guess was, either Caroline and Walt would be right back, declining to be sidelined by whatever Leigh proposed, or this would take a while. Possibly an indefinite while.

Oscar whined at her feet. She'd been doing her best to ignore the way he was circling them, trying to detect what was so interesting outside. She crossed to the back door and let him out into the yard. His safely fenced happy place. Where he deserved to be.

As the riptide persisted, stronger now than ever, the stairs were the soft ocean floor beneath her bare, swollen feet—chilled through, but even socks felt constraining these days, and just as well. This way she could feel the sand shifting, giving way with every step, each brush against the bottom a reminder that she had tried. She *had* tried. She could stop fooling herself into thinking the ground might become solid enough for her to drop anchor. Its claws would merely drag through the sludge with a uselessness she could no longer bear.

Doug, Leigh, now Caroline—they'd chased Brody away, or lured him, maybe. But could she blame them? It was unfair of her to expect someone so tiny to stay and hold so much weight.

She ran her fingers softly over his closed bedroom door as the undertow pulled her down the hall. The crocheted baby blue *B* Ecca had made still hung from the doorknob, and it swayed at her touch, like a half-hearted wave to someone you've already said good-bye to.

The current carried her past the bathroom, with its dreaded scale and mirrors and reminders of things her body's systems declined to do. Past the bedroom, with the heating blanket and sickly smell and vacant California king that reduced her to a fraction of what she'd been. A half of a couple.

She'd tried to tell them all:

She didn't do things by halves.

In her studio, one last wave deposited her in front of her mother's old nightstand, sturdy and reliable. It had stood by Ecca's side until the end, until the morning Sela had gone looking and found her still in bed, later than she'd ever have slept. Now it sat here at hers, so she wouldn't be alone. Sela had chosen carefully indeed, the things of her mother's she'd held on to. She crouched as low as the fluid in her joints would allow and reached into the corner of the bottom shelf, felt for the hand-carved pillbox Ecca had brought back, as a young twenty-something, from Europe.

"I knew I couldn't linger there forever. I always felt like a visitor, no matter how long I stayed," Ecca had told her. Sela had just that day been diagnosed, and she'd been sitting at the kitchen table of her childhood, hunched over lemon tea, letting the steam work at her tears. "I loved the places I lived there, but none of them felt like home. At the same time, I didn't want to come back—to face my awful parents and all the things I'd felt so eager to escape from. It's a desolate feeling, to want nothing more than to stay *somewhere,* but not be able to think of a single somewhere you'd like to be."

Ecca had placed the box on the table in front of Sela and pried open the hinged lid with a fingernail. "I brought this back with me, in case I never found a place."

Somehow, Sela had instantly known what those three tiny pills were. But her mother explained anyway: a guaranteed fatal dose or your lira back. Painless, quick, and unavailable stateside. Sela had recoiled, unable to comprehend that her mother—so at ease with her art, so in control of her world, so present for the people in her circle—had ever felt *that* lost.

"Did you ever take one?" She'd held her breath.

"There's no point in taking one. It's all three, or none at all."

"What happened then?" she'd asked, sniffing hard.

"I met your father." It was the only time Ecca had ever spoken of him voluntarily.

"And he was—?" Sela couldn't find the words for what she'd wanted to ask. *You loved him, after all? He showed you . . . something new? The value of life?*

Ecca had placed her open hand against the gentle rise of Sela's belly, where her pregnancy had barely begun to show. "Not him. You. He gave me you. A place to be."

Sela had marveled that a single touch could transmit so much love, so much hope. Not just to her but *through* her. She'd had no doubt that in that instant, Brody could feel the beating of her own mother's heart. Three generations of longing.

"This disease is scary and horrible and unfair, especially finding out now." Ecca's words had been somehow both soft and firm, like her touch. "But maybe it's *good* you didn't know before—it will be easier to bear now. Because you already have, right here, the reason you'll never have use for a box like this. Having someone to fight for is no small thing. It's everything."

"Then why," Sela had asked through fresh tears, "do you still have it?"

Ecca hadn't hesitated. "In case you ever needed to know."

The truth of that talk, the memory of that box, the contrast between the woman her mother had once been and the woman Sela knew her to be, all of it sustained her through the early, baffling months of her illness, through the remaining, hopeful months of her pregnancy.

And it haunted her from the day she was admitted to the hospital with preterm pain to the day she came across the box, not long after Ecca's funeral. For an instant, she'd been seized with fear—conjuring anew that horrible picture of Ecca so cold and still in her bed—but no, all three pills remained.

Ecca never would have left the world by choice. Unless, perhaps, Sela had left it first.

Her fingers closed around the wood's complicated surface now, and she slid to the floor, leaning into the heirloom shelves for comfort, bracing for the last tsunami of a wave.

The box was a clamshell in her hands, holding three pearls that were the only thing she could fathom trading her son's life for.

37

Caroline

Doug and I always thought we wanted a big family, but things didn't work out that way.

So many of the things Sela had told her were imprinted on Caroline's mind—as if on some level, she'd intuited all along that there was more to know, deeper to delve.

He reminds me of myself, Sela had written of Brody in one of her early letters. *The way I can tell he's dreaming his stuffed animals to life, bringing them along on his adventures. And of Doug, too, the way he acts like a little man of the house, sometimes even checking on me like I'm his responsibility, instead of the other way around.*

She remembered as clearly their heart-to-heart in person, on the subject of Doug, how things had fallen apart.

I just looked at him and realized we didn't see the world the same way anymore.

Absorbing the despondent look in Doug's eyes now, Caroline grasped the depth to which this was true.

Sela saw the world with Brody in it.

Doug saw it the way it actually was.

A piercing grief seized her, right at her core—for the little boy who had never become a little boy, for the mother who'd so clearly loved her child as fiercely as Caroline loved her own. Caroline hadn't needed to meet Brody for him to be real to her. The realization was like the release of a valve, and the air rushed out of her, taking with it her ability to speak.

But not Walt's.

"Do you mean to tell me," he breathed, "this woman made up a child? Trying to make herself—what, more sympathetic? More worthy of what she wanted Caroline to give?"

His initial rage at Sela, and all the suspicions Caroline had talked him out of, had reset. *What kind of mother,* he'd soon explode, *would use her dead baby for leverage?*

It was too cruel to say and too cruel to be true. Caroline knew it instantly. Sela was not that kind of mother.

She'd spoken of Brody with a love concentrated enough to make your teeth hurt. Helped Caroline's own children through things Caroline herself could not. In one short visit with her nieces and nephew, she'd encouraged their passions, eased their fears. Sela was a good mother. An enamored one.

A heartbroken one.

Leigh lifted her wet face from her hands to lock her steely eyes on Walt's. "*No.* It's not like that."

"She's a liar," Walt shot back.

"Not exactly," Doug said. But he nodded, as if this opinion was understandable.

"Back up," Caroline told Walt, finding her voice at last. "You jumped to this last time—"

"This time it's true."

"Sela isn't a liar," Leigh said. "She's sick. Sicker than you know."

Walt ignored her. "Hell, I'm starting to think last time it was true. She—"

"Please," Leigh cut him off. "This is part of the reason I brought you here. To have this out with us and not with her. Hear us out. Get the full story."

Caroline implored her husband with a look, and he held up his hands in surrender. She took the one that had been holding hers and clutched it between her own. He'd wanted to come, to do this together, so that's what they'd do. No more dividing.

"Why don't you start at the very beginning," Caroline said.

"I wish you really could," Leigh said automatically, as if she'd been waiting to get past the requisite present and back to the good times. "I wish you could have known her then."

It was the strangest thing. The woman Leigh and Doug painted a picture of wasn't the same shape or color as the one who'd written those long emails to Caroline, crossed state lines to meet her, begged forgiveness, and then run away. But Caroline could recognize the underpainting: the tone and intent and *heart* beneath the surface.

"Sela was so much fun," Doug said, his eyes far away. "There was no such thing as boring when she was around—not even a lazy kind of boring day, the kind you don't mind. She put her own twist on things you wouldn't even think could be another way." He turned to Leigh. "Remember how everything she made had a special name? Even just, like, grilled cheese?"

Leigh smiled—and though her sadness shone through, so did her affection. Looking at the two, anyone could have guessed correctly which had stayed and which had not been able to bear it. "If you were in her circle," she said, "you were treated to this whole little world of extra touches. A signature drink because it was Wednesday. A handmade card on your windshield at the end of a rough workday. A dinner 'reservation' that turned out to be a barefoot picnic." A clandestine outing to a neighboring resort's rooftop spa.

"I was completely taken with her," Doug said, almost as though he regretted it. "Done for. She could be exhausting to keep up with—but in that irresistibly lovable way you can't get mad at. Like a kid."

Impossible to hear that and not jump to what a good mom she'd have been. But no one said it.

"She's still about as fun as anyone in her shoes would be," Leigh pointed out. "As loyal, too. If anyone says *anything* bad about someone she loves, you'll never catch her giving in and admitting maybe her mom *was* too involved in her life, or maybe I *am* a lousy hostess, or maybe Doug *shouldn't* have left." He looked at his lap, clearly ashamed, though his reasons were starting to look more justifiable than Caroline could have imagined. "You know it's true," Leigh told him. "In a lot of ways, she's the same. It's us who can't cope well enough to just let her be."

Caroline couldn't help thinking of the night Walt had drawn that unlikely comparison between Sela and her father. An impression that she *must have really been something to see in her day,* he'd said. *Kind of a strange vibe to get from a younger person.*

"When she was diagnosed, I thought she should end the pregnancy," Doug said. "I'm not sure she ever forgave me that, even after . . . everything. The risks were high, though, and I thought maybe if we could manage her symptoms first, we could try again later, with precautions in place. But she wouldn't hear of it. She was furious at the suggestion."

His hands balled into fists. "It's not like I didn't want a family as badly as she did. By the time we got pregnant, it was all we talked about. I was on board, even with some risk—there's always a little risk, right? But this . . ." He shrugged. "Once I saw how adamant she was, I found the point impossible to argue, and it seemed unhealthy to pile on additional stress by fighting about it. Maybe if I'd insisted . . ."

"There's no reason to think there would've been a better outcome," Leigh said, as much to Caroline as to him. "There was no guarantee that her illness would worsen the way it did, or that he'd be born so early, but the probabilities were there."

Caroline cleared her throat. She didn't want to make them relive it, but she had to know how much truth there was in Sela's delusions or exaggerations or—whatever they were. Had Brody been born alive? Had they thought for a time he'd pull through?

"What exactly happened?" Walt asked for her. An apology and a question rolled into one.

Leigh looked to Doug, but he didn't speak.

"She did tell me Brody was born premature." Caroline's voice trembled. "I'm trying to remember now if I assumed he was okay, or if she implied it. . . ."

"He was never going to be okay," Doug said. "But he hung on. Long enough to make you hope, in spite of what they said. . . ." Tears came to his eyes, and he blinked them away. "It was torture. Watching him. Watching *her* watch him."

"I came only once, and the way she looked at me—" Leigh shook her head. "I was coming up on my due date, and felt like I was rubbing her face in it, even in trying to be there for her. I still do." She gestured at her baby bump, more pronounced now that she was seated.

"When Brody finally passed," Doug said, "Sela was still in bad shape herself. They were trying new meds to stabilize her blood pressure and other things, and she had to stay in the hospital."

"I've said this to her, but I don't know how anyone gets through that," Leigh said. "As a mother—incomprehensible agony." Caroline had heard stories of women who'd lost a baby in the delivery room, or the NICU, and then had to be wheeled out of the hospital alongside parents holding healthy newborns. The only thing worse she could think of was staying there, being tended to in some other wing, when you were supposed to be in the maternity ward.

When you were supposed to be headed home.

"The first couple times she referred to Brody like he was still with her, I ignored it," Doug said. "I literally couldn't—how could I—I was grieving too." He shook his head. "It wasn't just losing Brody. They told us she could never sustain a pregnancy again. To give up the idea and focus on getting her well. They said if she could regain her quality of life, we could explore other options then."

Caroline had wondered before what Doug was like. But never had she imagined him so full of raw emotion.

"I didn't want to kid myself that way," he continued. "Didn't want her to either, if I'm honest. It seemed far-fetched that anyone would approve an adoption for someone chronically ill. They might not call it terminal, but one way or the other . . ." He shrugged. "It was a huge disappointment, but I thought we'd be better off trying to accept it. To consider it a victory if we could live a relatively normal life for as long as possible, even if just the two of us."

"She didn't go for that, I take it." Caroline already knew the answer.

"Ha. Yeah. She was personally affronted by my efforts to accept it. At the same time, she kept pointing out that this was happening to her, not me. That I could still go off and have a family with someone else—not an option that had entered my mind. I loved Sela. This was the hand we'd been dealt: not *her, us*." He looked to Leigh, presumably for confirmation that he wasn't the deadbeat their visitors must have assumed, but she was lost in thought. His eyes pleaded with Caroline for understanding. "But sustaining that alone was . . . Even if you took her inner life or whatever you want to call it with Brody out of the equation, it *wasn't* sustainable. She looked at me like she wondered what I was still doing there. Frankly, she still does."

Sela had taken that tone with Caroline on the phone. After literally writing her off in Tennessee. Caroline had dismissed it as something she could hop in the car and resolve, but now she was unsure.

Unsure whether it was possible. Unsure whether she still wanted to try.

"I'm trying to comprehend exactly what this inner life you mention consists of," Walt said—slower now, more careful. "She was—what? Talking to an imaginary friend?"

Doug and Leigh shook their heads in unison. Caroline wondered when they'd first started conferring behind Sela's back. You could tell it was uncomfortable for both of them even now.

"It's hard to explain," Doug said. "She'd say or do some little, subtle thing, and all of a sudden you could tell where her mind was."

"She never forced the idea of Brody on anyone," Leigh said. "She kept him to herself. It was more like she'd slip up. I could never decide if she knew he wasn't real but sometimes got carried away pretending, or if the reality she constructed had tight borders. Either way . . . Rebecca thought it best if we all sort of went along with it." Her frown deepened.

"She called me *unimaginative,*" Doug said, his years-old disbelief still as palpable as if he were arguing the point to his late mother-in-law's face. "I honestly wondered if she was losing it too. She and Sela were so close it was understandable she'd get defensive, but this went beyond protecting her daughter." He again turned to Leigh for backup, and this time she gave it.

"It was almost like she was weirdly proud of Sela for creating a coping mechanism. Like, whatever works."

"You actually played along?" Walt was incredulous. "Acting like Brody was alive?"

"We never did that," Leigh said quickly. "Rebecca was adamant that we not challenge Sela, though. So we—gave her space."

A chill passed over Caroline as she remembered that late-night conversation she'd overheard in Lucy's bedroom.

My mother used to tell me that my imagination was my superpower. . . . When I couldn't stop the lonely or scary things happening in my brain, alone in my room, she suggested I use the superpower to pretend someone was with me.

Lucy had asked, with every ounce of her innocence: *Who?*

Sela's response had made so much sense. *Whoever you'd most like to have with you.*

They'd given her space, Doug said.

It sounded innocent enough.

But what they'd done equated to leaving her alone with *only* Brody for company. With *only* Brody for comfort.

"If you felt like her mother was letting her go off the deep end," Walt said, "or going over with her, why didn't you try to get her help?"

Doug and Leigh exchanged a look. "The specialists did coax her to a few postnatal therapy sessions, plus some counseling for us as a couple," he began. "But it didn't last long enough for me to realize the extent of . . . things. She was unreceptive, just sat there, and eventually refused to go back."

"That's it?" Caroline frowned. "I've noticed you're not exactly the unpushy type."

"That's not it," Leigh said. "But once a certain amount of time passed, we couldn't make *too* big a deal. Because of the points system—" Her voice broke on the last word, and Doug touched her shoulder. She jerked away, and he looked chastened, cleared his throat.

"Where Rebecca had us," he explained, "was with the transplant list. Once we understood how it works, and that Sela might end up on it—" He shook his head. "Generally, the youngest and healthiest get priority. But a mental health flag?"

"My God," Caroline whispered.

Doug looked up at the ceiling, as if some new, even worse revelation might fall on him.

"What are you supposed to do," Leigh asked through fresh tears, "when trying to help someone get better in one way means hurting their chances of getting better overall?"

"Would they really knock her down the list that far?" Walt's face crinkled. "I mean, given what she's been through . . . Maybe if she completed therapy, she'd earn the points back."

"Every transplant center makes its own guidelines, and I've never had an opportunity to get ours clarified, for obvious reasons," Doug said. "But my understanding is . . . even one point could cost her. Maybe her life. We didn't want to be responsible for that."

"Have you ever known American health care to be sympathetic? To do anything but look for excuses not to cover something?" Leigh fished a tissue from her pocket and wiped at her cheeks. "I was so scared to say or do the wrong thing, to make things worse, I didn't trust myself to be around her. It was too devastating. But leaving her to Rebecca . . . That turned out to be a short-term solution."

"I couldn't take it," Doug said. "I couldn't stay. Then Rebecca died, and I thought maybe, *maybe* I could go back and be there for Sela. Maybe with her enabler gone . . ." He trailed off.

"She was still—?" Caroline didn't know how to finish the thought either. What exactly was it Sela had been doing? Imagining? Acting? Dreaming while she was awake?

"She did seem better. But I couldn't tell for certain where her head was. And not knowing wasn't good enough."

He closed his eyes for a long moment, and when he opened them, Caroline knew somehow what he was about to say—and wished he wouldn't.

This must be how Sela felt.

"The other day, she gave me a scare again, but I talked myself out of it, told myself I was blowing things out of proportion, it was just a lapse. She'd had a bad string of days—physically, mentally.

Especially since Tennessee . . ." He wasn't thoughtless enough to finish. "She's been avoiding me, and frankly I took that as a good sign. When she's feeling the best is when she has the least tolerance for me." His attempt at levity fell flat.

"Sela is not a liar," Leigh said again. "The only person she's manipulated is herself. As far as I can tell, Brody has been a living, breathing part of her reality since long before she even considered looking for you. And honestly, she never felt comfortable reaching out to you. Doug and I practically forced her to."

Caroline waited for Walt to interject—a sarcastic *Thanks a lot,* perhaps—but he kept quiet.

"It's only since she found you that I've had that bad feeling again," Doug said. "Either she'd gotten good at hiding it but doesn't have the energy anymore, or it really did go away but now . . ."

"She's worse," Caroline finished. It was what Leigh had been trying to tell them, on Sela's front walk. It was why Leigh had brought her here.

If only any of them could have seen the look on Sela's face that Cincinnati afternoon on the stairs of their mothers' old high school. Caroline had posed the question she thought more wry than astute:

Did you know that before they used the clinical term depression, *they used to diagnose people with* nostalgia?

Sela hadn't looked interested or amused at the insight. She'd looked grateful. She'd looked *seen.*

Did it work? Lucy had asked Sela later that night. *What your mom said to do?*

Sela hadn't hesitated: *Like a charm.* She'd been glad even then for the peace of mind her strategy had managed to buy. Even at a price steeper than anyone should have to pay.

Walt slid his hand up Caroline's back. Even through her shirt, it felt clammy.

The hand of a terrified man.

"I think we should hold off," he began, "on going to see Sela until we've had a chance to wrap our minds around this. Maybe in the morning—"

But Caroline was already shaking her head. She faced Walt full on, trying to push down her own fear. To focus, first, on this.

"We can't. What if she saw us?"

"I'm pretty sure she did." Leigh's voice sliced the air between them. "The blinds moved when we pulled away."

"Why didn't you say something?" Caroline felt woozy. What must Sela think?

"I *had* to talk to you first." The knife edge of Leigh's voice had gone dull. "Find out what was what. And . . . let you know."

Caroline turned back to Walt. She wanted nothing more than to let him take her home. Even a hotel was too close to all of this.

But she couldn't.

"We have to go to her, Walt. We won't stay. We'll book a room for the night. But we need to hear her side, see how she is."

Leigh frowned. "I had to really work to get her to let me in earlier."

Doug held up his hand, revealing a key.

"If Sela finds a donor on her own," Caroline said quietly, "she doesn't need the list. It wouldn't matter how many points she had. Or had deducted."

No one dared answer. They all knew it was true, but also what it meant.

She might be Sela's best chance to get help.

With any of it.

38

Sela

"Mama?" Sela's eyes fluttered open. Brody knelt before her on the studio floor, smiling his crooked grin. The late-afternoon sun, light and golden here on the warm side of all these windows, caught the shine of his soft brown hair, as silky now as it had been at birth. "The *door,*" he told her, as if she'd been playing a silly game.

Had she been? She'd been sleeping so little. Feeling too much.

Her neck cricked in protest as she lifted her head from where it had lolled against the bookcase. She must have fallen asleep, here of all places. How long ago? An hour? Two?

A swift, efficient knock echoed from downstairs. The still-trying-to-be-polite kind that would soon turn to pounding. Then, the *what about me?* of Oscar's bark from the backyard.

She uncurled her legs in front of her, stretching her swollen joints, and a tiny box tumbled to the woven rug beneath her.

She blinked at it, as if it were a remotely familiar face she couldn't place.

"What's that?" Brody's little fingers reached for the intricately carved wood, and she sprang into motion, snatching it away before they could connect. She was not too disoriented for horror and relief to seize her. How could she have been so thoughtless as to leave this out? Even to have stored it in the first place on this low shelf, where he could reach?

But he hadn't reached. No harm done. If you were lucky, your parental missteps came with these reprieves—you could learn the lesson without paying the price. She smoothed Brody's hair, leaving his question unanswered, and scanned the room's higher points for a better hiding spot. Nothing as mundane and predictable as the medicine cabinet would do. Not when Leigh and Doug and now Caroline had become so insistently nosy.

Caroline. The realization jolted Sela to her feet. She'd been here, with Walt. Then gone, with Leigh. Sela moved her eyes quickly left to right a few times, a trick she'd learned to clear fog from the brain.

This was why she was here. But had she—

She opened the pillbox, counted. All three, still inside.

The pounding crescendoed downstairs, accompanied by a muffled call through the door, words she couldn't make out over Oscar's barking, more insistent now.

They were back, then. Just Caroline and Walt, or Leigh too? Damn it. Sela hadn't meant to stay. But she couldn't do anything about it now. Not on short notice, not in front of Brody.

"Mama?" Brody was pointing at the door, confused—but that didn't matter. What mattered was that he was *here.* A small miracle all over again. Tears pricked her eyes and she bent and gathered him in a fierce hug. He hadn't left her, then, without saying goodbye. Maybe he could stay after all.

That's what she wanted. For him to stay and them to go.

She carried him with her to the closet and tucked the box out of sight on the top shelf, behind a bin of plastic-sleeved prints she sometimes sold at art shows.

The release of the dead bolt clicked from downstairs, and a woman called her name. A voice she'd conjured more often than she'd heard it—narrating the emails she sent, laughing over conversations Sela wouldn't dare begin.

Caroline.

But Caroline couldn't have gotten in alone.

She hugged Brody tighter, rocking him. Why couldn't everyone let them be? They'd done it before—thoroughly. What made them so sure she needed them now? Arrogance was what it was. Superiority. She scrunched her face in determination, fighting back fresh tears.

The rattle of the back door in its frame. Excited retriever paws skidding on tile. Then: tentative footsteps on the stairs. She didn't have much time to pull herself together. Or to—what? More voices, male this time: Walt? And the unmistakable baritone of Doug. Brody heard it, too, tried to wriggle free. "Daddy!" But she didn't want to let him go. What if he liked things better Doug's way? He might slip—the way children of divorce did from one parent's house to the other's—from one parent's *reality* to the other's. What if he left for good this time?

She couldn't keep hold of him, though—so squirmy. He broke loose from her grip just as Leigh appeared in the doorway—cheeks flushed, face pinched with worry—and Caroline squeezed in behind her, filling the frame with such eager pity it took all Sela's self-control not to crawl under the desk behind her, plug her ears, and wail.

Leigh had told Caroline, all of it. Sela had suspected as much, yet seeing it splayed across her sister's face made it real.

"Oh, thank God," Leigh said, her hand flying to her chest. "When you didn't answer, and the house was so quiet, I thought—I don't know what I thought."

Sela's eyes darted around the room. Where had Brody gone? The corners waited in vacant shadow. Everything so empty, so still, that his absence squeezed her heart until she didn't know how it could still beat. Leigh and Caroline were blocking the exit—but had he slipped between their legs and run for Doug? Had Sela been too sidelined by panic to see him go?

No. He was nowhere.

Four expectant eyes locked on her face now, trying to be *there for her,* to be *here* for her. They didn't change the fact that she'd never been more alone.

"I must've fallen asleep," Sela mumbled, stealing a futile look into the closet once more. The words came out garbled.

Leigh frowned. "Here in the studio?"

Sela snapped to then, shooting all her hurt and confusion and fury into one laser look at Leigh. A look that said, *I'll sleep anywhere I please in the privacy of my home—which you've invaded.* A look that said, *You don't know what this is like, how this feels, and who are you to judge?* A look that said, *If you don't like it, why don't you leave?*

And by the way, I know what you've done. And it isn't okay.

Nothing is ever going to be okay.

Leigh shrank inward, reading her loud and clear. Sela should dial it back, show that she understood her friend meant well. She knew how to do that. She'd swallowed her envy and anguish and stayed at Leigh's side through two forays into early motherhood and another on the way—but she didn't have it in her just now. Not in front of Caroline.

Not without Brody.

"Heya, sis," Caroline said weakly. Sela's eyes followed the voice. Walt did not appear at Caroline's side, nor did Doug. They must have hung back, sent the women ahead. Typical.

"I said not to come."

But her sister didn't avert her gaze or flush the way Leigh had. She merely shrugged. "I said I needed to."

Caroline looked so *open*—her expression, her posture—the only way, Sela supposed, to leave room for so many unasked questions. They flowed from her sister in strands, wove themselves into braids, coiled around Sela's ankles until she feared that with a single tug, they might pull her legs out from under her.

"They told you I'm crazy." Might as well come out with it.

"Nobody said that," Leigh interjected, recovering from the stare-down. But Caroline's silence told Sela otherwise. She imagined the cords tightening around her ankles. A warning.

Then Doug *was* there. A hand on Leigh's shoulder, a panting dog at his feet. Even Oscar was eyeing Sela warily, not sure he should enter all the way.

"They needed to know," Doug said, too calmly. "That Brody isn't real."

Sela's breath caught as she stepped back, putting as much distance as she could between them until the hard edge of her mother's bookcase met her spine.

This. This was a one-sentence summation of everything that was wrong with Doug. Of all the reasons why he could *never* stay, even if he wanted to.

"He's *real,*" she snarled. She looked to Caroline. "You think I don't know," she said, voice warbling, "that he isn't alive? That he didn't survive?" Zero to sixty, she was shouting now. "That doesn't mean he isn't, wasn't, *real*! That doesn't mean I'm not a mother."

Oscar did come to her then, too sensitive not to. She dropped a hand onto his head. He was the only one she wasn't tired of reassuring.

Caroline's eyes filled—but not with guilty, frustrated tears, as Sela had seen too many times in Doug and even Leigh. All she saw reflected there was her own heartbreak.

"I told you I'd been pregnant," Sela pleaded, not wanting the mirror in her sister's eyes to cloud, to shatter. "I said I gave birth too soon. It was you who assumed the outcome had to have been good."

"I'm so sorry, Sela."

Sela could see she meant it. Caroline wasn't angry, or scared, the way everyone else seemed to be, even under the guise of empathy. Only sorry.

Had Caroline disputed her, Sela would have tried to explain. How from the moment she'd neglected to correct Caroline's logical but very wrong assumption, everything Sela had gone on to tell her was true. At least, it all *felt* true. Not a single story she'd relayed about Brody had been some tall tale invented on the spot. She'd drawn every quirk of his personality, every scrunch of his nose, from *memory*. The way he'd grown, the things he said and did, all of it had *happened* to Sela at some earlier moment, here in the studio, or curled in her bed, at her mother's boutique, walking to the park. She'd hidden those private moments away, sacred to mother and son alone—until Caroline came along.

What pure, freeing joy it had been to finally get to share Brody with someone. To gush, as any mother would, over his heroic little heart in ways she hadn't been able to with anyone else. The way Caroline did about her own kids, about childhood and motherhood and everything in between. Who could resist it, after that first, inadvertent taste? The chance to make those moments she and Brody shared in her mind even *more* real, if only for a precious while?

She knew Brody couldn't be with her—yet it didn't make sense. Because he *was* real.

If he weren't, that would mean this disease had taken everything she'd ever wanted, everything she could ever want to hope for again. It would mean there was nothing left of her. Nothing left for her. Except for the pillbox waiting in the closet.

"I'm not delusional," she said. The night she'd lain in her hospital room and listened to Doug and Ecca arguing outside the door, it was the only word he said that she made out loud and clear. She'd never discerned whether he'd been calling his wife or her mother the delusional one, but when she woke to find Doug gone, it made no difference.

"Brody *is* real, buried next to the spot where I will be one day. But I'd much rather live in a world with him in it. So I do."

Caroline nodded—Doug and Leigh and Walt and Oscar and the world around them fading away—and all that was left was the two of them.

Half sisters with no capacity for a half connection. All or nothing.

"I'm still here," Caroline said softly. A vote bravely cast for *all.*

But *all* would draw in Caroline in ways Sela could not abide.

"She says she told you," Doug interjected. Sela wouldn't look at him. Better to go on pretending he'd actually managed to leave her all the way. For all of their sakes. "That she's a prelim *match,* See. You have to talk to her, hear out her questions, see if—"

She shook her head, hard. "Stop telling me what I have to do. If she were your wife, would you want her to help me? To risk herself for *me*? Tell the truth!"

The answer was on his face. Finally. She had him.

No one had ever said it aloud to her: that maybe there was a reason people like Sela were at risk for being bumped down the transplant list. Maybe they *were* less deserving. Ranking people didn't seem right, but they did have to, somehow, so how else would they?

These were the things that no one said but everyone thought—and would never stop thinking, regardless of what happened from here.

She knew it was true, because *everyone* included her.

Even with a healthy kidney filtering the toxins inside of her, there would be things it could never filter. Things that would never again be pure.

"I tried to tell you," she said, speaking only to Caroline now. "I changed my mind. It was a good story, finding each other, but you don't need to stick around and see how it ends." She managed a smile—sad, but as reassuring as she could make it. It hadn't been that good of a story, anyway, on Caroline's end. What had signified hope and possibility for Sela had upended Caroline's entire belief system—in her parents' marriage, her mother's character, even her own partner and whether her first choice might've been a better one.

"No." Leigh sounded surprisingly strong, ready for a fight they'd been putting off for too long. "You're right that there are still things to work out, but—"

"I tried to prepare you for this," Sela interrupted. Leigh had moments, like on Brody's birthday, when she'd seemed to understand anew the depths of what Sela had lost. But if she didn't truly get it by now, she never would. "You know my mother didn't want this anyway."

"I know no such thing. And even if I did? I loved Rebecca, but she wasn't right about everything. If you think for a second *this*"—she gestured around the studio as if it were some twisted shrine—"is what she had in mind for you, you're wrong."

Ecca had let Brody stay. They never spoke of him, but Ecca had been the only other person to accept him. No one else ever would.

"You need help, Sela, one way or another. We're done going on like this." Leigh stepped back, into the bedroom, and for a second Sela thought she was leaving, storming out without actually storming. But she was only making way for someone else to get through.

Janie smiled at Sela—warmly, as if nothing unordinary was happening. As if she were about to take the microphone and step onto the stage, work the room. Doug opened his mouth to speak, and she turned on him the skeptical glare reserved for hecklers. Daring him to try.

He closed it.

"Leigh called me," Janie said, so casually she might have been crashing a party. "Sorry I'm late."

Sela hadn't realized she was trembling. All over. She searched the room once more for Brody. If Janie was going to take her away from here—was she?—he *had* to come, too.

Janie took her by the arm, reassuringly, and leaned in close. Janie, whose body gleaned its strength from her own sister's kidney. Janie, who had seen worse—depending on your definition of the word. Janie, who didn't suffer fools—including Sela.

"Sing it with me," she whispered directly into Sela's ear. "You can go your own way."

39

Caroline

In spite of everything, Walt and Caroline couldn't bring themselves to backtrack to the stoic chain hotels closer to the highway. Brevard was a town of inns, and the one where they landed was an inviting red brick from the mid-1800s, with two levels of white column–lined porches and clean, crisp accommodations. They'd requested the most tucked-away, out-of-earshot room available, and their lone third-story suite was updated tastefully, with all the right historical touches left in place—down to the oversized claw-foot tub stocked with spa-quality bath salts.

It was lost on them, all of it.

By the time they checked in, the sunset had faded to black. The day had been long enough to feel like a week, but Walt didn't stay to get settled. He dropped his duffel and announced he was heading out for provisions. When he returned a short time later with wine, cheese, olive oil, and a baguette—packaged neatly into a basket with glasses, plates, and utensils—she was still standing where he'd left her, at the window. Gazing at a view that could have been beautiful, if not obscured by the night.

"Not exactly dinner," he said. "But enough so we don't have to face the public." A polished wooden table divided two reading chairs in the sitting area at the far side of the bed, and he busied himself unpacking the spread there—pouring the wine, shaking herbs into the oil, slicing the bread and cheese. The inn owners had given him the works, but Caroline remained motionless at the window, unable to fathom eating but unwilling to say so. She understood the need he felt to *do* something.

"I'm so sorry I dragged you into this," she said, her words small in the stretch of room between them.

"You have nothing to be sorry about." His were surprisingly solid, strong by contrast, and they drew her, at last, into motion. Toward him. She dropped into one of the chairs, and he followed suit. Neither of them made a move toward the table.

"If I wasn't here, would you be staying at Sela's right now?" he asked. No judgment that she could detect. Only curiosity.

"I have no idea. I'm glad you are here, for what it's worth."

The silence lingered, thoughtfully. He leaned forward, over his knees. "You know, seeing Doug . . ." He raised his eyes to hers. "I could never leave you, Caroline, the way he's left her. Never. No matter what." She'd been bolstering herself for—what? A lecture? A rehashing of their collective horror and surprise? But not this—the thing she should have counted on.

Walt. Had things gotten so strange between them that she'd lost sight of him? He'd wanted to keep his guard up, keep her safe. But Walt, like the rest of them, was a human, a parent, not just a spouse but a friend and, more uncommon, good and sincere at all of the above.

"Being here in Brevard with you," he said, "I can see why you fell in love with the place. And I can't help but look at you here and wonder what *you* see. If you're picturing the other life you might have lived in these mountains, on these streets—because I'd be lying if I said I couldn't picture it. You and Keaton and—" She opened her mouth to object, but he held up a hand. "Who knows if you'd have met Sela any sooner, but even so . . . Things could have been totally different, all the way around. Would have been, very easily."

The fact that he of all people would voice her feelings somehow made them valid, even if she didn't want them to be. She nodded uneasily.

"With everything that's happened today, maybe this is selfish. I mean, I know it is." His voice dropped to a hush. "But I can't stop being grateful. I'm so relieved it never came to be."

She sunk into the plush back of the chair. Sela had been a lot of things to a lot of people: More than they bargained for. More than they could handle. More than their heart could hold. For Walt, she'd been a wake-up call. He'd looked at Sela today, truly seeing her at last, and his anger and fear had faded to empathy—and everything on the other side of it.

"I love you, Caroline. I love you in spite of our stupid plan that love didn't have to be part of the equation. I love you enough to want to do better at *everything* if that's what you need. I love you in ways I never intended. You can't tell me you seriously don't know that by now."

It was a strange world they'd created together, where falling in love with your wife meant breaking the rules. Yet she looked at him and saw how ridiculous it was that she needed to hear him say it in order to believe.

What kind of woman would be upset when her husband confesses that he's grown to love her *more* with time, a climb so steady they never stopped to notice the heights they'd reached, even as couples all around them lost hold, tumbling to their demise?

The same kind of woman who'd agree to marry a man she didn't love in the first place.

This was her chance, to not say it back. To use his breach of contract as an excuse for that do-over she'd caught herself stubbornly wishing for—with Keaton, maybe, or just with herself, alone at the wheel, calling the shots. Calling off her marriage didn't have to be as impossible as it seemed, even with the kids. Plenty of other people did and ended up far worse off than she and Walt could ever be. Sela and Doug, for instance.

Or, she could see this for what it was: a gift. The chance to choose each other all over again. Or, rather, for the first time, knowing all there was to know.

In a too-luxurious room for a too-depressing night, hundreds of miles from home, in the very place where she might have lived a parallel life quite comfortably, she realized: She wasn't here with Walt just because of the irreversible decisions that had been made for her.

It was because she loved him, too.

She loved him in a way she might have loved Keaton. In a way she was fairly sure she *could* have loved Keaton. But it was Walt who held her heart now.

Couldn't she relate to what Sela had been doing? Wasn't she guilty of the same? When she'd had to relearn who her parents were and what that meant for her, she'd dreamed up an alternate reality with Keaton. The one she'd been denied, against her will. She'd looked back at the marriage she'd arranged in its place and romanticized what she might have had instead. Romance, for one. But she already had it.

How about that.

There was no reason to be angry anymore. At Mom, Dad, Keaton, Walt, or even Sela. All she wanted was to pull them close, forgive them, and forget, impossible as it seemed.

Impossible as she knew it was.

"I seriously do," she said.

Caroline couldn't say which of them moved first, only that

suddenly they were in his chair together, given over to tears, arms around each other in a way she didn't want to end.

Later, they would find it in them to cut the bread. To sip the wine. To go back over the more unbelievable moments of this day. Entwined across their chairs, some part of them—their ankles, their fingers, her head in the crook of his arm—they'd debate, with abandon: Was it right for the system to deprioritize treatment for someone like Sela? Even if Caroline did want to help circumnavigate things, would a kidney be enough to save her troubled sister? What if she never recovered—and not just physically? What if Caroline's sacrifice was for nothing?

They asked questions no one could answer.

They voiced things they had to say but would never repeat.

When they'd exhausted the thread, they climbed into bed, lights out, and lay awake.

"You know how you said that you look at Doug and think you don't know how he could leave her?" Caroline ventured. "Even after . . . everything?" She took a deep breath. "I don't know if I can leave her either."

"I know." Walt took her hand across the sheets: a promise that he would not ask her to.

It wasn't Sela who preoccupied Caroline's thoughts on the way home. Nor was it Walt, though the new understanding between them filled the cabin of the car with a heat, a protective shield of sorts that brought an unexpected comfort. They hadn't stayed for brunch; hadn't lingered for the claw-foot tub. There'd been no question that they wouldn't return to Sela's now, but neither was there a question that they'd revisit the subject in the future.

They would.

When Sela was ready.

Not before.

Too many people had forced too many expectations upon poor Sela, and Caroline would not pile on. Nor would she repeat the mistake of staying away. She didn't know what had happened after they'd left Sela in Janie's capable hands last night, only that Janie and Leigh had promised to keep Caroline posted—now and from now on. She was thankful to have other ways to check on Sela now, a scrappy little team in her sister's corner.

Better still, with a clearer head today, she thought she might know someone who could help.

She left a message for Janie. And then her mind obeyed, for once, when she asked it to sit back and wait. It was easier now that she wasn't trapped in these thoughts alone.

For now, she and Walt had decided *not* to decide. When the time was right, they'd face it together, with a renewed commitment not only to each other but to all the things they had to be grateful for, in a world where fortune was distributed without regard to what was fair.

As they pointed the car north, then, it was no self-defensive trick that Sela was not the one filling her thoughts.

They belonged to the people she most wanted to get home to.

The people she'd awoken feeling desperately, ravenously hungry to hold.

Riley. Lucy. Owen. If she didn't have them . . .

If she woke up tomorrow and they were gone . . .

"*Please* can't I come?" Riley had begged when they left, wanting so badly to see Sela and her studio and her wisp of a wish of a son. Who could blame Riley for not understanding *but why not?* Caroline hadn't been free to explain. Riley didn't give up easily on anything she set her mind to—not on footwork on the field, not on letters on a canvas, and certainly not on people. She kept at things even when no one was watching to applaud her for it. You didn't have to be one of her younger siblings to look up to her.

And Lucy, she'd seemed to sense there was more to Sela than some vague past connection with her mom. There was, if hope was good for anything, a future connection with them all. Lucy's very essence was a reminder that there was more to life than light and dark. There was twilight, sparkle. That's what Sela's advice had helped her keep hold of. Even knowing what she did now, Caroline wouldn't take her sister's "superpower" words back or even disclaim them. As Sela had said, they worked.

Which left Owen, always trying to catch up, fueled by sheer innocence and energy. Caroline's deepest ache was to get back to her baby. She loved the way he stood out in any preschool crowd: Raised among such spirited sisters, you could spot him by his free will to play however he wanted, whatever he wanted, without regard to what was tough or cool. With a mom like Sela, Brody might have had that same magic; Caroline mourned that they'd never know.

Sela's was the kind of heartbreak anyone could imagine. But only a mother could *know:* that it was the absolute worst thing.

The thing you might never come back from.

The thing you might never want to, even if you could.

I want my mother, Sela had sobbed when they left, as Janie soothed her.

Some losses could be truly understood only by those who'd experienced what it was like to be responsible for the beating of a tiny heart—a heart that belonged to someone else but would never not also be yours. Some defeats were so thoroughly devastating, they could be shared only inside the kind of bond that could be neither replicated nor replaced.

But Sela had lost both sides of that, in such a short time. Maybe if she still had a mother to turn to . . .

Caroline would forgive her own. Outright. Her dad, too.

Somewhere between Ohio and North Carolina, she already had.

Janie rang her back. Caroline distracted herself with follow-up for a while, then laid her head on Walt's shoulder as he drove. Six yearning-filled hours later, he went alone to pick up the kids. Much as she wanted to see them, there was someone she needed first.

By the time she got up the front walk, Mom was waiting at the door. As if she'd been expecting her, tuned to those moments when her daughter could be nowhere but here.

"Caroline? Is everything—" She stopped short as she took Caroline in. Puffy face, no doubt. Drawn but determined. Lost and found at the same time.

"I need to talk to you," Caroline said simply. Then she was crying—ugly, full-throttle tears. Mom stepped back onto the rug, just as she had that morning everything changed, when Caroline found her here, fraught and furious in her nightgown.

But this time, she opened her arms.

Caroline stepped in.

"Okay," Mom whispered, crying now too. "Okay. We'll talk as much as you want. We'll talk it to death: Keaton, Walt, whatever you need. We'll talk you into hating me and then out of it again. We'll talk until I can convince you how sorry I am. Truly sorry."

If she'd repented this way from the start, where might they have ended up? This wasn't about that anymore.

But Mom wasn't going to stop now that she'd opened the floodgates. "I knew I was wrong, and I never meant . . . I just couldn't bear—" She shuddered with sobs. "I've messed everything up for you, haven't I?"

Caroline hugged her tighter, thinking what an odd thing it was for the roles to reverse, to offer comfort to the person she'd always sought it from.

Of course, a child did not have to grow into an adult to comfort her mother in the most essential ways.

"It's not that, Mom." She took a deep, shaky breath and pulled back to look her straight in the eyes. "It's Sela."

40

Sela

There was a difference between someone running scared and simply recognizing when it was time to back away. To breathe, take a break, afford space. Sela knew she had every reason to worry she might never see Caroline and Walt again.

But she didn't. In part because she was too frayed to expend the energy. In part because she understood they couldn't stay right then. And in part because Janie could.

Janie did.

I'll make some calls, Janie had said to Leigh. *I'll keep you updated,* she'd promised Caroline. *I'll take tonight,* she'd told Doug. But to Sela, Janie simply said, *I'll keep you company until we have a plan.* And then, with no mention of whether she'd had somewhere else to be for her Friday night or the whole of Saturday, she sank onto the couch and started browsing video apps, looking for a series neither of them had watched yet.

It was a little odd *not* resenting her presence. Sela wasn't so far gone that she didn't understand exactly why Janie would not leave her. She might have exploded, *I'm not going to hurt myself, okay? I'm just bereft. Just let me be bereft.* But instead, she agreed to a time-travel fantasy and managed to binge half the first season before drifting into exhaustion on the couch. Hours later, she awoke to find Janie still there, in the filtered sunlight. Awake-all-night caffeinated, smiling like it was no big thing.

Twenty-four hours in, calls had indeed been made. Caroline to Janie, clearing the idea. Caroline to a psychologist she'd met—a leap of blind faith. The psychologist, in turn, to Janie, trading questions. Then, Janie to Caroline: *Okay, worth a shot.* Rounds of muffled back-and-forth behind closed doors. Sela might have minded this, too, in an *I'm right here* sort of way—but she had the good sense to be grateful enough to keep mum. And so, the good nurse set her up in front of the webcam, secured the connection, and—the Sela baton securely passed—left to pick up dinner.

This call would determine what happened next. The big stuff, like whether she could keep her position on the list. And the little stuff, like whether Janie could go home and sleep.

No pressure.

She stared into the webcam, pulled the heated blanket around her lap, and nodded that she was ready to begin.

"Well, that gives me what I need to complete this initial evaluation."

At the other end of the video call, Dr. Kay Adams took off her reading glasses and set down her pen.

It could have gone a lot worse, Sela had to admit. Agreeing to things she knew to be true was easy enough. Even if they didn't *feel* true.

She didn't confuse the two, most of the time.

"Here's the deal," Dr. Kay said. She preferred not to be called Dr. Adams—*the Morticia jokes and finger snaps get old fast,* she'd explained. "Starting next week, I'm going to be in pretty rough shape. But I'll also have nothing but time on my hands. So, we'll aim for three video sessions a week, an hour each, but bear with me if I need to change a time based on what I feel up to. I'll also need your go-ahead for me to check in with Janie weekly—I won't violate your confidentiality as far as what's said in therapy, but I will check her own assessments against mine, since she's physically there, to be sure there isn't a vast gap between our impressions."

"What about when your recovery is over and you have real patients again?"

"Make no mistake, you will be a real patient. This might be off the insurance grid, and pro bono, and God I hate the term *unorthodox*. But the work you and I will be doing together will be necessary and real. As long as I feel you're making a sincere, honest effort, Janie and I will both keep this under wraps."

Her face burned at the phrasing: *a sincere, honest effort*. Perhaps Dr. Kay had already seen through her, right to the escape hatch she'd failed to mention on her closet shelf.

Plenty of sick people kept one, though, just in case. It was even legal in some states. That was not the unique thing about Sela. So maybe it went without saying. Plus, she hadn't lied when she said she wasn't having thoughts of using it. She hardly could when good people were putting themselves at risk for her, right now. Dr. Kay included.

"Can I ask why you'd do this for me? I mean—couldn't you lose your license or something?" She'd tried to ask the same of Janie. It was the only time she'd seen the nurse look angry with her, so she didn't press for an answer when none came.

Dr. Kay's eyes remained clear, sharp. "Thinking of turning me in?"

"Of course not. I just don't want to see anyone else in a bad spot because of me."

"So I hear." The doctor raised an eyebrow, undeterred. Might whoever was receiving her kidney next week get some of this clever efficiency? She seemed so no-nonsense, so sure.

"First, I believe there are more gray areas in life than many people—including those in my profession—prefer to acknowledge. Especially where the minds of highly creative people are concerned. Also pertaining here, I believe tragedy can shade us in the deepest grays for a while, whereas some of my colleagues see that darkness as more in the realm of black."

"So, you feel like you should, because you think you can?"

"Well, I hope I can. Your sister hopes I can. Nurse Janie hopes I can. I'd like to know if you hope I can."

Sela wasn't sure how to answer.

"You know, when Caroline called to ask if I might be willing to talk with you, she said I'd made some wrong assumptions about your relationship, the first time I met her. I felt bad at first, that I'd gone on about my own outreach to this stranger when it wasn't much different for you two—but you know, I don't think you're strangers after all. I don't need to see you together to see the connection. I hope you see it too."

"I see that I've complicated things for her in ways I wish I hadn't."

"Well, you can't help that you're her half sister, just like you can't help being your mother's daughter or your son's mother or your ex's ex. You're also you, full stop. We can't define ourselves solely by our relationships."

Sela could not remember the last time she'd come to any kind of full stop.

"Deal or no deal?" Dr. Kay tilted her head, pleasantly unsmiling.

Sela heard the rustling of paper carryout bags downstairs, signaling Janie's return. She was suddenly ravenous, aware of how long it had been since she'd enjoyed a meal.

Too long.

She nodded into the webcam. "Deal."

41

Caroline

"I saw. The way Fred and Rebecca looked at each other. Of course I saw." Mom sniffed hard, dabbing a balled-up tissue at her puffy cheeks, though they were dry now. She'd cried herself out long before she'd taken her turn to talk. "Honestly, everyone had to have seen. But for me—she was like a sister, the only person I'd let really know me, and let myself really know, until I met Fred. And he was . . . Well, he was all I wanted."

Her eyes searched Caroline's, but they were no longer pleading with her to understand. Only looking for some sign that one day she might.

"When she left, as if that might redeem her . . . I want to describe it as grief, but that's not right. Grieving someone I love, I take comfort in hearing their name still come up in conversation, and in sharing favorite memories. With Rebecca, I heard things, but tried my damnedest not to. If she came up, I changed the subject. If she wrote me, I tore it up unread. I gathered every postcard and note she'd ever sent me, every photo I could find with her in it, and threw them in a gas station dumpster. If I could have bleached her from my mind, I would have. But what I really wanted was to erase her from Fred's."

It seemed even Rebecca's death hadn't eased the searing pain of her betrayal. The decades since had left their imprint on Mom—the good days evident in her laugh lines, the bad nights shadowy in her creases. But when Caroline looked into that weary face, she could still see a young newlywed and expectant mother named Hannah determined to hold on to everything that had been promised her. Determined to avoid a household broken like the one she'd grown up in—not just for herself but for her daughter.

"Did you ever truly forgive Dad?"

Without hesitation, a nod. "Fred made a choice to do right by you and me, and that was the best I could hope for at that point. He went on to prove himself a fantastic dad, and a good husband, and after a while, I stopped doubting he'd follow through. Everything I'd wanted my life to be was right there, but I wouldn't have truly had it if I'd held on to that hurt. So I let it go."

"Until I started talking about moving to Brevard."

It wasn't a question.

"The day you started talking about Brevard was the day it hit me that you were grown, and what that meant. Fred had fulfilled his duty to us both. After more than two decades, no reasonable person could say he hadn't. Not even me."

Mom closed her eyes and inhaled slowly through her nose, contracting as her lips parted to let the breath go. It was as if every seemingly melodramatic, hallmark sigh over the years had been some miniature version of this: of having to mindfully stop herself from holding her breath.

"I was terrified," she whispered, "that if he crossed paths with Rebecca again, he wouldn't make the same choice."

Her eyes opened, pools of tears. "When I say that I saw the way he looked at her, what I mean is that I saw what was missing in the way he looked at me. That adoration had been there, between us, too—but always in me. It was always me." The pools spilled down her cheeks in smooth lines she didn't wipe away. "I couldn't take the risk of having them in the same city, even by happenstance, even for a day or two here and there. Not if I could help it. And I could help it, because I knew Rebecca feared all the same things for all the wrong reasons."

She grasped Caroline's hands between her own, which felt cold, and trembling, and frailer than they ever appeared—and, like so many other things about her, the exact same shape as Caroline's. "The way I saw it, I did what I had to do to keep my marriage safe. But I told myself it wouldn't cost you anything but a meaningless job. And that was a lie."

There it was, at last. Hannah Shively's version of the truth. Caroline could add it to Dad's, and Keaton's, Walt's, Sela's, her own. How many perspectives did you need before you could see the three-hundred-sixty-degree view of a life or even of a pivotal moment? This was not the last version left to tell—certainly they'd never know Rebecca's.

But it was the last one she wanted to hear.

Caroline stared down at their fingers. She'd been here for hours, long enough for the silent backdrop of her parents' house to turn from an empty echo to a peaceful respite and back again. Lucky as she'd been to catch Mom alone, Dad would be home soon. Walt and the kids were surely at the house by now, waiting for her to rejoin them for what was left of the weekend. It was time to go.

She wasn't sorry she hadn't let Mom explain before. If she needed to hear this, it was right for it to be today. When she had the wherewithal to be glad she'd never known enough to be quite this sad for her parents before. When her pride was far enough in check that though not everything had turned out for the best, she could be grateful for the things that had.

When she'd already forgiven but could do Mom the kindness of doing it again.

So, she did.

42

Sela

Sela wouldn't say therapy was helping, but she wouldn't say it wasn't. Sometimes, it even felt like something Ecca might have gotten behind—not like last time, when she'd worried those facing-facts sessions would be the thing to *give* Sela a real, all-the-way breakdown. This was in Ecca's language—*exploring the gray area*—and Sela was learning to accept how those shades had painted Ecca, too, thanks to Dr. Kay.

Sela had never seen someone so happy to be recovering from major surgery. Not that the therapist acknowledged her own state, or allowed Sela to, but the aura that had seemed so charged with purpose at the start had settled into something more satisfied, peaceful. She left Sela to come to realizations on her own.

For instance, that it *was* harder to live in a dreamworld when you were talking about the real one by appointment.

And damn near impossible on dialysis.

She spent so much time hooked to lines now, half her waking hours were supervised. Janie had been right about the upside of the grueling treatment: It put you in good company. Well, company, anyway. Might as well make the best of it.

None of the fellow patients were near Sela's age, but they were mostly grandparent types inclined to dote on her. The women knit her hats and scarves and pulled lotion from their purses when they saw the new dryness of her skin. The men doled out mints to combat nausea and shot bouncer-esque looks at Doug when he stopped in. They didn't know the whole story, of course—but his *we're still on the same health plan* line hadn't impressed. Sela didn't begrudge him checking on her. Leigh's pregnancy was in full swing now, and she had her own appointments to juggle. Someone had to report back to Caroline.

Sela would make sure the reports were good. Not because she'd agreed when Janie said that she had to be open to a potential donor's help, that Caroline was an adult with free will and Sela was not responsible for whatever she might decide. But because Sela had looked at Caroline on that last-ditch day in the studio and seen something so simultaneously simple and complex and new and yet unconditional, it could only have been sisterhood.

It came to her now not in emails or phone calls but in care packages. They made it seem okay that she and Caroline didn't know what to say to each other, that they'd temporarily taken to communicating secondhand, through Leigh; the gifts meant more than words. She took them with her to the dialysis center to unwrap there, something to look forward to. Books signed by the authors—*saw this woman speak at Joseph-Beth, picked up a copy for you.* Lip balms flavored with chocolate and caramel—*because there's more than one way to get a sugar fix.* And most recently, pictures drawn by her nieces and nephew. Lucy's made her stop and stare.

Rainbow Rain, Lucy had written across the bottom, each letter a different color. And that's what she'd drawn—periwinkle and red-orange and rose and sea foam and lemon-hued drops showering a house where a woman and a little girl stood in the yard, holding hands.

There was one child, eight-year-old Dustin, whose dialysis often overlapped with Sela's. She never got the full story on why he wasn't in the pediatric unit but gathered it had to do with circumstance, some exception—maybe a scheduling or transportation problem, as the closest one was some distance away. He was her favorite and also least favorite person in the little family the patients had become: Favorite because he was incapable of doubt that any of them would get well. Least favorite because she was not, and he was here, and nothing about that was fair.

She propped the picture on a little table opposite them, where they both could see it.

"I wish rain really did come down in colors," he mused. "That way, we wouldn't have to wait for the sun to come out before the storm is done. Real rainbows hardly ever happen."

It was such a treat, talking with a kid one-on-one; it had never escaped Sela that Leigh didn't trust her alone with hers. When the treatments left her with any energy, she took Oscar on walks to meet Leigh at the park and watch only "real" children play. She leaned into her sweet dog's companionship; Doug stopped taking him weekends, so she wouldn't be in the house alone.

Sela missed Brody. She missed the way a sense of calm washed over her at the sight of him. The comfort of his tiny hand in hers. The way his face lit up every time she dared dream aloud of a new adventure they might take together.

He never cared about the likelihood that they would never go.

He always knew, in a beyond-his-years way, that when it came to dreams, it was never too late.

43

Caroline

What do you do when a decision looms so large, you can't see around it?

You look through it. A filter, for everything.

You see a doctor and learn what you don't have a detectable predisposition for. Your suspicions are confirmed, though, that there's no way to really know. No guarantees.

You hug your kids as tight as they let you, as often as they let you. They don't seem to notice a change, or maybe they do. You sit with the fear that one day they'll need something you no longer have in your possession to give. You remind yourself how many levels of hypothetical this is, how even if they came to need a match, you might not be one, how you'd do everything in your power to find another way. How dicey it is to turn your back on an immediate need in the name of one that might never materialize.

Justifiable, maybe, but dicey nonetheless.

You get back to the rotation of big family dinners, behaving as if everything is normal until it almost is. Since the day you told your mom everything, crying your heart out, you haven't felt the urge to broach it with her again. You can't say you don't judge your parents, but you swallow your judgment; forgiveness tastes sweeter. You stop resenting your husband's family simply for being as decent as you once thought yours to be. You spend more time with your best friend, laugh louder and longer at Mo's off-color jokes.

You admire her, too, what a wonderful stepmother she is, though this heightens the tragedy of Sela dismissing her own prospects outright. Were Sela well, she might marry again. Someone with children, perhaps. There are so many ways to have a family. You've learned, too, that we never know when we'll be gifted things we didn't see coming, didn't think possible.

You take your time. You do not rush.

You write that letter of thanks and apology to your ex. It'll be the last he hears from you.

You think about how it felt that time a woman you didn't know, in a waiting room you didn't want to be in, mistook you and your stranger of a sister for the usual kind of siblings and called you lucky. You wonder if you really played along because you didn't feel like explaining—or if maybe, for an instant, that reality seemed preferable to the truth. Maybe you wanted to see what it felt like to try it on for size, pretend it was real. Or maybe you didn't want to see your disappointment reflected in that woman's eyes, knowing she, too, wanted to believe.

You read about photographers and artists who specialize in portraits of infants who never make it home. You wonder if Sela has such a picture of Brody—one perfect image of his perfect face, unmarked by wires or monitors or barriers. One in which no one would ever know he wasn't sleeping. You'd like to see it, if she does. If she can bear it, so can you.

When Christmas rolls around, you again divvy up the gift list with your husband. You don't joke about the best and worst one he ever chose, not knowing if it's funny yet, if it ever will be. You go to church, knowing you are missing something. You had once intended to be a Methodist, as your parents had. Your husband and kids come along, willing, inquisitive. You slip into your purse a leaflet, *What We Believe.* It clarifies what this version of God cares most about. Including, interestingly, what you do with your body. Sprinkle it with holy water; tattoo its skin; reduce it to ash when your soul is gone.

At home that night, you show your husband the section you were surprised to see. You weren't looking for it, but it found you.

> *Organ transplantation and donation are acts of charity, agape love, and self-sacrifice. We recognize the life-giving benefits of organ and tissue donation and encourage all people of faith to become donors as part of their love and ministry to others in need.*

He is not surprised.

Not then, and not a few days later, when he sits with you as you make the call to the clinic number you've saved, in case you would ever be brave enough or foolish enough to use it.

But neither of you sees it coming, what happens on the other end. They'll keep you on file, call you if something changes. As of now, though?

A match has already, newly been identified. All they're authorized to say is that things are moving ahead quite optimistically without you.

You hang up and cry: Relief and joy bind you to your husband, who is crying the same tears. Then you laugh, your foreheads pressed together. All that agony for nothing.

Except it wasn't.

It was for everything worth anything.

So you pick up the phone again, to finally hear her voice.

The sister whom you might, after all, get to keep.

Epilogue

Nine Months Later

The last Saturday of the summer, Sela awoke feeling as she had every day of the past three months post-transplant: free. To take deep, cleansing breaths of air-conditioned oxygen. To drink when she was thirsty, to eat food that tasted like food. To move without shivers of pain—or, rather, with pain she could identify, wait out. This, from the incision that hadn't quite healed. That, from adjusting to the new prescription. There, from yesterday's yoga.

Even with a distance to go, she could look around her empty bedroom in the just risen sun and flex the satisfied smile of a woman who's escaped the clutches of an unrelenting captor.

Which, for the time being, she had.

Pancakes. She had to check that she wasn't dreaming the smell—but there it was. Sweet and comforting as those lazy college taste tests at home with Leigh, as those special mornings out with Ecca. And that one time, with Brody. Silver dollars that day.

Janie wasn't the only one, it turned out, who took annual trips with her sister to commemorate their successful transplant. It was kind of a thing: not always a trip, but a dinner, a photo op, one of those fundraising walks, something symbolic for donor and recipient both to celebrate another year of health, another year of life.

Sela didn't think she and Caroline's mother would ever do that.

One could be grateful without building a relationship on that gratitude, just as one could give sincerely without the slightest desire to see strings attached.

The gift had never really been for Sela, of course. It was for Caroline. So she wouldn't have to, but also because she'd cared, more than anyone wanted her to, more than anyone thought she should. Because Brody—in perhaps his last, most noble act—had wriggled into his aunt's heart in a way that Hannah could not help seeing. If Hannah was looking to make right something in her own conscience as well, certainly nobody ever said so out loud.

Still, funnily enough, when Sela got the news—*donor identified!*—her first thought was of that advice issued from the podium at the Big Ask, Big Give seminar. That you might not need to ask: Just tell. She'd scoffed, but it proved true. Just not in any way she could have guessed.

Sela knew not how her father had taken it, whether he'd pushed back. The only facts that mattered were those that added up to a small miracle: that Caroline and Hannah had always been so physically alike, Hannah found herself wondering about the long shot that if one of them was a tissue match for Sela, the other might be, too—even without that same biological link. That though she fell on the upper end of the donor age range, she'd kept impeccable health, in part due to her husband's restrictions. One of the few things Sela begrudgingly owed to her father.

Besides, wasn't everyone driven by conscience, a little? Even those labeled *altruistic.*

The months leading up to the transplant were long, strained. Hannah's compatibility tests seemed to go on indefinitely, almost as if the medical team wouldn't stop until they found some reason to. Meanwhile, Sela had to complete a desensitization to boost her initially borderline compatibility with the donor kidney. So began an arm's-length phase between Sela and Caroline, between Sela and everyone invested in the outcome. A special kind of loneliness, but still less lonely than before.

She was glad that was behind her.

Stepping into her slippers and opening her door, she heard the bubbly chatter of the newly rested and the patter of Oscar, no doubt searching out scraps. She made her way downstairs and stopped in the kitchen doorway, surveying the scene.

This was Caroline's first visit since the surgery. For the procedure, Hannah had traveled to Sela's hospital—though the two met only once, right before go time. Sela's father was there, too, his body language angled sharply toward his wife and rightful daughter. But something in his expression seemed apologetic, as though he wished he could say more. He looked too familiar already, somehow, for her liking.

All Sela could manage was, *Thank you.* It was enough.

They'd gone back to Ohio at the first green light, and Caroline devoted herself to nursing her mom through recovery. Sela stayed in inpatient as long as she could, then arranged visits from an in-home nurse. Leigh made exactly one appearance before the baby came but still called every other day. Janie did, too. Ivy and the other Aesthetic artists organized a meal train. Friends from dialysis brought puzzles and board games and stayed to play. Doug's relief was palpable—he could move on now. He was seeing someone, though he never spoke of her. And even when only Oscar was left, Sela got by.

She no longer doubted that she could.

Now: Caroline was here, kids in tow, a fresh start all over again.

They still didn't know Sela was an aunt in more than a name, but who could ask for more? Having the gaggle of children gathered around the heap of pancakes on the table, Caroline at the stove warming maple syrup—it filled her house with *life.*

After seeing her through the worst of it, Dr. Kay had turned her over to a local practitioner, where Sela had therapy once a week in the open now. Mental health wasn't an unusual concern post-transplant; it was provided for. She talked about things she suspected other patients did—less about the past and more about the challenges of reentering the world of the healthier.

She leaned her head on the doorway, content to watch until they noticed her, feeling tearful for no single reason. Owen laughed at something Lucy said, and the way he threw back his head put Sela in mind of Ecca.

Then he turned, and she saw why. It wasn't Owen after all, but Brody, basking in the warmth of his cousins' presence. Of the family he'd never had. *They'd* never had.

He met her eye and beckoned her to join them.

Caroline crossed to the table, plunking a bowl of sugar-dusted strawberries onto the lazy Susan, and when she moved aside, Sela counted three little heads.

One, two, three. No Brody, only Owen.

"Good morning!" Caroline held up two steaming mugs. "Coffee?"

It smelled like heaven. Like a bold brew of something that had been forbidden for so long, you'd forgotten how much pleasure such a simple thing could bring.

A warm drink, with no limit to refills. A genuine smile, with no worried shadow. A newly open door, even if you couldn't quite bring yourself to close the one behind you.

Sela nodded and moved to take her seat at the table.

Acknowledgments

I owe a debt of gratitude to a number of people who helped to make this book possible.

Barbara Poelle believed in this story (and its author) from my first mention of the idea, and proved once again her ability to do the impossible when she made my family's one and only trip to Disney World *even more* memorable.

Alexandra Sehulster brought enthusiasm and insight to her acquisition of this project, and this manuscript is infinitely better for her collaboration and care in the editing process.

Megan Rader, as a registered dietitian specializing in renal care (and a good friend specializing in patience), was wonderfully gracious about a steady stream of "quick questions" coming at her in the form of texts, last-minute lunch dates, and phone calls. Her advice throughout was invaluable, as was her feedback on an early draft.

Amy Miller generously gave hours of time to speak with me about her experience as a kidney donor. Her openness was as invaluable as it was humbling, and I remain in awe of her generous, clear-eyed, unwavering spirit. I've witnessed the life-changing impact of her perspectives on many people who've been fortunate to cross her path, myself included.

Perry Malloy-Hall of the National Kidney Foundation kindly granted Amy's request to bring me as her guest to a power-packed The Big Ask: The Big Give workshop at Cincinnati Children's Hospital Medical Center. All of the panelists and featured speakers that day in November 2018 shone a bright light on the subject matter, and the NKF's print and online resources were invaluable aids in my research, as well.

In a time when I was devouring any related material I could get my hands on, Kim Dinan pointed me to the *Strangers* podcast's eye-opening four-part series (available in their archives, from January through March 2016) on Elizabeth and Mary and their altruistic match—fascinating listening for anyone interested in two strangers' real-life experiences with donation.

Note: While I've done my best to remain true to the real-life progression of chronic kidney disease and to the complex process of pursuing live organ donation, the fact that the experience is ultimately unique to every patient afforded me some leeway to take creative license for the sake of this fictional story, particularly where the timeline was concerned. (Likewise, the story's DNA test provider is imagined and not a proxy of any one existing company.) The aforementioned sources bear no responsibility for any perceived stretches, bends, or inaccuracies. If you'd like to learn more about the life-saving gift of kidney donation, visit www.kidney.org.

Astute beta readers Amy Fogelson and Lindsay Hiatt yet again went the extra mile in talking me through their notes and off the ledge.

My publishing team at St. Martin's Press—including Jen Enderlin, Katie Bassel, Erica Martirano, Brant Janeway, Alexis

Neuville, Mara Delgado-Sanchez, everyone at Macmillan Audio, and so many others—works tirelessly to introduce my work to new readers.

The Library Foundation of Cincinnati and Hamilton County awarded me the honor of serving as their 2019 Writer-in-Residence during the drafting and revising of much of this book.

The rock stars at Joseph-Beth Booksellers and The Bookshelf have been kind in their support of a locally based author, and I'm endlessly grateful for the opportunities they've afforded me—and for the welcoming open doors of thriving independent bookstores everywhere.

Fellow writers have amazed me with their wisdom, good humor, and generosity along the way, including the Tall Poppy Writers, the team at Career Authors, my *Writer's Digest* family, friends from 17 Scribes and WFWA, the Fiction Writers Co-op, and my Cin-Day sisterhood of Sharon Short, Katrina Kittle, and Kristina McBride.

My extended family makes a terrific team of cheerleaders: Love and thanks to the Yerega, Strawser, and Trachtenberg clans.

My husband, Scott, and our children are such good sports when it comes to this unpredictable career, with its odd hours and that dazed look I get when working through a plot problem in the middle of dinner. I love our life together, and I thank my lucky stars for you every day.